GREATEST WORKS OF

EDGAR ALLAN POE

CLASSICS

Reprint 2023

FINGERPRINT! CLASSICS
An imprint of Prakash Books India Pvt. Ltd

113/A, Darya Ganj,
New Delhi-110 002
Email: info@prakashbooks.com/sales@prakashbooks.com

facebook www.facebook.com/fingerprintpublishing
twitter www.twitter.com/FingerprintP
www.fingerprintpublishing.com

ISBN: 978 93 5440 146 6

Processed & printed in India

Born Edgar Poe on January 19, 1809, in Boston, Massachusetts, he was the second child of the American actor David Poe Jr. and the English actress Elizabeth Arnold Hopkins Poe. A year after his birth, his father deserted the family, and on December 8, 1811, Poe's mother died of tuberculosis. Though Poe was just two at that time, her death affected him deeply.

Left as orphans after Elizabeth's death, Poe and his two siblings were separated. Poe was fostered by John Allan, a Scottish merchant in Richmond, Virginia, and his wife, Frances Allan. He was baptized and the Allans named him 'Edgar Allan Poe.'

In 1815, the Allan family moved to Britain where Poe received classical education. Poe entered the University of Virginia in February 1826, taking classes in ancient and modern languages. Over the year, Poe accumulated gambling losses and drinking debts at the university and was forced to discontinue his education there. He returned to Richmond in 1827, only to meet with the news that his childhood sweetheart, Sarah Elmira Royster, was engaged.

Poe left his foster family and traveled to Boston in April 1827. A month later, unable to sustain himself, he joined the United States Army under the pseudonym Edgar A. Perry. In July of the same year, Poe published his first collection of poems called *Tamerlane and Other Poems.* The collection included his early poems inspired by the works of Lord Byron, and did not receive any critical attention.

After his foster mother's death in February 1829, John Allan helped Poe obtain an appointment at the United States Military Academy at West Point. The same year, before joining the academy, his second volume of verse titled *Al Aaraaf, Tamerlane, and Minor Poems* was published in Baltimore by Hatch & Dunning. This was his first commercially published collection.

In the later part of the next year, Poe was disowned by John Allan after his remarriage. Poe made up his mind to leave the academy and sought dismissal. In early 1831, Poe was court-martialed and expelled from West Point owing to his absence from classes and drills and negligence towards his duties. He moved to New York City after that, and in April, published his third collection titled *Poems* with Elam Bliss. It contained the early versions of some of his masterpieces including 'To Helen' and 'Israfel', and reprinted 'Tamerlane' and 'Al Aaraaf' among others.

Poe moved back to Baltimore where he stayed at his aunt Mrs. Maria Clemm's home, along with Henry, his cousin—Virginia, and his grandmother. Here, he began writing short stories. In May 1833, Poe offered his 'Tales of the Arabesque' (later titled *Tales of the Folio Club*) to the *New England Magazine*, only to have it rejected. Poe's short story 'MS. Found in a Bottle' won a literary prize of $50 in a writing contest conducted by the *Baltimore Saturday Visiter* in 1833.

Poe moved to Richmond in 1835. He began writing his only play, titled *Politician*, but did not finish it. In August of the same year, after being recommended by John P. Kennedy, an American novelist and politician, Poe began working with Thomas W. White as the assistant editor for the *Southern Literary Messenger.* He worked here till January 1837. In 1836, when Poe was twenty-six, he married his thirteen-year-old cousin Virginia, with his aunt's approval. He also began writing his only complete novel, *The Narrative of Arthur Gordon Pym*, which was published by Harper & Brothers in July 1838.

In 1839, Poe joined the *Burton's Gentleman's Magazine* as an assistant editor. His short story 'The Fall of the House of Usher' was published in the September 1839 issue of the magazine. An instant success, it is considered a masterpiece of American Gothic literature. In 1840, *Tales of the Grotesque and Arabesque*, a collection of his already printed short stories, was published in two volumes by Lea & Blanchard, a Philadelphia firm. He also prepared and published a prospectus for his own literary journal *The Penn*, renamed *The Stylus.* The journal was a dream of Poe, which never materialized.

Poe resigned from *Burton's Gentleman's Magazine* in 1841 and joined *Graham's Magazine* as an assistant. He continued to write and publish his tales and poems. 'The Murders in the Rue Morgue', published in the April 1841 issue of the *Graham's Magazine*, was considered the first detective story. The following year, Virginia fell ill, and Poe, who was already a regular drinker, began drinking excessively. All his attempts at finding a new job also failed.

Poe, along with Virginia, moved to New York in April 1844. In October of that year, Poe joined the *New York Evening Mirror*, where he worked for a brief period. On January 29, 1845, 'The Raven' was published in the *Evening Mirror*. Distinguished for its supernatural atmosphere, dramatic qualities, and musicality, this poem became a sensation and brought Poe considerable national fame.

Poe joined the editorial staff of *Broadway Journal*, a New York City newspaper, and later became its owner. During this period he revised and republished many of his short stories in the periodical. Poe also printed many of Frances Sargent Osgood's poems.

In July 1845, Evert A. Duyckinck, an American publisher and biographer, helped Poe in the selection of the stories to be included in *Tales*. Though Poe was not satisfied with Duyckinck's choices, *Tales*—published by Wiley and Putman—was a success.

On November 19, 1845, *The Raven and Other Poems* were published by the same publisher. This collection, dedicated to Miss Elizabeth Barrett (the future wife of Robert Browning), included the revised versions of many of his older poems in addition to the new ones. It brought him significant recognition.

In January of 1846, the *Broadway Journal* failed and ceased publication. Poe and Virginia shifted to a cottage in Fordham, New York, where Virginia's health deteriorated. Virginia Poe breathed her last on January 30, 1847, leaving Poe disturbed. After her death, he tried wooing the poet Sarah Helen Whitman, who admired Poe's stories. Poe wrote 'To Helen' for her, and they exchanged several letters and poems before he proposed to her. Though she accepted the proposal and the wedding date was decided, their relationship ended before that due to Poe's drunken binges and unpredictable behavior.

In March 1848, Poe published 'Eureka: A Prose Poem'. His longest work of non-fiction, it attempted to explain the universe and also discussed the relationship of man with the universe and God. His last major work, it was not well-received.

Drunken and penniless during his last days, Poe roamed on the streets of Baltimore, delirious. He died on October 7, 1849, in the

Washington College Hospital, and was buried in Westminster Hall. The circumstances leading to his death remain a mystery.

Edgar Allan Poe was a dreamer. A close contemporary of Washington Irving and Nathaniel Hawthorne, both the earliest stalwarts of American short story, Poe's literary career began with *Tamerlane and Other Poems* (1827) but it was his deftly plotted short stories which attracted attention. He was also a noticeable literary critic and an unwearying reviewer and essayist.

The recurring themes in his works—the death of women, bereavement, horror, madness, premature burial, decay, revival of the dead, life after death—are suggested to have resulted from his own life, which was a sequence of tragic events and frequent abandonments.

Poe has inspired and influenced writers across centuries. Many of his tales and poems have been adapted for motion pictures. More than a century and a half after Poe's death, his works still remain as fresh and scary, sending a frightening chill down the spines of his readers.

Contents

POEMS

Tales

Essays & Criticism

Letters

Poems

Tamerlane

[The original longer version of this poem first appeared in *Tamerlane and Other Poems* (1827). The revised shorter version was published in *Al Aaraaf, Tamerlane, and Minor Poems* (1829). This version was included in *The Raven and Other Poems* (1845).]

Kind solace in a dying hour!
  Such, father, is not (now) my theme—
I will not madly deem that power
    Of Earth may shrive me of the sin
    Unearthly pride hath revell'd in—
  I have no time to dote or dream:
You call it hope—that fire of fire!
It is but agony of desire:
If I *can* hope—Oh God! I can—
  Its fount is holier—more divine—
I would not call thee fool, old man,
  But such is not a gift of thine.

Know thou the secret of a spirit
  Bow'd from its wild pride into shame.
O yearning heart! I did inherit
  Thy withering portion with the fame,
The searing glory which hath shone
Amid the jewels of my throne,
Halo of Hell! and with a pain
Not Hell shall make me fear again—

O craving heart, for the lost flowers
And sunshine of my summer hours!
Th' undying voice of that dead time,
With its interminable chime,
Rings, in the spirit of a spell,
Upon thy emptiness—a knell.

I have not always been as now:
The fever'd diadem on my brow
  I claim'd and won usurpingly—
Hath not the same fierce heirdom given
  Rome to the Caesar—this to me?
    The heritage of a kingly mind,
And a proud spirit which hath striven
    Triumphantly with human kind.

On mountain soil I first drew life:
  The mists of the Taglay have shed
  Nightly their dews upon my head,
And, I believe, the winged strife
And tumult of the headlong air
Have nestled in my very hair.

So late from Heaven—that dew—it fell
  ('Mid dreams of an unholy night)
Upon me—with the touch of Hell,
  While the red flashing of the light
From clouds that hung, like banners, o'er,
  Appeared to my half-closing eye
  The pageantry of monarchy,
And the deep trumpet-thunder's roar
  Came hurriedly upon me, telling
    Of human battle, where my voice,
  My own voice, silly child!—was swelling
    (O! how my spirit would rejoice,
And leap within me at the cry)
The battle-cry of Victory!

The rain came down upon my head
    Unshelter'd—and the heavy wind
    Rendered me mad and deaf and blind.
It was but man, I thought, who shed
    Laurels upon me: and the rush—
The torrent of the chilly air
Gurgled within my ear the crush
    Of empires—with the captive's prayer—
The hum of suiters—and the tone
Of flattery 'round a sovereign's throne.

My passions, from that hapless hour,
    Usurp'd a tyranny which men
Have deem'd, since I have reach'd to power;
        My innate nature—be it so:
    But, father, there liv'd one who, then,
Then—in my boyhood—when their fire
        Burn'd with a still intenser glow,
(For passion must, with youth, expire)
    E'en *then* who knew this iron heart
    In woman's weakness had a part.

I have no words—alas!—to tell
The loveliness of loving well!
Nor would I now attempt to trace
The more than beauty of a face
Whose lineaments, upon my mind,
Are——shadows on th' unstable wind:
Thus I remember having dwelt
    Some page of early lore upon,
With loitering eye, till I have felt
The letters—with their meaning—melt
    To fantasies—with none.

O, she was worthy of all love!
    Love—as in infancy was mine—
'Twas such as angel minds above

Might envy; her young heart the shrine
On which my ev'ry hope and thought
Were incense—then a goodly gift,
For they were childish—and upright—
Pure——as her young example taught:
Why did I leave it, and, adrift,
Trust to the fire within, for light?

We grew in age—and love—together,
Roaming the forest, and the wild;
My breast her shield in wintry weather—
And, when the friendly sunshine smil'd,
And she would mark the opening skies,
I saw no Heaven—but in her eyes.

Young Love's first lesson is——the heart:
For 'mid that sunshine, and those smiles,
When, from our little cares apart,
And laughing at her girlish wiles,
I'd throw me on her throbbing breast,
And pour my spirit out in tears—
There was no need to speak the rest—
No need to quiet any fears
Of her—who ask'd no reason why,
But turn'd on me her quiet eye!

Yet *more* than worthy of the love
My spirit struggled with, and strove,
When, on the mountain peak, alone,
Ambition lent it a new tone—
I had no being—but in thee:
The world, and all it did contain
In the earth—the air—the sea—
Its joy—its little lot of pain
That was new pleasure—the ideal,
Dim, vanities of dreams by night—

And dimmer nothings which were real—
(Shadows—and a more shadowy light!)
Parted upon their misty wings,
And, so, confusedly, became
Thine image, and—a name—a name!
Two separate—yet most intimate things.

I was ambitious—have you known
The passion, father? You have not:
A cottager, I mark'd a throne
Of half the world as all my own,
And murmur'd at such lowly lot—
But, just like any other dream,
Upon the vapour of the dew
My own had past, did not the beam
Of beauty which did while it thro'
The minute—the hour—the day—oppress
My mind with double loveliness.

We walk'd together on the crown
Of a high mountain which look'd down
Afar from its proud natural towers
Of rock and forest, on the hills—
The dwindled hills! begirt with bowers
And shouting with a thousand rills.

I spoke to her of power and pride,
But mystically—in such guise
That she might deem it nought beside
The moment's converse; in her eyes
I read, perhaps too carelessly—
A mingled feeling with my own—
The flush on her bright cheek, to me
Seem'd to become a queenly throne
Too well that I should let it be
Light in the wilderness alone.

I wrapp'd myself in grandeur then,
  And donn'd a visionary crown—
    Yet it was not that Fantasy
    Had thrown her mantle over me—
But that, among the rabble—men,
    Lion ambition is chain'd down—
And crouches to a keeper's hand—
Not so in deserts where the grand
The wild—the terrible conspire
With their own breath to fan his fire.

Look 'round thee now on Samarcand!—
  Is not she queen of Earth? her pride
Above all cities? in her hand
  Their destinies? in all beside
Of glory which the world hath known
Stands she not nobly and alone?
Falling—her veriest stepping-stone
Shall form the pedestal of a throne—
And who her sovereign? Timour—he
  Whom the astonished people saw
Striding o'er empires haughtily
  A diadem'd outlaw—

O, human love! thou spirit given,
On Earth, of all we hope in Heaven!
Which fall'st into the soul like rain
Upon the Siroc wither'd plain,
And failing in thy power to bless
But leav'st the heart a wilderness!
Idea! which bindest life around
With music of so strange a sound
And beauty of so wild a birth—
Farewell! for I have won the Earth!

When Hope, the eagle that tower'd, could see
  No cliff beyond him in the sky,

His pinions were bent droopingly—
    And homeward turn'd his soften'd eye.
'Twas sunset: when the sun will part
There comes a sullenness of heart
To him who still would look upon
The glory of the summer sun.
That soul will hate the ev'ning mist,
So often lovely, and will list
To the sound of the coming darkness (known
To those whose spirits hearken) as one
Who, in a dream of night, *would* fly
But *cannot* from a danger nigh.

What tho' the moon—the white moon
Shed all the splendor of her noon,
Her smile is chilly—and *her* beam,
In that time of dreariness, will seem
(So like you gather in your breath)
A portrait taken after death.
And boyhood is a summer sun
Whose waning is the dreariest one—
For all we live to know is known,
And all we seek to keep hath flown—
Let life, then, as the day-flower, fall
With the noon-day beauty—which is all.

I reach'd my home—my home no more—
    For all had flown who made it so—
I pass'd from out its mossy door,
    And, tho' my tread was soft and low,
A voice came from the threshold stone
Of one whom I had earlier known—
    O, I defy thee, Hell, to show
    On beds of fire that burn below,
    A humbler heart—a deeper wo.
Father, I firmly do believe—
    I *know*—for Death, who comes for me

From regions of the blest afar,
Where there is nothing to deceive,
Hath left his iron gate ajar,
And rays of truth you cannot see
Are flashing thro' Eternity—
I do believe that Eblis hath
A snare in ev'ry human path—
Else how, when in the holy grove
I wandered of the idol, Love,
Who daily scents his snowy wings
With incense of burnt offerings
From the most unpolluted things,
Whose pleasant bowers are yet so riven
Above with trellic'd rays from Heaven
No mote may shun—no tiniest fly—
The light'ning of his eagle eye—
How was it that Ambition crept,
Unseen, amid the revels there,
Till growing bold, he laughed and leapt
In the tangles of Love's very hair?

Evening Star

[Published in *Tamerlane and Other Poems* (1827), this lyric poem was never printed again during Poe's lifetime.]

'Twas noontide of summer,
    And mid-time of night;
And stars, in their orbits,
    Shone pale, thro' the light
Of the brighter, cold moon,
    'Mid planets her slaves,
Herself in the Heavens,
    Her beam on the waves.
    I gaz'd awhile
    On her cold smile;
Too cold—too cold for me—
    There pass'd, as a shroud,
    A fleecy cloud,
And I turned away to thee,
    Proud Evening Star,
    In thy glory afar,
And dearer thy beam shall be;
    For joy to my heart
    Is the proud part
Thou bearest in Heav'n at night,
    And more I admire
    Thy distant fire,
Than that colder, lowly light.

Spirits of the Dead

[First published in *Tamerlane and Other Poems* (1827) with the title 'Visit of the Dead', it appeared with this title in *Al Aaraaf, Tamerlane, and Minor Poems* (1829).]

1

Thy soul shall find itself alone
'Mid dark thoughts of the grey tomb-stone—
Not one, of all the crowd, to pry
Into thine hour of secrecy:

2

Be silent in that solitude
    Which is not loneliness—for then
The spirits of the dead who stood
    In life before thee are again
In death around thee—and their will
Shall then overshadow thee: be still.

3

For the night—tho' clear—shall frown—
And the stars shall look not down,
From their high thrones in the Heaven,
With light like Hope to mortals given—

But their red orbs, without beam,
To thy weariness shall seem
As a burning and a fever
Which would cling to thee for ever:

4

Now are thoughts thou shalt not banish—
Now are visions ne'er to vanish—
From thy spirit shall they pass
No more—like dew-drop from the grass:

5

The breeze—the breath of God—is still—
And the mist upon the hill
Shadowy—shadowy—yet unbroken,
Is a symbol and a token—
How it hangs upon the trees,
A mystery of mysteries!—

Fairy-Land

[Published in *The Yankee and Boston Literary Gazette* in September 1829, it was included in *Al Aaraaf, Tamerlane, and Minor Poems* (1829), *Poems* (1831), and *The Raven and Other Poems* (1845).]

Dim vales—and shadowy floods—
And cloudy-looking woods,
Whose forms we can't discover
For the tears that drip all over
Huge moons there wax and wane—
Again—again—again—
Every moment of the night—
Forever changing places—
And they put out the star-light
With the breath from their pale faces.
About twelve by the moon-dial
One, more filmy than the rest
(A kind which, upon trial,
They have found to be the best)
Comes down—still down—and down
With its center on the crown
Of a mountain's eminence,
While its wide circumference
In easy drapery falls
Over hamlets, over halls,
Wherever they may be—

O'er the strange woods—o'er the sea—
Over spirits on the wing—
Over every drowsy thing—
And buries them up quite
In a labyrinth of light—
And then, how deep!—O, deep!
Is the passion of their sleep.
In the morning they arise,
And their moony covering
Is soaring in the skies,
With the tempests as they toss,
Like——almost any thing—
Or a yellow Albatross.
They use that moon no more
For the same end as before—
Videlicet a tent—
Which I think extravagant:
Its atomies, however,
Into a shower dissever,
Of which those butterflies,
Of Earth, who seek the skies,
And so come down again
(Never-contented things!)
Have brought a specimen
Upon their quivering wings.

Al Aaraaf*

[Written in his youth, it is Poe's longest poem. It was first published in his collection *Al Aaraaf, Tamerlane, and Minor Poems* in December 1829 and then, with revisions, in *Poems* (1831). This version is taken from *The Raven and Other Poems* (1845).]

Part I

O! Nothing earthly save the ray
(Thrown back from flowers) of Beauty's eye,
As in those gardens where the day
Springs from the gems of Circassy—
O! nothing earthly save the thrill
Of melody in woodland rill—
Or (music of the passion-hearted)
Joy's voice so peacefully departed
That like the murmur in the shell,
Its echo dwelleth and will dwell—
Oh, nothing of the dross of ours—
Yet all the beauty—all the flowers
That list our Love, and deck our bowers—
Adorn yon world afar, afar—
The wandering star.

* A star was discovered by Tycho Brahe which appeared suddenly in the heavens—attained, in a few days, a brilliancy surpassing that of Jupiter—then as suddenly disappeared, and has never been seen since.

'Twas a sweet time for Nesace—for there
Her world lay lolling on the golden air,
Near four bright suns—a temporary rest—
An oasis in desert of the blest.
Away—away—'mid seas of rays that roll
Empyrean splendor o'er th' unchained soul—
The soul that scarce (the billows are so dense)
Can struggle to its destin'd eminence—
To distant spheres, from time to time, she rode,
And late to ours, the favour'd one of God—
But, now, the ruler of an anchor'd realm,
She throws aside the sceptre—leaves the helm,
And, amid incense and high spiritual hymns,
Laves in quadruple light her angel limbs.

Now happiest, loveliest in yon lovely Earth,
Whence sprang the "Idea of Beauty" into birth,
(Falling in wreaths thro' many a startled star,
Like woman's hair 'mid pearls, until, afar,
It lit on hills Achaian, and there dwelt)
She look'd into Infinity—and knelt.
Rich clouds, for canopies, about her curled—
Fit emblems of the model of her world—
Seen but in beauty—not impeding sight
Of other beauty glittering thro' the light—
A wreath that twined each starry form around,
And all the opal'd air in colour bound.

All hurriedly she knelt upon a bed
Of flowers: of lilies such as rear'd the head
*On the fair Capo Deucato, and sprang
So eagerly around about to hang
Upon the flying footsteps of—deep pride—

* On Santa Maura—olim Deucadia.

[*]Of her who lov'd a mortal—and so died.
The Sephalica, budding with young bees,
Uprear'd its purple stem around her knees:
[†]And gemmy flower, of Trebizond misnam'd—
Inmate of highest stars, where erst it sham'd
All other loveliness: its honied dew
(The fabled nectar that the heathen knew)
Deliriously sweet, was dropp'd from Heaven,
And fell on gardens of the unforgiven
In Trebizond—and on a sunny flower
So like its own above that, to this hour,
It still remaineth, torturing the bee
With madness, and unwonted reverie:
In Heaven, and all its environs, the leaf
And blossom of the fairy plant, in grief
Disconsolate linger—grief that hangs her head,
Repenting follies that full long have fled,
Heaving her white breast to the balmy air,
Like guilty beauty, chasten'd, and more fair:
Nyctanthes too, as sacred as the light
She fears to perfume, perfuming the night:
[‡]And Clytia pondering between many a sun,
While pettish tears adown her petals run:
[§]And that aspiring flower that sprang on Earth—

---

* Sappho.

† This flower is much noticed by Lewenhoeck and Tournefort. The bee, feeding upon its blossom, becomes intoxicated.

‡ Clytia—The Chrysanthemum Peruvianum, or, to employ a better-known term, the turnsol—which continually turns towards the sun, covers itself, like Peru, the country from which it comes, with dewy clouds which cool and refresh its flowers during the most violent heat of the day.—*B. de St. Pierre.*

§ There is cultivated in the king's garden at Paris, a species of serpentine aloes without prickles, whose large and beautiful flower exhales a strong odor of the vanilla, during the time of its expansion, which is very short. It does not blow till towards the month of July—you then perceive it gradually open its petals—expand them—fade and die.—*St. Pierre.*

And died, ere scarce exalted into birth,
Bursting its odorous heart in spirit to wing
Its way to Heaven, from garden of a king:
*And Valisnerian lotus thither flown
From struggling with the waters of the Rhone:
†And thy most lovely purple perfume, Zante!
Isola d'oro!—Fior di Levante!
‡And the Nelumbo bud that floats for ever
With Indian Cupid down the holy river—
Fair flowers, and fairy! to whose care is given
§To bear the Goddess' song, in odors, up to Heaven:

"Spirit! that dwellest where,
    In the deep sky,
The terrible and fair,
    In beauty vie!
Beyond the line of blue—
    The boundary of the star
Which turneth at the view
    Of thy barrier and thy bar—
Of the barrier overgone
    By the comets who were cast
From their pride, and from their throne
    To be drudges till the last—
To be carriers of fire
    (The red fire of their heart)
With speed that may not tire
    And with pain that shall not part—
Who livest—*that* we know—

---

* There is found, in the Rhone, a beautiful lily of the Valisnerian kind. Its stem will stretch to the length of three or four feet—thus preserving its head above water in the swellings of the river.

† The Hyacinth.

‡ It is a fiction of the Indians, that Cupid was first seen floating in one of these down the river Ganges—and that he still loves the cradle of his childhood.

§ And golden vials full of odors which are the prayers of the saints.—*Rev. St. John.*

In Eternity—we feel—
But the shadow of whose brow
What spirit shall reveal?
Tho' the beings whom thy Nesace,
Thy messenger hath known
Have dream'd for thy Infinity
*A model of their own—
Thy will is done, Oh, God!
The star hath ridden high
Thro' many a tempest, but she rode
Beneath thy burning eye;
And here, in thought, to thee—
In thought that can alone
Ascend thy empire and so be
A partner of thy throne—
†By winged Fantasy,

---

* The Humanitarians held that God was to be understood as having a really human form.—*Vide Clarke's Sermons*, vol. 1, page 26, fol. edit.

The drift of Milton's argument, leads him to employ language which would appear, at first sight, to verge upon their doctrine; but it will be seen immediately, that he guards himself against the charge of having adopted one of the most ignorant errors of the dark ages of the church.—*Dr. Sumner's Notes on Milton's Christian Doctrine.*

This opinion, in spite of many testimonies to the contrary, could never have been very general. Andeus, a Syrian of Mesopotamia, was condemned for the opinion, as heretical. He lived in the beginning of the fourth century. His disciples were called Anthropmorphites.—*Vide Du Pin.*

Among Milton's poems are these lines:—

Dicite sacrorum præsides nemorum Deæ, &c.
Quis ille primus cujus ex imagine
Natura solers finxit humanum genus?
Eternus, incorruptus, æquævus polo,
Unusque et universus exemplar Dei.—And afterwards,
Non cui profundum Cæcitas lumen dedit
Dircæus augur vidit hunc alto sinu, &c.

† Seltsamen Tochter Jovis.
Seinem Schosskinde
Der Phantasie.—*Göethe.*

My embassy is given,
Till secrecy shall knowledge be
In the environs of Heaven."
She ceas'd—and buried then her burning cheek
Abash'd, amid the lilies there, to seek
A shelter from the fervor of His eye;
For the stars trembled at the Deity.
She stirr'd not—breath'd not—for a voice was there
How solemnly pervading the calm air!
A sound of silence on the startled ear
Which dreamy poets name "the music of the sphere."
Ours is a world of words: Quiet we call
"Silence"—which is the merest word of all.
All Nature speaks, and ev'n ideal things
Flap shadowy sounds from visionary wings—
But ah! not so when, thus, in realms on high
The eternal voice of God is passing by,
And the red winds are withering in the sky!

*"What tho' in worlds which sightless cycles run,
Link'd to a little system, and one sun—
Where all my love is folly and the crowd
Still think my terrors but the thunder cloud,
The storm, the earthquake, and the ocean-wrath—
(Ah! will they cross me in my angrier path?)
What tho' in worlds which own a single sun
The sands of Time grow dimmer as they run,
Yet thine is my resplendency, so given
To bear my secrets thro' the upper Heaven.
Leave tenantless thy crystal home, and fly,
With all thy train, athwart the moony sky—
†Apart—like fire-flies in Sicilian night,
And wing to other worlds another light!

---

* Sightless—too small to be seen—*Legge.*

† I have often noticed a peculiar movement of the fire-flies;—they will collect in a body and fly off, from a common center, into innumerable radii.

Divulge the secrets of thy embassy
To the proud orbs that twinkle—and so be
To ev'ry heart a barrier and a ban
Lest the stars totter in the guilt of man!"

Up rose the maiden in the yellow night,
The single-mooned eve!—on Earth we plight
Our faith to one love—and one moon adore—
The birth-place of young Beauty had no more.
As sprang that yellow star from downy hours
Up rose the maiden from her shrine of flowers,
And bent o'er sheeny mountain and dim plain
*Her way—but left not yet her Therasæan reign.

Part II

High on a mountain of enamell'd head—
Such as the drowsy shepherd on his bed
Of giant pasturage lying at his ease,
Raising his heavy eyelid, starts and sees
With many a mutter'd "hope to be forgiven"
What time the moon is quadrated in Heaven—
Of rosy head, that towering far away
Into the sunlit ether, caught the ray
Of sunken suns at eve—at noon of night,
While the moon danc'd with the fair stranger light—
Uprear'd upon such height arose a pile
Of gorgeous columns on th' unburthen'd air,
Flashing from Parian marble that twin smile
Far down upon the wave that sparkled there,
And nursled the young mountain in its lair.
†Of molten stars their pavement, such as fall

---

* Therasæa, or Therasea, the island mentioned by Seneca, which, in a moment, arose from the sea to the eyes of astonished mariners.

† Some star which, from the ruin'd roof
Of shak'd Olympus, by mischance, did fall.—*Milton.*

Thro' the ebon air, besilvering the pall
Of their own dissolution, while they die—
Adorning then the dwellings of the sky.
A dome, by linked light from Heaven let down,
Sat gently on these columns as a crown—
A window of one circular diamond, there,
Look'd out above into the purple air,
And rays from God shot down that meteor chain
And hallow'd all the beauty twice again,
Save when, between th' Empyrean and that ring,
Some eager spirit flapp'd his dusky wing.
But on the pillars Seraph eyes have seen
The dimness of this world: that greyish green
That Nature loves the best for Beauty's grave
Lurk'd in each cornice, round each architrave—
And every sculptur'd cherub thereabout
That from his marble dwelling peeréd out
Seem'd earthly in the shadow of his niche—
Achaian statues in a world so rich?
[*]Friezes from Tadmor and Persepolis—
From Balbec, and the stilly, clear abyss
[†]Of beautiful Gomorrah! O, the wave
Is now upon thee—but too late to save!

---

* Voltaire, in speaking of Persepolis, says, "Je connois bien l'admiration qu'inspirent ces ruines—mais un palais erigé au pied d'une chaine des rochers sterils—peut il être un chef d'oevure des arts!"

† "Oh! the wave"—Ula Degusi is the Turkish appellation; but, on its own shores, it is called Bahar Loth, or Almotanah. There were undoubtedly more than two cities englùphed in the "dead sea." In the valley of Siddim were five—Adrah, Zeboin, Zoar, Sodom and Gomorrah. Stephen of Byzantium mentions eight, and Strabo thirteeen, (engulphed)—but the last is out of all reason.

It is said, (Tacitus, Strabo, Josephus, Daniel of St. Saba, Nau, Maundrell, Troilo, D'Arvieux) that after an excessive drought, the vestiges of columns, walls, etc. are seen above the surface. At *any* season, such remains may be discovered by looking down into the transparent lake, and at such distances as would argue the existence of many settlements in the space now usurped by the 'Asphaltites.'

Sound loves to revel in a summer night:
Witness the murmur of the grey twilight
*That stole upon the ear, in Eyraco,
Of many a wild star-gazer long ago—
That stealeth ever on the ear of him
Who, musing, gazeth on the distance dim.
And sees the darkness coming as a cloud—
†Is not its form—its voice—most palpable and loud?

But what is this?—it cometh—and it brings
A music with it—'tis the rush of wings—
A pause—and then a sweeping, falling strain
And Nesace is in her halls again.
From the wild energy of wanton haste
Her cheeks were flushing, and her lips apart;
And zone that clung around her gentle waist
Had burst beneath the heaving of her heart.
Within the center of that hall to breathe
She paus'd and panted, Zanthe! all beneath,
The fairy light that kiss'd her golden hair
And long'd to rest, yet could but sparkle there!

‡Young flowers were whispering in melody
To happy flowers that night—and tree to tree;
Fountains were gushing music as they fell
In many a star-lit grove, or moon-lit dell;
Yet silence came upon material things—
Fair flowers, bright waterfalls and angel wings—
And sound alone that from the spirit sprang
Bore burthen to the charm the maiden sang:
"'Neath blue-bell or streamer—
Or tufted wild spray

---

* Eyraco—Chaldea.

† I have often thought I could distinctly hear the sound of the darkness as it stole over the horizon.

‡ Fairies use flowers for their charactery.—*Merry Wives of Windsor.*

That keeps, from the dreamer,
    *The moonbeam away—
Bright beings! that ponder,
    With half closing eyes,
On the stars which your wonder
    Hath drawn from the skies,
Till they glance thro' the shade, and
    Come down to your brow
Like——eyes of the maiden
    Who calls on you now—
Arise! from your dreaming
    In violet bowers,
To duty beseeming
    These star-litten hours—
And shake from your tresses
    Encumber'd with dew
The breath of those kisses
    That cumber them too—
(O! how, without you, Love!
    Could angels be blest?)
Those kisses of true love
    That lull'd ye to rest!
Up!—shake from your wing
    Each hindering thing:
The dew of the night—
    It would weigh down your flight;
And true love caresses—
    O! leave them apart!
They are light on the tresses,
    But lead on the heart.
Ligeia! Ligeia!
    My beautiful one!

---

* In Scripture is this passage—"The sun shall not harm thee by day, nor the moon by night." It is perhaps not generally known that the moon, in Egypt, has the effect of producing blindness to those who sleep with the face exposed to its rays, to which circumstance the passage evidently alludes.

Whose harshest idea
    Will to melody run,
O! is it thy will
    On the breezes to toss?
Or, capriciously still,
    *Like the lone Albatross,
Incumbent on night
    (As she on the air)
To keep watch with delight
    On the harmony there?

Ligeia! whatever
    Thy image may be,
No magic shall sever
    Thy music from thee.
Thou hast bound many eyes
    In a dreamy sleep—
But the strains still arise
    Which *thy* vigilance keep—
The sound of the rain
    Which leaps down to the flower,
And dances again
    In the rhythm of the shower—
†The murmur that springs
    From the growing of grass
Are the music of things—
    But are modell'd, alas!—
Away, then my dearest,
    O! hie thee away
To springs that lie clearest
    Beneath the moon-ray—

---

* The Albatross is said to sleep on the wing.

† I met with this idea in an old English tale, which I am now unable to obtain and quote from memory:—"The verie essence and, as it were, springe-heade, and origine of all musiche is the verie pleasaunte sounde which the trees of the forest do make when they growe."

To lone lake that smiles,
    In its dream of deep rest,
At the many star-isles
    That enjewel its breast—
Where wild flowers, creeping,
    Have mingled their shade,
On its margin is sleeping
    Full many a maid—
Some have left the cool glade, and
    *Have slept with the bee—
Arouse them my maiden,
    On moorland and lea—
Go! breathe on their slumber,
    All softly in ear,
The musical number
    They slumber'd to hear—
For what can awaken
    An angel so soon
Whose sleep hath been taken
    Beneath the cold moon,
As the spell which no slumber
    Of witchery may test,
The rythmical number
    Which lull'd him to rest?"

Spirits in wing, and angels to the view,
A thousand seraphs burst th' Empyrean thro',
Young dreams still hovering on their drowsy flight—

---

* The wild bee will not sleep in the shade if there be moonlight.
The rhyme in this verse, as in one about sixty lines before, has an appearance of affectation. It is, however, imitated from Sir W. Scott, or rather from Claud Halcro—in whose mouth I admired its effect:

O! were there an island,
    Tho' ever so wild
Where woman might smile, and
    No man be beguil'd, etc.

Seraphs in all but "Knowledge," the keen light
That fell, refracted, thro' thy bounds, afar
O Death! from eye of God upon that star:
Sweet was that error—sweeter still that death—
Sweet was that error—ev'n with *us* the breath
Of science dims the mirror of our joy—
To them 't were the Simoom, and would destroy—
For what (to them) availeth it to know
That Truth is Falsehood—or that Bliss is Woe?
Sweet was their death—with them to die was rife
With the last ecstacy of satiate life—
Beyond that death no immortality—
But sleep that pondereth and is not "to be"—
And there—oh! may my weary spirit dwell—
*Apart from Heaven's Eternity—and yet how far
from Hell!

What guilty spirit, in what shrubbery dim,
Heard not the stirring summons of that hymn?
But two: they fell: for Heaven no grace imparts
To those who hear not for their beating hearts.
A maiden-angel and her seraph-lover—
O! where (and ye may seek the wide skies over)

---

* With the Arabians there is a medium between Heaven and Hell, where men suffer no punishment, but yet do not attain that tranquil and even happiness which they suppose to be characteristic of heavenly enjoyment.

Un no rompido sueno—
Un dia puro—allegre—libre
Quiera—
Libre de amor—de zelo—
De odio—de esperanza—de rezelo.—*Luis Ponce de Leon.*

Sorrow is not excluded from "Al Aaraaf," but it is that sorrow which the living love to cherish for the dead, and which, in some minds, resembles the delirium of opium. The passionate excitement of Love and the buoyancy of spirit attendant upon intoxication are its less holy pleasures—the price of which, to those souls who make choice of "Al Aaraaf" as their residence after life, is final death and annihilation.

Was Love, the blind, near sober Duty known?
*Unguided Love hath fallen—'mid "tears of perfect moan."

He was a goodly spirit—he who fell:
A wanderer by moss-y-mantled well—
A gazer on the lights that shine above—
A dreamer in the moonbeam by his love:
What wonder? For each star is eye-like there,
And looks so sweetly down on Beauty's hair—
And they, and ev'ry mossy spring were holy
To his love-haunted heart and melancholy.
The night had found (to him a night of wo)
Upon a mountain crag, young Angelo—
Beetling it bends athwart the solemn sky,
And scowls on starry worlds that down beneath it lie.
Here sate he with his love—his dark eye bent
With eagle gaze along the firmament:
Now turn'd it upon her—but ever then
It trembled to the orb of EARTH again.

"Iante, dearest, see! how dim that ray!
How lovely 'tis to look so far away!
She seem'd not thus upon that autumn eve
I left her gorgeous halls—nor mourn'd to leave.
That eve—that eve—I should remember well—
The sun-ray dropp'd, in Lemnos, with a spell
On th' Arabesque carving of a gilded hall
Wherein I sate, and on the draperied wall—
And on my eye-lids—O the heavy light!
How drowsily it weigh'd them into night!
On flowers, before, and mist, and love they ran
With Persian Saadi in his Gulistan:

* There be tears of perfect moan
Wept for thee in Helicon.—*Milton.*

But O that light!—I slumber'd—Death, the while,
Stole o'er my senses in that lovely isle
So softly that no single silken hair
Awoke that slept—or knew that it was there.
The last spot of Earth's orb I trod upon
*Was a proud temple call'd the Parthenon—
More beauty clung around her column'd wall
†Than ev'n thy glowing bosom beats withal,
And when old Time my wing did disenthral
Thence sprang I—as the eagle from his tower,
And years I left behind me in an hour.
What time upon her airy bounds I hung
One half the garden of her globe was flung
Unrolling as a chart unto my view—
Tenantless cities of the desert too!
Ianthe, beauty crowded on me then,
And half I wish'd to be again of men."

"My Angelo! and why of them to be?
A brighter dwelling-place is here for thee—
And greener fields than in yon world above,
And women's loveliness—and passionate love."
"But, list, Ianthe! when the air so soft
‡Fail'd, as my pennon'd spirit leapt aloft,
Perhaps my brain grew dizzy—but the world
I left so late was into chaos hurl'd—
Sprang from her station, on the winds apart,
And roll'd, a flame, the fiery Heaven athwart.
Methought, my sweet one, then I ceased to soar
And fell—not swiftly as I rose before,
But with a downward, tremulous motion thro'
Light, brazen rays, this golden star unto!

* It was entire in 1687—the most elevated spot in Athens.

† Shadowing more beauty in their airy brows
Than have the white breasts of the Queen of Love.—*Marlowe.*

‡ Pennon—for pinion.—*Milton.*

Nor long the measure of my falling hours,
For nearest of all stars was thine to ours—
Dread star! that came, amid a night of mirth,
A red Dædalion on the timid Earth.

"We came—and to thy Earth—but not to us
Be given our lady's bidding to discuss:
We came, my love; around, above, below,
Gay fire-fly of the night we come and go,
Nor ask a reason save the angel-nod
She grants to us, as granted by her God—
But, Angelo, than thine grey Time unfurl'd
Never his fairy wing o'er fairier world!
Dim was its little disk, and angel eyes
Alone could see the phantom in the skies,
When first Al Aaraaf knew her course to be
Headlong thitherward o'er the starry sea—
But when its glory swell'd upon the sky,
As glowing Beauty's bust beneath man's eye,
We paus'd before the heritage of men,
And thy star trembled—as doth Beauty then!"

Thus, in discourse, the lovers whiled away
The night that waned and waned and brought
no day.
They fell: for Heaven to them no hope imparts
Who hear not for the beating of their hearts.

Romance

[First published as the 'Preface' to *Al Aaraaf, Tamerlane, and Minor Poems* (1829). An expanded version appeared as an 'Introduction' to *Poems* (1831). The original shorter version was published under the title 'Romance' in the August 30, 1845 issue of the *Broadway Journal* and was included in *The Raven and Other Poems* (1845).]

Romance, who loves to nod and sing,
With drowsy head and folded wing,
Among the green leaves as they shake
Far down within some shadowy lake,
To me a painted paroquet
Hath been—a most familiar bird—
Taught me my alphabet to say—
To lisp my very earliest word
While in the wild wood I did lie,
A child—with a most knowing eye.

Of late, eternal Condor years
So shake the very Heaven on high
With tumult as they thunder by,
I have no time for idle cares
Through gazing on the unquiet sky.
And when an hour with calmer wings
Its down upon thy spirit flings—

That little time with lyre and rhyme
To while away—forbidden things!
My heart would feel to be a crime
Unless it trembled with the strings.

Sonnet—To Science

[First appeared without a title in *Al Aaraaf, Tamerlane, and Minor Poems* (1829). This version was published in the August 2, 1845, issue of the *Broadway Journal.*]

Science! true daughter of Old Time thou art!
    Who alterest all things with thy peering eyes.
Why preyest thou thus upon the poet's heart,
    Vulture, whose wings are dull realities?
How should he love thee? or how deem thee wise,
    Who wouldst not leave him in his wandering
To seek for treasure in the jewelled skies
    Albeit he soared with an undaunted wing?
Hast thou not dragged Diana from her car?
    And driven the Hamadryad from the wood
To seek a shelter in some happier star?
    Hast thou not torn the Naiad from her flood,
The Elfin from the green grass, and from me
    The summer dream beneath the tamarind tree?

Lenore

[First published under the title 'A Pæan' in *Poems* (1831) and then in the January 1836 issue of the *Southern Literary Messenger.* Revised extensively numerous times. Appeared with the title 'Lenore' in the February 1843 issue of *The Pioneer,* a periodical published by James Russell Lowell. The final version was published in the *Broadway Journal* on August 16, 1845. The version below is taken from *The Raven and Other Poems* (1845).]

Ah, broken is the golden bowl! the spirit flown
 forever!
Let the bell toll!—a saintly soul floats on the
 Stygian river;
And, Guy De Vere, hast *thou* no tear?—weep now
 or never more!
See! on yon drear and rigid bier low lies thy love,
 Lenore!
Come! let the burial rite be read—the funeral song
 be sung!—
An anthem for the queenliest dead that ever died
 so young—
A dirge for her the doubly dead in that she died so
 young.

"Wretches! ye loved her for her wealth and hated
 her for her pride,

"And when she fell in feeble health, ye blessed
her—that she died!
"How *shall* the ritual, then, be read?—the requiem
how be sung
"By you—by yours, the evil eye,—by yours, the
slanderous tongue
"That did to death the innocent that died, and died
so young?"

Peccavimus; but rave not thus! and let a Sabbath song
Go up to God so solemnly the dead may feel
so wrong!
The sweet Lenore hath "gone before," with Hope,
that flew beside
Leaving thee wild for the dear child that should
have been thy bride—
For her, the fair and *debonair*, that now so
lowly lies,
The life upon her yellow hair but not within
her eyes—
The life still there, upon her hair—the death upon
her eyes.

"Avaunt! tonight my heart is light. No dirge will I
upraise,
"But waft the angel on her flight with a Pæan of
old days!
"Let *no* bell toll!—lest her sweet soul, amid its
hallowed mirth,
"Should catch the note, as it doth float—up from
the damnéd Earth.
"To friends above, from fiends below, the indignant
ghost is riven—
"From Hell unto a high estate far up within the
Heaven—
"From grief and groan, to a golden throne, beside
the King of Heaven."

The Sleeper

[First published with the title 'Irene' in *Poems* (1831). Revised and published in the *Southern Literary Messenger* in May 1836. It appeared as 'The Sleeper' in Philadelphia's *Saturday Chronicle* on May 22, 1841, after several revisions. This version was printed in the *Broadway Journal* on May 3, 1845.]

At midnight, in the month of June,
I stand beneath the mystic moon.
An opiate vapour, dewy, dim,
Exhales from out her golden rim,
And, softly dripping, drop by drop,
Upon the quiet mountain top,
Steals drowsily and musically
Into the universal valley.
The rosemary nods upon the grave;
The lily lolls upon the wave;
Wrapping the fog about its breast,
The ruin moulders into rest;
Looking like Lethe, see! the lake
A conscious slumber seems to take,
And would not, for the world, awake.
All Beauty sleeps!—and lo! where lies
(Her casement open to the skies)
Irene, with her Destinies!
Oh, lady bright! can it be right—
This window open to the night?

The wanton airs, from the tree-top,
Laughingly through the lattice drop—
The bodiless airs, a wizard rout,
Flit through thy chamber in and out,
And wave the curtain canopy
So fitfully—so fearfully—
Above the closed and fringed lid
'Neath which thy slumb'ring soul lies hid,
That, o'er the floor and down the wall,
Like ghosts the shadows rise and fall!
Oh, lady dear, hast thou no fear?
Why and what art thou dreaming here?
Sure thou art come o'er far-off seas,
A wonder to these garden trees!
Strange is thy pallor! strange thy dress!
Strange, above all, thy length of tress,
And this all solemn silentness!

The lady sleeps! Oh, may her sleep,
Which is enduring, so be deep!
Heaven have her in its sacred keep!
This chamber changed for one more holy,
This bed for one more melancholy,
I pray to God that she may lie
Forever with unopen'd eye,
While the dim sheeted ghosts go by!

My love, she sleeps! Oh, may her sleep,
As it is lasting, so be deep!
Soft may the worms about her creep!
Far in the forest, dim and old,
For her may some tall vault unfold—
Some vault that oft hath flung its black
And winged pannels fluttering back,
Triumphant, o'er the crested palls,
Of her grand family funerals—
Some sepulchre, remote, alone,

Against whose portal she hath thrown,
In childhood, many an idle stone—
Some tomb from out whose sounding door
She ne'er shall force an echo more,
Thrilling to think, poor child of sin!
It was the dead who groaned within.

To Helen

[First published in *Poems* (1831). Reprinted in the *Southern Literary Messenger* in March 1836. This revised version was included in *The Raven and Other Poems* (1845).]

Helen, thy beauty is to me
    Like those Nicean barks of yore,
That gently, o'er a perfumed sea,
    The weary way-worn wanderer bore
    To his own native shore.

On desperate seas long wont to roam,
    Thy hyacinth hair, thy classic face,
Thy Naiad airs have brought me home
    To the glory that was Greece,
And the grandeur that was Rome.

Lo! in yon brilliant window-niche
    How statue-like I see thee stand,
The agate lamp within thy hand!
    Ah, Psyche, from the regions which
    Are Holy-land!

The City in the Sea

[First published in *Poems* (1831) titled 'The Doomed City'. A revised version titled 'The City of Sin' appeared in the August 1836 issue of the *Southern Literary Messenger.* It appeared under this title in *The American Review: A Whig Journal* in April 1845 and the *Broadway Journal* in August 30, 1845. This version was published in *The Raven and Other Poems* (1845).]

Lo! Death has reared himself a throne
In a strange city lying alone
Far down within the dim West,
Where the good and the bad and the worst and the
 best
Have gone to their eternal rest.
There shrines and palaces and towers
(Time-eaten towers that tremble not!)
Resemble nothing that is ours.
Around, by lifting winds forgot,
Resignedly beneath the sky
The melancholy waters lie.

No rays from the holy heaven come down
On the long night-time of that town;
But light from out the lurid sea
Streams up the turrets silently—
Gleams up the pinnacles far and free—

Up domes—up spires—up kingly halls—
Up fanes—up Babylon-like walls—
Up shadowy long-forgotten bowers
Of scultured ivy and stone flowers—
Up many and many a marvelous shrine
Whose wreathed friezes intertwine
The viol, the violet, and the vine.

Resignedly beneath the sky
The melancholy waters lie.
So blend the turrets and shadows there
That all seem pendulous in air,
While from a proud tower in the town
Death looks gigantically down.

There open fanes and gaping graves
Yawn level with the luminous waves;
But not the riches there that lie
In each idol's diamond eye—
Not the gaily-jeweled dead
Tempt the waters from their bed;
For no ripples curl, alas!
Along that wilderness of glass—
No swellings tell that winds may be
Upon some far-off happier sea—
No heavings hint that winds have been
On seas less hideously serene.

But lo, a stir is in the air!
The wave—there is a movement there!
As if the towers had thrown aside,
In slightly sinking, the dull tide—
As if their tops had feebly given
A void within the filmy Heaven.
The waves have now a redder glow—
The hours are breathing faint and low—

And when, amid no earthly moans,
Down, down that town shall settle hence,
Hell, rising from a thousand thrones,
Shall do it reverence.

The Valley of Unrest

[First published as 'The Valley Nis' in *Poems* (1831) and later in the February 1836 issue of the *Southern Literary Messenger*. It appeared under the title 'The Valley of Unrest' in the April 1845 issue of the *American Whig Review* and September 6, 1845, issue of the *Broadway Journal*, and was included in *The Raven and Other Poems* (1845).]

Once it smiled a silent dell
Where the people did not dwell;
They had gone unto the wars,
Trusting to the mild-eyed stars,
Nightly, from their azure towers,
To keep watch above the flowers,
In the midst of which all day
The red sun-light lazily lay.
Now each visiter shall confess
The sad valley's restlessness.
Nothing there is motionless—
Nothing save the airs that brood
Over the magic solitude.
Ah, by no wind are stirred those trees
That palpitate like the chill seas
Around the misty Hebrides!
Ah, by no wind those clouds are driven
That rustle through the unquiet Heaven
Uneasily, from morn till even,

Over the violets there that lie
In myriad types of the human eye—
Over the lilies there that wave
And weep above a nameless grave!
They wave:—from out their fragrant tops
Eternal dews come down in drops.
They weep:—from off their delicate stems
Perennial tears descend in gems.

Hymn

[First published in Poe's tale 'Morella' in the April 1835 issue of the *Southern Literary Messenger.* Published as 'Catholic Hymn' in the *Broadway Journal* on August 16, 1845. This version appeared in *The Raven and Other Poems* (1845).]

At morn—at noon—at twilight dim—
Maria! thou hast heard my hymn!
In joy and wo—in good and ill—
Mother of God, be with me still!
When the Hours flew brightly by,
And not a cloud obscured the sky,
My soul, lest it should truant be,
Thy grace did guide to thine and thee;
Now, when storms of Fate o'ercast
Darkly my Present and my Past,
Let my Future radiant shine
With sweet hopes of thee and thine!

Bridal Ballad

[Published as 'Ballad' in the *Southern Literary Messenger* in January 1837 and the *Saturday Evening Post* on July 31, 1841. This version, with the title 'Bridal Ballad', was printed in the August 2, 1845, issue of the *Broadway Journal.*]

The ring is on my hand,
    And the wreath is on my brow;
Satins and jewels grand
Are all at my command,
    And I am happy now.

And my lord he loves me well;
    But, when first he breathed his vow,
I felt my bosom swell—
For the words rang as a knell,
And the voice seemed *his* who fell
In the battle down the dell,
    And who is happy now.

But he spoke to re-asure me,
    And he kissed my pallid brow,
While a reverie came o're me,
And to the church-yard bore me,
And I sighed to him before me,
Thinking him dead D'Elormie,
    "Oh, I am happy now!"

And thus the words were spoken,
    And this the plighted vow,
And, though my faith be broken,
And, though my heart be broken,
Behold the golden token
    That *proves* me happy now!

Would God I could awaken!
    For I dream I know not how,
And my soul is sorely shaken
Lest an evil step be taken,—
Lest the dead who is forsaken
    May not be happy now.

Sonnet—Silence

[First published in the *Philadelphia Saturday Courier* on January 4, 1840, under the title 'Silence, a Sonnet'. Revised and reprinted in the July 26, 1845, issue of the *Broadway Journal* and collected in *The Raven and Other Poems* (1845).]

There are some qualities—some incorporate things,
That have a double life, which thus is made
A type of that twin entity which springs
From matter and light, evinced in solid and shade.
There is a two-fold *Silence*—sea and shore—
Body and soul. One dwells in lonely places,
Newly with grass o'ergrown; some solemn graces,
Some human memories and tearful lore,
Render him terrorless: his name's "No More."
He is the corporate Silence: dread him not!
No power hath he of evil in himself;
But should some urgent fate (untimely lot!)
Bring thee to meet his shadow (nameless elf,
That haunteth the lone regions where hath trod
No foot of man,) commend thyself to God!

The Raven

[One of the most prominent poems ever written, it was first published with Poe's name in the January 29, 1845, issue of *The Evening Mirror*. An instant success, it brought Poe considerable national fame.]

Once upon a midnight dreary, while I pondered, weak and weary,
Over many a quaint and curious volume of forgotten lore,
While I nodded, nearly napping, suddenly there came a tapping,
As of some one gently rapping, rapping at my chamber door.
"'Tis some visiter," I muttered, "tapping at my chamber door—
Only this, and nothing more."

Ah, distinctly I remember it was in the bleak December,
And each separate dying ember wrought its ghost upon the floor.
Eagerly I wished the morrow;—vainly I had sought to borrow
From my books surcease of sorrow—sorrow for the lost Lenore—

For the rare and radiant maiden whom the angels name Lenore—
Nameless *here* for evermore.

And the silken, sad, uncertain rustling of each purple curtain
Thrilled me—filled me with fantastic terrors never felt before;
So that now, to still the beating of my heart, I stood repeating
"'Tis some visiter entreating entrance at my chamber door—
Some late visiter entreating entrance at my chamber door;—
This it is, and nothing more."

Presently my soul grew stronger; hesitating then no longer,
"Sir," said I, "or Madam, truly your forgiveness I implore;
But the fact is I was napping, and so gently you came rapping,
And so faintly you came tapping, tapping at my chamber door,
That I scarce was sure I heard you"—here I opened wide the door;——
Darkness there and nothing more.

Deep into that darkness peering, long I stood there wondering, fearing,
Doubting, dreaming dreams no mortal ever dared to dream before;
But the silence was unbroken, and the stillness gave no token,
And the only word there spoken was the whispered word, "Lenore!"

This I whispered, and an echo murmured back the word, "Lenore!"
Merely this, and nothing more.

Back into the chamber turning, all my soul within me burning,
Soon I heard again a tapping somewhat louder than before.
"Surely," said I, "surely that is something at my window lattice;
Let me see, then, what thereat is, and this mystery explore—
Let my heart be still a moment and this mystery explore;—
'Tis the wind and nothing more!"

Open here I flung the shutter, when, with many a flirt and flutter,
In there stepped a stately Raven of the saintly days of yore.
Not the least obeisance made he; not an instant stopped or stayed he;
But, with mien of lord or lady, perched above my chamber door—
Perched upon a bust of Pallas just above my chamber door—
Perched, and sat, and nothing more.

Then this ebony bird beguiling my sad fancy into smiling,
By the grave and stern decorum of the countenance it wore,
"Though thy crest be shorn and shaven, thou," I said, "are sure no craven,
Ghastly grim and ancient raven wandering from the Nightly shore—

Tell me what thy lordly name is on the Night's Plutonian shore!"
Quoth the Raven, "Nevermore."

Much I marvelled this ungainly fowl to hear discourse so plainly,
Though its answer little meaning—little relevancy bore;
For we cannot help agreeing that no living human being
Ever yet was blessed with seeing bird above his chamber door—
Bird or beast upon the sculptured bust above his chamber door,
With such name as "Nevermore."

But the Raven, sitting lonely on the placid bust, spoke only
That one word, as if his soul in that one word he did outpour.
Nothing farther then he uttered—not a feather then he fluttered—
Till I scarcely more than muttered "Other friends have flown before—
On the morrow *he* will leave me, as my hopes have flown before."
Then the bird said "Nevermore."

Startled at the stillness broken by reply so aptly spoken,
"Doubtless," said I, "what it utters is its only stock and store
Caught from some unhappy master whom unmerciful Disaster
Followed fast and followed faster till his songs one burden bore—

Till the dirges of his Hope that melancholy burden bore
Of 'Never—nevermore.'"

But the Raven still beguiling all my sad soul into smiling,
Straight I wheeled a cushioned seat in front of bird, and bust and door;
Then, upon the velvet sinking, I betook myself to linking
Fancy unto fancy, thinking what this ominous bird of yore—
What this grim, ungainly, ghastly, gaunt and ominous bird of yore
Meant in croaking "Nevermore."

This I sat engaged in guessing, but no syllable expressing
To the fowl whose fiery eyes now burned into my bosom's core;
This and more I sat divining, with my head at ease reclining
On the cushion's velvet lining that the lamplight gloated o'er,
But whose velvet violet lining with the lamplight gloating o'er,
She shall press, ah, nevermore!

Then, methought, the air grew denser, perfumed from an unseen censer
Swung by Angels whose faint foot-falls tinkled on the tufted floor.
"Wretch," I cried, "thy God hath lent thee—by these angels he hath sent thee
Respite—respite and nepenthe from thy memories of Lenore;

Quaff, oh quaff this kind nepenthe and forget this
lost Lenore!"
Quoth the Raven "Nevermore."

"Prophet!" said I, "thing of evil!—prophet still, if
bird or devil!—
Whether Tempter sent, or whether tempest tossed
thee here ashore,
Desolate yet all undaunted, on this desert land
enchanted—
On this home by Horror haunted—tell me truly, I
implore—
Is there—*is* there balm in Gilead?—tell me—tell
me, I implore!"
Quoth the Raven "Nevermore."

"Prophet!" said I, "thing of evil!—prophet still, if
bird or devil!
By that Heaven that bends above us—by that God
we both adore—
Tell this soul with sorrow laden if, within the
distant Aidenn,
It shall clasp a sainted maiden whom the angels
name Lenore—
Clasp a rare and radiant maiden whom the angels
name Lenore."
Quoth the Raven "Nevermore."

"Be that word our sign of parting, bird or fiend!" I
shrieked, upstarting—
"Get thee back into the tempest and the Night's
Plutonian shore!
Leave no black plume as a token of that lie thy soul
hath spoken!
Leave my loneliness unbroken!—quit the bust
above my door!

Take thy beak from out my heart, and take thy form
from off my door!"
Quoth the Raven "Nevermore."

And the Raven, never flitting, still is sitting, *still* is
sitting
On the pallid bust of Pallas just above my chamber
door;
And his eyes have all the seeming of a demon's that
is dreaming,
And the lamp-light o'er him streaming throws his
shadow on the floor;
And my soul from out that shadow that lies floating
on the floor
Shall be lifted—nevermore!

Eulalie—A Song

[First printed in *The American Review: A Whig Journal* in July 1845. Reprinted in the August 9, 1845, issue of the *Broadway Journal.*]

I dwelt alone
In a world of moan,
And my soul was a stagnant tide,
Till the fair and gentle Eulalie became my blushing bride—
Till the yellow-haired young Eulalie became my smiling bride.

Ah, less—less bright
The stars of the night
Than the eyes of the radiant girl,
And never a flake
That the vapor can make
With the moon-tints of purple and pearl,
Can vie with the modest Eulalie's most unregarded curl—
Can compare with the bright-eyed Eulalie's most humble and careless curl.

Now Doubt—now Pain
Come never again,

For her soul gives me sigh for sigh,
While all day long
Shines, bright and strong,
Astarté within the sky,
And ever to her dear Eulalie upturns her matron eye—
And ever to her young Eulalie upturns her violet eye.

A Valentine

[First published as 'To Her Whose Name is Written Below', in *The Evening Mirror* on February 21, 1846. An acrostic (taking the first letter of the first line, the second letter of the second line, and so on, we get the name Frances Sargent Osgood to whom the poem is dedicated), it was revised and published in the *Sartain's Union Magazine* and *The Flag of Our Union* in March 1849 with the title 'A Valentine'.]

At a 'Valentine Soiree,' in New York, the following enigmatical lines were received, among others, and read aloud to the company. The verses were enclosed in an envelope, addressed 'To her whose name is written within.' As no lady present could so read the riddle as to find her name written in it, the Valentine remained, and still remains, unclaimed. Can any of the readers of the FLAG discover for whom it is intended?

For her these lines are penned, whose luminous
    eyes,
Brightly expressive as the twins of Læda,
Shall find her own sweet name that, nestling, lies
Upon the page, enwrapped from every reader.
Search narrowly this rhyme, which holds a treasure
Divine—a talisman—an amulet
That must be worn at heart. Search well the
    measure;
The words—the letters themselves. Do not forget
The trivialest point, or you may lose your labor.

And yet there is in this no Gordian knot
Which one might not undo without a sabre
If one could merely understand the plot.
Enwritten upon this page whereon are peering
Such eager eyes, there lies, I say, *perdu*,
A well-known name, oft uttered in the hearing
Of poets, by poets; as the name is a poet's, too.
Its letters, although naturally lying—
Like the knight Pinto (Mendez Ferdinando)—
Still form a synonym for truth. Cease trying!
You will not read the riddle though you do the best
    you *can* do.

* Should there be no solution furnished of the above, we will give the key next week.

Ulalume: A Ballad

[First published anonymously in the December 1847 issue of the *American Whig Review*. This is the version reprinted by N. P. Willis, an American poet and editor, in the January 1, 1848, issue of the *Home Journal*. Its now-standard version (without the last stanza and with some minor revisions) was published in Griswold's edition of *Works* in 1850.]

[We do not know how many readers we have who will enjoy as we do, the following exquisitely piquant and skilful exercise of rarity and niceness of language. It is a poem which we find in the *American Review*, full of beauty and oddity of sentiment and versification, but a curiosity, (and a delicious one, we think,) in its philologic flavor. Who is the author?]

The skies they were ashen and sober;
    The leaves they were crisped and sere—
    The leaves they were withering and sere;
It was night in the lonesome October
    Of my most immemorial year;
It was hard by the dim lake of Auber,
    In the misty mid region of Weir—
It was down by the dank tarn of Auber,
    In the ghoul-haunted woodland of Weir.

Here once, through an alley Titanic,
    Of cypress, I roamed with my Soul—
    Of cypress, with Psyche, my Soul.

These were days when my heart was volcanic
    As the scoriac rivers that roll—
    As the lavas that restlessly roll
Their sulphurous currents down Yaanek
    In the ultimate climes of the pole—
That groan as they roll down Mount Yaanek
    In the realms of the boreal pole.

Our talk had been serious and sober,
    But our thoughts they were palsied and sere—
    Our memories were treacherous and sere—
For we knew not the month was October,
    And we marked not the night of the year—
    (Ah, night of all nights in the year!)
We noted not the dim lake of Auber—
    (Though once we had journeyed down here)—
We remembered not the dank tarn of Auber,
    Nor the ghoul-haunted woodland of Weir.

And now, as the night was senescent
    And star-dials pointed to morn—
    As the star-dials hinted of morn—
At the end of our path a liquescent
    And nebulous lustre was born.
Out of which a miraculous crescent
    Arose with a duplicate horn—
Astarte's bediamonded crescent
    Distinct with its duplicate horn.

And I said—"She is warmer than Dian:
    She rolls through an ether of sighs—
    She revels in a region of sighs:
She has seen that the tears are not dry on
    These cheeks, where the worm never dies,
And has come past the stars of the Lion
    To point us the path to the skies—
    To the Lethean peace of the skies—

Come up, in despite of the Lion,
To shine on us with her bright eyes—
Come up through the lair of the Lion,
With Love in her luminous eyes."

But Psyche, uplifting her finger,
Said—"Sadly this star I mistrust—
Her pallor I strangely mistrust:—
Oh, hasten!—oh, let us not linger!
Oh, fly!—let us fly!—for we must."
In terror she spoke, letting sink her
Wings till they trailed in the dust—
In agony sobbed, letting sink her
Plumes till they trailed in the dust—
Till they sorrowfully trailed in the dust.

I replied—"This is nothing but dreaming:
Let us on by this tremulous light!
Let us bathe in this crystalline light!
Its Sybilic splendor is beaming
With Hope and in Beauty tonight:—
See!—it flickers up the sky through the night!
Ah, we safely may trust to its gleaming,
And be sure it will lead us aright—
We safely may trust to a gleaming
That cannot but guide us aright,
Since it flickers up to Heaven through the night."

Thus I pacified Psyche and kissed her,
And tempted her out of her gloom—
And conquered her scruples and gloom;
And we passed to the end of the vista,
And were stopped by the door of a tomb—
By the door of a legended tomb;
And I said—"What is written, sweet sister,
On the door of this legended tomb?"

She replied—"Ulalume—Ulalume—
'Tis the vault of thy lost Ulalume!"

Then my heart it grew ashen and sober
    As the leaves that were crisped and sere—
    As the leaves that were withering and sere,
And I cried—"It was surely October
    On this very night of last year
    That I journeyed—I journeyed down here—
    That I brought a dread burden down here—
    On this night of all nights in the year,
    Oh, what demon has tempted me here?
Well I know, now, this dim lake of Auber—
    This misty mid region of Weir—
Well I know, now, this dank tarn of Auber,
    In the ghoul-haunted woodland of Weir."

Said we, then—the two, then—" Ah, can it
    Have been that the woodlandish ghouls—
    The pitiful, the merciful ghouls—
To bar up our way and to ban it
    From the secret that lies in these wolds—
    From the thing that lies hidden in these wolds—
Had drawn up the spectre of a planet
    From the limbo of lunary souls—
This sinfully scintillant planet
From the Hell of the planetary souls?"

A Dream within a Dream

[First published in *The Flag of Our Union*, a Boston-based weekly story paper, on March 31, 1849.]

Take this kiss upon the brow!
And, in parting from you now,
Thus much let me avow—
You are not wrong, who deem
That my days have been a dream;
Yet if Hope has flown away
In a night, or in a day,
In a vision, or in none,
Is it therefore the less *gone*?
All that we see or seem
Is but a dream within a dream.

I stand amid the roar
Of a surf-tormented shore,
And I hold within my hand
Grains of the golden sand—
How few! yet how they creep
Through my fingers to the deep,
While I weep—while I weep!
O God! can I not grasp
Them with a tighter clasp?

O God! can I not save
One from the pitiless wave?
Is *all* that we see or seem
But a dream within a dream?

Eldorado

[One of Poe's last poems, it was partly a reaction to the California Gold Rush. The poem first appeared in *The Flag of Our Union* on April 21, 1849.]

Gaily bedight,
A gallant knight,
In sunshine and in shadow,
Had journeyed long,
Singing a song,
In search of Eldorado.

But he grew old—
This knight so bold—
And o'er his heart a shadow
Fell, as he found
No spot of ground
That looked like Eldorado.

And, as his strength
Failed him at length,
He met a pilgrim shadow—
'Shadow,' said he,
'Where can it be—
This land of Eldorado?'
'Over the Mountains

Of the Moon,
Down the Valley of the Shadow,
Ride, boldly ride,'
The shade replied,—
'If you seek for Eldorado!'

For Annie

[Written for Mrs. Nancy Richmond, with whom Poe shared a platonic relationship. Published in *The Flag of Our Union* and *Home Journal* on April 28, 1849.]

Thank Heaven! the crisis—
The danger is past,
And the lingering illness
Is over at last—
And the fever called "Living"
Is conquered at last.

Sadly, I know
I am shorn of my strength,
And no muscle I move
As I lie at full length—
But no matter!—I feel
I am better at length.

And I rest so composedly
Now, in my bed,
That any beholder
Might fancy me dead—
Might start at beholding me,
Thinking me dead.
The moaning and groaning,
The sighing and sobbing,

Are quieted now,
    With that horrible throbbing
At heart:—ah, that horrible,
    Horrible throbbing!

The sickness—the nausea—
    The pitiless pain—
Have ceased with the fever
    That maddened my brain—
With the fever called "Living"
    That burned in my brain.

And oh! of all tortures
    That torture the worst
Has abated—the terrible
    Torture of thirst
For the naphthaline river
    Of Passion accurst:—
I have drank of a water
    That quenches all thirst:—

Of a water that flows,
    With a lullaby sound,
From a spring but a very few
    Feet under ground—
From a cavern not very far
    Down under ground.

And ah! let it never
    Be foolishly said
That my room it is gloomy
    And narrow my bed;
For man never slept
    In a different bed—
And, to *sleep*, you must slumber
    In just such a bed.

My tantalized spirit
    Here blandly reposes,
Forgetting, or never
    Regretting, its roses—
Its old agitations
    Of myrtles and roses:

For now, while so quietly
    Lying, it fancies
A holier odor
    About it, of pansies—
A rosemary odor,
    Commingled with pansies—
With rue and the beautiful
    Puritan pansies.

And so it lies happily,
    Bathing in many
A dream of the truth
    And the beauty of Annie—
Drowned in a bath
    Of the tresses of Annie.

She tenderly kissed me,
    She fondly caressed,
And then I fell gently
    To sleep on her breast—
Deeply to sleep
    From the heaven of her breast.

When the light was extinguished,
    She covered me warm,
And she prayed to the angels
    To keep me from harm—
To the queen of the angels
    To shield me from harm.

And I lie so composedly,
    Now, in my bed,
(Knowing her love)
    That you fancy me dead—
And I rest so contentedly,
    Now, in my bed,
(With her love at my breast)
    That you fancy me dead—
That you shudder to look at me,
    Thinking me dead:—

But my heart it is brighter
    Than all of the many
Stars in the sky,
    For it sparkles with Annie—
It glows with the light
    Of the love of my Annie—
With the thought of the light
    Of the eyes of my Annie.

Annabel Lee

[Concerning the themes of love, envy, and the death of a beautiful woman—which Poe considered "the most poetical topic in the world"—this was his last complete poem. It was first published as part of Griswold's obituary of Poe in *New-York Daily Tribune* on October 9, 1849. This is the original version.]

It was many and many a year ago,
    In a kingdom by the sea,
That a maiden there lived whom you may know
    By the name of Annabel Lee;—
And this maiden she lived with no other thought
    Than to love and be loved by me.

She was a child and *I* was a child,
    In this kingdom by the sea,
But we loved with a love that was more than love—
    I and my Annabel Lee—
With a love that the wingéd seraphs of Heaven
    Coveted her and me.

And this was the reason that, long ago,
    In this kingdom by the sea,
A wind blew out of a cloud by night
    Chilling my Annabel Lee;
So that her high-born kinsmen came

And bore her away from me,
To shut her up, in a sepulchre
In this kingdom by the sea.

The angels, not half so happy in Heaven,
Went envying her and me:—
Yes! that was the reason (as all men know,
In this kingdom by the sea)
That the wind came out of the cloud, chilling
And killing my Annabel Lee.

But our love it was stronger by far than the love
Of those who were older than we—
Of many far wiser than we—
And neither the angels in Heaven above
Nor the demons down under the sea
Can ever dissever my soul from the soul
Of the beautiful Annabel Lee:—

For the moon never beams without bringing me dreams
Of the beautiful Annabel Lee;
And the stars never rise but I see the bright eyes
Of the beautiful Annabel Lee;
And so, all the night-tide, I lie down by the side
Of my darling, my darling, my life and my bride
In her sepulchre there by the sea—
In her tomb by the side of the sea.

The Bells

[Suggesting the bell sounds as being representative of the stages of life from childhood to death, this onomatopoeic poem was published posthumously in the November 1849 issue of the *Sartain's Union Magazine.*]

I

Hear the sledges with the bells—
Silver bells!
What a world of merriment their melody foretells!
How they tinkle, tinkle, tinkle,
In the icy air of night!
While the stars that oversprinkle
All the heavens, seem to twinkle
With a crystalline delight;
Keeping time, time, time,
In a sort of Runic rhyme,
To the tintinnabulation that so musically wells
From the bells, bells, bells, bells,
Bells, bells, bells—
From the jingling and the tinkling of the bells.

II

Hear the mellow wedding bells
Golden bells!
What a world of happiness their harmony foretells!
Through the balmy air of night
How they ring out their delight!—
From the molten-golden notes,
And all in tune,
What a liquid ditty floats
To the turtle-dove that listens, while she gloats
On the moon!
Oh, from out the sounding cells,
What a gush of euphony voluminously wells!
How it swells!
How it dwells
On the Future!—how it tells
Of the rapture that impels
To the swinging and the ringing
Of the bells, bells, bells—
Of the bells, bells, bells, bells,
Bells, bells, bells—
To the rhyming and the chiming of the bells!

III

Hear the loud alarum bells—
Brazen bells!
What tale of terror, now, their turbulency tells!
In the startled ear of night
How they scream out their affright!
Too much horrified to speak,
They can only shriek, shriek,
Out of tune,

In a clamourous appealing to the mercy of the fire,
In a mad expostulation with the deaf and frantic
  fire,
Leaping higher, higher, higher,
With a desperate desire,
And a resolute endeavor
Now—now to sit, or never,
By the side of the pale-faced moon.
Oh, the bells, bells, bells!
What a tale their terror tells
Of Despair!
How they clang, and clash, and roar!
What a horror they outpour
On the bosom of the palpitating air!
Yet the ear, it fully knows,
By the twanging
And the clanging,
How the danger ebbs and flows;
Yet the ear distinctly tells,
In the jangling
And the wrangling,
How the danger sinks and swells,
By the sinking or the swelling in the anger of
  the bells—
Of the bells—
Of the bells, bells, bells, bells,
Bells, bells, bells—
In the clamour and the clangor of the bells!

IV

Hear the tolling of the bells—
Iron bells!
What a world of solemn thought their monody compels!
In the silence of the night,
How we shiver with affright
At the melancholy meaning of their tone!
For every sound that floats
From the rust within their throats
Is a groan.
And the people—ah, the people—
They that dwell up in the steeple,
All alone,
And who, tolling, tolling, tolling,
In that muffled monotone,
Feel a glory in so rolling
On the human heart a stone—
They are neither man nor woman—
They are neither brute nor human—
They are Ghouls:—
And their king it is who tolls:—
And he rolls, rolls, rolls, rolls,
Rolls
A pæan from the bells!
And his merry bosom swells
With the pæan of the bells!
And he dances, and he yells;
Keeping time, time, time,
In a sort of Runic rhyme,
To the pæan of the bells:—
Of the bells:
Keeping time, time, time,
In a sort of Runic rhyme,

To the throbbing of the bells—
Of the bells, bells, bells—
To the sobbing of the bells:—
Keeping time, time, time,
As he knells, knells, knells,
In a happy Runic rhyme,
To the rolling of the bells—
Of the bells, bells, bells:—
To the tolling of the bells—
Of the bells, bells, bells, bells,
Bells, bells, bells—
To the moaning and the groaning of the bells.

Alone

[Written by the 20-year-old Poe, this poem is often regarded autobiographical. Left untitled by him, it was published posthumously with this title in the *Scribner's Monthly* in September 1875.]

From childhood's hour I have not been
As others were—I have not seen
As others saw—I could not bring
My passions from a common spring—
From the same source I have not taken
My sorrow—I could not awaken
My heart to joy at the same tone—
And all I lov'd—*I* lov'd alone—
Then—in my childhood—in the dawn
Of a most stormy life—was drawn
From ev'ry depth of good and ill
The mystery which binds me still—
From the torrent, or the fountain—
From the red cliff of the mountain—
From the sun that 'round me roll'd
In its autumn tint of gold—
From the lightning in the sky
As it pass'd me flying by—
From the thunder, and the storm—

And the cloud that took the form
(When the rest of Heaven was blue)
Of a demon in my view—

Tales

MS. Found in a Bottle

[This adventure sea tale narrated by an unnamed narrator was the winning entry of a writing contest by the *Baltimore Saturday Visiter*, a weekly. It was published in the October 19, 1833, issue.]

Qui n'a plus qu'un moment a vivre
N'a plus rien a dissimuler.
—Quinault – Atys

Of my country and of my family I have little to say. Ill usage and length of years have driven me from the one, and estranged me from the other. Hereditary wealth afforded me an education of no common order, and a contemplative turn of mind enabled me to methodize the stores which early study very diligently garnered up. Beyond all things, the study of the German moralists gave me great delight; not from any ill-advised admiration of their eloquent madness, but from the ease with which my habits of rigid thought enabled me to detect their falsities. I have often been reproached with the aridity of my genius; a deficiency of imagination has been imputed to me as a crime; and the Pyrrhonism of my opinions has at all times rendered me notorious. Indeed, a strong relish for physical philosophy has, I fear, tinctured my mind with a very common error of this age—I mean the habit of referring occurrences, even the least susceptible of such reference, to the principles of that science. Upon the whole, no person could be less liable than myself to be led away from the severe precincts of truth by the *ignes fatui* of superstition. I have thought proper to premise thus much, lest the incredible tale I have to tell should be considered rather the raving of a crude imagination, than the positive experience of a mind to which the reveries of fancy have been a dead letter and a nullity.

After many years spent in foreign travel, I sailed in the year 18—, from the port of Batavia, in the rich and populous island of Java, on a voyage to the Archipelago of the Sunda Islands. I went as passenger—having no other inducement than a kind of nervous restlessness which haunted me as a fiend.

Our vessel was a beautiful ship of about four hundred tons, copper-fastened, and built at Bombay of Malabar teak. She was freighted with cotton-wool and oil, from the Laccadive Islands. We had also on board coir, jaggeree, ghee, cocoa-nuts, and a few cases of opium. The stowage was clumsily done, and the vessel consequently crank.

We got under way with a mere breath of wind, and for many days stood along the eastern coast of Java, without any other incident to beguile the monotony of our course than the occasional meeting with some of the small grabs of the Archipelago to which we were bound.

One evening, leaning over the taffrail, I observed a very singular, isolated cloud, to the N.W. It was remarkable, as well for its colour, as from its being the first we had seen since our departure from Batavia. I watched it attentively until sunset, when it spread all at once to the eastward and westward, girting in the horizon with a narrow strip of vapor, and looking like a long line of low beach. My notice was soon afterwards attracted by the dusky-red appearance of the moon, and the peculiar character of the sea. The latter was undergoing a rapid change, and the water seemed more than usually transparent. Although I could distinctly see the bottom, yet, heaving the lead, I found the ship in fifteen fathoms. The air now became intolerably hot, and was loaded with spiral exhalations similar to those arising from heat iron. As night came on, every breath of wind died away, and a more entire calm it is impossible to conceive. The flame of a candle burned upon the poop without the least perceptible motion, and a long hair, held between the finger and thumb, hung without the possibility of detecting a vibration. However, as the captain said he could perceive no indication of danger, and as we were drifting in bodily to shore, he ordered the sails to be furled, and the anchor let go. No watch was set, and the crew, consisting principally of Malays, stretched themselves deliberately upon deck. I went below—not without a full presentiment of evil. Indeed, every appearance warranted me in apprehending a Simoom. I told the captain my fears; but he paid no attention to what I said, and left me without deigning to give a reply. My uneasiness, however, prevented me from sleeping, and about midnight I went upon deck. As I placed my foot upon the upper step of the companion-ladder, I was startled by a loud, humming noise, like that occasioned by the rapid revolution of a mill-wheel, and before I could ascertain its meaning, I found the ship quivering to its center. In the next instant, a wilderness of foam hurled us upon our beam-ends, and, rushing over us fore and aft, swept the entire decks from stem to stern.

The extreme fury of the blast proved, in a great measure, the salvation of the ship. Although completely water-logged, yet, as her masts had gone by the board, she rose, after a minute, heavily from the sea, and, staggering awhile beneath the immense pressure of the tempest, finally righted.

By what miracle I escaped destruction, it is impossible to say. Stunned by the shock of the water, I found myself, upon recovery, jammed in between the stern-post and rudder. With great difficulty I gained my feet, and looking dizzily around, was, at first, struck with the idea of our being among breakers; so terrific, beyond the wildest imagination, was the whirlpool of mountainous and foaming ocean within which we were engulfed. After a while, I heard the voice of an old Swede, who had shipped with us at the moment of our leaving port. I hallooed to him with all my strength, and presently he came reeling aft. We soon discovered that we were the sole survivors of the accident. All on deck, with the exception of ourselves, had been swept overboard; the captain and mates must have perished as they slept, for the cabins were deluged with water. Without assistance, we could expect to do little for the security of the ship, and our exertions were at first paralyzed by the momentary expectation of going down. Our cable had, of course, parted like pack-thread, at the first breath of the hurricane, or we should have been instantaneously overwhelmed. We scudded with frightful velocity before the sea, and the water made clear breaches over us. The framework of our stern was shattered excessively, and, in almost every respect, we had received considerable injury; but to our extreme joy we found the pumps unchoked, and that we had made no great shifting of our ballast. The main fury of the blast had already blown over, and we apprehended little danger from the violence of the wind; but we looked forward to its total cessation with dismay; well believing, that,

in our shattered condition, we should inevitably perish in the tremendous swell which would ensue. But this very just apprehension seemed by no means likely to be soon verified. For five entire days and nights—during which our only subsistence was a small quantity of jaggeree, procured with great difficulty from the forecastle—the hulk flew at a rate defying computation, before rapidly succeeding flaws of wind, which, without equaling the first violence of the Simoom, were still more terrific than any tempest I had before encountered. Our course for the first four days was, with trifling variations, S.E. and by S.; and we must have run down the coast of New Holland. On the fifth day the cold became extreme, although the wind had hauled round a point more to the northward. The sun arose with a sickly yellow luster, and clambered a very few degrees above the horizon—emitting no decisive light. There were no clouds apparent, yet the wind was upon the increase, and blew with a fitful and unsteady fury. About noon, as nearly as we could guess, our attention was again arrested by the appearance of the sun. It gave out no light, properly so called, but a dull and sullen glow without reflection, as if all its rays were polarized. Just before sinking within the turgid sea, its central fires suddenly went out, as if hurriedly extinguished by some unaccountable power. It was a dim, sliver-like rim, alone, as it rushed down the unfathomable ocean.

We waited in vain for the arrival of the sixth day—that day to me has not arrived—to the Swede never did arrive. Thenceforward we were enshrouded in patchy darkness, so that we could not have seen an object at twenty paces from the ship. Eternal night continued to envelop us, all unrelieved by the phosphoric sea-brilliancy to which we had been accustomed in the tropics. We observed too, that, although the tempest continued to rage with unabated violence, there was no longer to be discovered the usual appearance of surf, or foam, which had hitherto attended us. All around were horror, and thick gloom, and a black sweltering desert of ebony. Superstitious terror crept by degrees into the spirit of the old Swede, and my own soul was wrapped up in silent wonder. We neglected all care of the ship, as worse than useless, and securing ourselves, as well as possible, to the stump of the mizzen-mast, looked out bitterly into the world of ocean. We had no means of calculating time, nor could we form any guess of our situation. We were, however, well aware of having made farther to the southward than any previous navigators, and felt great amazement at not meeting with the usual impediments of ice. In the meantime every moment threatened to be our last—every mountainous billow hurried to overwhelm us. The swell surpassed anything I had imagined possible, and that we were not instantly buried is a miracle. My companion spoke of the lightness of our cargo, and reminded me of the excellent qualities of our ship; but I could not help feeling the utter hopelessness of hope itself, and prepared myself gloomily for that death which I thought nothing could defer beyond an hour, as, with every knot of way the ship made, the swelling of the black stupendous seas became more dismally appalling. At times we gasped for breath at an elevation beyond the albatross—at times became dizzy with the velocity of our descent into some watery hell, where the air grew stagnant, and no sound disturbed the slumbers of the kraken.

We were at the bottom of one of these abysses, when a quick scream from my companion broke fearfully upon the night. "See! see!" cried he, shrieking in my ears, "Almighty God! see! see!" As he spoke, I became aware of a dull, sullen glare of red light which streamed down the sides of the vast chasm where we lay, and threw a fitful brilliancy upon our deck. Casting my eyes upwards, I beheld a spectacle which froze the current of my blood. At a terrific height directly above us, and upon the very verge of the precipitous descent, hovered a gigantic ship of, perhaps, four thousand tons. Although upreared upon the summit of a wave more than a hundred times her own altitude, her apparent size exceeded that of any ship of the line or East Indiaman in existence. Her huge hull was of a deep dingy black, unrelieved by any of the customary carvings of a ship. A single row of brass cannon protruded from her open ports, and dashed from their polished surfaces the fires of innumerable battle-lanterns, which swung to and fro about her rigging. But what mainly inspired us with horror and astonishment, was that she bore up under a press of sail in the very teeth of that supernatural sea, and of that ungovernable hurricane. When we first discovered her, her bows were alone to be seen, as she rose slowly from the dim and horrible gulf beyond her. For a moment of intense terror she paused upon the giddy pinnacle, as if in contemplation of her own sublimity, then trembled and tottered, and—came down.

At this instant, I know not what sudden self-possession came over my spirit. Staggering as far aft as I could, I awaited fearlessly the ruin that was to overwhelm. Our own vessel was at length ceasing from her struggles, and sinking with her head to the sea. The shock of the descending mass struck her, consequently, in that portion of her frame which was already under water, and the inevitable result was to hurl me, with irresistible violence, upon the rigging of the stranger.

As I fell, the ship hove in stays, and went about; and to the confusion ensuing I attributed my escape from the notice of the crew. With little difficulty I made my way unperceived to the main hatchway, which was partially open, and soon found an opportunity of secreting myself in the hold. Why I did so I can hardly tell. An indefinite sense of awe, which at first sight of the navigators of the ship had taken hold of my mind, was perhaps the principle of my concealment. I was unwilling to trust myself with a race of people who had offered, to the cursory glance I had taken, so many points of vague novelty, doubt, and apprehension. I therefore thought proper to contrive a hiding-place in the hold. This I did by removing a small portion of the shifting-boards, in such a manner as to afford me a convenient retreat between the huge timbers of the ship.

I had scarcely completed my work, when a footstep in the hold forced me to make use of it. A man passed by my place of concealment with a feeble and unsteady gait. I could not see his face, but had an opportunity of observing his general appearance. There was about it an evidence of great age and infirmity. His knees tottered beneath a load of years, and his entire frame quivered under the burthen. He muttered to himself, in a low broken tone, some words of a language which I could not understand, and groped in a corner among a pile of singular-looking instruments, and decayed charts of navigation. His manner was a wild mixture of the peevishness of second childhood, and the solemn dignity of a God. He at length went on deck, and I saw him no more.

A feeling, for which I have no name, has taken possession of my soul—a sensation which will admit of no analysis, to which the lessons of bygone times are inadequate, and for which I fear futurity itself will offer me no key. To a mind constituted like my own, the latter consideration is an evil. I shall never—I know that I shall never—be satisfied with regard to the nature of my conceptions. Yet it is not wonderful that these conceptions are indefinite, since they have their origin in sources so utterly novel. A new sense—a new entity is added to my soul.

It is long since I first trod the deck of this terrible ship, and the rays of my destiny are, I think, gathering to a focus. Incomprehensible men! Wrapped up in meditations of a kind which I cannot divine, they pass me by unnoticed. Concealment is utter folly on my part, for the people will not see. It was but just now that I passed directly before the eyes of the mate—it was no long while ago that I ventured into the captain's own private cabin, and took thence the materials with which I write, and have written. I shall from time to time continue this journal. It is true that I may not find an opportunity of transmitting it to the world, but I will not fail to make the endeavor. At the last moment I will enclose the MS. in a bottle, and cast it within the sea.

An incident has occurred which has given me new room for meditation. Are such things the operation of ungoverned chance? I had ventured upon deck and thrown myself down, without attracting any notice, among a pile of ratlin-stuff and old sails in the bottom of the yawl. While musing upon the singularity of my fate, I unwittingly daubed with a tar-brush the edges of a neatly-folded studding-sail which lay near me on a barrel. The studding-sail is now bent upon the ship, and the thoughtless touches of the brush are spread out into the word DISCOVERY.

I have made many observations lately upon the structure of the vessel. Although well armed, she is not, I think, a ship of war. Her rigging, build, and general equipment, all negative a supposition of this kind. What she is not, I can easily perceive; what she is, I fear it is impossible to say. I know not how it is, but in scrutinizing her strange model and singular cast of spars, her huge size and overgrown suits of canvas, her severely simple bow and antiquated stern, there will occasionally flash across my mind a sensation of familiar things, and there is always mixed up with such indistinct shadows of recollection, an unaccountable memory of old foreign chronicles and ages long ago.

I have been looking at the timbers of the ship. She is built of a material to which I am a stranger. There is a peculiar character about the wood which strikes me as rendering it unfit for the purpose to which it has been applied. I mean its extreme porousness, considered independently by the worm-eaten condition which is a consequence of navigation in these seas, and apart from the rottenness attendant upon age. It will appear perhaps an observation somewhat over-curious, but this wood would have every characteristic of Spanish oak, if Spanish oak were distended by any unnatural means.

In reading the above sentence a curious apothegm of an old weather-beaten Dutch navigator comes full upon my recollection. "It is as sure," he was wont to say, when any doubt was entertained of his veracity, "as sure as there is a sea where the ship itself will grow in bulk like the living body of the seaman."

About an hour ago, I made bold to thrust myself among a group of the crew. They paid me no manner of attention, and, although I stood in the very midst of them all, seemed utterly unconscious of my presence. Like the one I had at first seen in the hold, they all bore about them the marks of a hoary old age. Their knees trembled with infirmity; their shoulders were bent double with decrepitude; their shriveled skins rattled in the wind; their voices were low, tremulous and broken; their eyes glistened with the rheum of years; and their gray hairs streamed terribly in the tempest. Around them, on every part of the deck, lay scattered mathematical instruments of the most quaint and obsolete construction.

I mentioned some time ago the bending of a studding-sail. From that period the ship, being thrown dead off the wind, has continued her terrific course due south, with every rag of canvas packed upon her, from her trucks to her lower studding-sail booms, and rolling every moment her top-gallant yard-arms into the most appalling hell of water which it can enter into the mind of a man to imagine. I have just left the deck, where I find it impossible to maintain a footing, although the crew seem to experience little inconvenience. It appears to me a miracle of miracles that our enormous bulk is not swallowed up at once and for ever. We are surely doomed to hover continually upon the brink of eternity, without taking a final plunge into the abyss. From billows a thousand times more stupendous than any I have ever seen, we glide away with the facility of the arrowy sea-gull; and the colossal waters rear their heads above us like demons of the deep, but like demons confined to simple threats and forbidden to destroy. I am led to attribute these frequent escapes to the only natural cause which can account for such effect. I must suppose the ship to be within the influence of some strong current, or impetuous undertow.

I have seen the captain face to face, and in his own cabin—but, as I expected, he paid me no attention. Although in his appearance there is, to a casual observer, nothing which might bespeak him more or less than man—still a feeling of irrepressible reverence and awe mingled with the sensation of wonder with which I regarded him. In stature he is nearly my own height; that is, about five feet eight inches. He is of a well-knit and compact frame of body, neither robust nor remarkably otherwise.

But it is the singularity of the expression which reigns upon the face—it is the intense, the wonderful, the thrilling evidence of old age, so utter, so extreme, which excites within my spirit a sense—a sentiment ineffable. His forehead, although little wrinkled, seems to bear upon it the stamp of a myriad of years. His gray hairs are records of the past, and his grayer eyes are sybils of the future. The cabin floor was thickly strewn with strange, iron-clasped folios, and moldering instruments of science, and obsolete long-forgotten charts. His head was bowed down upon his hands, and he pored, with a fiery unquiet eye, over a paper which I took to be a commission, and which, at all events, bore the signature of a monarch. He muttered to himself, as did the first seaman whom I saw in the hold, some low peevish syllables of a foreign tongue, and although the speaker was close at my elbow, his voice seemed to reach my ears from the distance of a mile.

The ship and all in it are imbued with the spirit of Eld. The crew glide to and fro like the ghosts of buried centuries; their eyes have an eager and uneasy meaning; and when their fingers fall athwart my path in the wild glare of the battle-lanterns, I feel as I have never felt before, although I have been all my life a dealer in antiquities, and have imbibed the shadows of fallen columns at Balbec, and Tadmor, and Persepolis, until my very soul has become a ruin.

When I look around me I feel ashamed of my former apprehensions. If I trembled at the blast which has hitherto attended us, shall I not stand aghast at a warring of wind and ocean, to convey any idea of which the words tornado and simoom are trivial and ineffective? All in the immediate vicinity of the ship is the blackness of eternal night, and a chaos of foamless water; but, about a league on either side of us, may be seen, indistinctly and at intervals, stupendous ramparts of ice, towering away into the desolate sky, and looking like the walls of the universe.

As I imagined, the ship proves to be in a current; if that appellation can properly be given to a tide which, howling and shrieking by the white ice, thunders on to the southward with a velocity like the headlong dashing of a cataract. To conceive the horror of my sensations is, I presume, utterly impossible; yet a curiosity to penetrate the mysteries of these awful regions, predominates even over my despair, and will reconcile me to the most hideous aspect of death. It is evident that we are hurrying onwards to some exciting knowledge—some never-to-be-imparted secret, whose attainment is destruction. Perhaps this current leads us to the southern pole itself. It must be confessed that a supposition apparently so wild has every probability in its favor.

The crew pace the deck with unquiet and tremulous step; but there is upon their countenances an expression more of the eagerness of hope than of the apathy of despair.

In the meantime the wind is still in our poop, and, as we carry a crowd of canvas, the ship is at times lifted bodily from out the sea! Oh, horror upon horror!—the ice opens suddenly to the right, and to the left, and we are whirling dizzily, in immense concentric circles, round and round the borders of a gigantic amphitheater, the summit of whose walls is lost in the darkness and the distance. But little time will be left me to ponder upon my destiny! The circles rapidly grow small—we are plunging madly within the grasp of the whirlpool—and amid a roaring, and bellowing, and thundering of ocean and of tempest, the ship is quivering—O God! and—going down.

NOTE.—The 'MS. Found in a Bottle' was originally published in 1831, and it was not until many years afterwards that I became acquainted with the maps of Mercator, in which the ocean is represented as rushing, by four mouths, into the (northern) Polar Gulf, to be absorbed into the bowels of the earth; the Pole itself being represented by a black rock, towering to a prodigious height.

Ligeia

[Narrated by an unnamed, unreliable narrator, this Gothic-styled satire was first published in September 18, 1838, issue of the *Baltimore American Museum*. It was collected in the *Tales of Grotesque and Arabesque* (1840). A revised version, including the poem 'The Conqueror Worm', was published in the February 15, 1845, issue of *The New World*. This is the version printed in the *Broadway Journal* on September 27, 1845.]

> And the will therein lieth, which dieth not. Who knoweth the mysteries of the will, with its vigor? For God is but a great will pervading all things by nature of its intentness. Man doth not yield himself to the angels, nor unto death utterly, save only through the weakness of his feeble will.
>
> —JOSEPH GLANVILL

I cannot, for my soul, remember how, when, or even precisely where, I first became acquainted with the lady Ligeia. Long years have since elapsed, and my memory is feeble through much suffering. Or, perhaps, I cannot *now* bring these points to mind, because, in truth, the character of my beloved, her rare learning, her singular yet placid cast of beauty, and the thrilling and enthralling eloquence of her low musical language, made their way into my heart by paces so steadily and stealthily progressive that they have been unnoticed and unknown. Yet I believe that I met her first and most frequently in some large, old, decaying city near the Rhine. Of her family—I have surely heard her speak. That it is of a remotely ancient date cannot be doubted. Ligeia! Ligeia! Buried in studies of a nature more than all else adapted to deaden impressions of the outward world, it is by that sweet word alone—by Ligeia—that I bring before mine eyes in fancy the image of her who is no more. And now, while I write, a recollection flashes upon me that I have *never known* the paternal name of her who was my friend and my betrothed, and who became the partner of my studies, and finally the wife of my bosom. Was it a playful charge on the part of my Ligeia? or was it a test of my strength of affection, that I should institute no inquiries upon this point? or was it rather a caprice of my own—a wildly romantic offering on the shrine of the most passionate devotion? I but indistinctly recall the fact itself—what wonder that I have utterly forgotten the circumstances which originated or attended it? And, indeed, if ever that spirit which is entitled *Romance*—if ever she, the wan and the misty-winged *Ashtophet* of idolatrous Egypt, presided, as they tell, over marriages ill-omened, then most surely she presided over mine.

There is one dear topic, however, on which my memory fails me not. It is the *person* of Ligeia. In stature she was tall, somewhat slender, and, in her latter days, even emaciated. I would in vain attempt to portray the majesty, the quiet ease, of her demeanor, or the incomprehensible lightness and elasticity of her footfall. She came and departed as a shadow. I was never made aware of her entrance into my closed study save by the dear music of her low sweet voice, as she placed her marble hand upon my shoulder. In beauty of face no maiden ever equalled her. It was the radiance of an opium dream—an airy and spirit-lifting vision more wildly divine than the phantasies which hovered about the slumbering souls of the daughters of Delos. Yet her features were not of that regular mould which we have been falsely taught to worship in the classical labors of the heathen. "There is no exquisite beauty," says Bacon, Lord Verulam, speaking truly of all the forms and *genera* of beauty, "without some *strangeness* in the proportion." Yet, although I saw that the features of Ligeia were not of a classic regularity—although I perceived that her loveliness was indeed "exquisite," and felt that there was much of "strangeness" pervading it, yet I have tried in vain to detect the irregularity and to trace home my own perception of "the strange." I examined the contour of the lofty and pale forehead—it was faultless—how cold indeed that word when applied to a majesty so divine!—the skin rivalling the purest ivory, the commanding extent and repose, the gentle prominence of the regions above the temples; and then the raven-black, the glossy, the luxuriant and naturally-curling tresses, setting forth the full force of the Homeric epithet, "hyacinthine!" I looked at the delicate outlines of the nose—and nowhere but in the graceful medallions of the Hebrews had I beheld a similar perfection. There were the same luxurious smoothness of surface, the same scarcely perceptible tendency to the aquiline, the same harmoniously curved nostrils speaking the free spirit. I regarded the sweet mouth. Here was indeed the triumph of all things heavenly—the magnificent turn of the short upper lip—the soft, voluptuous slumber of the under—the dimples which sported, and the colour which spoke—the teeth glancing back, with a brilliancy almost startling, every ray of the holy light which fell upon them in her serene and placid, yet most exultingly radiant of all smiles. I scrutinized the formation of the chin—and here, too, I found the gentleness of breadth, the softness and the majesty, the fullness and the spirituality, of the Greek—the contour which the God Apollo revealed but in a dream, to Cleomenes, the son of the Athenian. And then I peered into the large eyes of Ligeia.

For eyes we have no models in the remotely antique. It might have been, too, that in these eyes of my beloved lay the secret to which Lord Verulam alludes. They were, I must believe, far larger than the ordinary eyes of our own race. They were even fuller than the fullest of the gazelle eyes of the tribe of the valley of Nourjahad. Yet it was only at intervals—in moments of intense excitement—that this peculiarity became more than slightly noticeable in Ligeia. And at such moments was her beauty—in my heated fancy thus it appeared perhaps—the beauty of beings either above or apart from the earth—the beauty of the fabulous Houri of the Turk. The hue of the orbs was the most brilliant of black, and, far over them, hung jetty lashes of great length. The brows, slightly irregular in outline, had the same tint. The "strangeness," however, which I found in the eyes, was of a nature distinct from the formation, or the colour, or the brilliancy of the features, and must, after all, be referred to the *expression.* Ah, word of no meaning! behind whose vast latitude of mere sound we intrench our ignorance of so much of the spiritual. The expression of the eyes of Ligeia! How for long hours have I pondered upon it! How have I, through the whole of a midsummer night, struggled to fathom it! What was it—that something more profound than the well of Democritus—which lay far within the pupils of my beloved? What *was* it? I was possessed with a passion to discover. Those eyes! those large, those shining, those divine orbs! they became to me twin stars of Leda, and I to them devoutest of astrologers.

There is no point, among the many incomprehensible anomalies of the science of mind, more thrillingly exciting than the fact—never, I believe, noticed in the schools—that, in our endeavors to recall to memory something long forgotten, we often find ourselves *upon the very verge* of remembrance, without being able, in the end, to remember. And thus how frequently, in my intense scrutiny of Ligeia's eyes, have I felt approaching the full knowledge of their expression—felt it approaching—yet not quite be mine—and so at length entirely depart! And (strange, oh strangest mystery of all!) I found, in the commonest objects of the universe, a circle of analogies to that expression. I mean to say that, subsequently to the period when Ligeia's beauty passed into my spirit, there dwelling as in a shrine, I derived, from many existences in the material world, a sentiment such as I felt always aroused within me by her large and luminous orbs. Yet not the more could I define that sentiment, or analyze, or even steadily view it. I recognized it, let me repeat, sometimes in the survey of a rapidly-growing vine—in the contemplation of a moth, a butterfly, a chrysalis, a stream of running water. I have felt it in the ocean; in the falling of a meteor. I have felt it in the glances of unusually aged people. And there are one or two stars in heaven—(one especially, a star of the sixth magnitude, double and changeable, to be found near the large star in Lyra) in a telescopic scrutiny of which I have been made aware of the feeling. I have been filled with it by certain sounds from stringed instruments, and not unfrequently by passages from books. Among innumerable other instances, I well remember something in a volume of Joseph Glanvill, which (perhaps merely from its quaintness—who shall say?) never failed to inspire me with the sentiment;—"And the will therein lieth, which dieth not. Who knoweth the mysteries of the will, with its vigor? For God is but a great will pervading all things by nature of its intentness. Man doth not yield him to the angels, nor unto death utterly, save only through the weakness of his feeble will."

Length of years, and subsequent reflection, have enabled me to trace, indeed, some remote connection between this passage in the English moralist and a portion of the character of Ligeia. An *intensity* in thought, action, or speech, was possibly, in her, a result, or at least an index, of that gigantic volition which, during our long intercourse, failed to give other and more immediate evidence of its existence. Of all the women whom I have ever known, she, the outwardly calm, the ever-placid Ligeia, was the most violently a prey to the tumultuous vultures of stern passion. And of such passion I could form no estimate, save by the miraculous expansion of those eyes which at once so delighted and appalled me—by the almost magical melody, modulation, distinctness and placidity of her very low voice—and by the fierce energy (rendered doubly effective by contrast with her manner of utterance) of the wild words which she habitually uttered.

I have spoken of the learning of Ligeia: it was immense—such as I have never known in woman. In the classical tongues was she deeply proficient, and as far as my own acquaintance extended in regard to the modern dialects of Europe, I have never known her at fault. Indeed upon any theme of the most admired, because simply the most abstruse of the boasted erudition of the academy, have I *ever* found Ligeia at fault? How singularly—how thrillingly, this one point in the nature of my wife has forced itself, at this late period only, upon my attention! I said her knowledge was such as I have never known in woman—but where breathes the man who has traversed, and successfully, *all* the wide areas of moral, physical, and mathematical science? I saw not then what I now clearly perceive, that the acquisitions of Ligeia were gigantic, were astounding; yet I was sufficiently aware of her infinite supremacy to resign myself, with a child-like confidence, to her guidance through the chaotic world of metaphysical investigation at which I was most busily occupied during the earlier years of our marriage. With how vast a triumph—with how vivid a delight—with how much of all that is ethereal in hope—did I *feel*, as she bent over me in studies but little sought—but less known—that delicious vista by slow degrees expanding before me, down whose long, gorgeous, and all untrodden path, I might at length pass onward to the goal of a wisdom too divinely precious not to be forbidden!

How poignant, then, must have been the grief with which, after some years, I beheld my well-grounded expectations take wings to themselves and fly away! Without Ligeia I was but as a child groping benighted. Her presence, her readings alone, rendered vividly luminous

the many mysteries of the transcendentalism in which we were immersed. Wanting the radiant luster of her eyes, letters, lambent and golden, grew duller than Saturnian lead. And now those eyes shone less and less frequently upon the pages over which I pored. Ligeia grew ill. The wild eyes blazed with a too—too glorious effulgence; the pale fingers became of the transparent waxen hue of the grave, and the blue veins upon the lofty forehead swelled and sank impetuously with the tides of the most gentle emotion. I saw that she must die—and I struggled desperately in spirit with the grim Azrael. And the struggles of the passionate wife were, to my astonishment, even more energetic than my own. There had been much in her stern nature to impress me with the belief that, to her, death would have come without its terrors;—but not so. Words are impotent to convey any just idea of the fierceness of resistance with which she wrestled with the Shadow. I groaned in anguish at the pitiable spectacle. I would have soothed—I would have reasoned; but, in the intensity of her wild desire for life,—for life—*but* for life—solace and reason were alike the uttermost of folly. Yet not until the last instance, amid the most convulsive writhings of her fierce spirit, was shaken the external placidity of her demeanor. Her voice grew more gentle—grew more low—yet I would not wish to dwell upon the wild meaning of the quietly uttered words. My brain reeled as I hearkened entranced, to a melody more than mortal—to assumptions and aspirations which mortality had never before known.

That she loved me I should not have doubted; and I might have been easily aware that, in a bosom such as hers, love would have reigned no ordinary passion. But in death only, was I fully impressed with the strength of her affection. For long hours, detaining my hand, would she pour out before me the overflowing of a heart whose more than passionate devotion amounted to idolatry. How had I deserved to be so blessed by such confessions?—how had I deserved to be so cursed with the removal of my beloved in the hour of her making them? But upon this subject I cannot bear to dilate. Let me say only, that in Ligeia's more than womanly abandonment to a love, alas! all unmerited, all unworthily bestowed, I at length recognized the principle of her longing with so wildly earnest a desire for the life which was now fleeing so rapidly away. It is this wild longing—it is this eager vehemence of desire for life—*but* for life—that I have no power to portray—no utterance capable of expressing.

At high noon of the night in which she departed, beckoning me, peremptorily, to her side, she bade me repeat certain verses composed by herself not many days before. I obeyed her.—They were these:*

Lo! 't is a gala night
    Within the lonesome latter years—
An angel throng, bewinged, bedight
    In veils, and drown'd in tears,
Sit in a theatre, to see
    A play of hopes and fears,
While the orchestra breathes fitfully
    The music of the spheres.

Mimes, in the form of God on high,
    Mutter and mumble low,
And hither and thither fly—
    Mere puppets they, who come and go
At bidding of vast formless things
    That shift the scenery to and fro,
Flapping from out their Condor wings
    Invisible Wo!

That motley drama!—oh, be sure
    It shall not be forgot!
With its Phantom chas'd forever more,
    By a crowd that seize it not,
Through a circle that ever returneth in
    To the self-same spot,
And much of Madness, and more of Sin,
    And Horror the soul of the plot.

But see, amid the mimic rout
    A crawling shape intrude!
A blood-red thing that writhes from out

* This poem was first published in *Graham's Magazine* in January 1843 under the title 'The Conqueror Worm'.—Ed.

The scenic solitude!
It writhes!—it writhes!—with mortal pangs
The mimes become its food,
And the seraphs sob at vermin fangs
In human gore imbued.

Out—out are the lights—out all!
And, over each quivering form,
The curtain, a funeral pall,
Comes down with the rush of a storm,
And the angels, all pallid and wan,
Uprising, unveiling, affirm
That the play is the tragedy, "Man,"
And its hero the Conqueror Worm.

"O God!" half shrieked Ligeia, leaping to her feet and extending her arms aloft with a spasmodic movement, as I made an end of these lines—"O God! O Divine Father!—shall these things be undeviatingly so?—shall this Conqueror be not once conquered? Are we not part and parcel in Thee? Who—who knoweth the mysteries of the will with its vigor? Man doth not yield him to the angels, *nor unto death utterly*, save only through the weakness of his feeble will."

And now, as if exhausted with emotion, she suffered her white arms to fall, and returned solemnly to her bed of Death. And as she breathed her last sighs, there came mingled with them a low murmur from her lips. I bent to them my ear and distinguished, again, the concluding words of the passage in Glanvill—"*Man doth not yield him to the angels, nor unto death utterly, save only through the weakness of his feeble will.*"

She died;—and I, crushed into the very dust with sorrow, could no longer endure the lonely desolation of my dwelling in the dim and decaying city by the Rhine. I had no lack of what the world calls wealth. Ligeia had brought me far more, very far more than ordinarily falls to the lot of mortals. After a few months, therefore, of weary and aimless wandering, I purchased, and put in some repair, an abbey, which I shall not name, in one of the wildest and least frequented portions of fair England. The gloomy and dreary grandeur of the building, the almost savage aspect of the domain, the many melancholy and time-honored memories connected with both, had much in unison with the feelings of utter abandonment which had driven me into that remote and unsocial region of the country. Yet although the external abbey, with its verdant decay hanging about it, suffered but little alteration, I gave way, with a child-like perversity, and perchance with a faint hope of alleviating my sorrows, to a display of more than regal magnificence within.—For such follies, even in childhood, I had imbibed a taste and now they came back to me as if in the dotage of grief. Alas, I feel how much even of incipient madness might have been discovered in the gorgeous and fantastic draperies, in the solemn carvings of Egypt, in the wild cornices and furniture, in the Bedlam patterns of the carpets of tufted gold! I had become a bounden slave in the trammels of opium, and my labors and my orders had taken a colouring from my dreams. But these absurdities I must not pause to detail. Let me speak only of that one chamber, ever accursed, whither in a moment of mental alienation, I led from the altar as my bride—as the successor of the unforgotten Ligeia—the fair-haired and blue-eyed Lady Rowena Trevanion, of Tremaine.

There is no individual portion of the architecture and decoration of that bridal chamber which is not now visibly before me. Where were the souls of the haughty family of the bride, when, through thirst of gold, they permitted to pass the threshold of an apartment *so* bedecked, a maiden and a daughter so beloved? I have said that I minutely remember the details of the chamber—yet I am sadly forgetful on topics of deep moment—and here there was no system, no keeping, in the fantastic display, to take hold upon the memory. The room lay in a high turret of the castellated abbey, was pentagonal in shape, and of capacious size. Occupying the whole southern face of the pentagon was the sole window—an immense sheet of unbroken glass from Venice—a single pane, and tinted of a leaden hue, so that the rays of either the sun or moon, passing through it, fell with a ghastly lustre on the objects within. Over the upper portion of this huge window, extended the trellice-work of an aged vine, which clambered up the massy walls of the turret. The ceiling, of gloomy-looking oak, was excessively lofty, vaulted, and elaborately fretted with the wildest and most grotesque specimens of a semi-Gothic, semi-Druidical device. From out the most central recess of this melancholy vaulting, depended, by a single chain of gold with long links, a huge censer of the same metal, Saracenic in pattern, and with many perforations so contrived that there writhed in and out of them, as if endued with a serpent vitality, a continual succession of parti-coloured fires.

Some few ottomans and golden candelabra, of Eastern figure, were in various stations about—and there was the couch, too—the bridal couch—of an Indian model, and low, and sculptured of solid ebony, with a pall-like canopy above. In each of the angles of the chamber stood on end a gigantic sarcophagus of black granite, from the tombs of the kings over against Luxor, with their aged lids full of immemorial sculpture. But in the draping of the apartment lay, alas! the chief phantasy of all. The lofty walls, gigantic in height—even unproportionably so—were hung from summit to foot, in vast folds, with a heavy and massive-looking tapestry—tapestry of a material which was found alike as a carpet on the floor, as a covering for the ottomans and the ebony bed, as a canopy for the bed, and as the gorgeous volutes of the curtains which partially shaded the window. The material was the richest cloth of gold. It was spotted all over, at irregular intervals, with arabesque figures, about a foot in diameter, and wrought upon the cloth in patterns of the most jetty black. But these figures partook of the true character of the arabesque only when regarded from a single point of view. By a contrivance now common, and indeed traceable to a very remote period of antiquity, they were made changeable in aspect. To one entering the room, they bore the appearance of simple monstrosities; but upon a farther advance, this appearance gradually departed; and step by step, as the visiter moved his station in the chamber, he saw himself surrounded by an endless succession of the ghastly forms which belong to the superstition of the Norman, or arise in the guilty slumbers of the monk. The phantasmagoric effect was vastly heightened by the artificial introduction of a strong continual current of wind behind the draperies—giving a hideous and uneasy animation to the whole.

In halls such as these—in a bridal chamber such as this—I passed, with the Lady of Tremaine, the unhallowed hours of the first month of our marriage—passed them with but little disquietude. That my wife dreaded the fierce moodiness of my temper—that she shunned me and loved me but little—I could not help perceiving; but it gave me rather pleasure than otherwise. I loathed her with a hatred belonging more to demon than to man. My memory flew back, (oh, with what intensity of regret!) to Ligeia, the beloved, the august, the beautiful, the entombed.

I reveled in recollections of her purity, of her wisdom, of her lofty, her ethereal nature, of her passionate, her idolatrous love. Now, then, did my spirit fully and freely burn with more than all the fires of her own. In the excitement of my opium dreams (for I was habitually fettered in the shackles of the drug) I would call aloud upon her name, during the silence of the night, or among the sheltered recesses of the glens by day, as if, through the wild eagerness, the solemn passion, the consuming ardour of my longing for the departed, I could restore her to the pathway she had abandoned—ah, *could* it be forever?—upon the earth.

About the commencement of the second month of the marriage, the Lady Rowena was attacked with sudden illness, from which her recovery was slow. The fever which consumed her rendered her nights uneasy; and in her perturbed state of half-slumber, she spoke of sounds, and of motions, in and about the chamber of the turret, which I concluded had no origin save in the distemper of her fancy, or perhaps in the phantasmagoric influences of the chamber itself. She became at length convalescent—finally well. Yet but a brief period elapsed, ere a second more violent disorder again threw her upon a bed of suffering; and from this attack her frame, at all times feeble, never altogether recovered. Her illnesses were, after this epoch, of alarming character, and of more alarming recurrence, defying alike the knowledge and the great exertions of her physicians. With the increase of the chronic disease which had thus, apparently, taken too sure hold upon her constitution to be eradicated by human means, I could not fail to observe a similar increase in the nervous irritation of her temperament, and in her excitability by trivial causes of fear. She spoke again, and now more frequently and pertinaciously, of the sounds—of the slight sounds—and of the unusual motions among the tapestries, to which she had formerly alluded.

One night, near the closing in of September, she pressed this distressing subject with more than usual emphasis upon my attention. She had just awakened from an unquiet slumber, and I had been watching, with feelings half of anxiety, half of vague terror, the workings of her emaciated countenance. I sat by the side of her ebony bed, upon one of the ottomans of India. She partly arose, and spoke, in an earnest low whisper, of sounds which she *then* heard, but which I could not hear—of motions which she *then* saw, but which I could not perceive. The wind was rushing hurriedly behind the tapestries, and I wished to show her (what, let me confess it, I could not *all* believe) that those almost inarticulate breathings, and those very gentle variations of the figures upon the wall, were but the natural effects of that customary rushing of the wind. But a deadly pallor, overspreading her face, had proved to me that my exertions to reassure her would be fruitless. She appeared to be fainting, and no attendants were within call. I remembered where was deposited a decanter of light wine which had been ordered by her physicians, and hastened across the chamber to procure it. But, as I stepped beneath the light of the censer, two circumstances of a startling nature attracted my attention. I had felt that some palpable although invisible object had passed lightly by my person; and I saw that there lay upon the golden carpet, in the very middle of the rich luster thrown from the censer, a shadow—a faint, indefinite shadow of angelic aspect—such as might be fancied for the shadow of a shade. But I was wild with the excitement of an immoderate dose of opium, and heeded these things but little, nor spoke of them to Rowena. Having found the wine, I recrossed the chamber, and poured out a goblet-ful, which I held to the lips of the fainting lady. She had now partially recovered, however, and took the vessel herself, while I sank upon an ottoman near me, with my eyes fastened upon her person. It was then that I became distinctly aware of a gentle foot-fall upon the carpet, and near the couch; and in a second thereafter, as Rowena was in the act of raising the wine to her lips, I saw, or may have dreamed that I saw, fall within the goblet, as if from some invisible spring in the atmosphere of the room, three or four large drops of a brilliant and ruby coloured fluid. If this I saw—not so Rowena. She swallowed the wine unhesitatingly, and I forbore to speak to her of a circumstance which must, after all, I considered, have been but the suggestion of a vivid imagination, rendered morbidly active by the terror of the lady, by the opium, and by the hour.

Yet I cannot conceal it from my own perception that, immediately subsequent to the fall of the ruby-drops, a rapid change for the worse took place in the disorder of my wife; so that, on the third subsequent night, the hands of her menials prepared her for the tomb, and on the fourth, I sat alone, with her shrouded body, in that fantastic chamber which had received her as my bride.—Wild visions, opium-engendered, flitted, shadow-like, before me. I gazed with unquiet eye upon the sarcophagi in the angles of the room, upon the varying figures of the drapery, and upon the writhing of the parti-coloured fires in the censer overhead. My eyes then fell, as I called to mind the circumstances of a former night, to the spot beneath the glare of the censer where I had seen the faint traces of the shadow. It was there, however, no longer; and breathing with greater freedom, I turned my glances to the pallid and rigid figure upon the bed. Then rushed upon me a thousand memories of Ligeia—and then came back upon my heart, with the turbulent violence of a flood, the whole of that unutterable wo with which I had regarded *her* thus enshrouded. The night waned; and still, with a bosom full of bitter thoughts of the one only and supremely beloved, I remained gazing upon the body of Rowena.

It might have been midnight, or perhaps earlier, or later, for I had taken no note of time, when a sob, low, gentle, but very distinct, startled me from my revery.—I *felt* that it came from the bed of ebony—the bed of death. I listened in an agony of superstitious terror—but there was no repetition of the sound. I strained my vision to detect any motion in the corpse—but there was not the slightest perceptible. Yet I could not have been deceived. I *had* heard the noise, however faint, and my soul was awakened within me. I resolutely and perseveringly kept my attention riveted upon the body. Many minutes elapsed before any circumstance occurred tending to throw light upon the mystery. At length it became evident that a slight, a very feeble, and barely noticeable tinge of colour had flushed up within the cheeks, and along the sunken small veins of the eyelids. Through a species of unutterable horror and awe, for which the language of mortality has no sufficiently energetic expression, I felt my heart cease to beat, my limbs grow rigid where I sat. Yet a sense of duty finally operated to restore my self-possession. I could no longer doubt that we had been precipitate in our preparations—that Rowena still lived. It was necessary that some immediate exertion be made; yet the turret was altogether apart from the portion of the abbey tenanted by the servants—there were none within call—I had no means of summoning them to my aid without leaving the room for many minutes—and this I could not venture to do. I therefore struggled alone in my endeavors to call back the spirit still hovering. In a short period it was certain, however, that a relapse had taken place; the colour disappeared from both eyelid and cheek, leaving a wanness even more than that of marble; the lips became doubly shriveled and pinched up in the ghastly expression of death; a repulsive clamminess and coldness overspread rapidly the surface of the body; and all the usual rigorous stiffness immediately supervened. I fell back with a shudder upon the couch from which I had been so startlingly aroused, and again gave myself up to passionate waking visions of Ligeia.

An hour thus elapsed when (could it be possible?) I was a second time aware of some vague sound issuing from the region of the bed. I listened—in extremity of horror. The sound came again—it was a sigh. Rushing to the corpse, I saw—distinctly saw—a tremor upon the lips. In a minute afterward they relaxed, disclosing a bright line of the pearly teeth. Amazement now struggled in my bosom with the profound awe which had hitherto reigned there alone. I felt that my vision grew dim, that my reason wandered; and it was only by a violent effort that I at length succeeded in nerving myself to the task which duty thus once more had pointed out. There was now a partial glow upon the forehead and upon the cheek and throat; a perceptible warmth pervaded the whole frame; there was even a slight pulsation at the heart. The lady *lived*; and with redoubled ardour I betook myself to the task of restoration. I chafed and bathed the temples and the hands, and used every exertion which experience, and no little medical reading, could suggest. But in vain. Suddenly, the colour fled, the pulsation ceased, the lips resumed the expression of the dead, and, in an instant afterward, the whole body took upon itself the icy chilliness, the livid hue, the intense rigidity, the sunken outline, and all the loathsome peculiarities of that which has been, for many days, a tenant of the tomb.

And again I sunk into visions of Ligeia—and again, (what marvel that I shudder while I write?) *again* there reached my ears a low sob from the region of the ebony bed. But why shall I minutely detail the unspeakable horrors of that night? Why shall I pause to relate how, time after time, until near the period of the gray dawn, this hideous drama of revivification was repeated; how each terrific relapse was only into a sterner and apparently more irredeemable death; how each agony wore the aspect of a struggle with some invisible foe; and how each struggle was succeeded by I know not what of wild change in the personal appearance of the corpse? Let me hurry to a conclusion.

The greater part of the fearful night had worn away, and she who had been dead, once again stirred—and now more vigorously than hitherto, although arousing from a dissolution more appalling in its utter hopelessness than any. I had long ceased to struggle or to move, and remained sitting rigidly upon the ottoman, a helpless prey to a whirl of violent emotions, of which extreme awe was perhaps the least terrible, the least consuming. The corpse, I repeat, stirred, and now more vigorously than before. The hues of life flushed up with unwonted energy into the countenance—the limbs relaxed—and, save that the eyelids were yet pressed heavily together, and that the bandages and draperies of the grave still imparted their charnel character to the figure, I might have dreamed that Rowena had indeed shaken off, utterly, the fetters of Death. But if this idea was not, even then, altogether adopted, I could at least doubt no longer, when, arising from the bed, tottering, with feeble steps, with closed eyes, and with the manner of one bewildered in a dream, the thing that was enshrouded advanced bodily and palpably into the middle of the apartment.

I trembled not—I stirred not—for a crowd of unutterable fancies connected with the air, the stature, the demeanor of the figure, rushing hurriedly through my brain, had paralyzed—had chilled me into stone. I stirred not—but gazed upon the apparition. There was a mad disorder in my thoughts—a tumult unappeasable. Could it, indeed, be the *living* Rowena who confronted me? Could it indeed be Rowena *at all*—the fair-haired, the blue-eyed Lady Rowena Trevanion of Tremaine? Why, *why* should I doubt it? The bandage lay heavily about the mouth—but then might it not be the mouth of the breathing Lady of Tremaine? And the cheeks—there were the roses as in her noon of life—yes, these might indeed be the fair cheeks of the living Lady of Tremaine. And the chin, with its dimples, as in health, might it not be hers?—but *had she then grown taller since her malady?* What inexpressible madness seized me with that thought? One bound, and I had reached her feet! Shrinking from my touch, she let fall from her head, unloosened, the ghastly cerements which had confined it, and there streamed forth, into the rushing atmosphere of the chamber, huge masses of long and dishevelled hair; *it was blacker than the raven wings of the midnight!* And now slowly opened *the eyes* of the figure which stood before me. "Here then, at least," I shrieked aloud, "can I never—can I never be mistaken—these are the full, and the black, and the wild eyes—of my lost love—of the lady—of the LADY LIGEIA!"

The Fall of the House of Usher

[An outstanding work of American gothic literature, this gruesome short story narrated by an unnamed narrator was published in *Burton's Gentleman's Magazine* in September 1839.]

Son coeur est un luth suspendu;
Sitôt qu'on le touche il rèsonne.

—De Béranger

During the whole of a dull, dark, and soundless day in the autumn of the year, when the clouds hung oppressively low in the heavens, I had been passing alone, on horseback, through a singularly dreary tract of country; and at length found myself, as the shades of the evening drew on, within view of the melancholy House of Usher. I know not how it was—but, with the first glimpse of the building, a sense of insufferable gloom pervaded my spirit. I say insufferable; for the feeling was unrelieved by any of that half-pleasurable, because poetic, sentiment, with which the mind usually receives even the sternest natural images of the desolate or terrible. I looked upon the scene before me—upon the mere house, and the simple landscape features of the domain—upon the bleak walls—upon the vacant eye-like windows—upon a few rank sedges—and upon a few white trunks of decayed trees—with an utter depression of soul which I can compare to no earthly sensation more properly than to the after-dream of the reveler upon opium—the bitter lapse into everyday life—the hideous dropping off of the veil. There was an iciness, a sinking, a sickening of the heart—an unredeemed dreariness of thought which no goading of the imagination could torture into aught of the sublime. What was it—I paused to think—what was it that so unnerved me in the contemplation of the House of Usher? It was a mystery all insoluble; nor could I grapple with the shadowy fancies that crowded upon me as I pondered. I was forced to fall back upon the unsatisfactory conclusion, that while, beyond doubt, there *are* combinations of very simple natural objects which have the power of thus affecting us, still the analysis of this power lies among considerations beyond our depth. It was possible, I reflected, that a mere different arrangement of the particulars of the scene, of the details of the picture, would be sufficient to modify, or perhaps to annihilate its capacity for sorrowful impression; and, acting upon this idea, I reined my horse to the precipitous brink of a black and lurid tarn that lay in unruffled luster by the dwelling, and gazed down—but with a shudder even more thrilling than before—upon the remodeled and inverted images of the gray sedge, and the ghastly tree-stems, and the vacant and eye-like windows.

Nevertheless, in this mansion of gloom I now proposed to myself a sojourn of some weeks. Its proprietor, Roderick Usher, had been one of my boon companions in boyhood; but many years had elapsed since our last meeting. A letter, however, had lately reached me in a distant part of the country—a letter from him—which, in its wildly importunate nature, had admitted of no other than a personal reply. The MS. gave evidence of nervous agitation. The writer spoke of acute bodily illness—of a mental disorder which oppressed him—and of an earnest desire to see me, as his best, and indeed his only personal friend, with a view of attempting, by the cheerfulness of my society, some alleviation of his malady. It was the manner in which all this, and much more, was said—it was the apparent *heart* that went with his request—which allowed me no room for hesitation; and I accordingly obeyed forthwith what I still considered a very singular summons.

Although, as boys, we had been even intimate associates, yet I really knew little of my friend. His reserve had been always excessive and habitual. I was aware, however, that his very ancient family had been noted, time out of mind, for a peculiar sensibility of temperament, displaying itself, through long ages, in many works of exalted art, and manifested, of late, in repeated deeds of munificent yet unobtrusive charity, as well as in a passionate devotion to the intricacies, perhaps even more than to the orthodox and easily recognizable beauties, of musical science. I had learned, too, the very remarkable fact, that the stem of the Usher race, all time-honored as it was, had put forth, at no period, any enduring branch; in other words, that the entire family lay in the direct line of descent, and had always, with very trifling and very temporary variation, so lain. It was this deficiency, I considered, while running over in thought the perfect keeping of the character of the premises with the accredited character of the people, and while speculating upon the possible influence which the one, in the long lapse of centuries, might have exercised upon the other—it was this deficiency, perhaps, of collateral issue, and the consequent undeviating transmission, from sire to son, of the patrimony with the name, which had, at length, so identified the two as to merge the original title of the estate in the quaint and equivocal appellation of the "House of Usher"—an appellation which seemed to include, in the minds of the peasantry who used it, both the family and the family mansion.

I have said that the sole effect of my somewhat childish experiment—that of looking down within the tarn—had been to deepen the first singular impression. There can be no doubt that the consciousness of the rapid increase of my superstition—for why should I not so term it?—served mainly to accelerate the increase itself. Such, I have long known, is the paradoxical law of all sentiments having terror as a basis. And it might have been for this reason only, that, when I again uplifted my eyes to the house itself, from its image in the pool, there grew in my mind a strange fancy—a fancy so ridiculous, indeed, that I but mention it to show the vivid force of the sensations which oppressed me. I had so worked upon my imagination as really to believe that about the whole mansion and domain there hung an atmosphere peculiar to themselves and their immediate vicinity—an atmosphere which had no affinity with the air of heaven, but which had reeked up from the decayed trees, and the gray wall, and the silent tarn—a pestilent and mystic vapor, dull, sluggish, faintly discernible, and leaden-hued.

Shaking off from my spirit what *must* have been a dream, I scanned more narrowly the real aspect of the building. Its principal feature seemed to be that of an excessive antiquity. The discolouration of ages had been great. Minute fungi overspread the whole exterior, hanging in a fine tangled web-work from the eaves. Yet all this was apart from any extraordinary dilapidation. No portion of the masonry had fallen; and there appeared to be a wild inconsistency between its still perfect adaptation of parts, and the crumbling condition of the individual stones. In this there was much that reminded me of the specious totality of old wood-work which has rotted for long years in some neglected vault, with no disturbance from the breath of the external air. Beyond this indication of extensive decay, however, the fabric gave little token of instability. Perhaps the eye of a scrutinizing observer might have discovered a barely perceptible fissure, which, extending from the roof of the building in front, made its way down the wall in a zigzag direction, until it became lost in the sullen waters of the tarn.

Noticing these things, I rode over a short causeway to the house. A servant in waiting took my horse, and I entered the Gothic archway of the hall. A valet, of stealthy step, thence conducted me, in silence, through many dark and intricate passages in my progress to the *studio* of his master. Much that I encountered on the way contributed, I know not how, to heighten the vague sentiments of which I have already spoken. While the objects around me—while the carvings of the ceilings, the somber tapestries of the walls, the ebon blackness of the floors, and the phantasmagoric armorial trophies which rattled as I strode, were but matters to which, or to such as which, I had been accustomed from my infancy—while I hesitated not to acknowledge how familiar was all this—I still wondered to find how unfamiliar were the fancies which ordinary images were stirring up. On one of the staircases, I met the physician of the family. His countenance, I thought, wore a mingled expression of low cunning and perplexity. He accosted me with trepidation and passed on. The valet now threw open a door and ushered me into the presence of his master.

The room in which I found myself was very large and lofty. The windows were long, narrow, and pointed, and at so vast a distance from the black oaken floor as to be altogether inaccessible from within. Feeble gleams of encrimsoned light made their way through the trellised panes, and served to render sufficiently distinct the more prominent objects around; the eye, however, struggled in vain to reach the remoter angles of the chamber, or the recesses of the vaulted and fretted ceiling. Dark draperies hung upon the walls. The general furniture was profuse, comfortless, antique, and tattered. Many books and musical instruments lay scattered about, but failed to give any vitality to the scene. I felt that I breathed an atmosphere of sorrow. An air of stern, deep, and irredeemable gloom hung over and pervaded all.

Upon my entrance, Usher arose from a sofa on which he had been lying at full length, and greeted me with a vivacious warmth which had much in it, I at first thought, of an overdone cordiality—of the constrained effort of the *ennuyé* man of the world. A glance, however, at his countenance, convinced me of his perfect sincerity. We sat down; and for some moments, while he spoke not, I gazed upon him with a feeling half of pity, half of awe. Surely, man had never before so terribly altered, in so brief a period, as had Roderick Usher! It was with difficulty that I could bring myself to admit the identity of the wan being before me with the companion of my early boyhood. Yet the character of his face had been at all times remarkable. A cadaverousness of complexion; an eye large, liquid, and luminous beyond comparison; lips somewhat thin and very pallid, but of a surpassingly beautiful curve; a nose of a delicate Hebrew model, but with a breadth of nostril unusual in similar formations; a finely molded chin, speaking, in its want of prominence, of a want of moral energy; hair of a more than web-like softness and tenuity; these features, with an inordinate expansion above the regions of the temple, made up altogether a countenance not easily to be forgotten. And now in the mere exaggeration of the prevailing character of these features, and of the expression they were wont to convey, lay so much of change that I doubted to whom I spoke. The now ghastly pallor of the skin, and the now miraculous luster of the eye, above all things startled and even awed me. The silken hair, too, had been suffered to grow all unheeded, and as, in its wild gossamer texture, it floated rather than fell about the face, I could not, even with effort, connect its arabesque expression with any idea of simple humanity.

In the manner of my friend I was at once struck with an incoherence—an inconsistency; and I soon found this to arise from a series of feeble and futile struggles to overcome an habitual trepidancy—an excessive nervous agitation. For something of this nature I had indeed been prepared, no less by his letter, than by reminiscences of certain boyish traits, and by conclusions deduced from his peculiar physical conformation and temperament. His action was alternately vivacious and sullen. His voice varied rapidly from a tremulous indecision (when the animal spirits seemed utterly in abeyance) to that species of energetic concision—that abrupt, weighty, unhurried, and hollow-sounding enunciation—that leaden, self-balanced and perfectly modulated guttural utterance, which may be observed in the lost drunkard, or the irreclaimable eater of opium, during the periods of his most intense excitement.

It was thus that he spoke of the object of my visit, of his earnest desire to see me, and of the solace he expected me to afford him. He entered, at some length, into what he conceived to be the nature of his malady. It was, he said, a constitutional and a family evil, and one for which he despaired to find a remedy—a mere nervous affection, he immediately added, which would undoubtedly soon pass off. It displayed itself in a host of unnatural sensations. Some of these, as he detailed them, interested and bewildered me; although, perhaps, the terms, and the general manner of the narration had their weight. He suffered much from a morbid acuteness of the senses; the most insipid food was alone endurable; he could wear only garments of certain texture; the odors of all flowers were oppressive; his eyes were tortured by even a faint light; and there were but peculiar sounds, and these from stringed instruments, which did not inspire him with horror.

To an anomalous species of terror I found him a bounden slave. "I shall perish," said he, "I *must* perish in this deplorable folly. Thus, thus, and not otherwise, shall I be lost. I dread the events of the future, not in themselves, but in their results. I shudder at the thought of any, even the most trivial, incident, which may operate upon this intolerable agitation of soul. I have, indeed, no abhorrence of danger, except in its absolute effect—in terror. In this unnerved—in this pitiable condition—I feel that the period will sooner or later arrive when I must abandon life and reason together, in some struggle with the grim phantasm, FEAR."

I learned, moreover, at intervals, and through broken and equivocal hints, another singular feature of his mental condition. He was enchained by certain superstitious impressions in regard to the dwelling which he tenanted, and whence, for many years, he had never ventured forth—in regard to an influence whose supposititious force was conveyed in terms too shadowy here to be re-stated—an influence which some peculiarities in the mere form and substance of his family mansion, had, by dint of long sufferance, he said, obtained over his spirit—an effect which the *physique* of the gray walls and turrets, and of the dim tarn into which they all looked down, had, at length, brought about upon the *morale* of his existence.

He admitted, however, although with hesitation, that much of the peculiar gloom which thus afflicted him could be traced to a more natural and far more palpable origin—to the severe and long-continued illness—indeed to the evidently approaching dissolution—of a tenderly beloved sister—his sole companion for long years—his last and only relative on earth. "Her decease," he said, with a bitterness which I can never forget, "would leave him (him the hopeless and the frail) the last of the ancient race of the Ushers." While he spoke, the Lady Madeline (for so was she called) passed slowly through a remote portion of the apartment, and, without having noticed my presence, disappeared. I regarded her with an utter astonishment not unmingled with dread—and yet I found it impossible to account for such feelings. A sensation of stupor oppressed me, as my eyes followed her retreating steps. When a door, at length, closed upon her, my glance sought instinctively and eagerly the countenance of the brother—but he had buried his face in his hands, and I could only perceive that a far more than ordinary wanness had overspread the emaciated fingers through which trickled many passionate tears.

The disease of the Lady Madeline had long baffled the skill of her physicians. A settled apathy, a gradual wasting away of the person, and frequent although transient affections of a partially cataleptical character, were the unusual diagnosis. Hitherto she had steadily borne up against the pressure of her malady, and had not betaken herself finally to bed; but, on the closing in of the evening of my arrival at the house, she succumbed (as her brother told me at night with inexpressible agitation) to the prostrating power of the destroyer; and I learned that the glimpse I had obtained of her person would thus probably be the last I should obtain—that the lady, at least while living, would be seen by me no more.

For several days ensuing, her name was unmentioned by either Usher or myself; and during this period I was busied in earnest endeavors to alleviate the melancholy of my friend. We painted and read together; or I listened, as if in a dream, to the wild improvisations of his speaking guitar. And thus, as a closer and still closer intimacy admitted me more unreservedly into the recesses of his spirit, the more bitterly did I perceive the futility of all attempt at cheering a mind from which darkness, as if an inherent positive quality, poured forth upon all objects of the moral and physical universe, in one unceasing radiation of gloom.

I shall ever bear about me a memory of the many solemn hours I thus spent alone with the master of the House of Usher. Yet I should fail in any attempt to convey an idea of the exact character of the studies, or of the occupations, in which he involved me, or led me the way. An excited and highly distempered ideality threw a sulphurous luster over all. His long improvised dirges will ring forever in my ears. Among other things, I hold painfully in mind a certain singular perversion and amplification of the wild air of the last waltz of Von Weber. From the paintings over which his elaborate fancy brooded, and which grew, touch by touch, into vagueness at which I shuddered the more thrillingly, because I shuddered knowing not why;—from these paintings (vivid as their images now are before me) I would in vain endeavor to educe more than a small portion which should lie within the compass of merely written words. By the utter simplicity, by the nakedness of his designs, he arrested and overawed attention. If ever mortal painted an idea, that mortal was Roderick Usher. For me at least—in the circumstances then surrounding me—there arose out of the pure abstractions which the hypochondriac contrived to throw upon his canvass, an intensity of intolerable awe, no shadow of which felt I ever yet in the contemplation of the certainly glowing yet too concrete reveries of Fuseli.

One of the phantasmagoric conceptions of my friend, partaking not so rigidly of the spirit of abstraction, may be shadowed forth, although feebly, in words. A small picture presented the interior of an immensely long and rectangular vault or tunnel, with low walls, smooth, white, and without interruption or device. Certain accessory points of the design served well to convey the idea that this excavation lay at an exceeding depth below the surface of the earth. No outlet was observed in any portion of its vast extent, and no torch, or other artificial source of light was discernible; yet a flood of intense rays rolled throughout, and bathed the whole in a ghastly and inappropriate splendor.

I have just spoken of that morbid condition of the auditory nerve which rendered all music intolerable to the sufferer, with the exception of certain effects of stringed instruments. It was, perhaps, the narrow limits to which he thus confined himself upon the guitar, which gave birth, in great measure, to the fantastic character of his performances. But the fervid *facility* of his *impromptus* could not be so accounted for. They must have been, and were, in the notes, as well as in the words of his wild fantasias (for he not unfrequently accompanied himself with rhymed verbal improvisations), the result of that intense mental collectedness and concentration to which I have previously alluded as observable only in particular moments of the highest artificial excitement. The words of one of these rhapsodies I have easily remembered. I was, perhaps, the more forcibly impressed with it, as he gave it, because, in the under or mystic current of its meaning, I fancied that I perceived, and for the first time, a full consciousness on the part of Usher, of the tottering of his lofty reason upon her throne. The verses, which were entitled "The Haunted Palace,"* ran very nearly, if not accurately, thus:

I

In the greenest of our valleys,
    By good angels tenanted,
Once a fair and stately palace—
    Radiant palace—reared its head.
In the monarch Thought's dominion—
    It stood there!
Never seraph spread a pinion
    Over fabric half so fair.

II

Banners yellow, glorious, golden,
    On its roof did float and flow;
(This—all this—was in the olden
    Time long ago)
And every gentle air that dallied,
    In that sweet day,
Along the ramparts plumed and pallid,
    A winged odor went away.

III

Wanderers in that happy valley
    Through two luminous windows saw
Spirits moving musically
    To a lute's well-tunèd law,

* This poem was first published in the *American Museum* in April 1839.—Ed.

Round about a throne, where sitting
    (Porphyrogene!)
In state his glory well befitting,
    The ruler of the realm was seen.

IV

And all with pearl and ruby glowing
    Was the fair palace door,
Through which came flowing, flowing, flowing,
    And sparkling evermore,
A troop of Echoes whose sweet duty
    Was but to sing,
In voices of surpassing beauty,
    The wit and wisdom of their king.

V

But evil things, in robes of sorrow,
    Assailed the monarch's high estate;
(Ah, let us mourn, for never morrow
    Shall dawn upon him, desolate!)
And, round about his home, the glory
    That blushed and bloomed
Is but a dim-remembered story
    Of the old time entombed.

VI

And travelers now within that valley,
    Through the red-litten windows, see
Vast forms that move fantastically
    To a discordant melody;
While, like a rapid ghastly river,
    Through the pale door,
A hideous throng rush out forever,
    And laugh—but smile no more.

I well remember that suggestions arising from this ballad, led us into a train of thought wherein there became manifest an opinion of Usher's which I mention not so much on account of its novelty (for other men* have thought thus), as on account of the pertinacity with which he maintained it. This opinion, in its general form, was that of the sentience of all vegetable things. But, in his disordered fancy, the idea had assumed a more daring character, and trespassed, under certain conditions, upon the kingdom of inorganization. I lack words to express the full extent, or the earnest *abandon* of his persuasion. The belief, however, was connected (as I have previously hinted) with the gray stones of the home of his forefathers. The conditions of the sentience had been here, he imagined, fulfilled in the method of collocation of these stones—in the order of their arrangement, as well as in that of the many *fungi* which overspread them, and of the decayed trees which stood around—above all, in the long undisturbed endurance of this arrangement, and in its reduplication in the still waters of the tarn. Its evidence—the evidence of the sentience—was to be seen, he said, (and I here started as he spoke) in the gradual yet certain condensation of an atmosphere of their own about the waters and the walls. The result was discoverable, he added, in that silent, yet importunate and terrible influence which for centuries had molded the destinies of his family, and which made *him* what I now saw him—what he was. Such opinions need no comment, and I will make none.

Our books—the books which, for years, had formed no small portion of the mental existence of the invalid—were, as might be supposed, in strict keeping with this character of phantasm. We pored together over such works as the *Ververt et Chartreuse* of Gresset; the *Belphegor* of Machiavelli; the *Heaven and Hell* of Swedenborg; the *Subterranean Voyage of Nicholas Klimm* by Holberg; the *Chiromancy* of Robert Flud, of Jean D'Indaginé, and of De la Chambre; the *Journey into the Blue Distance* of Tieck; and the *City of the Sun* of Campanella. One favorite volume was a small octavo edition of the *Directorium Inquisitorium*, by the Dominican Eymeric de Gironne; and there were passages in *Pomponius Mela*, about the old African Satyrs and Aegipans, over which Usher would sit dreaming for hours. His chief delight, however, was found in the perusal of an exceedingly rare and

* Watson, Dr. Percival, Spallanzani, and especially the Bishop of Landaff. See *Chemical Essays*, vol. v.

curious book in quarto Gothic—the manual of a forgotten church—the *Vigiliae Mortuorum secundum Chorum Ecclesiæ Maguntinae.*

I could not help thinking of the wild ritual of this work, and of its probable influence upon the hypochondriac, when, one evening, having informed me abruptly that the Lady Madeline was no more, he stated his intention of preserving her corpse for a fortnight, (previously to its final interment,) in one of the numerous vaults within the main walls of the building. The worldly reason, however, assigned for this singular proceeding, was one which I did not feel at liberty to dispute. The brother had been led to his resolution (so he told me) by consideration of the unusual character of the malady of the deceased, of certain obtrusive and eager inquiries on the part of her medical men, and of the remote and exposed situation of the burial-ground of the family. I will not deny that when I called to mind the sinister countenance of the person whom I met upon the staircase, on the day of my arrival at the house, I had no desire to oppose what I regarded as at best but a harmless, and by no means an unnatural, precaution.

At the request of Usher, I personally aided him in the arrangements for the temporary entombment. The body having been encoffined, we two alone bore it to its rest. The vault in which we placed it (and which had been so long unopened that our torches, half smothered in its oppressive atmosphere, gave us little opportunity for investigation) was small, damp, and entirely without means of admission for light; lying, at great depth, immediately beneath that portion of the building in which was my own sleeping apartment. It had been used, apparently, in remote feudal times, for the worst purposes of a donjon-keep, and, in later days, as a place of deposit for powder, or some other highly combustible substance, as a portion of its floor, and the whole interior of a long archway through which we reached it, were carefully sheathed with copper. The door, of massive iron, had been, also, similarly protected. Its immense weight caused an unusually sharp grating sound, as it moved upon its hinges.

Having deposited our mournful burden upon tressels within this region of horror, we partially turned aside the yet unscrewed lid of the coffin, and looked upon the face of the tenant. A striking similitude between the brother and sister now first arrested my attention; and Usher, divining, perhaps, my thoughts, murmured out some few words from which I learned that the deceased and himself had been twins, and that sympathies of a scarcely intelligible nature had always existed between them. Our glances, however, rested not long upon the dead—for we could not regard her unawed. The disease which had thus entombed the lady in the maturity of youth, had left, as usual in all maladies of a strictly cataleptical character, the mockery of a faint blush upon the bosom and the face, and that suspiciously lingering smile upon the lip which is so terrible in death. We replaced and screwed down the lid, and, having secured the door of iron, made our way, with toil, into the scarcely less gloomy apartments of the upper portion of the house.

And now, some days of bitter grief having elapsed, an observable change came over the features of the mental disorder of my friend. His ordinary manner had vanished. His ordinary occupations were neglected or forgotten. He roamed from chamber to chamber with hurried, unequal, and objectless step. The pallor of his countenance had assumed, if possible, a more ghastly hue—but the luminousness of his eye had utterly gone out. The once occasional huskiness of his tone was heard no more; and a tremulous quaver, as if of extreme terror, habitually characterized his utterance. There were times, indeed, when I thought his unceasingly agitated mind was laboring with some oppressive secret, to divulge which he struggled for the necessary courage. At times, again, I was obliged to resolve all into the mere inexplicable vagaries of madness, for I beheld him gazing upon vacancy for long hours, in an attitude of the profoundest attention, as if listening to some imaginary sound. It was no wonder that his condition terrified—that it infected me. I felt creeping upon me, by slow yet certain degrees, the wild influences of his own fantastic yet impressive superstitions.

It was, especially, upon retiring to bed late in the night of the seventh or eighth day after the placing of the lady Madeline within the donjon, that I experienced the full power of such feelings. Sleep came not near my couch—while the hours waned and waned away. I struggled to reason off the nervousness which had dominion over me. I endeavored to believe that much, if not all of what I felt, was due to the bewildering influence of the gloomy furniture of the room—of the dark and tattered draperies, which, tortured into motion by the breath of a rising tempest, swayed fitfully to and fro upon the walls, and rustled uneasily about the decorations of the bed. But my efforts were fruitless. An irrepressible tremor gradually pervaded my frame; and, at length, there sat upon my very heart an incubus of utterly causeless alarm. Shaking this off with a gasp and a struggle, I uplifted myself upon the pillows, and, peering earnestly within the intense darkness of the chamber, harkened—I know not why, except that an instinctive spirit prompted me—to certain low and indefinite sounds which came, through the pauses of the storm, at long intervals, I knew not whence. Overpowered by an intense sentiment of horror, unaccountable yet unendurable, I threw on my clothes with haste (for I felt that I should sleep no more during the night), and endeavored to arouse myself from the pitiable condition into which I had fallen, by pacing rapidly to and fro through the apartment.

I had taken but few turns in this manner, when a light step on an adjoining staircase arrested my attention. I presently recognized it as that of Usher. In an instant afterward he rapped, with a gentle touch, at my door, and entered, bearing a lamp. His countenance was, as usual, cadaverously wan—but, moreover, there was a species of mad hilarity in his eyes—an evidently restrained *hysteria* in his whole demeanor. His air appalled me—but anything was preferable to the solitude which I had so long endured, and I even welcomed his presence as a relief.

"And you have not seen it?" he said abruptly, after having stared about him for some moments in silence—"you have not then seen it?—but, stay! you shall." Thus speaking, and having carefully shaded his lamp, he hurried to one of the casements, and threw it freely open to the storm.

The impetuous fury of the entering gust nearly lifted us from our feet. It was, indeed, a tempestuous yet sternly beautiful night, and one wildly singular in its terror and its beauty. A whirlwind had apparently collected its force in our vicinity; for there were frequent and violent alterations in the direction of the wind; and the exceeding density of the clouds (which hung so low as to press upon the turrets of the house) did not prevent our perceiving the life-like velocity with which they flew careering from all points against each other, without passing away into the distance. I say that even their exceeding density did not prevent our perceiving this—yet we had no glimpse of the moon or stars—nor was there any flashing forth of the lightning. But the under surfaces of the huge masses of agitated vapor, as well as all terrestrial objects immediately around us, were glowing in the unnatural light of a faintly luminous and distinctly visible gaseous exhalation which hung about and enshrouded the mansion.

"You must not—you shall not behold this!" said I, shudderingly, to Usher, as I led him, with a gentle violence, from the window to a seat. "These appearances, which bewilder you, are merely electrical phenomena not uncommon—or it may be that they have their ghastly origin in the rank miasma of the tarn. Let us close this casement;—the air is chilling and dangerous to your frame. Here is one of your favorite romances. I will read, and you shall listen;—and so we will pass away this terrible night together."

The antique volume which I had taken up was the *Mad Trist* of Sir Launcelot Canning; but I had called it a favorite of Usher's more in sad jest than in earnest; for, in truth, there is little in its uncouth and unimaginative prolixity which could have had interest for the lofty and spiritual ideality of my friend. It was, however, the only book immediately at hand; and I indulged a vague hope that the excitement which now agitated the hypochondriac, might find relief (for the history of mental disorder is full of similar anomalies) even in the extremeness of the folly which I should read. Could I have judged, indeed, by the wild overstrained air of vivacity with which he harkened, or apparently harkened, to the words of the tale, I might well have congratulated myself upon the success of my design.

I had arrived at that well-known portion of the story where Ethelred, the hero of the Trist, having sought in vain for peaceable admission into the dwelling of the hermit, proceeds to make good an entrance by force. Here, it will be remembered, the words of the narrative run thus:

"And Ethelred, who was by nature of a doughty heart, and who was now mighty withal, on account of the powerfulness of the wine which he had drunken, waited no longer to hold parley with the hermit, who, in sooth, was of an obstinate and maliceful turn, but, feeling the rain upon his shoulders, and fearing the rising of the tempest, uplifted his mace outright, and, with blows, made quickly room in the plankings of the door for his gauntleted hand; and now pulling therewith sturdily, he so cracked, and ripped, and tore all asunder, that the noise of the dry and hollow-sounding wood alarumed and reverberated throughout the forest."

At the termination of this sentence I started, and for a moment, paused; for it appeared to me (although I at once concluded that my excited fancy had deceived me)—it appeared to me that, from some very remote portion of the mansion, there came, indistinctly, to my ears, what might have been, in its exact similarity of character, the echo (but a stifled and dull one certainly) of the very cracking and ripping sound which Sir Launcelot had so particularly described. It was, beyond doubt, the coincidence alone which had arrested my attention; for, amid the rattling of the sashes of the casements, and the ordinary commingled noises of the still increasing storm, the sound, in itself, had nothing, surely, which should have interested or disturbed me. I continued the story:

"But the good champion Ethelred, now entering within the door, was sore enraged and amazed to perceive no signal of the maliceful hermit; but, in the stead thereof, a dragon of a scaly and prodigious demeanor, and of a fiery tongue, which sate in guard before a palace of gold, with a floor of silver; and upon the wall there hung a shield of shining brass with this legend enwritten—

Who entereth herein, a conqueror hath bin;
Who slayeth the dragon, the shield he shall win.

And Ethelred uplifted his mace, and struck upon the head of the dragon, which fell before him, and gave up his pesty breath, with a shriek so horrid and harsh, and withal so piercing, that Ethelred had fain to close his ears with his hands against the dreadful noise of it, the like whereof was never before heard."

Here again I paused abruptly, and now with a feeling of wild amazement—for there could be no doubt whatever that, in this instance, I did actually hear (although from what direction it proceeded I found it impossible to say) a low and apparently distant, but harsh, protracted, and most unusual screaming or grating sound—the exact counterpart of what my fancy had already conjured up for the dragon's unnatural shriek as described by the romancer.

Oppressed, as I certainly was, upon the occurrence of this second and most extraordinary coincidence, by a thousand conflicting sensations, in which wonder and extreme terror were predominant, I still retained sufficient presence of mind to avoid exciting, by any observation, the sensitive nervousness of my companion. I was by no means certain that he had noticed the sounds in question; although, assuredly, a strange alteration had, during the last few minutes, taken place in his demeanor. From a position fronting my own, he had gradually brought round his chair, so as to sit with his face to the door of the chamber; and thus

I could but partially perceive his features, although I saw that his lips trembled as if he were murmuring inaudibly. His head had dropped upon his breast—yet I knew that he was not asleep, from the wide and rigid opening of the eye as I caught a glance of it in profile. The motion of his body, too, was at variance with this idea—for he rocked from side to side with a gentle yet constant and uniform sway. Having rapidly taken notice of all this, I resumed the narrative of Sir Launcelot, which thus proceeded:

"And now, the champion, having escaped from the terrible fury of the dragon, bethinking himself of the brazen shield, and of the breaking up of the enchantment which was upon it, removed the carcass from out of the way before him, and approached valorously over the silver pavement of the castle to where the shield was upon the wall; which in sooth tarried not for his full coming, but feel down at his feet upon the silver floor, with a mighty great and terrible ringing sound."

No sooner had these syllables passed my lips, than—as if a shield of brass had indeed, at the moment, fallen heavily upon a floor of silver—I became aware of a distinct, hollow, metallic, and clangorous, yet apparently muffled reverberation. Completely unnerved, I leaped to my feet; but the measured rocking movement of Usher was undisturbed. I rushed to the chair in which he sat. His eyes were bent fixedly before him, and throughout his whole countenance there reigned a stony rigidity. But, as I placed my hand upon his shoulder, there came a strong shudder over his whole person; a sickly smile quivered about his lips; and I saw that he spoke in a low, hurried, and gibbering murmur, as if unconscious of my presence. Bending closely over him, I at length drank in the hideous import of his words.

"Not hear it?—yes, I hear it, and *have* heard it. Long—long—long—many minutes, many hours, many days, have I heard it—yet I dared not—oh, pity me, miserable wretch that I am!—I dared not—I *dared* not speak! *We have put her living in the tomb!* Said I not that my senses were acute? I *now* tell you that I heard her first feeble movements in the hollow coffin. I heard them—many, many days ago—yet I dared not—*I dared not speak!* And now—tonight—Ethelred—ha! ha!—the breaking of the hermit's door, and the death-cry of the dragon, and the clangor of the shield!—say, rather, the rending of her coffin, and the grating of the iron hinges of her prison, and her struggles within the coppered archway of the vault! Oh whither shall I fly? Will she not be here anon? Is she not hurrying to upbraid me for my haste? Have I not heard her footstep on the stair? Do I not distinguish that heavy and horrible beating of her heart? MADMAN!"—here he sprang furiously to his feet, and shrieked out his syllables, as if in the effort he were giving up his soul—"MADMAN! I TELL YOU THAT SHE NOW STANDS WITHOUT THE DOOR!"

As if in the superhuman energy of his utterance there had been found the potency of a spell—the huge antique panels to which the speaker pointed, threw slowly back, upon the instant, their ponderous and ebony jaws. It was the work of the rushing gust—but then without those doors there DID stand the lofty and enshrouded figure of the Lady Madeline of Usher. There was blood upon her white robes, and the evidence of some bitter struggle upon every portion of her emaciated frame. For a moment she remained trembling and reeling to and fro upon the threshold—then, with a low moaning cry, fell heavily inward upon the person of her brother, and in her violent and now final death-agonies, bore him to the floor a corpse, and a victim to the terrors he had anticipated.

From that chamber, and from that mansion, I fled aghast. The storm was still abroad in all its wrath as I found myself crossing the old causeway. Suddenly there shot along the path a wild light, and I turned to see whence a gleam so unusual could have issued; for the vast house and its shadows were alone behind me. The radiance was that of the full, setting, and blood-red moon, which now shone vividly through that once barely-discernible fissure, of which I have before spoken as extending from the roof of the building, in a zigzag direction, to the base. While I gazed, this fissure rapidly widened—there came a fierce breath of the whirlwind—the entire orb of the satellite burst at once upon my sight—my brain reeled as I saw the mighty walls rushing asunder—there was a long tumultuous shouting sound like the voice of a thousand waters—and the deep and dank tarn at my feet closed sullenly and silently over the fragments of the "HOUSE OF USHER."

The Murders in the Rue Morgue

[Considered a precursor of detective fiction, it is one of Poe's tales of ratiocination. Featuring the first detective in fiction, C. Auguste Dupin, this was first published in *Graham's Magazine* in April 1841.]

> What song the Syrens sang, or what name Achilles assumed when he hid himself among women, although puzzling questions, are not beyond *all* conjecture.
>
> —Sir Thomas Browne, *Urn-Burial*

The mental features discoursed of as the analytical, are, in themselves, but little susceptible of analysis. We appreciate them only in their effects. We know of them, among other things, that they are always to their possessor, when inordinately possessed, a source of the liveliest enjoyment. As the strong man exults in his physical ability, delighting in such exercises as call his muscles into action, so glories the analyst in that moral activity which *disentangles*. He derives pleasure from even the most trivial occupations bringing his talent into play. He is fond of enigmas, of conundrums, of hieroglyphics; exhibiting in his solutions of each a degree of *acumen* which appears to the ordinary apprehension preternatural. His results, brought about by the very soul and essence of method, have, in truth, the whole air of intuition.

The faculty of re-solution is possibly much invigorated by mathematical study, and especially by that highest branch of it which, unjustly, and merely on account of its retrograde operations, has been called, as if *par excellence*, analysis. Yet to calculate is not in itself to analyze. A chess-player, for example, does the one without effort at the other. It follows that the game of chess, in its effects upon mental character, is greatly misunderstood. I am not now writing a treatise, but simply prefacing a somewhat peculiar narrative by observations very much at random. I will, therefore, take occasion to assert that the higher powers of the reflective intellect are more decidedly and more usefully tasked by the unostentatious game of draughts than by all the elaborate frivolity of chess. In this latter, where the pieces have different and *bizarre* motions, with various and variable values, what is only complex is mistaken (a not unusual error) for what is profound. The *attention* is here called powerfully into play. If it flag for an instant, an oversight is committed resulting in injury or defeat. The possible moves being not only manifold but involute, the chances of such oversights are multiplied; and in nine cases out of ten it is the more concentrative rather than the more acute player who conquers. In draughts, on the contrary, where the moves are *unique* and have but little variation, the probabilities of inadvertence are diminished, and the mere attention being left comparatively unemployed, what advantages are obtained by either party are obtained by superior *acumen*. To be less abstract—Let us suppose a game of draughts where the pieces are reduced to four kings, and where, of course, no oversight is to be expected. It is obvious that here the victory can be decided (the players being at all equal) only by some *recherché* movement, the result of some strong exertion of the intellect. Deprived of ordinary resources, the analyst throws himself into the spirit of his opponent, identifies himself therewith, and not unfrequently sees thus, at a glance, the sole methods (sometime indeed absurdly simple ones) by which he may seduce into error or hurry into miscalculation.

Whist has long been noted for its influence upon what is termed the calculating power; and men of the highest order of intellect have been known to take an apparently unaccountable delight in it, while eschewing chess as frivolous. Beyond doubt there is nothing of a similar nature so greatly tasking the faculty of analysis. The best chess-player in Christendom *may* be little more than the best player of chess; but proficiency in whist implies capacity for success in all those more important undertakings where mind struggles with mind. When I say proficiency, I mean that perfection in the game which includes a comprehension of *all* the sources whence legitimate advantage may be derived. These are not only manifold but multiform, and lie frequently among recesses of thought altogether inaccessible to the ordinary understanding. To observe attentively is to remember distinctly; and, so far, the concentrative chess-player will do very well at whist; while the rules of Hoyle (themselves based upon the mere mechanism of the game) are sufficiently and generally comprehensible. Thus to have a retentive memory, and to proceed by "the book," are points commonly regarded as the sum total of good playing. But it is in matters beyond the limits of mere rule that the skill of the analyst is evinced. He makes, in silence, a host of observations and inferences. So, perhaps, do his companions; and the difference in the extent of the information obtained, lies not so much in the validity of the inference as in the quality of the observation. The necessary knowledge is that of *what* to observe. Our player confines himself not at all; nor, because the game is the object, does he reject deductions from things external to the game. He examines the countenance of his partner, comparing it carefully with that of each of his opponents. He considers the mode of assorting the cards in each hand; often counting trump by trump, and honor by honor, through the glances bestowed by their holders upon each. He notes every variation of face as the play progresses, gathering a fund of thought from the differences in the expression of certainty, of surprise, of triumph, or of chagrin. From the manner of gathering up a trick he judges whether the person taking it can make another in the suit. He recognizes what is played through feint, by the air with which it is thrown upon the table. A casual or inadvertent word; the accidental dropping or turning of a card, with the accompanying anxiety or carelessness in regard to its concealment; the counting of the tricks, with the order of their arrangement; embarrassment, hesitation, eagerness or trepidation—all afford, to his apparently intuitive perception, indications of the true state of affairs. The first two or three rounds having been played, he is in full possession of the contents of each hand, and thenceforward puts down his cards with as absolute a precision of purpose as if the rest of the party had turned outward the faces of their own.

The analytical power should not be confounded with ample ingenuity; for while the analyst is necessarily ingenious, the ingenious man is often remarkably incapable of analysis. The constructive or combining power, by which ingenuity is usually manifested, and to which the phrenologists (I believe erroneously) have assigned a separate organ, supposing it a primitive faculty, has been so frequently seen in those whose intellect bordered otherwise upon idiocy, as to have attracted general observation among writers on morals. Between ingenuity and the analytic ability there exists a difference far greater, indeed, than that between the fancy and the imagination, but of a character very strictly analogous. It will be found, in fact, that the ingenious are always fanciful, and the *truly* imaginative never otherwise than analytic.

The narrative which follows will appear to the reader somewhat in the light of a commentary upon the propositions just advanced.

Residing in Paris during the spring and part of the summer of 18—, I there became acquainted with a Monsieur C. Auguste Dupin. This young gentleman was of an excellent—indeed of an illustrious family, but, by a variety of untoward events, had been reduced to such poverty that the energy of his character succumbed beneath it, and he ceased to bestir himself in the world, or to care for the retrieval of his fortunes. By courtesy of his creditors, there still remained in his possession a small remnant of his patrimony; and, upon the income arising from this, he managed, by means of a rigorous economy, to procure the necessaries of life, without troubling himself about its superfluities. Books, indeed, were his sole luxuries, and in Paris these are easily obtained.

Our first meeting was at an obscure library in the Rue Montmartre, where the accident of our both being in search of the same very rare and very remarkable volume, brought us into closer communion. We saw each other again and again. I was deeply interested in the little family history which he detailed to me with all that candour which a Frenchman indulges whenever mere self is his theme. I was astonished, too, at the vast extent of his reading; and, above all, I felt my soul enkindled within me by the wild fervor, and the vivid freshness of his imagination. Seeking in Paris the objects I then sought, I felt that the society of such a man would be to me a treasure beyond price; and this feeling I frankly confided to him. It was at length arranged that we should live together during my stay in the city; and as my worldly circumstances were somewhat less embarrassed than his own, I was permitted to be at the expense of renting, and furnishing in a style which suited the rather fantastic gloom of our common temper, a time-eaten and grotesque mansion, long deserted through superstitions into which we did not inquire, and tottering to its fall in a retired and desolate portion of the Faubourg St. Germain.

Had the routine of our life at this place been known to the world, we should have been regarded as madmen—although, perhaps, as madmen of a harmless nature. Our seclusion was perfect. We admitted no visiters. Indeed the locality of our retirement had been carefully kept a secret from my own former associates; and it had been many years since Dupin had ceased to know or be known in Paris. We existed within ourselves alone.

It was a freak of fancy in my friend (for what else shall I call it?) to be enamored of the Night for her own sake; and into this *bizarrerie*, as into all his others, I quietly fell; giving myself up to his wild whims with a perfect *abandon*. The sable divinity would not herself dwell with us always; but we could counterfeit her presence. At the first dawn of the morning we closed all the messy shutters of our old building; lighting a couple of tapers which, strongly perfumed, threw out only the ghastliest and feeblest of rays. By the aid of these we then busied our souls in dreams—reading, writing, or conversing, until warned by the clock of the advent of the true Darkness. Then we sallied forth into the streets arm in arm, continuing the topics of the day, or roaming far and wide until a late hour, seeking, amid the wild lights and shadows of the populous city, that infinity of mental excitement which quiet observation can afford.

At such times I could not help remarking and admiring (although from his rich ideality I had been prepared to expect it) a peculiar analytic ability in Dupin. He seemed, too, to take an eager delight in its exercise—if not exactly in its display—and did not hesitate to confess the pleasure thus derived. He boasted to me, with a low chuckling laugh, that most men, in respect to himself, wore windows in their bosoms, and was wont to follow up such assertions by direct and very startling proofs of his intimate knowledge of my own. His manner at these moments was frigid and abstract; his eyes were vacant in expression; while his voice, usually a rich tenor, rose into a treble which would have sounded petulantly but for the deliberateness and entire distinctness of the enunciation. Observing him in these moods, I often dwelt meditatively upon the old philosophy of the Bi-Part Soul, and amused myself with the fancy of a double Dupin—the creative and the resolvent.

Let it not be supposed, from what I have just said, that I am detailing any mystery, or penning any romance. What I have described in the

Frenchman, was merely the result of an excited, or perhaps of a diseased intelligence. But of the character of his remarks at the periods in question an example will best convey the idea.

We were strolling one night down a long dirty street in the vicinity of the Palais Royal. Being both, apparently, occupied with thought, neither of us had spoken a syllable for fifteen minutes at least. All at once Dupin broke forth with these words:

"He is a very little fellow, that's true, and would do better for the *Théâtre des Variétés*."

"There can be no doubt of that," I replied unwittingly, and not at first observing (so much had I been absorbed in reflection) the extraordinary manner in which the speaker had chimed in with my meditations. In an instant afterward I recollected myself, and my astonishment was profound.

"Dupin," said I, gravely, "this is beyond my comprehension. I do not hesitate to say that I am amazed, and can scarcely credit my senses. How was it possible you should know I was thinking of——?" Here I paused, to ascertain beyond a doubt whether he really knew of whom I thought.

"Of Chantilly," said he, "why do you pause? You were remarking to yourself that his diminutive figure unfitted him for tragedy."

This was precisely what had formed the subject of my reflections. Chantilly was a *quondam* cobbler of the Rue St. Denis, who, becoming stage-mad, had attempted the *rôle* of Xerxes, in Crébillon's tragedy so called, and been notoriously Pasquinaded for his pains.

"Tell me, for Heaven's sake," I exclaimed, "the method—if method there is—by which you have been enabled to fathom my soul in this matter." In fact I was even more startled than I would have been willing to express.

"It was the fruiterer," replied my friend, "who brought you to the conclusion that the mender of soles was not of sufficient height for Xerxes *et id genus omne*."

"The fruiterer!—you astonish me—I know no fruiterer whomsoever."

"The man who ran up against you as we entered the street—it may have been fifteen minutes ago."

I now remembered that, in fact, a fruiterer, carrying upon his head a large basket of apples, had nearly thrown me down, by accident, as we passed from the Rue C—into the thoroughfare where we stood; but what this had to do with Chantilly I could not possibly understand.

There was not a particle of *charlatanerie* about Dupin. "I will explain," he said, "and that you may comprehend all clearly, we will first retrace the course of your meditations, from the moment in which I spoke to you until that of the *rencontre* with the fruiterer in question. The larger links of the chain run thus—Chantilly, Orion, Dr. Nichols, Epicurus, Stereotomy, the street stones, the fruiterer."

There are few persons who have not, at some period of their lives, amused themselves in retracing the steps by which particular conclusions of their own minds have been attained. The occupation is often full of interest; and he who attempts it for the first time is astonished by the apparently illimitable distance and incoherence between the starting-point and the goal. What, then, must have been my amazement when I heard the Frenchman speak what he had just spoken, and when I could not help acknowledging that he had spoken the truth. He continued:

"We had been talking of horses, if I remember aright, just before leaving the Rue C—. This was the last subject we discussed. As we crossed into this street, a fruiterer, with a large basket upon his head, brushing quickly past us, thrust you upon a pile of paving stones collected at a spot where the causeway is undergoing repair. You stepped upon one of the loose fragments, slipped, slightly strained your ankle, appeared vexed or sulky, muttered a few words, turned to look at the pile, and then proceeded in silence. I was not particularly attentive to what you did; but observation has become with me, of late, a species of necessity.

"You kept your eyes upon the ground—glancing, with a petulant expression, at the holes and ruts in the pavement (so that I saw you were still thinking of the stones), until we reached the little alley called Lamartine, which has been paved, by way of experiment, with the overlapping and riveted blocks. Here your countenance brightened up, and, perceiving your lips move, I could not doubt that you murmured the word 'stereotomy,' a term very affectedly applied to this species of pavement. I knew that you could not say to yourself 'stereotomy' without being brought to think of atomies, and thus of the theories of Epicurus; and since, when we discussed this subject not very long ago, I mentioned to you how singularly, yet with how little notice, the vague guesses of that noble Greek had met with confirmation in the late nebular cosmogony, I felt that you could not avoid casting your eyes upward to the great *nebula* in Orion, and I certainly expected that you would do so. You did look up; and I was now assured that I had correctly followed your steps. But in that bitter *tirade* upon Chantilly, which appeared in yesterday's *Musée*, the satirist, making some disgraceful allusions to the cobbler's change of name upon assuming the buskin, quoted a Latin line about which we have often conversed. I mean the line—

Perdidit antiquum litera sonum.

"I had told you that this was in reference to Orion, formerly written Urion; and, from certain pungencies connected with this explanation, I was aware that you could not have forgotten it. It was clear, therefore, that you would not fail to combine the two ideas of Orion and Chantilly. That you did combine them I saw by the character of the smile which passed over your lips. You thought of the poor cobbler's immolation. So far, you had been stooping in your gait; but now I saw you draw yourself up to your full height. I was then sure that you reflected upon the diminutive figure of Chantilly. At this point I interrupted your meditations to remark that as, in fact, he was a very little fellow—that Chantilly—he would do better at the *Théâtre des Variétés*."

Not long after this, we were looking over an evening edition of the *Gazette des Tribunaux*, when the following paragraphs arrested our attention.

"Extraordinary Murders.—This morning, about three o'clock, the inhabitants of the Quartier St. Roch were aroused from sleep by a succession of terrific shrieks, issuing, apparently, from the fourth story of a house in the Rue Morgue, known to be in the sole occupancy of one Madame L'Espanaye, and her daughter Mademoiselle Camille L'Espanaye. After some delay, occasioned by a fruitless attempt to procure admission in the usual manner, the gateway was broken in with a crowbar, and eight or ten of the neighbors entered accompanied by two *gendarmes*. By this time the cries had ceased; but, as the party rushed up the first flight of stairs, two or more rough voices in angry contention were distinguished and seemed to proceed from the upper part of the house. As the second landing was reached, these sounds, also, had ceased and everything remained perfectly quiet. The party spread themselves and hurried from room to room. Upon arriving at a large back chamber in the fourth story, (the door of which, being found locked, with the key inside, was forced open,) a spectacle presented itself which struck every one present not less with horror than with astonishment.

"The apartment was in the wildest disorder—the furniture broken and thrown about in all directions. There was only one bedstead; and from this the bed had been removed, and thrown into the middle of the floor. On a chair lay a razor, besmeared with blood. On the hearth were two or three long and thick tresses of grey human hair, also dabbled in blood, and seeming to have been pulled out by the roots. Upon the floor were found four Napoleons, an earring of topaz, three large silver spoons, three smaller of *métal d'Alger*, and two bags, containing nearly four thousand francs in gold. The drawers of a *bureau*, which stood in one corner were open, and had been, apparently, rifled, although many articles still remained in them. A small iron safe was discovered under the *bed* (not under the bedstead). It was open, with the key still in the door. It had no contents beyond a few old letters, and other papers of little consequence.

"Of Madame L'Espanaye no traces were here seen; but an unusual quantity of soot being observed in the fireplace, a search was made in the chimney, and (horrible to relate!) the corpse of the daughter, head downward, was dragged therefrom; it having been thus forced up the narrow aperture for a considerable distance. The body was quite warm. Upon examining it, many excoriations were perceived, no doubt occasioned by the violence with which it had been thrust up and disengaged. Upon the face were many severe scratches, and, upon the throat, dark bruises, and deep indentations of finger nails, as if the deceased had been throttled to death.

"After a thorough investigation of every portion of the house, without farther discovery, the party made its way into a small paved yard in the rear of the building, where lay the corpse of the old lady, with her throat so entirely cut that, upon an attempt to raise her, the head fell off. The body, as well as the head, was fearfully mutilated—the former so much so as scarcely to retain any semblance of humanity.

"To this horrible mystery there is not as yet, we believe, the slightest clew."

The next day's paper had these additional particulars.

"THE TRAGEDY IN THE RUE MORGUE.—Many individuals have been examined in relation to this most extraordinary and frightful affair [The word '*affaire*' has not yet, in France, that levity of import which it conveys with us], "but nothing whatever has transpired to throw light upon it. We give below all the material testimony elicited.

"*Pauline Dubourg*, laundress, deposes that she has known both the deceased for three years, having washed for them during that period. The old lady and her daughter seemed on good terms—very affectionate towards each other. They were excellent pay. Could not speak in regard to their mode or means of living. Believed that Madame L. told fortunes for a living. Was reputed to have money put by. Never met any persons in the house when she called for the clothes or took them home. Was sure that they had no servant in employ. There appeared to be no furniture in any part of the building except in the fourth story.

"*Pierre Moreau*, tobacconist, deposes that he has been in the habit of selling small quantitics of tobacco and snuff to Madame L'Espanaye for nearly four years. Was born in the neighborhood, and has always resided there. The deceased and her daughter had occupied the house in which the corpses were found for more than six years. It was formerly occupied by a jeweler, who underlet the upper rooms to various persons. The house was the property of Madame L. She became dissatisfied with the abuse of the premises by her tenant, and moved into them herself, refusing to let any portion. The old lady was childish. Witness had seen the daughter some five or six times during the six years. The two lived an exceedingly retired life—were reputed to have money. Had heard it said among the neighbors that Madame L. told fortunes—did not believe it. Had never seen any person enter the door except the old lady and her daughter, a porter once or twice, and a physician some eight or ten times.

"Many other persons, neighbors, gave evidence to the same effect. No one was spoken of as frequenting the house. It was not known whether there were any living connexions of Madame L. and her daughter. The shutters of the front windows were seldom opened. Those in the rear were always closed, with the exception of the large back room, fourth story. The house was a good house—not very old.

"*Isidore Muset, gendarme*, deposes that he was called to the house about three o'clock in the morning, and found some twenty or thirty persons at the gateway, endeavoring to gain admittance. Forced it open, at length, with a bayonet—not with a crowbar. Had but little difficulty in getting it open, on account of its being a double or folding gate, and bolted neither at bottom nor top. The shrieks were continued until the gate was forced—and then suddenly ceased. They seemed to be screams of some person (or persons) in great agony—were loud and drawn out, not short and quick. Witness led the way upstairs. Upon reaching the first landing, heard two voices in loud and angry contention—the one a gruff voice, the other much shriller—a very strange voice. Could distinguish some words of the former, which was that of a Frenchman. Was positive that it was not a woman's voice. Could distinguish the words '*sacré*' and '*diable*.' The shrill voice was that of a foreigner. Could not be sure whether it was the voice of a man or of a woman. Could not make out what was said, but believed the language to be Spanish. The state of the room and of the bodies was described by this witness as we described them yesterday.

"*Henri Duval*, a neighbor, and by trade a silversmith, deposes that he was one of the party who first entered the house. Corroborates the testimony of Muset in general. As soon as they forced an entrance, they reclosed the door, to keep out the crowd, which collected very fast, notwithstanding the lateness of the hour. The shrill voice, this witness thinks, was that of an Italian. Was certain it was not French. Could not be sure that it was a man's voice. It might have been a woman's. Was not acquainted with the Italian language. Could not distinguish the words, but was convinced by the intonation that the speaker was an Italian. Knew Madame L. and her daughter. Had conversed with both frequently. Was sure that the shrill voice was not that of either of the deceased.

"—*Odenheimer, restaurateur*. This witness volunteered his testimony. Not speaking French, was examined through an interpreter. Is a native of Amsterdam. Was passing the house at the time of the shrieks. They lasted for several minutes—probably ten. They were long and loud—very awful and distressing. Was one of those who entered the building. Corroborated the previous evidence in every respect but one. Was sure that the shrill voice was that of a man—of a Frenchman. Could not distinguish the words uttered. They were loud and quick—unequal—spoken apparently in fear as well as in anger. The voice was harsh—not so much shrill as harsh. Could not call it a shrill voice. The gruff voice said repeatedly '*sacré*,' '*diable*,' and once '*mon Dieu*.'

"*Jules Mignaud*, banker, of the firm of Mignaud et Fils, Rue Deloraine. Is the elder Mignaud. Madame L'Espanaye had some property. Had opened an account with his banking house in the spring of the year—(eight years previously). Made frequent deposits in small sums. Had checked for nothing until the third day before her death, when she took out in person the sum of 4000 francs. This sum was paid in gold, and a clerk went home with the money.

"*Adolphe Le Bon*, clerk to Mignaud et Fils, deposes that on the day in question, about noon, he accompanied Madame L'Espanaye to her residence with the 4000 francs, put up in two bags. Upon the door being opened, Mademoiselle L. appeared and took from his hands one of the bags, while the old lady relieved him of the other. He then bowed and departed. Did not see any person in the street at the time. It is a bye-street—very lonely.

"*William Bird*, tailor, deposes that he was one of the party who entered the house. Is an Englishman. Has lived in Paris two years. Was one of the first to ascend the stairs. Heard the voices in contention. The gruff voice was that of a Frenchman. Could make out several words, but cannot now remember all. Heard distinctly '*sacré*' and '*mon Dieu*.' There was a sound at the moment as if of several persons struggling—a scraping and scuffling sound. The shrill voice was very loud—louder than the gruff one. Is sure that it was not the voice of an Englishman. Appeared to be that of a German. Might have been a woman's voice. Does not understand German.

"Four of the above-named witnesses, being recalled, deposed that the door of the chamber in which was found the body of Mademoiselle L. was locked on the inside when the party reached it. Everything was perfectly silent—no groans or noises of any kind. Upon forcing the door no person was seen. The windows, both of the back and front room, were down and firmly fastened from within. A door between the two rooms was closed, but not locked. The door leading from the front room into the passage was locked, with the key on the inside. A small room in the front of the house, on the fourth story, at the head of the passage was open, the door being ajar. This room was crowded with old beds, boxes, and so forth. These were carefully removed and searched. There was not an inch of any portion of the house which was not carefully searched. Sweeps were sent up and down the chimneys. The house was a four-story one, with garrets (*mansardes.*) A trap-door on the roof was nailed down very securely—did not appear to have been opened for years. The time elapsing between the hearing of the voices in contention and the breaking open of the room door, was variously stated by the witnesses. Some made it as short as three minutes—some as long as five. The door was opened with difficulty.

"*Alfonzo Garcio*, undertaker, deposes that he resides in the Rue Morgue. Is a native of Spain. Was one of the party who entered the house. Did not proceed upstairs. Is nervous, and was apprehensive of the consequences of agitation. Heard the voices in contention. The gruff voice was that of a Frenchman. Could not distinguish what was said. The shrill voice was that of an Englishman—is sure of this. Does not understand the English language, but judges by the intonation.

"*Alberto Montani*, confectioner, deposes that he was among the first to ascend the stairs. Heard the voices in question. The gruff voice was that of a Frenchman. Distinguished several words. The speaker appeared to be expostulating. Could not make out the words of the shrill voice. Spoke quick and unevenly. Thinks it the voice of a Russian. Corroborates the general testimony. Is an Italian. Never conversed with a native of Russia.

"Several witnesses, recalled, here testified that the chimneys of all the rooms on the fourth story were too narrow to admit the passage of a human being. By 'sweeps' were meant cylindrical sweeping brushes, such as are employed by those who clean chimneys. These brushes were passed up and down every flue in the house. There is no back passage by which any one could have descended while the party proceeded upstairs. The body of Mademoiselle L'Espanaye was so firmly wedged in the chimney that it could not be got down until four or five of the party united their strength.

"*Paul Dumas*, physician, deposes that he was called to view the bodies about daybreak. They were both then lying on the sacking of the bedstead in the chamber where Mademoiselle L. was found. The corpse of the young lady was much bruised and excoriated. The fact that it had been thrust up the chimney would sufficiently account for these appearances. The throat was greatly chafed. There were several deep scratches just below the chin, together with a series of livid spots which were evidently the impression of fingers. The face was fearfully discoloured, and the eye-balls protruded. The tongue had been partially bitten through. A large bruise was discovered upon the pit of the stomach, produced, apparently, by the pressure of a knee. In the opinion of M. Dumas, Mademoiselle L'Espanaye had been throttled to death by some person or persons unknown. The corpse of the mother was horribly mutilated. All the bones of the right leg and arm were more or less shattered. The left *tibia* much splintered, as well as all the ribs of the left side. Whole body dreadfully bruised and discoloured. It was not possible to say how the injuries had been inflicted. A heavy club of wood, or a broad bar of iron—a chair—any large, heavy, and obtuse weapon would have produced such results, if wielded by the hands of a very powerful man. No woman could have inflicted the blows with any weapon. The head of the deceased, when seen by witness, was entirely separated from the body, and was also greatly shattered. The throat had evidently been cut with some very sharp instrument—probably with a razor.

"*Alexandre Etienne*, surgeon, was called with M. Dumas to view the bodies. Corroborated the testimony, and the opinions of M. Dumas.

"Nothing farther of importance was elicited, although several other persons were examined. A murder so mysterious, and so perplexing in all its particulars, was never before committed in Paris—if indeed a murder has been committed at all. The police are entirely at fault—an unusual occurrence in affairs of this nature. There is not, however, the shadow of a clew apparent."

The evening edition of the paper stated that the greatest excitement still continued in the Quartier St. Roch—that the premises in question had been carefully re-searched, and fresh examinations of witnesses instituted, but all to no purpose. A postscript, however, mentioned that Adolphe Le Bon had been arrested and imprisoned—although nothing appeared to criminate him, beyond the facts already detailed.

Dupin seemed singularly interested in the progress of this affair—at least so I judged from his manner, for he made no comments. It was only after the announcement that Le Bon had been imprisoned, that he asked me my opinion respecting the murders.

I could merely agree with all Paris in considering them an insoluble mystery. I saw no means by which it would be possible to trace the murderer.

"We must not judge of the means," said Dupin, "by this shell of an examination. The Parisian police, so much extolled for *acumen*, are cunning, but no more. There is no method in their proceedings, beyond the method of the moment. They make a vast parade of measures; but, not unfrequently, these are so ill adapted to the objects proposed, as to put us in mind of Monsieur Jourdain's calling for his *robe-de-chambre—pour mieux entendre la musique.* The results attained by them are not unfrequently surprising, but, for the most part, are brought about by simple diligence and activity. When these qualities are unavailing, their schemes fail. Vidocq, for example, was a good guesser and a persevering man. But, without educated thought, he erred continually by the very intensity of his investigations. He impaired his vision by holding the object too close. He might see, perhaps, one or two points with unusual clearness, but in so doing he, necessarily, lost sight of the matter as a whole. Thus there is such a thing as being too profound. Truth is not always in a well. In fact, as regards the more important knowledge, I do believe that she is invariably superficial. The depth lies in the valleys where we seek her, and not upon the mountain-tops where she is found. The modes and sources of this kind of error are well typified in the contemplation of the heavenly bodies. To look at a star by glances—to view it in a side-long way, by turning toward it the exterior portions of the *retina* (more susceptible of feeble impressions of light than the interior), is to behold the star distinctly—is to have the best appreciation of its luster—a luster which grows dim just in proportion as we turn our vision *fully* upon it. A greater number of rays actually fall upon the eye in the latter case, but, in the former, there is the more refined capacity for comprehension. By undue profundity we perplex and enfeeble thought; and it is possible to make even Venus herself vanish from the firmament by a scrutiny too sustained, too concentrated, or too direct.

"As for these murders, let us enter into some examinations for ourselves, before we make up an opinion respecting them. An inquiry will afford us amusement," [I thought this an odd term, so applied, but said nothing] "and, besides, Le Bon once rendered me a service for which I am not ungrateful. We will go and see the premises with our own eyes. I know G—, the Prefect of Police, and shall have no difficulty in obtaining the necessary permission."

The permission was obtained, and we proceeded at once to the Rue Morgue. This is one of those miserable thoroughfares which intervene between the Rue Richelieu and the Rue St. Roch. It was late in the afternoon when we reached it; as this quarter is at a great distance from that in which we resided. The house was readily found; for there were still many persons gazing up at the closed shutters, with an objectless curiosity, from the opposite side of the way. It was an ordinary Parisian house, with a gateway, on one side of which was a glazed watch-box, with a sliding panel in the window, indicating a *loge de concierge.* Before going in we walked up the street, turned down an alley, and then, again turning, passed in the rear of the building—Dupin, meanwhile examining the whole neighborhood, as well as the house, with a minuteness of attention for which I could see no possible object.

Retracing our steps, we came again to the front of the dwelling, rang, and, having shown our credentials, were admitted by the agents in charge. We went upstairs—into the chamber where the body of Mademoiselle L'Espanaye had been found, and where both the deceased still lay. The disorders of the room had, as usual, been suffered to exist. I saw nothing beyond what had been stated in the *Gazette des Tribunaux.* Dupin scrutinized everything—not excepting the bodies of the victims. We then went into the other rooms, and into the yard; a *gendarme* accompanying us throughout. The examination occupied us until dark, when we took our departure. On our way home my companion stepped in for a moment at the office of one of the daily papers.

I have said that the whims of my friend were manifold, and that *Je les ménageais*:—for this phrase there is no English equivalent. It was his humor, now, to decline all conversation on the subject of the murder, until about noon the next day. He then asked me, suddenly, if I had observed anything *peculiar* at the scene of the atrocity.

There was something in his manner of emphasizing the word "peculiar," which caused me to shudder, without knowing why.

"No, nothing *peculiar*," I said; "nothing more, at least, than we both saw stated in the paper."

"The *Gazette*," he replied, "has not entered, I fear, into the unusual horror of the thing. But dismiss the idle opinions of this print. It appears to me that this mystery is considered insoluble, for the very reason which should cause it to be regarded as easy of solution—I mean for the *outré* character of its features. The police are confounded by the seeming absence of motive—not for the murder itself—but for the atrocity of the murder. They are puzzled, too, by the seeming impossibility of reconciling the voices heard in contention, with the facts that no one was discovered upstairs but the assassinated Mademoiselle L'Espanaye, and that there were no means of egress without the notice of the party ascending. The wild disorder of the room; the corpse thrust, with the head downward, up the chimney; the frightful mutilation of the body of the old lady; these considerations, with those just mentioned, and others which I need not mention, have sufficed to paralyze the powers, by putting completely at fault the boasted *acumen*, of the government agents. They have fallen into the gross but common error of confounding the unusual with the abstruse. But it is by these deviations from the plane of the ordinary, that reason feels its way, if at all, in its search for the true. In investigations such as we are now pursuing, it should not be so much asked 'what has occurred,' as 'what has occurred that has never occurred before.' In fact, the facility with which I shall arrive, or have arrived, at the solution of this mystery, is in the direct ratio of its apparent insolubility in the eyes of the police."

I stared at the speaker in mute astonishment.

"I am now awaiting," continued he, looking toward the door of our apartment—"I am now awaiting a person who, although perhaps not the perpetrator of these butcheries, must have been in some measure implicated in their perpetration. Of the worst portion of the crimes committed, it is probable that he is innocent. I hope that I am right in this supposition; for upon it I build my expectation of reading the entire riddle. I look for the man here—in this room—every moment. It is true that he may not arrive; but the probability is that he will. Should he come, it will be necessary to detain him. Here are pistols; and we both know how to use them when occasion demands their use."

I took the pistols, scarcely knowing what I did, or believing what I heard, while Dupin went on, very much as if in a soliloquy. I have already spoken of his abstract manner at such times. His discourse was addressed to myself; but his voice, although by no means loud, had that intonation which is commonly employed in speaking to someone at a great distance. His eyes, vacant in expression, regarded only the wall.

"That the voices heard in contention," he said, "by the party upon the stairs, were not the voices of the women themselves, was fully proved by the evidence. This relieves us of all doubt upon the question whether the old lady could have first destroyed the daughter and afterward have committed suicide. I speak of this point chiefly for the sake of method; for the strength of Madame L'Espanaye would have been utterly unequal to the task of thrusting her daughter's corpse up the chimney as it was found; and the nature of the wounds upon her own person entirely preclude the idea of self-destruction. Murder, then, has been committed by some third party; and the voices of this third party were those heard in contention. Let me now advert—not to the whole testimony respecting these voices—but to what was *peculiar* in that testimony. Did you observe anything peculiar about it?"

I remarked that, while all the witnesses agreed in supposing the gruff voice to be that of a Frenchman, there was much disagreement in regard to the shrill, or, as one individual termed it, the harsh voice.

"That was the evidence itself," said Dupin, "but it was not the peculiarity of the evidence. You have observed nothing distinctive. Yet there *was* something to be observed. The witnesses, as you remark, agreed about the gruff voice; they were here unanimous. But in regard to the shrill voice, the peculiarity is—not that they disagreed—but that, while an Italian, an Englishman, a Spaniard, a Hollander, and a Frenchman attempted to describe it, each one spoke of it as that *of a foreigner*. Each is sure that it was not the voice of one of his own countrymen. Each likens it—not to the voice of an individual of any nation with whose language he is conversant—but the converse. The Frenchman supposes it the voice of a Spaniard, and 'might have distinguished some words *had he been acquainted with the Spanish*.' The Dutchman maintains it to have been that of a Frenchman; but we find it stated that '*not understanding French this witness was examined through an interpreter*.' The Englishman thinks it the voice of a German, and '*does not understand German*.' The Spaniard 'is sure' that it was that of an Englishman, but 'judges by the intonation' altogether, '*as he has no knowledge of the English*.' The Italian believes it the voice of a Russian, but '*has never conversed with a native of Russia*.' A second Frenchman differs, moreover, with the first, and is positive that the voice was that of an Italian; but, *not being cognizant of that tongue*, is, like the Spaniard, 'convinced by the intonation.' Now, how strangely unusual must that voice have really been, about which such testimony as this *could* have been elicited!—in whose *tones*, even, denizens of the five great divisions of Europe could recognize nothing familiar! You will say that it might have been the voice of an Asiatic—of an African. Neither Asiatics nor Africans abound in Paris;

but, without denying the inference, I will now merely call your attention to three points. The voice is termed by one witness 'harsh rather than shrill.' It is represented by two others to have been 'quick and *unequal.*' No words—no sounds resembling words—were by any witness mentioned as distinguishable.

"I know not," continued Dupin, "what impression I may have made, so far, upon your own understanding; but I do not hesitate to say that legitimate deductions even from this portion of the testimony—the portion respecting the gruff and shrill voices—are in themselves sufficient to engender a suspicion which should give direction to all farther progress in the investigation of the mystery. I said 'legitimate deductions'; but my meaning is not thus fully expressed. I designed to imply that the deductions are the *sole* proper ones, and that the suspicion arises *inevitably* from them as the single result. What the suspicion is, however, I will not say just yet. I merely wish you to bear in mind that, with myself, it was sufficiently forcible to give a definite form—a certain tendency—to my inquiries in the chamber.

"Let us now transport ourselves, in fancy, to this chamber. What shall we first seek here? The means of egress employed by the murderers. It is not too much to say that neither of us believe in preternatural events. Madame and Mademoiselle L'Espanaye were not destroyed by spirits. The doers of the deed were material, and escaped materially. Then how? Fortunately, there is but one mode of reasoning upon the point, and that mode *must* lead us to a definite decision. Let us examine, each by each, the possible means of egress. It is clear that the assassins were in the room where Mademoiselle L'Espanaye was found, or at least in the room adjoining, when the party ascended the stairs. It is then only from these two apartments that we have to seek issues. The police have laid bare the floors, the ceilings, and the masonry of the walls, in every direction. No *secret* issues could have escaped their vigilance. But not trusting to *their* eyes, I examined with my own. There were, then, no secret issues. Both doors leading from the rooms into the passage were securely locked, with the keys inside. Let us turn to the chimneys. These, although of ordinary width for some eight or ten feet above the hearths, will not admit, throughout their extent, the body of a large cat. The impossibility of egress, by means already stated, being thus absolute, we are reduced to the windows. Through those of the front room no one could have escaped without notice from the crowd in the street. The murderers *must* have passed, then, through those of the back room. Now, brought to this conclusion in so unequivocal a manner as we are, it is not our part, as reasoners, to reject it on account of apparent 'impossibilities'. It is only left for us to prove that these apparent 'impossibilities' are, in reality, not such.

"There are two windows in the chamber. One of them is unobstructed by furniture, and is wholly visible. The lower portion of the other is hidden from view by the head of the unwieldy bedstead which is thrust close up against it. The former was found securely fastened from within. It resisted the utmost force of those who endeavored to raise it. A large gimlet-hole had been pierced in its frame to the left, and a very stout nail was found fitted therein, nearly to the head. Upon examining the other window, a similar nail was seen similarly fitted in it; and a vigorous attempt to raise this sash, failed also. The police were now entirely satisfied that egress had not been in these directions. And, *therefore*, it was thought a matter of supererogation to withdraw the nails and open the windows.

"My own examination was somewhat more particular, and was so for the reason I have just given—because here it was, I knew, that all apparent impossibilities *must* be proved to be not such in reality.

"I proceeded to think thus—*a posteriori*. The murderers *did* escape from one of these windows. This being so, they could not have refastened the sashes from the inside, as they were found fastened;—the consideration which put a stop, through its obviousness, to the scrutiny of the police in this quarter. Yet the sashes *were* fastened. They *must*, then, have the power of fastening themselves. There was no escape from this conclusion. I stepped to the unobstructed casement, withdrew the nail with some difficulty and attempted to raise the sash. It resisted all my efforts, as I had anticipated. A concealed spring must, I now know, exist; and this corroboration of my idea convinced me that my premises at least, were correct, however mysterious still appeared the circumstances attending the nails. A careful search soon brought to light the hidden spring. I pressed it, and, satisfied with the discovery, forbore to upraise the sash.

"I now replaced the nail and regarded it attentively. A person passing out through this window might have reclosed it, and the spring would have caught—but the nail could not have been replaced. The conclusion was plain, and again narrowed in the field of my investigations. The assassins *must* have escaped through the other window. Supposing, then, the springs upon each sash to be the same, as was probable, there *must* be found a difference between the nails, or at least between the modes of their fixture. Getting upon the sacking of the bedstead, I looked over the head-board minutely at the second casement. Passing my hand down behind the board, I readily discovered and pressed the spring, which was, as I had supposed, identical in character with its neighbor. I now looked at the nail. It was as stout as the other, and apparently fitted in the same manner—driven in nearly up to the head.

"You will say that I was puzzled; but, if you think so, you must have misunderstood the nature of the inductions. To use a sporting phrase, I had not been once 'at fault.' The scent had never for an instant been lost. There was no flaw in any link of the chain. I had traced the secret to its ultimate result—and that result was *the nail*. It had, I say, in every respect, the appearance of its fellow in the other window; but this fact was an absolute nullity (conclusive us it might seem to be) when compared with the consideration that here, at this point, terminated the clew. 'There *must* be something wrong,' I said, 'about the nail.' I touched it; and the head, with about a quarter of an inch of the shank, came off in my fingers. The rest of the shank was in the gimlet-hole where it had been broken off. The fracture was an old one (for its edges were encrusted with rust), and had apparently been accomplished by the blow of a hammer, which had partially embedded, in the top of the bottom sash, the head portion of the nail. I now carefully replaced this head portion in the indentation whence I had taken it, and the resemblance to a perfect nail was complete—the fissure was invisible. Pressing the spring, I gently raised the sash for a few inches; the head went up with it, remaining firm in its bed. I closed the window, and the semblance of the whole nail was again perfect.

"The riddle, so far, was now unriddled. The assassin had escaped through the window which looked upon the bed. Dropping of its own accord upon his exit (or perhaps purposely closed), it had become fastened by the spring; and it was the retention of this spring which had been mistaken by the police for that of the nail—farther inquiry being thus considered unnecessary.

"The next question is that of the mode of descent. Upon this point I had been satisfied in my walk with you around the building. About five feet and a half from the casement in question there runs a lightning-rod. From this rod it would have been impossible for any one to reach the window itself, to say nothing of entering it. I observed, however, that the shutters of the fourth story were of the peculiar kind called by Parisian carpenters *ferrades*—a kind rarely employed at the present day, but frequently seen upon very old mansions at Lyons and Bordeaux. They are in the form of an ordinary door (a single, not a folding door), except that the upper half is latticed or worked in open trellis—thus affording an excellent hold for the hands. In the present instance these shutters are fully three feet and a half broad. When we saw them from the rear of the house, they were both about half open—that is to say, they stood off at right angles from the wall. It is probable that the police, as well as myself, examined the back of the tenement; but, if so, in looking at these *ferrades* in the line of their breadth (as they must have done), they did not perceive this great breadth itself, or, at all events, failed to take it into due consideration. In fact, having once satisfied themselves that no egress could have been made in this quarter, they would naturally bestow here a very cursory examination. It was clear to me, however, that the shutter belonging to the window at the head of the bed, would, if swung fully back to the wall, reach to within two feet of the lightning-rod. It was also evident that, by exertion of a very unusual degree of activity and courage, an entrance into the window, from the rod, might have been thus effected.—By reaching to the distance of two feet and a half (we now suppose the shutter open to its whole extent) a robber might have taken a firm grasp upon the trellis-work. Letting go, then, his hold upon the rod, placing his feet securely against the wall, and springing boldly from it, he might have swung the shutter so as to close it, and, if we imagine the window open at the time, might even have swung himself into the room.

"I wish you to bear especially in mind that I have spoken of a *very* unusual degree of activity as requisite to success in so hazardous and so difficult a feat. It is my design to show you, first, that the thing might possibly have been accomplished:—but, secondly and *chiefly*, I wish to impress upon your understanding the *very extraordinary*—the almost preternatural character of that agility which could have accomplished it.

"You will say, no doubt, using the language of the law, that 'to make out my case' I should rather undervalue, than insist upon a full estimation of the activity required in this matter. This may be the practice in law, but it is not the usage of reason. My ultimate object is only the truth. My immediate purpose is to lead you to place in juxtaposition, that *very unusual* activity of which I have just spoken with that *very peculiar* shrill (or harsh) and *unequal* voice, about whose nationality no two persons could be found to agree, and in whose utterance no syllabification could be detected."

At these words a vague and half-formed conception of the meaning of Dupin flitted over my mind. I seemed to be upon the verge of comprehension without power to comprehend—as men, at times, find themselves upon the brink of remembrance without being able, in the end, to remember. My friend went on with his discourse.

"You will see," he said, "that I have shifted the question from the mode of egress to that of ingress. It was my design to convey the idea that both were effected in the same manner, at the same point. Let us now revert to the interior of the room. Let us survey the appearances here. The drawers of the bureau, it is said, had been rifled, although many articles of apparel still remained within them. The conclusion here is absurd. It is a mere guess—a very silly one—and no more. How are we to know that the articles found in the drawers were not all these drawers had originally contained? Madame L'Espanaye and her daughter lived an exceedingly retired life—saw no company—seldom went out—had little use for numerous changes of habiliment. Those found were at least of as good quality as any likely to be possessed by these ladies. If a thief had taken any, why did he not take the best—why did he not take all? In a word, why did he abandon four thousand francs in gold to encumber himself with a bundle of linen? The gold *was* abandoned. Nearly the whole sum mentioned by Monsieur Mignaud, the banker, was discovered, in bags, upon the floor. I wish you, therefore, to discard from your thoughts the blundering idea of *motive*, engendered in the brains of the police by that portion of the evidence which speaks of money delivered at the door of the house. Coincidences ten times as remarkable as this (the delivery of the money, and murder committed within three days upon the party receiving it), happen to all of us every hour of our lives, without attracting even momentary notice. Coincidences, in general, are great stumbling-blocks in the way of that class of thinkers who have been educated to know nothing of the theory of probabilities—that theory to which the most glorious objects of human research are indebted for the most glorious of illustration. In the present instance, had the gold been gone, the fact of its delivery three days before would have formed something more than a coincidence. It would have been corroborative of this idea of motive. But, under the real circumstances of the case, if we are to suppose gold the motive of this outrage, we must also imagine the perpetrator so vacillating an idiot as to have abandoned his gold and his motive together.

"Keeping now steadily in mind the points to which I have drawn your attention—that peculiar voice, that unusual agility, and that startling absence of motive in a murder so singularly atrocious as this—let us glance at the butchery itself. Here is a woman strangled to death by manual strength, and thrust up a chimney, head downward. Ordinary assassins employ no such modes of murder as this. Least of all, do they thus dispose of the murdered. In the manner of thrusting the corpse up the chimney, you will admit that there was something *excessively outré*—something altogether irreconcilable with our common notions of human action, even when we suppose the actors the most depraved of men. Think, too, how great must have been that strength which could have thrust the body *up* such an aperture so forcibly that the united vigor of several persons was found barely sufficient to drag it *down!*

"Turn, now, to other indications of the employment of a vigor most marvelous. On the hearth were thick tresses—very thick tresses—of gray human hair. These had been torn out by the roots. You are aware of the great force necessary in tearing thus from the head even twenty or thirty hairs together. You saw the locks in question as well as myself. Their roots (a hideous sight!) were clotted with fragments of the flesh of the scalp—sure token of the prodigious power which had been exerted in uprooting perhaps half a million of hairs at a time. The throat of the old lady was not merely cut, but the head absolutely severed from the body: the instrument was a mere razor. I wish you also to look at the *brutal* ferocity of these deeds. Of the bruises upon the body of Madame L'Espanaye I do not speak. Monsieur Dumas, and his worthy coadjutor Monsieur Etienne, have pronounced that they were inflicted by some obtuse instrument; and so far these gentlemen are very correct. The obtuse instrument was clearly the stone pavement in the yard, upon which the victim had fallen from the window which looked in upon the bed. This idea, however simple it may now seem, escaped the police for the same reason that the breadth of the shutters escaped them—because, by the affair of the nails, their perceptions had been hermetically sealed against the possibility of the windows having ever been opened at all.

"If now, in addition to all these things, you have properly reflected upon the odd disorder of the chamber, we have gone so far as to combine the ideas of an agility astounding, a strength superhuman, a ferocity brutal, a butchery without motive, a *grotesquerie* in horror absolutely alien from humanity, and a voice foreign in tone to the ears of men of many nations, and devoid of all distinct or intelligible syllabification. What result, then, has ensued? What impression have I made upon your fancy?"

I felt a creeping of the flesh as Dupin asked me the question. "A madman," I said, "has done this deed—some raving maniac, escaped from a neighboring *Maison de Santé*."

"In some respects," he replied, "your idea is not irrelevant. But the voices of madmen, even in their wildest paroxysms, are never found to tally with that peculiar voice heard upon the stairs. Madmen are of some nation, and their language, however incoherent in its words, has always the coherence of syllabification. Besides, the hair of a madman is not such as I now hold in my hand. I disentangled this little tuft from the rigidly clutched fingers of Madame L'Espanaye. Tell me what you can make of it."

"Dupin!" I said, completely unnerved; "this hair is most unusual—this is no *human* hair."

"I have not asserted that it is," said he; "but, before we decide this point, I wish you to glance at the little sketch I have here traced upon this paper. It is a facsimile drawing of what has been described in one portion of the testimony as 'dark bruises, and deep indentations of fingernails,' upon the throat of Mademoiselle L'Espanaye, and in another, (by Messrs Dumas and Etienne), as a 'series of livid spots, evidently the impression of fingers.'

"You will perceive," continued my friend, spreading out the paper upon the table before us, "that this drawing gives the idea of a firm and fixed hold. There is no *slipping* apparent. Each finger has retained—possibly until the death of the victim—the fearful grasp by which it originally embedded itself. Attempt, now, to place all your fingers, at the same time, in the respective impressions as you see them."

I made the attempt in vain.

"We are possibly not giving this matter a fair trial," he said. "The paper is spread out upon a plane surface; but the human throat is cylindrical. Here is a billet of wood, the circumference of which is about that of the throat. Wrap the drawing around it, and try the experiment again."

I did so; but the difficulty was even more obvious than before. "This," I said, "is the mark of no human hand."

"Read now," replied Dupin, "this passage from Cuvier."

It was a minute anatomical and generally descriptive account of the large fulvous Ourang-Outang of the East Indian Islands. The gigantic stature, the prodigious strength and activity, the wild ferocity, and the imitative propensities of these mammalia are sufficiently well known to all. I understood the full horrors of the murder at once.

"The description of the digits," said I, as I made an end of reading, "is in exact accordance with this drawing. I see that no animal but an Ourang-Outang, of the species here mentioned, could have impressed the indentations as you have traced them. This tuft of tawny hair, too, is identical in character with that of the beast of Cuvier. But I cannot possibly comprehend the particulars of this frightful mystery. Besides, there were *two* voices heard in contention, and one of them was unquestionably the voice of a Frenchman."

"True; and you will remember an expression attributed almost unanimously, by the evidence, to this voice,—the expression, '*Mon Dieu!*' This, under the circumstances, has been justly characterized by one of the witnesses (Montani, the confectioner,) as an expression of remonstrance or expostulation. Upon these two words, therefore, I have mainly built my hopes of a full solution of the riddle. A Frenchman was cognizant of the murder. It is possible—indeed it is far more than probable—that he was innocent of all participation in the bloody transactions which took place. The Ourang-Outang may have escaped from him. He may have traced it to the chamber; but, under the agitating circumstances which ensued, he could never have recaptured it. It is still at large. I will not pursue these guesses—for I have no right to call them more—since the shades of reflection upon which they are based are scarcely of sufficient depth to be appreciable by my own intellect, and since I could not pretend to make them intelligible to the understanding of another. We will call them guesses then, and speak of them as such. If the Frenchman in question is indeed, as I suppose, innocent of this atrocity, this advertisement which I left last night, upon our return home, at the office of *Le Monde*, (a paper devoted to the shipping interest, and much sought by sailors), will bring him to our residence."

He handed me a paper, and I read thus:

> CAUGHT—*In the Bois de Boulogne, early in the morning of the—* *inst.* (the morning of the murder), *a very large, tawny Ourang-Outang of the Bornese species. The owner (who is ascertained to be a sailor, belonging to a Maltese vessel), may have the animal again, upon identifying it satisfactorily and paying a few charges arising from its capture and keeping. Call at No. ——, Rue ——, Faubourg St. Germain—au troisième.*

"How was it possible," I asked, "that you should know the man to be a sailor, and belonging to a Maltese vessel?"

"I do *not* know it," said Dupin. "I am not *sure* of it. Here, however, is a small piece of ribbon, which from its form, and from its greasy appearance, has evidently been used in tying the hair in one of those long *queues* of which sailors are so fond. Moreover, this knot is one which few besides sailors can tie, and is peculiar to the Maltese. I picked the ribbon up at the foot of the lightning-rod. It could not have belonged to either of the deceased. Now if, after all, I am wrong in my induction from this ribbon, that the Frenchman was a sailor belonging to a Maltese vessel, still I can have done no harm in saying what I did in the advertisement. If I am in error, he will merely suppose that I have been misled by some circumstance into which he will not take the trouble to inquire. But if I am right, a great point is gained. Cognizant although innocent of the murder, the Frenchman will naturally hesitate about replying to the advertisement—about demanding the Ourang-Outang. He will reason thus:—'I am innocent; I am poor; my Ourang-Outang is of great value—to one in my circumstances a fortune of itself—why should I lose it through idle apprehensions of danger? Here it is, within my grasp. It was found in the Bois de Boulogne—at a vast distance from the scene of that butchery. How can it ever be suspected that a brute beast should have done the deed? The police are at fault—they have failed to procure the slightest clew. Should they even trace the animal, it would be impossible to prove me cognizant of the murder, or to implicate me in guilt on account of that cognizance. Above all, *I am known.* The advertiser designates me as the possessor of the beast. I am not sure to what limit his knowledge may extend. Should I avoid claiming a property of so great value, which it is known that I possess, I will render the animal at least, liable to suspicion. It is not my policy to attract attention either to myself or to the beast. I will answer the advertisement, get the Ourang-Outang, and keep it close until this matter has blown over.'"

At this moment we heard a step upon the stairs.

"Be ready," said Dupin, "with your pistols, but neither use them nor show them until at a signal from myself."

The front door of the house had been left open, and the visiter had entered, without ringing, and advanced several steps upon the staircase. Now, however, he seemed to hesitate. Presently we heard him descending. Dupin was moving quickly to the door, when we again heard him coming up. He did not turn back a second time, but stepped up with decision, and rapped at the door of our chamber.

"Come in," said Dupin, in a cheerful and hearty tone.

A man entered. He was a sailor, evidently—a tall, stout, and muscular-looking person, with a certain dare-devil expression of countenance, not altogether unprepossessing. His face, greatly sunburnt, was more than half hidden by whisker and *mustachio.* He had with him a huge oaken cudgel, but appeared to be otherwise unarmed. He bowed awkwardly, and bade us "good evening," in French accents, which, although somewhat Neufchatelish, were still sufficiently indicative of a Parisian origin.

"Sit down, my friend," said Dupin. "I suppose you have called about the Ourang-Outang. Upon my word, I almost envy you the possession of him; a remarkably fine, and no doubt a very valuable animal. How old do you suppose him to be?"

The sailor drew a long breath, with the air of a man relieved of some intolerable burden, and then replied, in an assured tone:

"I have no way of telling—but he can't be more than four or five years old. Have you got him here?"

"Oh no, we had no conveniences for keeping him here. He is at a livery stable in the Rue Dubourg, just by. You can get him in the morning. Of course you are prepared to identify the property?"

"To be sure I am, sir."

"I shall be sorry to part with him," said Dupin.

"I don't mean that you should be at all this trouble for nothing, sir," said the man. "Couldn't expect it. Am very willing to pay a reward for the finding of the animal—that is to say, anything in reason."

"Well," replied my friend, "that is all very fair, to be sure. Let me think!—what should I have? Oh! I will tell you. My reward shall be this.

You shall give me all the information in your power about these murders in the Rue Morgue."

Dupin said the last words in a very low tone, and very quietly. Just as quietly, too, he walked toward the door, locked it and put the key in his pocket. He then drew a pistol from his bosom and placed it, without the least flurry, upon the table.

The sailor's face flushed up as if he were struggling with suffocation. He started to his feet and grasped his cudgel; but the next moment he fell back into his seat, trembling violently, and with the countenance of death itself. He spoke not a word. I pitied him from the bottom of my heart.

"My friend," said Dupin, in a kind tone, "you are alarming yourself unnecessarily—you are indeed. We mean you no harm whatever. I pledge you the honor of a gentleman, and of a Frenchman, that we intend you no injury. I perfectly well know that you are innocent of the atrocities in the Rue Morgue. It will not do, however, to deny that you are in some measure implicated in them. From what I have already said, you must know that I have had means of information about this matter—means of which you could never have dreamed. Now the thing stands thus. You have done nothing which you could have avoided—nothing, certainly, which renders you culpable. You were not even guilty of robbery, when you might have robbed with impunity. You have nothing to conceal. You have no reason for concealment. On the other hand, you are bound by every principle of honor to confess all you know. An innocent man is now imprisoned, charged with that crime of which you can point out the perpetrator."

The sailor had recovered his presence of mind, in a great measure, while Dupin uttered these words; but his original boldness of bearing was all gone.

"So help me God," said he, after a brief pause, "I will tell you all I know about this affair—but I do not expect you to believe one half I say—I would be a fool indeed if I did. Still, I *am* innocent, and I will make a clean breast if I die for it."

What he stated was, in substance, this. He had lately made a voyage to the Indian Archipelago. A party, of which he formed one, landed at Borneo, and passed into the interior on an excursion of pleasure. Himself and a companion had captured the Ourang-Outang. This companion dying, the animal fell into his own exclusive possession. After great trouble, occasioned by the intractable ferocity of his captive during the home voyage, he at length succeeded in lodging it safely at his own residence in Paris, where, not to attract toward himself the unpleasant curiosity of his neighbors, he kept it carefully secluded, until such time as it should recover from a wound in the foot, received from a splinter on board ship. His ultimate design was to sell it.

Returning home from some sailors' frolic the night, or rather in the morning of the murder, he found the beast occupying his own bedroom, into which it had broken from a closet adjoining, where it had been, as was thought, securely confined. Razor in hand, and fully lathered, it was sitting before a looking-glass, attempting the operation of shaving, in which it had no doubt previously watched its master through the keyhole of the closet. Terrified at the sight of so dangerous a weapon in the possession of an animal so ferocious, and so well able to use it, the man, for some moments, was at a loss what to do. He had been accustomed, however, to quiet the creature, even in its fiercest moods, by the use of a whip, and to this he now resorted. Upon sight of it, the Ourang-Outang sprang at once through the door of the chamber, down the stairs, and thence, through a window, unfortunately open, into the street.

The Frenchman followed in despair; the ape, razor still in hand, occasionally stopping to look back and gesticulate at its pursuer, until the latter had nearly come up with it. It then again made off. In this manner the chase continued for a long time. The streets were profoundly quiet, as it was nearly three o'clock in the morning. In passing down an alley in the rear of the Rue Morgue, the fugitive's attention was arrested by a light gleaming from the open window of Madame L'Espanaye's chamber, in the fourth story of her house. Rushing to the building, it perceived the lightning-rod, clambered up with inconceivable agility, grasped the shutter, which was thrown fully back against the wall, and, by its means, swung itself directly upon the headboard of the bed. The whole feat did not occupy a minute. The shutter was kicked open again by the Ourang-Outang as it entered the room.

The sailor, in the meantime, was both rejoiced and perplexed. He had strong hopes of now recapturing the brute, as it could scarcely escape from the trap into which it had ventured, except by the rod, where it might be intercepted as it came down. On the other hand, there was much cause for anxiety as to what it might do in the house. This latter reflection urged the man still to follow the fugitive. A lightning rod is ascended without difficulty, especially by a sailor; but, when he had arrived as high as the window, which lay far to his left, his career was stopped; the most that he could accomplish was to reach over so as to obtain a glimpse of the interior of the room. At this glimpse he nearly fell from his hold through excess of horror. Now it was that those hideous shrieks arose upon the night, which had startled from slumber the inmates of the Rue Morgue. Madame L'Espanaye and her daughter, habited in their night clothes, had apparently been occupied in arranging some papers in the iron chest already mentioned, which had been wheeled into the middle of the room. It was open, and its contents lay beside it on the floor. The victims must have been sitting with their backs toward the window; and, from the time elapsing between the ingress of the beast and the screams, it seems probable that it was not immediately perceived. The flapping-to of the shutter would naturally have been attributed to the wind.

As the sailor looked in, the gigantic animal had seized Madame L'Espanaye by the hair (which was loose, as she had been combing it), and was flourishing the razor about her face, in imitation of the motions of a barber. The daughter lay prostrate and motionless; she had swooned. The screams and struggles of the old lady (during which the hair was torn from her head) had the effect of changing the probably pacific purposes of the Ourang-Outang into those of wrath. With one determined sweep of its muscular arm it nearly severed her head from her body. The sight of blood inflamed its anger into frenzy. Gnashing its teeth, and flashing fire from its eyes, it flew upon the body of the girl, and embedded its fearful talons in her throat, retaining its grasp until she expired. Its wandering and wild glances fell at this moment upon the head of the bed, over which the face of its master, rigid with horror, was just discernible. The fury of the beast, who no doubt bore still in mind the dreaded whip, was instantly converted into fear. Conscious of having deserved punishment, it seemed desirous of concealing its bloody deeds, and skipped about the chamber in an agony of nervous agitation; throwing down and breaking the furniture as it moved, and dragging the bed from the bedstead. In conclusion, it seized first the corpse of the daughter, and thrust it up the chimney, as it was found; then that of the old lady, which it immediately hurled through the window headlong.

As the ape approached the casement with its mutilated burden, the sailor shrank aghast to the rod, and, rather gliding than clambering down

it, hurried at once home—dreading the consequences of the butchery, and gladly abandoning, in his terror, all solicitude about the fate of the Ourang-Outang. The words heard by the party upon the staircase were the Frenchman's exclamations of horror and affright, commingled with the fiendish jabberings of the brute.

I have scarcely anything to add. The Ourang-Outang must have escaped from the chamber, by the rod, just before the break of the door. It must have closed the window as it passed through it. It was subsequently caught by the owner himself, who obtained for it a very large sum at the *Jardin des Plantes.* Le Bon was instantly released, upon our narration of the circumstances (with some comments from Dupin) at the *bureau* of the Prefect of Police. This functionary, however well disposed to my friend, could not altogether conceal his chagrin at the turn which affairs had taken, and was fain to indulge in a sarcasm or two, about the propriety of every person minding his own business.

"Let him talk," said Dupin, who had not thought it necessary to reply. "Let him discourse; it will ease his conscience, I am satisfied with having defeated him in his own castle. Nevertheless, that he failed in the solution of this mystery, is by no means that matter for wonder which he supposes it; for, in truth, our friend the Prefect is somewhat too cunning to be profound. In his wisdom is no *stamen.* It is all head and no body, like the pictures of the Goddess Laverna,—or, at best, all head and shoulders, like a codfish. But he is a good creature after all. I like him especially for one masterstroke of cant, by which he has attained his reputation for ingenuity. I mean the way he has '*de nier ce qui est, et d'expliquer ce qui n'est pas.*'"*

---

* Rousseau, *Nouvelle Heloise.*

Eleonora

[Considered autobiographical by many, this tale was first published as 'Eleonora: A Fable' in the literary annual *The Gift: A Christmas and New Year's Present for 1842*. A modified version was published in the May 24, 1845, issue of the *Broadway Journal*.]

Sub conservatione formae specificae salva anima.
—Raymond Lully

I am come of a race noted for vigor of fancy and ardour of passion. Men have called me mad; but the question is not yet settled, whether madness is or is not the loftiest intelligence—whether much that is glorious—whether all that is profound—does not spring from disease of thought—from *moods* of mind exalted at the expense of the general intellect. They who dream by day are cognizant of many things which escape those who dream only by night. In their gray visions they obtain glimpses of eternity, and thrill, in awaking, to find that they have been upon the verge of the great secret. In snatches, they learn something of the wisdom which is of good, and more of the mere knowledge which is of evil. They penetrate, however, rudderless or compassless, into the vast ocean of the "light ineffable" and again, like the adventures of the Nubian geographer, "*agressi sunt mare tenebrarum, quid in eo esset exploraturi*."

We will say, then, that I am mad. I grant, at least, that there are two distinct conditions of my mental existence—the condition of a lucid reason, not to be disputed, and belonging to the memory of events forming the first epoch of my life—and a condition of shadow and doubt, appertaining to the present, and to the recollection of what constitutes the second great era of my being. Therefore, what I shall tell of the earlier period, believe; and to what I may relate of the later time, give only such credit as may seem due; or doubt it altogether; or, if doubt it ye cannot, then play unto its riddle the Oedipus.

She whom I loved in youth, and of whom I now pen calmly and distinctly these remembrances, was the sole daughter of the only sister of my mother long departed. Eleonora was the name of my cousin. We had always dwelled together, beneath a tropical sun, in the Valley of the Many-Colored Grass. No unguided footstep ever came upon that vale; for it lay far away up among a range of giant hills that hung beetling around about it, shutting out the sunlight from its sweetest recesses. No path was trodden in its vicinity; and, to reach our happy home, there was need of putting back, with force, the foliage of many thousands of forest trees, and of crushing to death the glories of many millions of fragrant flowers. Thus it was that we lived all alone, knowing nothing of the world without the valley—I, and my cousin, and her mother.

From the dim regions beyond the mountains at the upper end of our encircled domain, there crept out a narrow and deep river, brighter than all save the eyes of Eleonora; and, winding stealthily about in mazy courses, it passed away, at length, through a shadowy gorge, among hills still dimmer than those whence it had issued. We called it the "River of Silence": for there seemed to be a hushing influence in its flow. No murmur arose from its bed, and so gently it wandered along, that the pearly pebbles upon which we loved to gaze, far down within its bosom, stirred not at all, but lay in a motionless content, each in its own old station, shining on gloriously forever.

The margin of the river, and of the many dazzling rivulets that glided, through devious ways, into its channel, as well as the spaces that extended from the margins away down into the depths of the streams until they reached the bed of pebbles at the bottom—these spots, not less than the whole surface of the valley, from the river to the mountains that girdled it in, were carpeted all by a soft green grass, thick, short, perfectly even, and vanilla-perfumed, but so besprinkled throughout with the yellow buttercup, the white daisy, the purple violet, and the ruby-red asphodel, that its exceeding beauty spoke to our hearts in loud tones, of the love and of the glory of God.

And, here and there, in groves about this grass, like wildernesses of dreams, sprang up fantastic trees, whose tall slender stems stood not upright, but slanted gracefully towards the light that peered at noon-day into the center of the valley. Their bark was speckled with the vivid alternate splendor of ebony and silver, and was smoother than all save the cheeks of Eleonora; so that but for the brilliant green of the huge leaves that spread from their summits in long, tremulous lines, dallying with the Zephyrs, one might have fancied them giant serpents of Syria doing homage to their Sovereign the Sun.

Hand in hand about this valley, for fifteen years, roamed I with Eleonora before Love entered within our hearts. It was one evening at the close of the third lustrum of her life, and of the fourth of my own, that we sat, locked in each other's embrace, beneath the serpent-like trees, and looked down within the waters of the River of Silence at our images therein. We spoke no words during the rest of that sweet day; and our words even upon the morrow were tremulous and few. We had drawn the God Eros from that wave, and now we felt that he had enkindled within us the fiery souls of our forefathers. The passions which had for centuries distinguished our race, came thronging with the fancies for which they had been equally noted, and together breathed a delirious bliss over the Valley of the Many-Colored Grass. A change fell upon all things. Strange, brilliant flowers, star-shaped, burst out upon the trees where no flowers had been known before. The tints of the green carpet deepened; and when, one by one, the white daisies shrank away, there sprang up in place of them, ten by ten of the ruby-red asphodel. And life arose in our paths; for the tall flamingo, hitherto unseen, with all gay glowing birds, flaunted his scarlet plumage before us. The golden and silver fish haunted the river, out of the bosom of which issued, little by little, a murmur that swelled, at length, into a lulling melody more divine than that of the harp of Æolus—sweeter than all save the voice of Eleonora. And now, too, a voluminous cloud, which we had long watched in the regions of Hesper, floated out thence, all gorgeous in crimson and gold, and settling in peace above us, sank, day by day, lower and lower, until its edges rested upon the tops of the mountains, turning all their dimness into magnificence, and shutting us up, as if forever, within a magic prison-house of grandeur and of glory.

The loveliness of Eleonora was that of the Seraphim; but she was a maiden artless and innocent as the brief life she had led among the flowers. No guile disguised the fervor of love which animated her heart, and she examined with me its inmost recesses as we walked together in the Valley of the Many-Colored Grass, and discoursed of the mighty changes which had lately taken place therein.

At length, having spoken one day, in tears, of the last sad change which must befall Humanity, she thenceforward dwelt only upon this one sorrowful theme, interweaving it into all our converse, as, in the songs of the bard of Schiraz, the same images are found occurring, again and again, in every impressive variation of phrase.

She had seen that the finger of Death was upon her bosom—that, like the ephemeron, she had been made perfect in loveliness only to die; but the terrors of the grave, to her, lay solely in a consideration which she revealed to me, one evening at twilight, by the banks of the River of Silence. She grieved to think that, having entombed her in the Valley of the Many-Colored Grass, I would quit forever its happy recesses, transferring the love which now was so passionately her own to some maiden of the outer and every-day world. And, then and there, I threw myself hurriedly at the feet of Eleonora, and offered up a vow, to herself and to Heaven, that I would never bind myself in marriage to any daughter of Earth—that I would in no manner prove recreant to her dear memory, or to the memory of the devout affection with which she had blessed me. And I called the Mighty Ruler of the Universe to witness the pious solemnity of my vow. And the curse which I invoked of *Him* and of her, a saint in Helusion, should I prove traitorous to that promise, involved a penalty the exceeding great horror of which will not permit me to make record of it here. And the bright eyes of Eleonora grew brighter at my words; and she sighed as if a deadly burthen had been taken from her breast; and she trembled and very bitterly wept; but she made acceptance of the vow, (for what was she but a child?) and it made easy to her the bed of her death. And she said to me, not many days afterwards, tranquilly dying, that, because of what I had done for the comfort of her spirit she would watch over me in that spirit when departed, and, if so it were permitted her return to me visibly in the watches of the night; but, if this thing were, indeed, beyond the power of the souls in Paradise, that she would, at least, give me frequent indications of her presence; sighing upon me in the evening winds, or filling the air which I breathed with perfume from the censers of the angels. And, with these words upon her lips, she yielded up her innocent life, putting an end to the first epoch of my own.

Thus far I have faithfully said. But as I pass the barrier in Time's path, formed by the death of my beloved, and proceed with the second era of my existence, I feel that a shadow gathers over my brain, and I mistrust the perfect sanity of the record. But let me on.—Years dragged themselves along heavily, and still I dwelled within the Valley of the Many-Colored Grass;—but a second change had come upon all things. The star-shaped flowers shrank into the stems of the trees, and appeared no more. The tints of the green carpet faded; and, one by one, the ruby-red asphodels withered away; and there sprang up, in place of them, ten by ten, dark, eye-like violets, that writhed uneasily and were ever encumbered with dew. And Life departed from our paths; for the tall flamingo flaunted no longer his scarlet plumage before us, but flew sadly from the vale into the hills, with all the gay glowing birds that had arrived in his company. And the golden and silver fish swam down through the gorge at the lower end of our domain and bedecked the sweet river never again. And the lulling melody that had been softer than the wind-harp of Æolus, and more divine than all save the voice of Eleonora, it died little by little away, in murmurs growing lower and lower, until the stream returned, at length, utterly, into the solemnity of its original silence. And then, lastly, the voluminous cloud uprose, and, abandoning the tops of the mountains to the dimness of old, fell back into the regions of Hesper, and took away all its manifold golden and gorgeous glories from the Valley of the Many-Colored Grass.

Yet the promises of Eleonora were not forgotten; for I heard the sounds of the swinging of the censers of the angels; and streams of a holy perfume floated ever and ever about the valley; and at lone hours, when my heart beat heavily, the winds that bathed my brow came unto me laden with soft sighs; and indistinct murmurs filled often the night air, and once—oh, but once only! I was awakened from a slumber, like the slumber of death, by the pressing of spiritual lips upon my own.

But the void within my heart refused, even thus, to be filled. I longed for the love which had before filled it to overflowing. At length the valley *pained* me through its memories of Eleonora, and I left it forever for the vanities and the turbulent triumphs of the world.

***

I found myself within a strange city, where all things might have served to blot from recollection the sweet dreams I had dreamed so long in the Valley of the Many-Colored Grass. The pomps and pageantries of a stately court, and the mad clangor of arms, and the radiant loveliness of women, bewildered and intoxicated my brain. But as yet my soul had proved true to its vows, and the indications of the presence of Eleonora were still given me in the silent hours of the night. Suddenly these manifestations they ceased, and the world grew dark before mine eyes, and I stood aghast at the burning thoughts which possessed, at the terrible temptations which beset me; for there came from some far, far distant and unknown land, into the gay court of the king I served, a maiden to whose beauty my whole recreant heart yielded at once—at whose footstool I bowed down without a struggle, in the most ardent, in the most abject worship of love. What indeed was my passion for the young girl of the valley in comparison with the fervor, and the delirium, and the spirit-lifting ecstasy of adoration with which I poured out my whole soul in tears at the feet of the ethereal Ermengarde?—Oh bright was the seraph Ermengarde! and in that knowledge I had room for none other.—Oh divine was the angel Ermengarde! and as I looked down into the depths of her memorial eyes, I thought only of them—and *of her.*

I wedded;—nor dreaded the curse I had invoked; and its bitterness was not visited upon me. And once—but once again in the silence of the night; there came through my lattice the soft sighs which had forsaken me; and they modelled themselves into familiar and sweet voice, saying:

"Sleep in peace!—for the Spirit of Love reigneth and ruleth, and, in taking to thy passionate heart her who is Ermengarde, thou art absolved, for reasons which shall be made known to thee in Heaven, of thy vows unto Eleonora."

The Masque of the Red Death

[Published in *Graham's Magazine* in May 1842 with the title 'The Mask of the Red Death: A fantasy', this story of predicament is influenced by Horace Walpole's *The Castle of Otranto,* which is the first Gothic novel. In 1845, 'Mask' was changed to 'Masque' and the subtitle was deleted.]

The "Red Death" had long devastated the country. No pestilence had ever been so fatal, or so hideous. Blood was its Avatar and its seal—the redness and the horror of blood. There were sharp pains, and sudden dizziness, and then profuse bleeding at the pores, with dissolution. The scarlet stains upon the body and especially upon the face of the victim, were the pest ban which shut him out from the aid and from the sympathy of his fellow-men. And the whole seizure, progress and termination of the disease, were the incidents of half an hour.

But the Prince Prospero was happy and dauntless and sagacious. When his dominions were half depopulated, he summoned to his presence a thousand hale and light-hearted friends from among the knights and dames of his court, and with these retired to the deep seclusion of one of his castellated abbeys. This was an extensive and magnificent structure, the creation of the prince's own eccentric yet august taste. A strong and lofty wall girdled it in. This wall had gates of iron. The courtiers, having entered, brought furnaces and massy hammers and welded the bolts. They resolved to leave means neither of ingress nor egress to the sudden impulses of despair or of frenzy from within. The abbey was amply provisioned. With such precautions the courtiers might bid defiance to contagion. The external world could take care of itself. In the meantime it was folly to grieve, or to think. The prince had provided all the appliances of pleasure. There were buffoons, there were improvisatori, there were ballet-dancers, there were musicians, there was Beauty, there was wine. All these and security were within. Without was the "Red Death."

It was toward the close of the fifth or sixth month of his seclusion, and while the pestilence raged most furiously abroad, that the Prince Prospero entertained his thousand friends at a masked ball of the most unusual magnificence.

It was a voluptuous scene, that masquerade. But first let me tell of the rooms in which it was held. There were seven—an imperial suite. In many palaces, however, such suites form a long and straight vista, while the folding doors slide back nearly to the walls on either hand, so that the view of the whole extent is scarcely impeded. Here the case was very different; as might have been expected from the duke's love of the bizarre. The apartments were so irregularly disposed that the vision embraced but little more than one at a time. There was a sharp turn at every twenty or thirty yards, and at each turn a novel effect. To the right and left, in the middle of each wall, a tall and narrow Gothic window looked out upon a closed corridor which pursued the windings of the suite. These windows were of stained glass whose colour varied in accordance with the prevailing hue of the decorations of the chamber into which it opened. That at the eastern extremity was hung, for example, in blue—and vividly blue were its windows. The second chamber was purple in its ornaments and tapestries, and here the panes were purple. The third was green throughout, and so were the casements. The fourth was furnished and lighted with orange—the fifth with white—the sixth with violet. The seventh apartment was closely shrouded in black velvet tapestries that hung all over the ceiling and down the walls, falling in heavy folds upon a carpet of the same material and hue. But in this chamber only, the colour of the windows failed to correspond with the decorations. The panes here were scarlet—a deep blood colour. Now in no one of the seven apartments was there any lamp or candelabrum, amid the profusion of golden ornaments that lay scattered to and fro or depended from the roof. There was no light of any kind emanating from lamp or candle within the suite of chambers.

But in the corridors that followed the suite, there stood, opposite to each window, a heavy tripod, bearing a brazier of fire that projected its rays through the tinted glass and so glaringly illumined the room. And thus were produced a multitude of gaudy and fantastic appearances. But in the western or black chamber the effect of the firelight that streamed upon the dark hangings through the blood-tinted panes, was ghastly in the extreme, and produced so wild a look upon the countenances of those who entered, that there were few of the company bold enough to set foot within its precincts at all.

It was in this apartment, also, that there stood against the western wall, a gigantic clock of ebony. Its pendulum swung to and fro with a dull, heavy, monotonous clang; and when the minute-hand made the circuit of the face, and the hour was to be stricken, there came from the brazen lungs of the clock a sound which was clear and loud and deep and exceedingly musical, but of so peculiar a note and emphasis that, at each lapse of an hour, the musicians of the orchestra were constrained to pause, momentarily, in their performance, to hearken to the sound; and thus the waltzers perforce ceased their evolutions; and there was a brief disconcert of the whole gay company; and, while the chimes of the clock yet rang, it was observed that the giddiest grew pale, and the more aged and sedate passed their hands over their brows as if in confused reverie or meditation. But when the echoes had fully ceased, a light laughter at once pervaded the assembly; the musicians looked at each other and smiled as if at their own nervousness and folly, and made whispering vows, each to the other, that the next chiming of the clock should produce in them no similar emotion; and then, after the lapse of sixty minutes, (which embrace three thousand and six hundred seconds of the Time that flies,) there came yet another chiming of the clock, and then were the same disconcert and tremulousness and meditation as before.

But, in spite of these things, it was a gay and magnificent revel. The tastes of the duke were peculiar. He had a fine eye for colours and effects. He disregarded the *decora* of mere fashion. His plans were bold and fiery, and his conceptions glowed with barbaric luster. There are some who would have thought him mad. His followers felt that he was not. It was necessary to hear and see and touch him to be *sure* that he was not.

He had directed, in great part, the moveable embellishments of the seven chambers, upon occasion of this great fête; and it was his own guiding taste which had given character to the masqueraders. Be sure they were grotesque. There were much glare and glitter and piquancy and phantasm—much of what has been since seen in *Hernani.* There were arabesque figures with unsuited limbs and appointments. There were delirious fancies such as the madman fashions. There were much of the beautiful, much of the wanton, much of the bizarre, something of the terrible, and not a little of that which might have excited disgust. To and fro in the seven chambers there stalked, in fact, a multitude of dreams. And these—the dreams—writhed in and about, taking hue from the rooms, and causing the wild music of the orchestra to seem as the echo of their steps. And, anon, there strikes the ebony clock which stands in the hall of the velvet. And then, for a moment, all is still, and all is silent save the voice of the clock. The dreams are stiff-frozen as they stand. But the echoes of the chime die away—they have endured but an instant—and a light, half-subdued laughter floats after them as they depart. And now again the music swells, and the dreams live, and writhe to and fro more merrily than ever, taking hue from the many-tinted windows through which stream the rays from the tripods. But to the chamber which lies most westwardly of the seven, there are now none of the maskers who venture; for the night is waning away; and there flows a ruddier light through the blood-coloured panes; and the blackness of the sable drapery appals; and to him whose foot falls upon the sable carpet, there comes from the near clock of ebony a muffled peal more solemnly emphatic than any which reaches *their* ears who indulge in the more remote gaieties of the other apartments.

But these other apartments were densely crowded, and in them beat feverishly the heart of life. And the revel went whirlingly on, until at length there commenced the sounding of midnight upon the clock. And then the music ceased, as I have told; and the evolutions of the waltzers were quieted; and there was an uneasy cessation of all things as before. But now there were twelve strokes to be sounded by the bell of the clock; and thus it happened, perhaps, that more of thought crept, with more of time, into the meditations of the thoughtful among those who reveled. And thus, too, it happened, perhaps, that before the last echoes of the last chime had utterly sunk into silence, there were many individuals in the crowd who had found leisure to become aware of the presence of a masked figure which had arrested the attention of no single individual before. And the rumor of this new presence having spread itself whisperingly around, there arose at length from the whole company a buzz, or murmur, expressive of disapprobation and surprise—then, finally, of terror, of horror, and of disgust.

In an assembly of phantasms such as I have painted, it may well be supposed that no ordinary appearance could have excited such sensation. In truth the masquerade license of the night was nearly unlimited; but the figure in question had out-Heroded Herod, and gone beyond the bounds of even the prince's indefinite decorum. There are chords in the hearts of the most reckless which cannot be touched without emotion. Even with the utterly lost, to whom life and death are equally jests, there are matters of which no jest can be made. The whole company, indeed, seemed now deeply to feel that in the costume and bearing of the stranger neither wit nor propriety existed. The figure was tall and gaunt, and shrouded from head to foot in the habiliments of the grave. The mask which concealed the visage was made so nearly to resemble the countenance of a stiffened corpse that the closest scrutiny must have had difficulty in detecting the cheat. And yet all this might have been endured, if not approved, by the mad revelers around. But the mummer had gone so far as to assume the type of the Red Death. His vesture was dabbled in *blood*—and his broad brow, with all the features of the face, was besprinkled with the scarlet horror.

When the eyes of Prince Prospero fell upon this spectral image (which, with a slow and solemn movement, as if more fully to sustain its role, stalked to and fro among the waltzers) he was seen to be convulsed in the first moment with a strong shudder either of terror or distaste; but, in the next, his brow reddened with rage.

"Who dares?" he demanded hoarsely of the courtiers who stood near him—"who dares insult us with this blasphemous mockery? Seize him and unmask him—that we may know whom we have to hang, at sunrise, from the battlements!"

It was in the eastern or blue chamber in which stood the Prince Prospero as he uttered these words. They rang throughout the seven rooms loudly and clearly—for the prince was a bold and robust man, and the music had become hushed at the waving of his hand.

It was in the blue room where stood the prince, with a group of pale courtiers by his side. At first, as he spoke, there was a slight rushing movement of this group in the direction of the intruder, who at the moment was also near at hand, and now, with deliberate and stately step, made closer approach to the speaker. But from a certain nameless awe with which the mad assumptions of the mummer had inspired the whole party, there were found none who put forth hand to seize him; so that, unimpeded, he passed within a yard of the prince's person; and, while the vast assembly, as if with one impulse, shrank from the centers of the rooms to the walls, he made his way uninterruptedly, but with the same solemn and measured step which had distinguished him from the first, through the blue chamber to the purple—through the purple to the green—through the green to the orange—through this again to the white—and even thence to the violet, ere a decided movement had been made to arrest him. It was then, however, that the Prince Prospero, maddening with rage and the shame of his own momentary cowardice, rushed hurriedly through the six chambers, while none followed him on account of a deadly terror that had seized upon all. He bore aloft a drawn dagger, and had approached, in rapid impetuosity, to within three or four feet of the retreating figure, when the latter, having attained the extremity of the velvet apartment, turned suddenly and confronted his pursuer. There was a sharp cry—and the dagger dropped gleaming upon the sable carpet, upon which, instantly afterwards, fell prostrate in death the Prince Prospero. Then, summoning the wild courage of despair, a throng of the revelers at once threw themselves into the black apartment, and, seizing the mummer, whose tall figure stood erect and motionless within the shadow of the ebony clock, gasped in unutterable horror at finding the grave cerements and corpse-like mask which they handled with so violent a rudeness, untenanted by any tangible form.

And now was acknowledged the presence of the Red Death. He had come like a thief in the night. And one by one dropped the revelers in the blood-bedewed halls of their revel, and died each in the despairing posture of his fall. And the life of the ebony clock went out with that of the last of the gay. And the flames of the tripods expired. And Darkness and Decay and the Red Death held illimitable dominion over all.

ARackham

The Pit and the Pendulum

[Published in *The Gift: A Christmas and New Year's Present for 1843* in 1842, this horror short story studies the effect terror has on the narrator.]

Impia tortorum longos hic turba furores
Sanguinis innocui, non satiata, aluit.
Sospite nunc patriâ, fracto nunc funeris antro,
Mors ubi dira fuit vita salusque patent.

—Quatrain composed for the gates of
a market to be erected upon the site
of the Jacobin Club House at Paris

I was sick—sick unto death with that long agony; and when they at length unbound me, and I was permitted to sit, I felt that my senses were leaving me. The sentence—the dread sentence of death—was the last of distinct accentuation which reached my ears. After that, the sound of the inquisitorial voices seemed merged in one dreamy indeterminate hum. It conveyed to my soul the idea of *revolution*—perhaps from its association in fancy with the burr of a mill wheel. This only for a brief period; for presently I heard no more. Yet, for a while, I saw; but with how terrible an exaggeration! I saw the lips of the black-robed judges. They appeared to me white—whiter than the sheet upon which I trace these words—and thin even to grotesqueness; thin with the intensity of their expression of firmness, of immoveable resolution, of stern contempt of human torture. I saw that the decrees of what to me was Fate, were still issuing from those lips. I saw them writhe with a deadly locution. I saw them fashion the syllables of my name; and I shuddered because no sound succeeded. I saw, too, for a few moments of delirious horror, the soft and nearly imperceptible waving of the sable draperies which enwrapped the walls of the apartment. And then my vision fell upon the seven tall candles upon the table. At first they wore the aspect of charity, and seemed white and slender angels who would save me; but then, all at once, there came a most deadly nausea over my spirit, and I felt every fibre in my frame thrill as if I had touched the wire of a galvanic battery, while the angel forms became meaningless specters, with heads of flame, and I saw that from them there would be no help. And then there stole into my fancy, like a rich musical note, the thought of what sweet rest there must be in the grave. The thought came gently and stealthily, and it seemed long before it attained full appreciation; but just as my spirit came at length properly to feel and entertain it, the figures of the judges vanished, as if magically, from before me; the tall candles sank into nothingness; their flames went out utterly; the blackness of darkness supervened; all sensations appeared swallowed up in a mad rushing descent as of the soul into Hades. Then silence, and stillness, night were the universe.

I had swooned; but still will not say that all of consciousness was lost. What of it there remained I will not attempt to define, or even to describe; yet all was not lost. In the deepest slumber—no! In delirium—no! In a swoon—no! In death—no! even in the grave all *is not lost*. Else there is no immortality for man. Arousing from the most profound of slumbers, we break the gossamer web of *some* dream. Yet in a second afterward (so frail may that web have been), we remember not that we have dreamed. In the return to life from the swoon there are two stages; first, that of the sense of mental or spiritual; secondly, that of the sense of physical, existence. It seems probable that if, upon reaching the second stage, we could recall the impressions of the first, we should find these impressions eloquent in memories of the gulf beyond. And that gulf is—what? How at least shall we distinguish its shadows from those of the tomb? But if the impressions of what I have termed the first stage are not at will recalled, yet, after long interval, do they not come unbidden, while we marvel whence they come? He who has never swooned, is not he who finds strange palaces and wildly familiar faces in coals that glow; is not he who beholds floating in mid-air the sad visions that the many may not view; is not he who ponders

over the perfume of some novel flower—is not he whose brain grows bewildered with the meaning of some musical cadence which has never before arrested his attention.

Amid frequent and thoughtful endeavors to remember; amid earnest struggles to regather some token of the state of seeming nothingness into which my soul had lapsed, there have been moments when I have dreamed of success; there have been brief, very brief periods when I have conjured up remembrances which the lucid reason of a later epoch assures me could have had reference only to that condition of seeming unconsciousness. These shadows of memory tell, indistinctly, of tall figures that lifted and bore me in silence down—down—still down—till a hideous dizziness oppressed me at the mere idea of the interminableness of the descent. They tell also of a vague horror at my heart, on account of that heart's unnatural stillness. Then comes a sense of sudden motionlessness throughout all things; as if those who bore me (a ghastly train!) had outrun, in their descent, the limits of the limitless, and paused from the wearisomeness of their toil. After this I call to mind flatness and dampness; and then all is *madness*—the madness of a memory which busies itself among forbidden things.

Very suddenly there came back to my soul motion and sound—the tumultuous motion of the heart, and, in my ears, the sound of its beating. Then a pause in which all is blank. Then again sound, and motion, and touch—a tingling sensation pervading my frame. Then the mere consciousness of existence, without thought—a condition which lasted long. Then, very suddenly, *thought*, and shuddering terror, and earnest endeavor to comprehend my true state. Then a strong desire to lapse into insensibility. Then a rushing revival of soul and a successful effort to move. And now a full memory of the trial, of the judges, of the sable draperies, of the sentence, of the sickness, of the swoon. Then entire forgetfulness of all that followed; of all that a later day and much earnestness of endeavor have enabled me vaguely to recall.

So far, I had not opened my eyes. I felt that I lay upon my back, unbound. I reached out my hand, and it fell heavily upon something damp and hard. There I suffered it to remain for many minutes, while I strove to imagine where and what I could be. I longed, yet dared not to employ my vision. I dreaded the first glance at objects around me. It was not that I feared to look upon things horrible, but that I grew aghast lest there should be *nothing* to see. At length, with a wild desperation at heart, I quickly unclosed my eyes. My worst thoughts, then, were confirmed. The blackness of eternal night encompassed me. I struggled for breath. The intensity of the darkness seemed to oppress and stifle me. The atmosphere was intolerably close. I still lay quietly, and made effort to exercise my reason. I brought to mind the inquisitorial proceedings, and attempted from that point to deduce my real condition. The sentence had passed; and it appeared to me that a very long interval of time had since elapsed. Yet not for a moment did I suppose myself actually dead. Such a supposition, notwithstanding what we read in fiction, is altogether inconsistent with real existence;—but where and in what state was I? The condemned to death, I knew, perished usually at the *autos-da-fé*, and one of these had been held on the very night of the day of my trial. Had I been remanded to my dungeon, to await the next sacrifice, which would not take place for many months? This I at once saw could not be. Victims had been in immediate demand. Moreover, my dungeon, as well as all the condemned cells at Toledo, had stone floors, and light was not altogether excluded.

A fearful idea now suddenly drove the blood in torrents upon my heart, and for a brief period, I once more relapsed into insensibility. Upon recovering, I at once started to my feet, trembling convulsively in every fiber. I thrust my arms wildly above and around me in all directions. I felt nothing; yet dreaded to move a step, lest I should be impeded by the walls of a *tomb*. Perspiration burst from every pore, and stood in cold big beads upon my forehead. The agony of suspense grew at length intolerable, and I cautiously moved forward, with my arms extended, and my eyes straining from their sockets, in the hope of catching some faint ray of light. I proceeded for many paces; but still all was blackness and vacancy. I breathed more freely. It seemed evident that mine was not, at least, the most hideous of fates.

And now, as I still continued to step cautiously onward, there came thronging upon my recollection a thousand vague rumors of the horrors of Toledo. Of the dungeons there had been strange things narrated—fables I had always deemed them—but yet strange, and too ghastly to repeat, save in a whisper. Was I left to perish of starvation in this subterranean world of darkness; or what fate, perhaps even more fearful, awaited me? That the result would be death, and a death of more than customary bitterness,

I knew too well the character of my judges to doubt. The mode and the hour were all that occupied or distracted me.

My outstretched hands at length encountered some solid obstruction. It was a wall, seemingly of stone masonry—very smooth, slimy, and cold. I followed it up; stepping with all the careful distrust with which certain antique narratives had inspired me. This process, however, afforded me no means of ascertaining the dimensions of my dungeon; as I might make its circuit, and return to the point whence I set out, without being aware of the fact; so perfectly uniform seemed the wall. I therefore sought the knife which had been in my pocket, when led into the inquisitorial chamber, but it was gone; my clothes had been exchanged for a wrapper of coarse serge. I had thought of forcing the blade in some minute crevice of the masonry, so as to identify my point of departure. The difficulty, nevertheless, was but trivial; although, in the disorder of my fancy, it seemed at first insuperable. I tore a part of the hem from the robe and placed the fragment at full length, and at right angles to the wall. In groping my way around the prison, I could not fail to encounter this rag upon completing the circuit. So, at least I thought: but I had not counted upon the extent of the dungeon, or upon my own weakness. The ground was moist and slippery. I staggered onward for some time, when I stumbled and fell. My excessive fatigue induced me to remain prostrate; and sleep soon overtook me as I lay.

Upon awaking and stretching forth an arm, I found beside me a loaf and a pitcher with water. I was too much exhausted to reflect upon this circumstance, but ate and drank with avidity. Shortly afterward, I resumed my tour around the prison, and with much toil came at last upon the fragment of the serge. Up to the period when I fell, I had counted fifty-two paces, and upon resuming my walk, I had counted forty-eight more—when I arrived at the rag. There were in all, then, a hundred paces; and, admitting two paces to the yard, I presumed the dungeon to be fifty yards in circuit. I had met, however, with many angles in the wall, and thus I could form no guess at the shape of the vault; for vault I could not help supposing it to be.

I had little object—certainly no hope—in these researches; but a vague curiosity prompted me to continue them. Quitting the wall, I resolved to cross the area of the enclosure. At first I proceeded with extreme caution, for the floor, although seemingly of solid material, was treacherous with slime. At length, however, I took courage, and did not hesitate to step firmly; endeavoring to cross in as direct a line as possible. I had advanced some ten or twelve paces in this manner, when the remnant of the torn hem of my robe became entangled between my legs. I stepped on it, and fell violently on my face.

In the confusion attending my fall, I did not immediately apprehend a somewhat startling circumstance, which yet, in a few seconds afterward, and while I still lay prostrate, arrested my attention. It was this—my chin rested upon the floor of the prison, but my lips and the upper portion of my head, although seemingly at a less elevation than the chin, touched nothing. At the same time my forehead seemed bathed in a clammy vapor, and the peculiar smell of decayed fungus arose to my nostrils. I put forward my arm, and shuddered to find that I had fallen at the very brink of a circular pit, whose extent, of course, I had no means of ascertaining at the moment. Groping about the masonry just below the margin, I succeeded in dislodging a small fragment, and let it fall into the abyss. For many seconds I hearkened to its reverberations as it dashed against the sides of the chasm in its descent; at length there was a sullen plunge into water, succeeded by loud echoes. At the same moment there came a sound resembling the quick opening, and as rapid closing of a door overhead, while a faint gleam of light flashed suddenly through the gloom, and as suddenly faded away.

I saw clearly the doom which had been prepared for me, and congratulated myself upon the timely accident by which I had escaped. Another step before my fall, and the world had seen me no more. And the death just avoided was of that very character which I had regarded as fabulous and frivolous in the tales respecting the Inquisition. To the victims of its tyranny, there was the choice of death with its direst physical agonies, or death with its most hideous moral horrors. I had been reserved for the latter. By long suffering my nerves had been unstrung, until I trembled at the sound of my own voice, and had become in every respect a fitting subject for the species of torture which awaited me.

Shaking in every limb, I groped my way back to the wall; resolving there to perish rather than risk the terrors of the wells, of which my imagination now pictured many in various positions about the dungeon. In other conditions of mind I might have had courage to end my misery at once by a plunge into one of these abysses; but now I was the veriest of cowards. Neither could I forget what I had read of these pits—that the *sudden* extinction of life formed no part of their most horrible plan.

Agitation of spirit kept me awake for many long hours; but at length I again slumbered. Upon arousing, I found by my side, as before, a loaf and a pitcher of water. A burning thirst consumed me, and I emptied the vessel at a draught. It must have been drugged; for scarcely had I drunk, before I became irresistibly drowsy. A deep sleep fell upon me—a sleep like that of death. How long it lasted of course, I know not; but when, once again, I unclosed my eyes, the objects around me were visible. By a wild sulphurous luster, the origin of which I could not at first determine, I was enabled to see the extent and aspect of the prison.

In its size I had been greatly mistaken. The whole circuit of its walls did not exceed twenty-five yards. For some minutes this fact occasioned me a world of vain trouble; vain indeed! for what could be of less importance, under the terrible circumstances which environed me, than the mere dimensions of my dungeon? But my soul took a wild interest in trifles, and I busied myself in endeavors to account for the error I had committed in my measurement. The truth at length flashed upon me. In my first attempt at exploration I had counted fifty-two paces, up to the period when I fell; I must then have been within a pace or two of the fragment of serge; in fact, I had nearly performed the circuit of the vault. I then slept, and upon awaking, I must have returned upon my steps—thus supposing the circuit nearly double what it actually was. My confusion of mind prevented me from observing that I began my tour with the wall to the left, and ended it with the wall to the right.

I had been deceived, too, in respect to the shape of the enclosure. In feeling my way I had found many angles, and thus deduced an idea of great irregularity; so potent is the effect of total darkness upon one arousing from lethargy or sleep! The angles were simply those of a few slight depressions, or niches, at odd intervals. The general shape of the prison was square. What I had taken for masonry seemed now to be iron, or some other metal, in huge plates, whose sutures or joints occasioned the depression. The entire surface of this metallic enclosure was rudely daubed in all the hideous and repulsive devices to which the charnel superstition of the monks has given rise. The figures of fiends in aspects of menace, with skeleton forms, and other more really fearful images, overspread and disfigured the walls. I observed that the outlines of these monstrosities were sufficiently distinct, but that the colours seemed faded and blurred, as if from the effects of a damp atmosphere. I now noticed the floor, too, which was of stone. In the center yawned the circular pit from whose jaws I had escaped; but it was the only one in the dungeon.

All this I saw indistinctly and by much effort, for my personal condition had been greatly changed during slumber. I now lay upon my back, and at full length, on a species of low framework of wood. To this I was securely bound by a long strap resembling a surcingle. It passed in many convolutions about my limbs and body, leaving at liberty only my head, and my left arm to such extent that I could, by dint of much exertion, supply myself with food from an earthen dish which lay by my side on the floor. I saw, to my horror, that the pitcher had been removed. I say to my horror—for I was consumed with intolerable thirst. This thirst it appeared to be the design of my persecutors to stimulate—for the food in the dish was meat pungently seasoned.

Looking upward, I surveyed the ceiling of my prison. It was some thirty or forty feet overhead, and constructed much as the side walls. In one of its panels a very singular figure riveted my whole attention. It was the painted figure of Time as he is commonly represented, save that, in lieu of a scythe, he held what, at a casual glance, I supposed to be the pictured image of a huge pendulum such as we see on antique clocks. There was something, however, in the appearance of this machine which caused me to regard it more attentively. While I gazed directly upward at it (for its position was immediately over my own), I fancied that I saw it in motion. In an instant afterward the fancy was confirmed. Its sweep was brief, and of course slow. I watched it for some minutes, somewhat in fear, but more in wonder. Wearied at length with observing its dull movement, I turned my eyes upon the other objects in the cell.

A slight noise attracted my notice, and, looking to the floor, I saw several enormous rats traversing it. They had issued from the well, which lay just within view to my right. Even then, while I gazed, they came up in troops, hurriedly, with ravenous eyes, allured by the scent of the meat. From this it required much effort and attention to scare them away.

It might have been half an hour, perhaps even an hour (for I could take but imperfect note of time), before I again cast my eyes upward. What I then saw confounded and amazed me. The sweep of the pendulum had increased in extent by nearly a yard. As a natural consequence, its velocity was also much greater. But what mainly disturbed me was the idea that had perceptibly *descended.* I now observed—with what horror it is needless to say—that its nether extremity was formed of a crescent of glittering steel, about a foot in length from horn to horn; the horns upward, and the under edge evidently as keen as that of a razor. Like a razor also, it seemed massive and heavy, tapering from the edge into a solid and broad structure above. It was appended to a weighty rod of brass, and the whole *hissed* as it swung through the air.

I could no longer doubt the doom prepared for me by monkish ingenuity in torture. My cognizance of the pit had become known to the inquisitorial agents—*the pit,* whose horrors had been destined for so bold a recusant as myself—*the pit,* typical of hell, and regarded by rumor as the Ultima Thule of all their punishments. The plunge into this pit I had avoided by the merest of accidents, I knew that surprise, or entrapment into torment, formed an important portion of all the grotesquerie of these dungeon deaths. Having failed to fall, it was no part of the demon plan to hurl me into the abyss; and thus (there being no alternative) a different and a milder destruction awaited me. Milder! I half smiled in my agony as I thought of such application of such a term.

What boots it to tell of the long, long hours of horror more than mortal, during which I counted the rushing oscillations of the steel! Inch by inch—line by line—with a descent only appreciable at intervals that seemed ages—down and still down it came! Days passed—it might have been that many days passed—ere it swept so closely over me as to fan me with its acrid breath. The odor of the sharp steel forced itself into my nostrils. I prayed—I wearied heaven with my prayer for its more speedy descent. I grew frantically mad, and struggled to force myself upward against the sweep of the fearful scimitar. And then I fell suddenly calm, and lay smiling at the glittering death, as a child at some rare bauble.

There was another interval of utter insensibility; it was brief; for upon again lapsing into life, there had been no perceptible descent in the pendulum. But it might have been long; for I knew there were demons who took note of my swoon, and who could have arrested the vibration at pleasure. Upon my recovery, too, I felt very—oh, inexpressibly sick and weak, as if through long inanition. Even amid the agonies of that period, the human nature craved food. With painful effort I outstretched my left arm as far as my bonds permitted, and took possession of the small remnant which had been spared me by the rats. As I put a portion of it within my lips, there rushed to my mind a half-formed thought of joy—of hope. Yet what business had *I* with hope? It was, as I say, a half-formed thought—man has many such, which are never completed. I felt that it was of joy—of hope; but felt also that it had perished in its formation. In vain I struggled to perfect—to regain it. Long suffering had nearly annihilated all my ordinary powers of mind. I was an imbecile—an idiot.

The vibration of the pendulum was at right angles to my length. I saw that the crescent was designed to cross the region of the heart. It would fray the serge of my robe—it would return and repeat its operations—again—and again. Notwithstanding its terrifically wide sweep (some thirty feet or more) and the hissing vigor of its descent, sufficient to sunder these very walls of iron, still the fraying of my robe would be all that, for several minutes, it would accomplish. And at this thought I paused. I dared not go farther than this reflection. I dwelt upon it with a pertinacity of attention—as if, in so dwelling, I could arrest *here* the descent of the steel. I forced myself to ponder upon the sound of the crescent as it should pass across the garment—upon the peculiar thrilling sensation which the friction of cloth produces on the nerves. I pondered upon all this frivolity until my teeth were on edge.

Down—steadily down it crept. I took a frenzied pleasure in contrasting its downward with its lateral velocity. To the right—to the left—far and wide—with the shriek of a damned spirit; to my heart, with the stealthy pace of the tiger! I alternately laughed and howled as the one or the other idea grew predominant.

Down—certainly, relentlessly down! It vibrated within three inches of my bosom! I struggled violently, furiously, to free my left arm. This was free only from the elbow to the hand. I could reach the latter, from the platter beside me, to my mouth, with great effort, but no farther. Could I have broken the fastenings above the elbow, I would have seized and attempted to arrest the pendulum. I might as well have attempted to arrest an avalanche!

Down—still unceasingly—still inevitably down! I gasped and struggled at each vibration. I shrank convulsively at its every sweep. My eyes followed its outward or upward whirls with the eagerness of the most unmeaning despair; they closed themselves spasmodically at the descent, although death would have been a relief, oh! how unspeakable! Still I quivered in every nerve to think how slight a sinking of the machinery would precipitate that keen, glistening axe upon my bosom. It was *hope* that prompted the nerve to quiver—the frame to shrink. It was *hope*—the hope that triumphs on the rack—that whispers to the death-condemned even in the dungeons of the Inquisition.

I saw that some ten or twelve vibrations would bring the steel in actual contact with my robe, and with this observation there suddenly came over my spirit all the keen, collected calmness of despair. For the first time during many hours—or perhaps days—*I thought.* It now occurred to me that the bandage, or surcingle, which enveloped me, was *unique.* I was tied by no separate cord. The first stroke of the razor-like crescent athwart any portion of the band, would so detach it that it might be unwound from my person by means of my left hand. But how fearful, in that case, the proximity of the steel! The result of the slightest struggle how deadly! Was it likely, moreover, that the minions of the torturer had not foreseen and provided for this possibility? Was it probable that the bandage crossed my bosom in the track of the pendulum? Dreading to find my faint and, as it seemed, my last hope frustrated, I so far elevated my head as to obtain a distinct view of my breast. The surcingle enveloped my limbs and body close in all directions—*save in the path of the destroying crescent.*

Scarcely had I dropped my head back into its original position, when there flashed upon my mind what I cannot better describe than as the unformed half of that idea of deliverance to which I have previously alluded, and of which a moiety only floated indeterminately through my brain when I raised food to my burning lips. The whole thought was now present—feeble, scarcely sane, scarcely definite—but still entire. I proceeded at once, with the nervous energy of despair, to attempt its execution.

For many hours the immediate vicinity of the low framework upon which I lay had been literally swarming with rats. They were wild, bold, ravenous; their red eyes glaring upon me as if they waited but for motionlessness on my part to make me their prey. "To what food," I thought, "have they been accustomed in the well?"

They had devoured, in spite of all my efforts to prevent them, all but a small remnant of the contents of the dish. I had fallen into an habitual see-saw, or wave of the hand about the platter; and, at length, the unconscious uniformity of the movement deprived it of effect. In their

voracity the vermin frequently fastened their sharp fangs in my fingers. With the particles of the oily and spicy viand which now remained, I thoroughly rubbed the bandage wherever I could reach it; then, raising my hand from the floor, I lay breathlessly still.

At first the ravenous animals were startled and terrified at the change—at the cessation of movement. They shrank alarmedly back; many sought the well. But this was only for a moment. I had not counted in vain upon their voracity. Observing that I remained without motion, one or two of the boldest leaped upon the framework, and smelt at the surcingle. This seemed the signal for a general rush. Forth from the well they hurried in fresh troops. They clung to the wood—they overran it, and leaped in hundreds upon my person. The measured movement of the pendulum disturbed them not at all. Avoiding its strokes they busied themselves with the anointed bandage. They pressed—they swarmed upon me in ever accumulating heaps. They writhed upon my throat; their cold lips sought my own; I was half stifled by their thronging pressure; disgust, for which the world has no name, swelled my bosom, and chilled, with a heavy clamminess, my heart. Yet one minute, and I felt that the struggle would be over. Plainly I perceived the loosening of the bandage. I knew that in more than one place it must be already severed. With a more than human resolution I lay *still.*

Nor had I erred in my calculations—nor had I endured in vain. I at length felt that I was *free.* The surcingle hung in ribbons from my body. But the stroke of the pendulum already pressed upon my bosom. It had divided the serge of the robe. It had cut through the linen beneath. Twice again it swung, and a sharp sense of pain shot through every nerve. But the moment of escape had arrived. At a wave of my hand my deliverers hurried tumultuously away. With a steady movement—cautious, sidelong, shrinking, and slow—I slid from the embrace of the bandage and beyond the reach of the scimitar. For the moment, at least, *I was free.*

Free!—and in the grasp of the Inquisition! I had scarcely stepped from my wooden bed of horror upon the stone floor of the prison, when the motion of the hellish machine ceased and I beheld it drawn up, by some invisible force, through the ceiling. This was a lesson which I took desperately to heart. My every motion was undoubtedly watched. Free!—I had but escaped death in one form of agony, to be delivered unto worse than death in some other. With that thought I rolled my eyes nervously around on the barriers of iron that hemmed me in. Something unusual—some change which, at first, I could not appreciate distinctly—it was obvious, had taken place in the apartment. For many minutes of a dreamy and trembling abstraction, I busied myself in vain, unconnected conjecture. During this period, I became aware, for the first time, of the origin of the sulphurous light which illumined the cell. It proceeded from a fissure, about half an inch in width, extending entirely around the prison at the base of the walls, which thus appeared, and were, completely separated from the floor. I endeavored, but of course in vain, to look through the aperture.

As I arose from the attempt, the mystery of the alteration in the chamber broke at once upon my understanding. I have observed that, although the outlines of the figures upon the walls were sufficiently distinct, yet the colours seemed blurred and indefinite. These colours had now assumed, and were momentarily assuming, a startling and most intense brilliancy, that gave to the spectral and fiendish portraitures an aspect that might have thrilled even firmer nerves than my own. Demon eyes, of a wild and ghastly vivacity, glared upon me in a thousand directions, where none had been visible before, and gleamed with the lurid luster of a fire that I could not force my imagination to regard as unreal.

Unreal!—Even while I breathed there came to my nostrils the breath of the vapor of heated iron! A suffocating odor pervaded the prison! A deeper glow settled each moment in the eyes that glared at my agonies! A richer tint of crimson diffused itself over the pictured horrors of blood! I panted! I gasped for breath! There could be no doubt of the design of my tormentors—oh! most unrelenting! oh! most demoniac of men! I shrank from the glowing metal to the center of the cell. Amid the thought of the fiery destruction that impended, the idea of the coolness of the well came over my soul like balm. I rushed to its deadly brink. I threw my straining vision below. The glare from the enkindled roof illumined its inmost recesses. Yet, for a wild moment, did my spirit refuse to comprehend the meaning of what I saw. At length it forced—it wrestled its way into my soul—it burned itself in upon my shuddering reason. Oh! for a voice to speak!—oh! horror!—oh! any horror but this! With a shriek, I rushed from the margin, and buried my face in my hands—weeping bitterly.

The heat rapidly increased, and once again I looked up, shuddering as with a fit of the ague. There had been a second change in the cell—and now the change was obviously in the *form.* As before, it was in vain that I, at first, endeavored to appreciate or understand what was taking place. But not long was I left in doubt. The Inquisitorial vengeance had been hurried by my two-fold escape, and there was to be no more dallying with the King of Terrors. The room had been square. I saw that two of its iron angles were now acute—two, consequently, obtuse. The fearful difference quickly increased with a low rumbling or moaning sound. In an instant the apartment had shifted its form into that of a lozenge. But the alteration stopped not here—I neither hoped nor desired it to stop. I could have clasped the red walls to my bosom as a garment of eternal peace. "Death," I said, "any death but that of the pit!" Fool! might I have not known that into the pit it was the object of the burning iron to urge me? Could I resist its glow? or, if even that, could I withstand its pressure? And now, flatter and flatter grew the lozenge, with a rapidity that left me no time for contemplation. Its center, and of course, its greatest width, came just over the yawning gulf. I shrank back—but the closing walls pressed me resistlessly onward. At length for my seared and writhing body there was no longer an inch of foothold on the firm floor of the prison. I struggled no more, but the agony of my soul found vent in one loud, long, and final scream of despair. I felt that I tottered upon the brink—I averted my eyes—

There was a discordant hum of human voices! There was a loud blast as of many trumpets! There was a harsh grating as of a thousand thunders! The fiery walls rushed back! An outstretched arm caught my own as I fell, fainting, into the abyss. It was that of General Lasalle. The French army had entered Toledo. The Inquisition was in the hands of its enemies.

The Tell-Tale Heart

[This story of antagonism narrated by an unnamed unreliable narrator was first published in January 1843 in James Russell Lowell's *The Pioneer.* One of Poe's most famous stories, it is regarded as a classic in Gothic fiction.]

True!—nervous—very, very dreadfully nervous I had been and am; but why *will* you say that I am mad? The disease had sharpened my senses—not destroyed—not dulled them. Above all was the sense of hearing acute. I heard all things in the heaven and in the earth. I heard many things in hell. How, then, am I mad? Hearken! and observe how healthily—how calmly I can tell you the whole story.

It is impossible to say how first the idea entered my brain; but once conceived, it haunted me day and night. Object there was none. Passion there was none. I loved the old man. He had never wronged me. He had never given me insult. For his gold I had no desire. I think it was his eye! yes, it was this! He had the eye of a vulture—a pale blue eye, with a film over it. Whenever it fell upon me, my blood ran cold; and so by degrees—very gradually—I made up my mind to take the life of the old man, and thus rid myself of the eye forever.

Now this is the point. You fancy me mad. Madmen know nothing. But you should have seen *me.* You should have seen how wisely I proceeded—with what caution—with what foresight—with what dissimulation I went to work! I was never kinder to the old man than during the whole week before I killed him. And every night, about midnight, I turned the latch of his door and opened it—oh so gently! And then, when I had made an opening sufficient for my head, I put in a dark lantern, all closed, closed, that no light shone out, and then I thrust in my head. Oh, you would have laughed to see how cunningly I thrust it in! I moved it slowly—very, very slowly, so that I might not disturb the old man's sleep. It took me an hour to place my whole head within the opening so far that I could see him as he lay upon his bed. Ha! would a madman have been so wise as this? And then, when my head was well in the room, I undid the lantern cautiously—oh, so cautiously—cautiously (for the hinges creaked)—I undid it just so much that a single thin ray fell upon the vulture eye. And this I did for seven long nights—every night just at midnight—but I found the eye always closed; and so it was impossible to do the work; for it was not the old man who vexed me, but his Evil Eye. And every morning, when the day broke, I went boldly into the chamber, and spoke courageously to him, calling him by name in a hearty tone, and inquiring how he has passed the night. So you see he would have been a very profound old man, indeed, to suspect that every night, just at twelve, I looked in upon him while he slept.

Upon the eighth night I was more than usually cautious in opening the door. A watch's minute hand moves more quickly than did mine. Never before that night had I *felt* the extent of my own powers—of my sagacity. I could scarcely contain my feelings of triumph. To think that there I was, opening the door, little by little, and he not even to dream of my secret deeds or thoughts. I fairly chuckled at the idea; and perhaps he heard me; for he moved on the bed suddenly, as if startled. Now you may think that I drew back—but no. His room was as black as pitch with the thick darkness (for the shutters were close fastened, through fear of robbers), and so I knew that he could not see the opening of the door, and I kept pushing it on steadily, steadily.

I had my head in, and was about to open the lantern, when my thumb slipped upon the tin fastening, and the old man sprang up in bed, crying out—"Who's there?"

I kept quite still and said nothing. For a whole hour I did not move a muscle, and in the meantime I did not hear him lie down. He was still sitting up in the bed listening;—just as I have done, night after night, hearkening to the death watches in the wall.

Presently I heard a slight groan, and I knew it was the groan of mortal terror. It was not a groan of pain or of grief—oh, no!—it was the low stifled sound that arises from the bottom of the soul when overcharged with awe. I knew the sound well. Many a night, just at midnight, when all the world slept, it has welled up from my own bosom, deepening, with its dreadful echo, the terrors that distracted me. I say I knew it well. I knew what the old man felt, and pitied him, although I chuckled at heart. I knew that he had been lying awake ever since the first slight noise, when he had turned in the bed. His fears had been ever since growing upon him. He had been trying to fancy them causeless, but could not. He had been saying to himself—"It is nothing but the wind in the chimney, it is only a mouse crossing the floor," or "It is merely a cricket which has made a single chirp." Yes, he had been trying to comfort himself with these suppositions: but he had found all in vain. *All in vain*; because Death, in approaching him had stalked with his black shadow before him, and enveloped the victim. And it was the mournful influence of the unperceived shadow that caused him to feel—although he neither saw nor heard—to *feel* the presence of my head within the room.

When I had waited a long time, very patiently, without hearing him lie down, I resolved to open a little—a very, very little crevice in the lantern. So I opened it—you cannot imagine how stealthily, stealthily—until, at length a simple dim ray, like the thread of the spider, shot from out the crevice and fell full upon the vulture eye.

It was open—wide, wide open—and I grew furious as I gazed upon it. I saw it with perfect distinctness—all a dull blue, with a hideous veil over it that chilled the very marrow in my bones; but I could see nothing else of the old man's face or person: for I had directed the ray as if by instinct, precisely upon the damned spot.

And have I not told you that what you mistake for madness is but over-acuteness of the sense?—now, I say, there came to my ears a low, dull, quick sound, such as a watch makes when enveloped in cotton. I knew that sound well, too. It was the beating of the old man's heart. It increased my fury, as the beating of a drum stimulates the soldier into courage.

But even yet I refrained and kept still. I scarcely breathed. I held the lantern motionless. I tried how steadily I could maintain the ray upon the eye. Meantime the hellish tattoo of the heart increased. It grew quicker and quicker, and louder and louder every instant. The old man's terror *must* have been extreme! It grew louder, I say, louder every moment!—do you mark me well I have told you that I am nervous: so I am. And now at the dead hour of the night, amid the dreadful silence of that old house, so strange a noise as this excited me to uncontrollable terror. Yet, for some minutes longer I refrained and stood still. But the beating grew louder, louder! I thought the heart must burst. And now a new anxiety seized me—the sound would be heard by a neighbor! The old man's hour had come! With a loud yell, I threw open the lantern and leaped into the room. He shrieked once—once only. In an instant I dragged him to the floor, and pulled the heavy bed over him. I then smiled gaily, to find the deed so far done. But, for many minutes, the heart beat on with a muffled sound. This, however, did not vex me; it would not be heard through the wall. At length it ceased. The old man was dead. I removed the bed and examined the corpse. Yes, he was stone, stone dead. I placed my hand upon the heart and held it there many minutes. There was no pulsation. He was stone dead. His eye would trouble me no more.

If still you think me mad, you will think so no longer when I describe the wise precautions I took for the concealment of the body. The night waned, and I worked hastily, but in silence. First of all I dismembered the corpse. I cut off the head and the arms and the legs.

I then took up three planks from the flooring of the chamber, and deposited all between the scantlings. I then replaced the boards so cleverly, so cunningly, that no human eye—not even *his*—could have detected anything wrong. There was nothing to wash out—no stain of any kind—no blood-spot whatever. I had been too wary for that. A tub had caught all—ha! ha!

When I had made an end of these labors, it was four o'clock—still dark as midnight. As the bell sounded the hour, there came a knocking at the street door. I went down to open it with a light heart—for what had I *now* to fear? There entered three men, who introduced themselves, with perfect suavity, as officers of the police. A shriek had been heard by a neighbor during the night; suspicion of foul play had been aroused; information had been lodged at the police office, and they (the officers) had been deputed to search the premises.

I smiled—for *what* had I to fear? I bade the gentlemen welcome. The shriek, I said, was my own in a dream. The old man, I mentioned, was absent in the country. I took my visiters all over the house. I bade them search—search *well*. I led them, at length, to *his* chamber. I showed them his treasures, secure, undisturbed. In the enthusiasm of my confidence, I brought chairs into the room, and desired them *here* to rest from their fatigues, while I myself, in the wild audacity of my perfect triumph, placed my own seat upon the very spot beneath which reposed the corpse of the victim.

The officers were satisfied. My *manner* had convinced them. I was singularly at ease. They sat, and while I answered cheerily, they chatted of familiar things. But, ere long, I felt myself getting pale and wished them gone. My head ached, and I fancied a ringing in my ears: but still they sat and still chatted. The ringing became more distinct:—It continued and became more distinct: I talked more freely to get rid of the feeling; but it continued and gained definiteness—until, at length, I found that the noise was *not* within my ears.

No doubt I now grew *very* pale; but I talked more fluently, and with a heightened voice. Yet the sound increased—and what could I do? It was *a low, dull, quick sound—much such a sound as a watch makes when enveloped in cotton.* I gasped for breath—and yet the officers heard it not. I talked more quickly, more vehemently; but the noise steadily increased. I arose and argued about trifles, in a high key and with violent gesticulations; but the noise steadily increased. Why *would* they not be gone? I paced the floor to and fro with heavy strides, as if excited to fury by the observations of the men—but the noise steadily increased. Oh God! what *could* I do? I foamed—I raved—I swore! I swung the chair upon which I had been sitting, and grated it upon the boards, but the noise arose over all and continually increased. It grew louder—louder—*louder*! And still the men chatted pleasantly, and smiled. Was it possible they heard not? Almighty God!—no, no! They heard!—they suspected!—they *knew*!—they were making a mockery of my horror!—this I thought, and this I think. But anything was better than this agony! Anything was more tolerable than this derision! I could bear those hypocritical smiles no longer! I felt that I must scream or die! and now—again!—hark! louder! louder! louder! *louder*!

"Villains!" I shrieked, "dissemble no more! I admit the deed! Tear up the planks! here, here!—It is the beating of his hideous heart!"

The Gold-Bug

[The winning entry in a writing contest sponsored by the *Philadelphia Dollar Newspaper*, this short story was published in the newspaper in two instalments: on June 21 and June 28, 1843. A lightning success, it was one of his most widely read works.]

What ho! what ho! this fellow is dancing mad!
He hath been bitten by the Tarantula.
—*All in the Wrong*

Many years ago, I contracted an intimacy with a Mr. William Legrand. He was of an ancient Huguenot family, and had once been wealthy; but a series of misfortunes had reduced him to want. To avoid the mortification consequent upon his disasters, he left New Orleans, the city of his forefathers, and took up his residence at Sullivan's Island, near Charleston, South Carolina.

This Island is a very singular one. It consists of little else than the sea sand, and is about three miles long. Its breadth at no point exceeds a quarter of a mile. It is separated from the main land by a scarcely perceptible creek, oozing its way through a wilderness of reeds and slime, a favorite resort of the marsh hen. The vegetation, as might be supposed, is scant, or at least dwarfish. No trees of any magnitude are to be seen. Near the western extremity, where Fort Moultrie stands, and where are some miserable frame buildings, tenanted, during summer, by the fugitives from Charleston dust and fever, may be found, indeed, the bristly palmetto; but the whole island, with the exception of this western point, and a line of hard, white beach on the seacoast, is covered with a dense undergrowth of the sweet myrtle, so much prized by the horticulturists of England. The shrub here often attains the height of fifteen or twenty feet, and forms an almost impenetrable coppice, burthening the air with its fragrance.

In the inmost recesses of this coppice, not far from the eastern or more remote end of the island, Legrand had built himself a small hut, which he occupied when I first, by mere accident, made his acquaintance. This soon ripened into friendship—for there was much in the recluse to excite interest and esteem. I found him well educated, with unusual powers of mind, but infected with misanthropy, and subject to perverse moods of alternate enthusiasm and melancholy. He had with him many books, but rarely employed them. His chief amusements were gunning and fishing, or sauntering along the beach and through the myrtles, in quest of shells or entomological specimens;—his collection of the latter might have been envied by a Swammerdamm. In these excursions he was usually accompanied by an old negro, called Jupiter, who had been manumitted before the reverses of the family, but who could be induced, neither by threats nor by promises, to abandon what he considered his right of attendance upon the footsteps of his young "Massa Will." It is not improbable that the relatives of Legrand, conceiving him to be somewhat unsettled in intellect, had contrived to instil this obstinacy into Jupiter, with a view to the supervision and guardianship of the wanderer.

The winters in the latitude of Sullivan's Island are seldom very severe, and in the fall of the year it is a rare event indeed when a fire is considered necessary. About the middle of October, 18—, there occurred, however, a day of remarkable chilliness. Just before sunset I scrambled my way through the evergreens to the hut of my friend, whom I had not visited for several weeks—my residence being, at that time, in Charleston, a distance of nine miles from the Island, while the facilities of passage and re-passage were very far behind those of the present day. Upon reaching the hut I rapped, as was my custom, and getting no reply, sought for the key where I knew it was secreted, unlocked the door and went in. A fine fire was blazing upon the hearth. It was a novelty, and by no means an ungrateful one. I threw off an overcoat, took an arm-chair by the crackling logs, and awaited patiently the arrival of my hosts.

Soon after dark they arrived, and gave me a most cordial welcome. Jupiter, grinning from ear to ear, bustled about to prepare some marsh-hens for supper. Legrand was in one of his fits—how else shall I term them?—of enthusiasm. He had found an unknown bivalve, forming a new genus, and, more than this, he had hunted down and secured, with Jupiter's assistance, a *scarabæus* which he believed to be totally new, but in respect to which he wished to have my opinion on the morrow.

"And why not tonight?" I asked, rubbing my hands over the blaze, and wishing the whole tribe of *scarabæi* at the devil.

"Ah, if I had only known you were here!" said Legrand, "but it's so long since I saw you; and how could I foresee that you would pay me a visit this very night of all others? As I was coming home I met Lieutenant G—, from the fort, and, very foolishly, I lent him the bug; so it will be impossible for you to see it until the morning. Stay here tonight, and I will send Jup down for it at sunrise. It is the loveliest thing in creation!"

"What?—sunrise?"

"Nonsense! no!—the bug. It is of a brilliant gold colour—about the size of a large hickory-nut—with two jet black spots near one extremity of the back, and another, somewhat longer, at the other. The *antennæ* are—"

"Dey aint *no* tin in him, Massa Will, I keep a tellin on you," here interrupted Jupiter; "de bug is a goole bug, solid, ebery bit of him, inside and all, sep him wing—neber feel half so hebby a bug in my life."

"Well, suppose it is, Jup," replied Legrand, somewhat more earnestly, it seemed to me, than the case demanded, "is that any reason for your letting the birds burn? The colour"—here he turned to me—"is really almost enough to warrant Jupiter's idea. You never saw a more brilliant metallic luster than the scales emit—but of this you cannot judge till tomorrow. In the meantime I can give you some idea of the shape." Saying this, he seated himself at a small table, on which were a pen and ink, but no paper. He looked for some in a drawer, but found none.

"Never mind," said he at length, "this will answer;" and he drew from his waistcoat pocket a scrap of what I took to be very dirty foolscap, and made upon it a rough drawing with the pen. While he did this, I retained my seat by the fire, for I was still chilly. When the design was complete, he handed it to me without rising. As I received it, a loud growl was heard, succeeded by a scratching at the door. Jupiter opened it, and a large Newfoundland, belonging to Legrand, rushed in, leaped upon my shoulders, and loaded me with caresses; for I had shown him much attention during previous visits.

When his gambols were over, I looked at the paper, and, to speak the truth, found myself not a little puzzled at what my friend had depicted.

"Well!" I said, after contemplating it for some minutes, "this *is* a strange *scarabæus*, I must confess: new to me: never saw anything like it before—unless it was a skull, or a death's-head—which it more nearly resembles than anything else that has come under *my* observation."

"A death's-head!" echoed Legrand. "Oh—yes—well, it has something of that appearance upon paper, no doubt. The two upper black spots look like eyes, eh? and the longer one at the bottom like a mouth—and then the shape of the whole is oval."

"Perhaps so," said I; "but, Legrand, I fear you are no artist. I must wait until I see the beetle itself, if I am to form any idea of its personal appearance."

"Well, I don't know," said he, a little nettled, "I draw tolerably—*should* do it at least—have had good masters, and flatter myself that I am not quite a blockhead."

"But, my dear fellow, you are joking then," said I, "this is a very passable *skull*—indeed, I may say that it is a very *excellent* skull, according to the vulgar notions about such specimens of physiology—and your *scarabæus* must be the queerest *scarabæus* in the world if it resembles it. Why, we may get up a very thrilling bit of superstition upon this hint. I presume you will call the bug *scarabæus caput hominis*, or something of that kind—there are many similar titles in the Natural Histories. But where are the antennæ you spoke of?"

"The *antennæ*!" said Legrand, who seemed to be getting unaccountably warm upon the subject; "I am sure you must see the *antennæ*. I made them as distinct as they are in the original insect, and I presume that is sufficient."

"Well, well," I said, "perhaps you have—still I don't see them;" and I handed him the paper without additional remark, not wishing to ruffle his temper; but I was much surprised at the turn affairs had taken; his ill humor puzzled me—and, as for the drawing of the beetle, there were positively *no antennæ* visible, and the whole *did* bear a very close resemblance to the ordinary cuts of a death's-head.

He received the paper very peevishly, and was about to crumple it, apparently to throw it in the fire, when a casual glance at the design seemed suddenly to rivet his attention. In an instant his face grew violently red—in another as excessively pale. For some minutes he continued to scrutinize the drawing minutely where he sat. At length he arose, took a candle from the table, and proceeded to seat himself upon a sea-chest in the farthest corner of the room. Here again he made an anxious examination of the paper; turning it in all directions. He said nothing, however, and his conduct greatly astonished me; yet I thought it prudent not to exacerbate the growing moodiness of his temper by any comment. Presently he took from his coat pocket a wallet, placed the paper carefully in it, and deposited both in a writing-desk, which he locked. He now grew more composed in his demeanor; but his original air of enthusiasm had quite disappeared. Yet he seemed not so much sulky as abstracted. As the evening wore away he became more and more absorbed in reverie, from which no sallies of mine could arouse him. It had been my intention to pass the night at the hut, as I had frequently done before, but, seeing my host in this mood, I deemed it proper to take leave. He did not press me to remain, but, as I departed, he shook my hand with even more than his usual cordiality.

It was about a month after this (and during the interval I had seen nothing of Legrand) when I received a visit, at Charleston, from his man, Jupiter. I had never seen the good old negro look so dispirited, and I feared that some serious disaster had befallen my friend.

"Well, Jup," said I, "what is the matter now?—how is your master?"

"Why, to speak de troof, massa, him not so berry well as mought be."

"Not well! I am truly sorry to hear it. What does he complain of?"

"Dar! dat's it!—him neber plain of notin—but him berry sick for all dat."

"*Very* sick, Jupiter!—why didn't you say so at once? Is he confined to bed?"

"No, dat he aint!—he aint find nowhar—dat's just whar de shoe pinch—my mind is got to be berry hebby bout poor Massa Will."

"Jupiter, I should like to understand what it is you are talking about. You say your master is sick. Hasn't he told you what ails him?"

"Why, massa, taint worf while for to git mad about de matter—Massa Will say noffin at all aint de matter wid him—but den what make him go about looking dis here way, wid he head down and he soldiers up, and as white as a gose? And den he keep a syphon all de time—"

"Keeps a what, Jupiter?"

"Keeps a syphon wid de figgurs on de slate—de queerest figgurs I ebber did see. Ise gittin to be skeered, I tell you. Hab for to keep mighty tight eye pon him noovers. Todder day he gib me slip fore de sun up and was gone de whole ob de blessed day. I had a big stick ready cut for to gib him deuced good beating when he did come—but Ise sich a fool dat I hadn't de heart arter all—he look so berry poorly."

"Eh?—what?—ah yes!—upon the whole I think you had better not be too severe with the poor fellow—don't flog him, Jupiter—he can't very well stand it—but can you form no idea of what has occasioned this illness, or rather this change of conduct? Has anything unpleasant happened since I saw you?"

"No, massa, dey aint bin noffin unpleasant *since* den—'twas *fore* den I'm feared—'twas de berry day you was dare."

"How? what do you mean?"

"Why, massa, I mean de bug—dare now."

"The what?"

"De bug—I'm berry sartain dat Massa Will bin bit somewhere bout de head by dat goole-bug."

"And what cause have you, Jupiter, for such a supposition?"

"Claws enuff, massa, and mouth too. I nebber did see sick a deuced bug—he kick and he bite ebery ting what cum near him. Massa Will cotch him fuss, but had for to let him go gin mighty quick, I tell you—den was de time he must ha got de bite. I did n't like de look oh de bug mouff, myself, no how, so I would n't take hold ob him wid my finger, but I cotch him wid a piece ob paper dat I found. I rap him up in de paper and stuff piece ob it in he mouff—dat was de way."

"And you think, then, that your master was really bitten by the beetle, and that the bite made him sick?"

"I don't tink noffin about it—I nose it. What make him dream bout de goole so much, if taint cause he bit by de goole-bug? Ise heerd bout dem goole-bugs fore dis."

"But how do you know he dreams about gold?"

"How I know? why cause he talk about it in he sleep—dat's how I nose."

"Well, Jup, perhaps you are right; but to what fortunate circumstance am I to attribute the honor of a visit from you today?"

"What de matter, massa?"

"Did you bring any message from Mr. Legrand?"

"No, massa, I bring dis here pissel;" and here Jupiter handed me a note which ran thus:

> MY DEAR—
>
> Why have I not seen you for so long a time? I hope you have not been so foolish as to take offence at any little *brusquerie* of mine; but no, that is improbable.
>
> Since I saw you I have had great cause for anxiety. I have something to tell you, yet scarcely know how to tell it, or whether I should tell it at all.
>
> I have not been quite well for some days past, and poor old Jup annoys me, almost beyond endurance, by his well-meant attentions. Would you believe it?—he had prepared a huge stick, the other day, with which to chastise me for giving him the slip, and spending the day, *solus*, among the hills on the main land. I verily believe that my ill looks alone saved me a flogging.
>
> I have made no addition to my cabinet since we met.
>
> If you can, in any way, make it convenient, come over with Jupiter. *Do* come. I wish to see you *tonight*, upon business of importance. I assure you that it is of the *highest* importance.
>
> —Ever yours,
> WILLIAM LEGRAND

There was something in the tone of this note which gave me great uneasiness. Its whole style differed materially from that of Legrand. What could he be dreaming of? What new crotchet possessed his excitable brain? What "business of the highest importance" could *he* possibly have to transact? Jupiter's account of him boded no good. I dreaded lest the continued pressure of misfortune had, at length, fairly unsettled the reason of my friend. Without a moment's hesitation, therefore, I prepared to accompany the negro.

Upon reaching the wharf, I noticed a scythe and three spades, all apparently new, lying in the bottom of the boat in which we were to embark.

"What is the meaning of all this, Jup?" I inquired.

"Him syfe, massa, and spade."

"Very true; but what are they doing here?"

"Him de syfe and de spade what Massa Will sis pon my buying for him in de town, and de debbils own lot of money I had to gib for em."

"But what, in the name of all that is mysterious, is your 'Massa Will' going to do with scythes and spades?"

"Dat's more dan *I* know, and debbil take me if I don't blieve 'tis more dan he know, too. But it's all cum ob do bug."

Finding that no satisfaction was to be obtained of Jupiter, whose whole intellect seemed to be absorbed by "de bug," I now stepped into the boat and made sail. With a fair and strong breeze we soon ran into the little cove to the northward of Fort Moultrie, and a walk of some two miles brought us to the hut. It was about three in the afternoon when we arrived. Legrand had been awaiting us in eager expectation. He grasped my hand with a nervous empressement which alarmed me and strengthened the suspicions already entertained. His countenance was pale even to ghastliness, and his deep-set eyes glared with unnatural lustre. After some inquiries respecting his health, I asked him, not knowing what better to say, if he had yet obtained the scarabæus from Lieutenant G—.

"Oh, yes," he replied, colouring violently, "I got it from him the next morning. Nothing should tempt me to part with that *scarabæus.* Do you know that Jupiter is quite right about it?"

"In what way?" I asked, with a sad foreboding at heart.

"In supposing it to be a bug of *real gold.*" He said this with an air of profound seriousness, and I felt inexpressibly shocked.

"This bug is to make my fortune," he continued, with a triumphant smile, "to reinstate me in my family possessions. Is it any wonder, then, that I prize it? Since Fortune has thought fit to bestow it upon me, I have only to use it properly and I shall arrive at the gold of which it is the index. Jupiter; bring me that *scarabæus*!"

"What! de bug, massa? I'd rudder not go fer trubble dat bug—you mus git him for your own self." Hereupon Legrand arose, with a grave and stately air, and brought me the beetle from a glass case in which it was enclosed. It was a beautiful *scarabæus*, and, at that time, unknown to naturalists—of course a great prize in a scientific point of view. There were two round, black spots near one extremity of the back, and a long one near the other. The scales were exceedingly hard and glossy, with all the appearance of burnished gold. The weight of the insect was very remarkable, and, taking all things into consideration, I could hardly blame Jupiter for his opinion respecting it; but what to make of Legrand's concordance with that opinion, I could not, for the life of me, tell.

"I sent for you," said he, in a grandiloquent tone, when I had completed my examination of the beetle, "I sent for you, that I might have your counsel and assistance in furthering the views of Fate and of the bug—"

"My dear Legrand," I cried, interrupting him, "you are certainly unwell, and had better use some little precautions. You shall go to bed, and I will remain with you a few days, until you get over this. You are feverish and—"

"Feel my pulse," said he.

I felt it, and, to say the truth, found not the slightest indication of fever.

"But you may be ill and yet have no fever. Allow me this once to prescribe for you. In the first place, go to bed. In the next—"

"You are mistaken," he interposed, "I am as well as I can expect to be under the excitement which I suffer. If you really wish me well, you will relieve this excitement."

"And how is this to be done?"

"Very easily. Jupiter and myself are going upon an expedition into the hills, upon the main land, and, in this expedition we shall need the aid of some person in whom we can confide. You are the only one we can trust. Whether we succeed or fail, the excitement which you now perceive in me will be equally allayed."

"I am anxious to oblige you in any way," I replied; "but do you mean to say that this infernal beetle has any connection with your expedition into the hills?"

"It has."

"Then, Legrand, I can become a party to no such absurd proceeding."

"I am sorry—very sorry—for we shall have to try it by ourselves."

"Try it by yourselves! The man is surely mad!—but stay!—how long do you propose to be absent?"

"Probably all night. We shall start immediately, and be back, at all events, by sunrise."

"And will you promise me, upon your honor, that when this freak of yours is over, and the bug business (good God!) settled to your satisfaction, you will then return home and follow my advice implicitly, as that of your physician?"

"Yes; I promise; and now let us be off, for we have no time to lose."

With a heavy heart I accompanied my friend. We started about four o'clock—Legrand, Jupiter, the dog, and myself. Jupiter had with him the scythe and spades—the whole of which he insisted upon carrying—more through fear, it seemed to me, of trusting either of the implements within reach of his master, than from any excess of industry or complaisance. His demeanor was dogged in the extreme, and "dat deuced bug" were the sole words which escaped his lips during the journey. For my own part, I had charge of a couple of dark lanterns, while Legrand contented himself with the *scarabæus*, which he carried attached to the end of a bit of whip-cord; twirling it to and fro, with the air of a conjuror, as he went. When I observed this last, plain evidence of my friend's aberration of mind, I could scarcely refrain from tears. I thought it best, however, to humor his fancy, at least for the present, or until I could adopt some more energetic measures with a chance of success. In the mean time I endeavored, but all in vain, to sound him in regard to the object of the expedition. Having succeeded in inducing me to accompany him, he seemed unwilling to hold conversation upon any topic of minor importance, and to all my questions vouchsafed no other reply than "we shall see!"

We crossed the creek at the head of the island by means of a skiff; and, ascending the high grounds on the shore of the main land, proceeded in a northwesterly direction, through a tract of country excessively wild and desolate, where no trace of a human footstep was to be seen. Legrand led the way with decision; pausing only for an instant, here and there, to consult what appeared to be certain landmarks of his own contrivance upon a former occasion.

In this manner we journeyed for about two hours, and the sun was just setting when we entered a region infinitely more dreary than any yet seen. It was a species of table land, near the summit of an almost inaccessible hill, densely wooded from base to pinnacle, and interspersed with huge crags that appeared to lie loosely upon the soil, and in many cases were prevented from precipitating themselves into the valleys below, merely by the support of the trees against which they reclined. Deep ravines, in various directions, gave an air of still sterner solemnity to the scene.

The natural platform to which we had clambered was thickly overgrown with brambles, through which we soon discovered that it would have been impossible to force our way but for the scythe; and Jupiter, by direction of his master, proceeded to clear for us a path to the foot of an enormously tall tulip-tree, which stood, with some eight or ten oaks, upon the level, and far surpassed them all, and all other trees which I had then ever seen, in the beauty of its foliage and form, in the wide spread of its branches, and in the general majesty of its appearance. When we reached this tree, Legrand turned to Jupiter, and asked him if he thought he could climb it. The old man seemed a little staggered by the question, and for some moments made no reply. At length he approached the huge trunk, walked slowly around it, and examined it with minute attention. When he had completed his scrutiny, he merely said,

"Yes, massa, Jup climb any tree he ebber see in he life."

"Then up with you as soon as possible, for it will soon be too dark to see what we are about."

"How far mus go up, massa?" inquired Jupiter.

"Get up the main trunk first, and then I will tell you which way to go—and here—stop! take this beetle with you."

"De bug, Massa Will!—de goole-bug!" cried the negro, drawing back in dismay—"what for mus tote de bug way up de tree?—d—n if I do!"

"If you are afraid, Jup, a great big negro like you, to take hold of a harmless little dead beetle, why you can carry it up by this string—but, if you do not take it up with you in some way, I shall be under the necessity of breaking your head with this shovel."

"What de matter now, massa?" said Jup, evidently shamed into compliance; "always want for to raise fuss wid old nigger. Was only funnin any how. *Me* feered de bug! what I keer for de bug?" Here he took cautiously hold of the extreme end of the string, and, maintaining the insect as far from his person as circumstances would permit, prepared to ascend the tree.

In youth, the tulip-tree, or *Liriodendron Tulipferum*, the most magnificent of American foresters, has a trunk peculiarly smooth, and often rises to a great height without lateral branches; but, in its riper age, the bark becomes gnarled and uneven, while many short limbs make their appearance on the stem. Thus the difficulty of ascension, in the present case, lay more in semblance than in reality. Embracing the huge cylinder, as closely as possible, with his arms and knees, seizing with his hands some projections, and resting his naked toes upon others, Jupiter, after one or two narrow escapes from falling, at length wriggled himself into the first great fork, and seemed to consider the whole business as virtually accomplished. The risk of the achievement was, in fact, now over, although the climber was some sixty or seventy feet from the ground.

"Which way mus go now, Massa Will?" he asked.

"Keep up the largest branch—the one on this side," said Legrand. The negro obeyed him promptly, and apparently with but little trouble; ascending higher and higher, until no glimpse of his squat figure could be obtained through the dense foliage which enveloped it. Presently his voice was heard in a sort of halloo.

"How much fudder is got for go?"

"How high up are you?" asked Legrand.

"Ebber so fur," replied the negro; "can see de sky fru de top ob de tree."

"Never mind the sky, but attend to what I say. Look down the trunk and count the limbs below you on this side. How many limbs have you passed?"

"One, two, tree, four, fibe—I done pass fibe big limb, massa, pon dis side."

"Then go one limb higher."

In a few minutes the voice was heard again, announcing that the seventh limb was attained.

"Now, Jup," cried Legrand, evidently much excited, "I want you to work your way out upon that limb as far as you can. If you see anything strange, let me know."

By this time what little doubt I might have entertained of my poor friend's insanity, was put finally at rest. I had no alternative but to conclude him stricken with lunacy, and I became seriously anxious about getting him home. While I was pondering upon what was best to be done, Jupiter's voice was again heard.

"Mos feerd for to ventur pon dis limb berry far—tis dead limb putty much all de way."

"Did you say it was a *dead* limb, Jupiter?" cried Legrand in a quavering voice.

"Yes, massa, him dead as de door-nail—done up for sartain—done departed dis here life."

"What in the name heaven shall I do?" asked Legrand, seemingly in the greatest distress.

"Do!" said I, glad of an opportunity to interpose a word, "why come home and go to bed. Come now!—that's a fine fellow. It's getting late, and, besides, you remember your promise."

"Jupiter," cried he, without heeding me in the least, "do you hear me?"

"Yes, Massa Will, hear you ebber so plain."

"Try the wood well, then, with your knife, and see if you think it *very* rotten."

"Him rotten, massa, sure nuff," replied the negro in a few moments, "but not so berry rotten as mought be. Mought ventur out leetle way pon de limb by myself, dat's true."

"By yourself!—what do you mean?"

"Why I mean de bug. 'Tis *berry* hebby bug. Spose I drop him down fuss, and den de limb won't break wid just de weight ob one nigger."

"You infernal scoundrel!" cried Legrand, apparently much relieved, "what do you mean by telling me such nonsense as that? As sure as you drop that beetle I'll break your neck. Look here, Jupiter, do you hear me?"

"Yes, massa, needn't hollo at poor nigger dat style."

"Well! now listen!—if you will venture out on the limb as far as you think safe, and not let go the beetle, I'll make you a present of a silver dollar as soon as you get down."

"I'm gwine, Massa Will—deed I is," replied the negro very promptly—"mos out to the eend now."

"Out to the end!" here fairly screamed Legrand, "do you say you are out to the end of that limb?"

"Soon be to de eend, massa,—o-o-o-o-oh! Lorgol-a-marcy! what is dis here pon de tree?"

"Well!" cried Legrand, highly delighted, "what is it?"

"Why taint noffin but a skull—somebody bin lef him head up de tree, and de crows done gobble ebery bit ob de meat off."

"A skull, you say!—very well!—how is it fastened to the limb?—what holds it on?"

"Sure nuff, massa; mus look. Why dis berry curous sarcumstance, pon my word—dare's a great big nail in de skull, what fastens ob it on to de tree."

"Well now, Jupiter, do exactly as I tell you—do you hear?"

"Yes, massa."

"Pay attention, then!—find the left eye of the skull."

"Hum! hoo! dat's good! why dare aint no eye lef at all."

"Curse your stupidity! do you know your right hand from your left?"

"Yes, I nose dat—nose all bout dat—tis my lef hand what I chops de wood wid."

"To be sure! you are left-handed; and your left eye is on the same side as your left hand. Now, I suppose, you can find the left eye of the skull, or the place where the left eye has been. Have you found it?"

Here was a long pause. At length the negro asked,

"Is de lef eye of de skull pon de same side as de lef hand of de skull, too?—cause de skull aint got not a bit ob a hand at all—nebber mind! I got de lef eye now—here de lef eye! what mus do wid it?"

"Let the beetle drop through it, as far as the string will reach—but be careful and not let go your hold of the string."

"All dat done, Massa Will; mighty easy ting for to put de bug fru de hole—look out for him dare below!"

During this colloquy no portion of Jupiter's person could be seen; but the beetle, which he had suffered to descend, was now visible at the end of the string, and glistened, like a globe of burnished gold, in the last rays of the setting sun, some of which still faintly illumined the eminence upon which we stood. The scarabæus hung quite clear of any branches, and, if allowed to fall, would have fallen at our feet. Legrand immediately took the scythe, and cleared with it a circular space, three or four yards in diameter, just beneath the insect, and, having accomplished this, ordered Jupiter to let go the string and come down from the tree.

Driving a peg, with great nicety, into the ground, at the precise spot where the beetle fell, my friend now produced from his pocket a tape measure. Fastening one end of this at that point of the trunk, of the tree which was nearest the peg, he unrolled it till it reached the peg, and thence farther unrolled it, in the direction already established by the two points of the tree and the peg, for the distance of fifty feet—Jupiter clearing away the brambles with the scythe. At the spot thus attained a second peg was driven, and about this, as a center, a rude circle, about four feet in diameter, described. Taking now a spade himself, and giving one to Jupiter and one to me, Legrand begged us to set about digging as quickly as possible.

To speak the truth, I had no especial relish for such amusement at any time, and, at that particular moment, would most willingly have declined it; for the night was coming on, and I felt much fatigued with the exercise already taken; but I saw no mode of escape, and was fearful of disturbing my poor friend's equanimity by a refusal. Could I have depended, indeed, upon Jupiter's aid, I would have had no hesitation in attempting to get the lunatic home by force; but I was too well assured of the old negro's disposition, to hope that he would assist me, under any circumstances, in a personal contest with his master. I made no doubt that the latter had been infected with some of the innumerable Southern superstitions about money buried, and that his phantasy had received confirmation by the finding of the *scarabæus*, or, perhaps, by Jupiter's obstinacy in maintaining it to be "a bug of real gold." A mind disposed to lunacy would readily be led away by such suggestions—especially if chiming in with favorite preconceived ideas—and then I called to mind the poor fellow's speech about the beetle's being "the index of his fortune." Upon the whole, I was sadly vexed and puzzled, but, at length, I concluded to make a virtue of necessity—to dig with a good will, and thus the sooner to convince the visionary, by ocular demonstration, of the fallacy of the opinions he entertained.

The lanterns having been lit, we all fell to work with a zeal worthy a more rational cause; and, as the glare fell upon our persons and implements, I could not help thinking how picturesque a group we composed, and how strange and suspicious our labors must have appeared to any interloper who, by chance, might have stumbled upon our whereabouts.

We dug very steadily for two hours. Little was said; and our chief embarrassment lay in the yelpings of the dog, who took exceeding interest in our proceedings. He, at length, became so obstreperous that we grew fearful of his giving the alarm to some stragglers in the vicinity;—or, rather, this was the apprehension of Legrand;—for myself, I should have rejoiced at any interruption which might have enabled me to get the wanderer home. The noise was, at length, very effectually silenced by Jupiter, who, getting out of the hole with a dogged air of deliberation, tied the brute's mouth up with one of his suspenders, and then returned, with a grave chuckle, to his task.

When the time mentioned had expired, we had reached a depth of five feet, and yet no signs of any treasure became manifest. A general pause ensued, and I began to hope that the farce was at an end. Legrand, however, although evidently much disconcerted, wiped his brow thoughtfully and recommenced. We had excavated the entire circle of four feet diameter, and now we slightly enlarged the limit, and went to the farther depth of two feet. Still nothing appeared. The gold-seeker, whom I sincerely pitied, at length clambered from the pit, with the bitterest disappointment imprinted upon every feature, and proceeded, slowly and reluctantly, to put on his coat, which he had thrown off at the beginning of his labor. In the mean time I made no remark. Jupiter, at a signal from his master, began to gather up his tools. This done, and the dog having been unmuzzled, we turned in profound silence towards home.

We had taken, perhaps, a dozen steps in this direction, when, with a loud oath, Legrand strode up to Jupiter, and seized him by the collar. The astonished negro opened his eyes and mouth to the fullest extent, let fall the spades, and fell upon his knees.

"You scoundrel," said Legrand, hissing out the syllables from between his clenched teeth—"you infernal black villain!—speak, I tell you!—answer me this instant, without prevarication!—which—which is your left eye?"

"Oh, my golly, Massa Will! aint dis here my lef eye for sartain?" roared the terrified Jupiter, placing his hand upon his right organ of vision, and holding it there with a desperate pertinacity, as if in immediate dread of his master's attempt at a gouge.

"I thought so!—I knew it! hurrah!" vociferated Legrand, letting the negro go, and executing a series of curvets and caracols, much to the astonishment of his valet, who, arising from his knees, looked, mutely, from his master to myself, and then from myself to his master.

"Come! we must go back," said the latter, "the game's not up yet;" and he again led the way to the tulip-tree.

"Jupiter," said he, when we reached its foot, "come here! was the skull nailed to the limb with the face outwards, or with the face to the limb?"

"De face was out, massa, so dat de crows could get at de eyes good, widout any trouble."

"Well, then, was it this eye or that through which you dropped the beetle?"—here Legrand touched each of Jupiter's eyes.

"'T was dis eye, massa—de lef eye—jis as you tell me," and here it was his right eye that the negro indicated.

"That will do—must try it again."

Here my friend, about whose madness I now saw, or fancied that I saw, certain indications of method, removed the peg which marked the spot where the beetle fell, to a spot about three inches to the westward of its former position. Taking, now, the tape measure from the nearest point of the trunk to the peg, as before, and continuing the extension in a straight line to the distance of fifty feet, a spot was indicated, removed, by several yards, from the point at which we had been digging.

Around the new position a circle, somewhat larger than in the former instance, was now described, and we again set to work with the spades. I was dreadfully weary, but, scarcely understanding what had occasioned the change in my thoughts, I felt no longer any great aversion from the labor imposed. I had become most unaccountably interested—nay, even excited. Perhaps there was something, amid all the extravagant demeanor of Legrand—some air of forethought, or of deliberation, which impressed me. I dug eagerly, and now and then caught myself actually looking, with something that very much resembled expectation, for the fancied treasure, the vision of which had demented my unfortunate companion. At a period when such vagaries of thought most fully possessed me, and when we had been at work perhaps an hour and a half, we were again interrupted by the violent howlings of the dog. His uneasiness, in the first instance, had been, evidently, but the result of playfulness or caprice, but he now assumed a bitter and serious tone. Upon Jupiter's again attempting to muzzle him, he made furious resistance, and, leaping into the hole, tore up the mould frantically with his claws. In a few seconds he had uncovered a mass of human bones, forming two complete skeletons, intermingled with several buttons of metal, and what appeared to be the dust of decayed woollen. One or two strokes of a spade upturned the blade of a large Spanish knife, and, as we dug farther, three or four loose pieces of gold and silver coin came to light.

At sight of these the joy of Jupiter could scarcely be restrained, but the countenance of his master wore an air of extreme disappointment He urged us, however, to continue our exertions, and the words were hardly uttered when I stumbled and fell forward, having caught the toe of my boot in a large ring of iron that lay half buried in the loose earth.

We now worked in earnest, and never did I pass ten minutes of more intense excitement. During this interval we had fairly unearthed an oblong chest of wood, which, from its perfect preservation and wonderful hardness, had plainly been subjected to some mineralizing process—perhaps that of the Bi-chloride of Mercury. This box was three feet and a half long, three feet broad, and two and a half feet deep. It was firmly secured by bands of wrought iron, riveted, and forming a kind of open trelliswork over the whole. On each side of the chest, near the top, were three rings of iron—six in all—by means of which a firm hold could be obtained by six persons. Our utmost united endeavors served only to disturb the coffer very slightly in its bed. We at once saw the impossibility of removing so great a weight. Luckily, the sole fastenings of the lid consisted of two sliding bolts. These we drew back—trembling and panting with anxiety. In an instant, a treasure of incalculable value lay gleaming before us. As the rays of the lanterns fell within the pit, there flashed upwards a glow and a glare, from a confused heap of gold and of jewels, that absolutely dazzled our eyes.

I shall not pretend to describe the feelings with which I gazed. Amazement was, of course, predominant. Legrand appeared exhausted with excitement, and spoke very few words. Jupiter's countenance wore, for some minutes, as deadly a pallor as it is possible, in nature of things, for any negro's visage to assume. He seemed stupefied—thunder-stricken. Presently he fell upon his knees in the pit, and, burying his naked arms up to the elbows in gold, let them there remain, as if enjoying the luxury of a bath. At length, with a deep sigh, he exclaimed, as if in a soliloquy,

"And dis all cum ob de goole-bug! de putty goole bug! de poor little goole-bug, what I boosed in dat sabage kind ob style! Aint you shamed ob yourself, nigger?—answer me dat!"

It became necessary, at last, that I should arouse both master and valet to the expediency of removing the treasure. It was growing late, and it behooved us to make exertion, that we might get everything housed before daylight. It was difficult to say what should be done, and much time was spent in deliberation—so confused were the ideas of all. We, finally, lightened the box by removing two thirds of its contents, when we were enabled, with some trouble, to raise it from the hole. The articles taken out were deposited among the brambles, and the dog left to guard them, with strict orders from Jupiter neither, upon any pretence, to stir from the spot, nor to open his mouth until our return. We then hurriedly made for home with the chest; reaching the hut in safety, but after excessive toil, at one o'clock in the morning. Worn out as we were, it was not in human nature to do more immediately. We rested until two, and had supper; starting for the hills immediately afterwards, armed with three stout sacks, which, by good luck, were upon the premises. A little before four we arrived at the pit, divided the remainder of the booty, as equally as might be, among us, and, leaving the holes unfilled, again set out for the hut, at which, for the second time, we deposited our golden burthens, just as the first faint streaks of the dawn gleamed from over the tree-tops in the East.

We were now thoroughly broken down; but the intense excitement of the time denied us repose. After an unquiet slumber of some three or four hours' duration, we arose, as if by preconcert, to make examination of our treasure.

The chest had been full to the brim, and we spent the whole day, and the greater part of the next night, in a scrutiny of its contents. There had been nothing like order or arrangement. Everything had been heaped in promiscuously. Having assorted all with care, we found ourselves possessed of even vaster wealth than we had at first supposed. In coin there was rather more than four hundred and fifty thousand dollars—estimating the value of the pieces, as accurately as we could, by the tables of the period. There was not a particle of silver. All was gold of antique date and of great variety—French, Spanish, and German money, with a few English guineas, and some counters, of which we had never seen specimens before. There were several very large and heavy coins, so worn that we could make nothing of their inscriptions. There was no American money. The value of the jewels we found more difficulty in estimating. There were diamonds—some of them exceedingly large and fine—a hundred and ten in all, and not one of them small; eighteen rubies of remarkable brilliancy;—three hundred and ten emeralds, all very beautiful; and twenty-one sapphires, with an opal. These stones had all been broken from their settings and thrown loose in the chest.

The settings themselves, which we picked out from among the other gold, appeared to have been beaten up with hammers, as if to prevent identification. Besides all this, there was a vast quantity of solid gold ornaments;—nearly two hundred massive finger- and ear-rings;—rich chains—thirty of these, if I remember;—eighty-three very large and heavy crucifixes;—five gold censers of great value;—a prodigious golden punch bowl, ornamented with richly chased vine-leaves and Bacchanalian figures; with two sword-handles exquisitely embossed, and many other smaller articles which I cannot recollect. The weight of these valuables exceeded three hundred and fifty pounds avoirdupois; and in this estimate I have not included one hundred and ninety-seven superb gold watches; three of the number being worth each five hundred dollars, if one. Many of them were very old, and as time keepers valueless; the works having suffered, more or less, from corrosion—but all were richly jeweled and in cases of great worth. We estimated the entire contents of the chest, that night, at a million and a half of dollars; and upon the subsequent disposal of the trinkets and jewels (a few being retained for our own use), it was found that we had greatly undervalued the treasure.

When, at length, we had concluded our examination, and the intense excitement of the time had, in some measure, subsided, Legrand, who saw that I was dying with impatience for a solution of this most extraordinary riddle, entered into a full detail of all the circumstances connected with it.

"You remember;" said he, "the night when I handed you the rough sketch I had made of the *scarabæus*. You recollect also, that I became quite vexed at you for insisting that my drawing resembled a death's-head. When you first made this assertion I thought you were jesting; but afterwards I called to mind the peculiar spots on the back of the insect, and admitted to myself that your remark had some little foundation in fact. Still, the sneer at my graphic powers irritated me—for I am considered a good artist—and, therefore, when you handed me the scrap of parchment, I was about to crumple it up and throw it angrily into the fire."

"The scrap of paper, you mean," said I.

"No; it had much of the appearance of paper, and at first I supposed it to be such, but when I came to draw upon it, I discovered it, at once, to be a piece of very thin parchment. It was quite dirty, you remember. Well, as I was in the very act of crumpling it up, my glance fell upon the sketch at which you had been looking, and you may imagine my astonishment when

I perceived, in fact, the figure of a death's-head just where, it seemed to me, I had made the drawing of the beetle. For a moment I was too much amazed to think with accuracy. I knew that my design was very different in detail from this—although there was a certain similarity in general outline. Presently I took a candle, and seating myself at the other end of the room, proceeded to scrutinize the parchment more closely. Upon turning it over, I saw my own sketch upon the reverse, just as I had made it. My first idea, now, was mere surprise at the really remarkable similarity of outline—at the singular coincidence involved in the fact, that unknown to me, there should have been a skull upon the other side of the parchment, immediately beneath my figure of the *scarabæus*, and that this skull, not only in outline, but in size, should so closely resemble my drawing. I say the singularity of this coincidence absolutely stupefied me for a time. This is the usual effect of such coincidences. The mind struggles to establish a connexion—a sequence of cause and effect—and, being unable to do so, suffers a species of temporary paralysis. But, when I recovered from this stupor, there dawned upon me gradually a conviction which startled me even far more than the coincidence. I began distinctly, positively, to remember that there had been no drawing upon the parchment when I made my sketch of the *scarabæus*. I became perfectly certain of this; for I recollected turning up first one side and then the other, in search of the cleanest spot. Had the skull been then there, of course I could not have failed to notice it. Here was indeed a mystery which I felt it impossible to explain; but, even at that early moment, there seemed to glimmer, faintly, within the most remote and secret chambers of my intellect, a glow-worm-like conception of that truth which last night's adventure brought to so magnificent a demonstration. I arose at once, and putting the parchment securely away, dismissed all farther reflection until I should be alone.

"When you had gone, and when Jupiter was fast asleep, I betook myself to a more methodical investigation of the affair. In the first place I considered the manner in which the parchment had come into my possession. The spot where we discovered the *scarabæus* was on the coast of the main land, about a mile eastward of the island, and but a short distance above high water mark. Upon my taking hold of it, it gave me a sharp bite, which caused me to let it drop. Jupiter, with his accustomed caution, before seizing the insect, which had flown towards him, looked about him for a leaf, or something of that nature, by which to take hold of it. It was at this moment that his eyes, and mine also, fell upon the scrap of parchment, which I then supposed to be paper. It was lying half buried in the sand, a corner sticking up. Near the spot where we found it, I observed the remnants of the hull of what appeared to have been a ship's long boat. The wreck seemed to have been there for a very great while; for the resemblance to boat timbers could scarcely be traced.

"Well, Jupiter picked up the parchment, wrapped the beetle in it, and gave it to me. Soon afterwards we turned to go home, and on the way met Lieutenant G—. I showed him the insect, and he begged me to let him take it to the fort. Upon my consenting, he thrust it forthwith into his waistcoat pocket, without the parchment in which it had been wrapped, and which I had continued to hold in my hand during his inspection. Perhaps he dreaded my changing my mind, and thought it best to make sure of the prize at once—you know how enthusiastic he is on all subjects connected with Natural History. At the same time, without being conscious of it, I must have deposited the parchment in my own pocket.

"You remember that when I went to the table, for the purpose of making a sketch of the beetle, I found no paper where it was usually kept. I looked in the drawer, and found none there. I searched my pockets, hoping to find an old letter, when my hand fell upon the parchment. I thus detail the precise mode in which it came into my possession; for the circumstances impressed me with peculiar force.

"No doubt you will think me fanciful—but I had already established a kind of *connection*. I had put together two links of a great chain. There was a boat lying upon a sea-coast, and not far from the boat was a parchment—*not a paper*—with a skull depicted upon it. You will, of course, ask 'where is the connection?' I reply that the skull, or death's-head, is the well-known emblem of the pirate. The flag of the death's head is hoisted in all engagements.

"I have said that the scrap was parchment, and not paper. Parchment is durable—almost imperishable. Matters of little moment are rarely consigned to parchment; since, for the mere ordinary purposes of drawing or writing, it is not nearly so well adapted as paper. This reflection suggested some meaning—some relevancy—in the death's-head. I did not fail to observe, also, the *form* of the parchment. Although one of its corners had been, by some accident, destroyed, it could be seen that the original form was oblong. It was just such a slip, indeed, as might have been chosen for a memorandum—for a record of something to be long remembered and carefully preserved."

"But," I interposed, "you say that the skull was *not* upon the parchment when you made the drawing of the beetle. How then do you trace any connection between the boat and the skull—since this latter, according to your own admission, must have been designed (God only knows how or by whom) at some period subsequent to your sketching the *scarabæus*?"

"Ah, hereupon turns the whole mystery; although the secret, at this point, I had comparatively little difficulty in solving. My steps were sure, and could afford but a single result. I reasoned, for example, thus: When I drew the *scarabæus*, there was no skull apparent upon the parchment. When I had completed the drawing I gave it to you, and observed you narrowly until you returned it. *You*, therefore, did not design the skull, and no one else was present to do it. Then it was not done by human agency. And nevertheless it was done.

"At this stage of my reflections I endeavored to remember, and *did* remember, with entire distinctness, every incident which occurred about the period in question. The weather was chilly (oh rare and happy accident!), and a fire was blazing upon the hearth. I was heated with exercise and sat near the table. You, however, had drawn a chair close to the chimney. Just as I placed the parchment in your hand, and as you were in the act of inspecting it, Wolf, the Newfoundland, entered, and leaped upon your shoulders. With your left hand you caressed him and kept him off, while your right, holding the parchment, was permitted to fall listlessly between your knees, and in close proximity to the fire. At one moment I thought the blaze had caught it, and was about to caution you, but, before I could speak, you had withdrawn it, and were engaged in its examination. When I considered all these particulars, I doubted not for a moment that heat had been the agent in bringing to light, upon the parchment, the skull which I saw designed upon it. You are well aware that chemical preparations exist, and have existed time out of mind, by means of which it is possible to write upon either paper or vellum, so that the characters shall become visible only when subjected to the action of fire. Zaffre, digested in *aqua regia*, and diluted with four times its weight of water, is sometimes employed; a green tint results. The regulus of cobalt, dissolved in spirit of niter, gives a red. These colours disappear at longer or shorter intervals after the material written upon cools, but again become apparent upon the re-application of heat.

"I now scrutinized the death's-head with care. Its outer edges—the edges of the drawing nearest the edge of the vellum—were far more distinct than the others. It was clear that the action of the caloric had been imperfect or unequal. I immediately kindled a fire, and subjected every portion of the parchment to a glowing heat. At first, the only effect was the strengthening of the faint lines in the skull; but, upon persevering in the experiment, there became visible, at the corner of the slip, diagonally opposite to the spot in which the death's-head was delineated, the figure of what I at first supposed to be a goat. A closer scrutiny, however, satisfied me that it was intended for a kid."

"Ha! ha!" said I, "to be sure I have no right to laugh at you—a million and a half of money is too serious a matter for mirth—but you are not about to establish a third link in your chain—you will not find any especial connection between your pirates and a goat—pirates, you know, have nothing to do with goats; they appertain to the farming interest."

"But I have just said that the figure was *not* that of a goat."

"Well, a kid then—pretty much the same thing."

"Pretty much, but not altogether," said Legrand. "You may have heard of one *Captain* Kidd. I at once looked upon the figure of the animal as a kind of punning or hieroglyphical signature. I say signature; because its position upon the vellum suggested this idea. The death's-head at the corner diagonally opposite, had, in the same manner, the air of a stamp, or seal. But I was sorely put out by the absence of all else—of the body to my imagined instrument—of the text for my context."

"I presume you expected to find a letter between the stamp and the signature."

"Something of that kind. The fact is, I felt irresistibly impressed with a presentiment of some vast good fortune impending. I can scarcely say why. Perhaps, after all, it was rather a desire than an actual belief;—but do you know that Jupiter's silly words, about the bug being of solid gold, had a remarkable effect upon my fancy? And then the series of accidents and coincidences—these were so *very* extraordinary. Do you observe how mere an accident it was that these events should have occurred upon the sole day of all the year in which it has been, or may be, sufficiently cool for fire, and that without the fire, or without the intervention of the dog at the precise moment in which he appeared, I should never have become aware of the death's-head, and so never the possessor of the treasure?"

"But proceed—I am all impatience."

"Well; you have heard, of course, the many stories current—the thousand vague rumors afloat about money buried, somewhere upon the Atlantic coast, by Kidd and his associates. These rumors must have had some foundation in fact. And that the rumors have existed so long and so continuous, could have resulted, it appeared to me, only from the circumstance of the buried treasure still *remaining* entombed. Had Kidd concealed his plunder for a time, and afterwards reclaimed it, the rumors would scarcely have reached us in their present unvarying form. You will observe that the stories told are all about money-seekers, not about money-finders. Had the pirate recovered his money, there the affair would have dropped. It seemed to me that some accident—say the loss of a memorandum indicating its locality—had deprived him of the means of recovering it, and that this accident had become known to his followers, who otherwise might never have heard that treasure had been concealed at all, and who, busying themselves in vain, because unguided attempts, to regain it, had given first birth, and then universal currency, to the reports which are now so common. Have you ever heard of any important treasure being unearthed along the coast?"

"Never."

"But that Kidd's accumulations were immense, is well known. I took it for granted, therefore, that the earth still held them; and you will scarcely be surprised when I tell you that I felt a hope, nearly amounting to certainty, that the parchment so strangely found, involved a lost record of the place of deposit."

"But how did you proceed?"

"I held the vellum again to the fire, after increasing the heat; but nothing appeared. I now thought it possible that the coating of dirt might have something to do with the failure; so I carefully rinsed the parchment by pouring warm water over it, and, having done this, I placed it in a tin pan, with the skull downwards, and put the pan upon a furnace of lighted charcoal. In a few minutes, the pan having become thoroughly heated, I removed the slip, and, to my inexpressible joy, found it spotted, in several places, with what appeared to be figures arranged in lines. Again I placed it in the pan, and suffered it to remain another minute. Upon taking it off, the whole was just as you see it now."

Here Legrand, having re-heated the parchment, submitted it to my inspection. The following characters were rudely traced, in a red tint, between the death's-head and the goat:

53‡‡†305))6*;4826)4‡.)4‡);806*;48†8¶60))85;1‡(;:‡
8†83(88)5†;46(;88*96*?;8)*‡(;485);5*†2:*‡(;4956*
2(5*—4)8¶8*;4069285);)6†8)4‡‡;1(‡9;48081;8:8‡1;4
8†85;4)485†528806*81(‡9;48;(88;4(‡?34;48)4‡;161;:
188;‡?;

"But," said I, returning him the slip, "I am as much in the dark as ever. Were all the jewels of Golconda awaiting me upon my solution of this enigma, I am quite sure that I should be unable to earn them."

"And yet," said Legrand, "the solution is by no means so difficult as you might be lead to imagine from the first hasty inspection of the characters. These characters, as any one might readily guess, form a cipher—that is to say, they convey a meaning; but then, from what is known of Kidd, I could not suppose him capable of constructing any of the more abstruse cryptographs. I made up my mind, at once, that this was of a simple species—such, however, as would appear, to the crude intellect of the sailor, absolutely insoluble without the key."

"And you really solved it?"

"Readily; I have solved others of an abstruseness ten thousand times greater. Circumstances, and a certain bias of mind, have led me to take interest in such riddles, and it may well be doubted whether human ingenuity can construct an enigma of the kind which human ingenuity may not, by proper application, resolve. In fact, having once established connected and legible characters, I scarcely gave a thought to the mere difficulty of developing their import.

"In the present case—indeed in all cases of secret writing—the first question regards the *language* of the cipher; for the principles of solution, so far, especially, as the more simple ciphers are concerned, depend upon, and are varied by, the genius of the particular idiom. In general, there is no alternative but experiment (directed by probabilities) of every tongue known to him who attempts the solution, until the true one be attained. But, with the cipher now before us, all difficulty was removed by the signature. The pun upon the word 'Kidd' is appreciable in no other language than the English. But for this consideration I should have begun my attempts with the Spanish and French, as the tongues in which a secret of this kind would most naturally have been written by a pirate of the Spanish main. As it was, I assumed the cryptograph to be English.

"You observe there are no divisions between the words. Had there been divisions, the task would have been comparatively easy. In such case I should have commenced with a collation and analysis of the shorter words, and, had a word of a single letter occurred, as is most likely, (*a* or *I*, for example,) I should have considered the solution as assured. But, there being no division, my first step was to ascertain the predominant letters, as well as the least frequent. Counting all, I constructed a table, thus:

Of the character 8	there are	33.
;	"	26.
4	"	19.
‡)	"	16.
*	"	13.
5	"	12.
6	"	11.
† 1	"	8.
0	"	6.
9 2	"	5.
:3	"	4.
?	"	3.
¶	"	2.
—.	"	1.

"Now, in English, the letter which most frequently occurs is *e*. Afterwards, succession runs thus: *a o i d h n r s t u y c f g l m w b k p q x z*. *E* predominates so remarkably that an individual sentence of any length is rarely seen, in which it is not the prevailing character.

"Here, then, we leave, in the very beginning, the groundwork for something more than a mere guess. The general use which may be made of the table is obvious—but, in this particular cipher, we shall only very partially require its aid. As our predominant character is 8, we will commence by assuming it as the *e* of the natural alphabet. To verify the supposition, let us observe if the 8 be seen often in couples—for *e* is doubled with great frequency in English—in such words, for example, as 'meet,' 'fleet,' 'speed,' 'seen,' 'been,' 'agree,' &c. In the present instance we see it doubled no less than five times, although the cryptograph is brief.

"Let us assume 8, then, as *e*. Now, of all *words* in the language, 'the' is most usual; let us see, therefore, whether there are not repetitions of any three characters, in the same order of collocation, the last of them being 8. If we discover repetitions of such letters, so arranged, they will most probably represent the word 'the.' Upon inspection, we find no less than seven such arrangements, the characters being ;48. We may, therefore, assume that ; represents *t*, 4 represents *h*, and 8 represents *e*—the last being now well confirmed. Thus a great step has been taken.

"But, having established a single word, we are enabled to establish a vastly important point; that is to say, several commencements and terminations of other words. Let us refer, for example, to the last instance but one, in which the combination ;48 occurs—not far from the end of the cipher. We know that the ; immediately ensuing is the commencement of a word, and, of the six characters succeeding this 'the,' we are cognizant of no less than five. Let us set these characters down, thus, by the letters we know them to represent, leaving a space for the unknown—

t eeth.

"Here we are enabled, at once, to discard the '*th*,' as forming no portion of the word commencing with the first *t*; since, by experiment of the entire alphabet for a letter adapted to the vacancy, we perceive that no word can be formed of which this *th* can be a part. We are thus narrowed into

t ee,

and, going through the alphabet, if necessary, as before, we arrive at the word 'tree,' as the sole possible reading. We thus gain another letter, *r*, represented by (, with the words 'the tree' in juxtaposition.

"Looking beyond these words, for a short distance, we again see the combination ;48, and employ it by way of *termination* to what immediately precedes. We have thus this arrangement:

the tree ;4(‡?34 the,

or, substituting the natural letters, where known, it reads thus:

the tree thr‡?3h the.

"Now, if, in place of the unknown characters, we leave blank spaces, or substitute dots, we read thus:

the tree thr . . . h the,

when the word '*through*' makes itself evident at once. But this discovery gives us three new letters, *o*, *u*, and *g*, represented by ‡, ? and 3.

"Looking now, narrowly, through the cipher for combinations of known characters, we find, not very far from the beginning, this arrangement,

83(88, or egree,

which, plainly, is the conclusion of the word 'degree,' and gives us another letter, *d*, represented by †.

"Four letters beyond the word 'degree,' we perceive the combination

;46(;88.

"Translating the known characters, and representing the unknown by dots, as before, we read thus:

th. rtee.

an arrangement immediately suggestive of the word 'thirteen,' and again furnishing us with two new characters, *i* and *n*, represented by 6 and *.

"Referring, now, to the beginning of the cryptograph, we find the combination,

53‡‡†.

"Translating, as before, we obtain

.good,

which assures us that the first letter is *A*, and that the first two words are 'A good.'

"To avoid confusion, it is now time that we arrange our key, as far as discovered, in a tabular form, to avoid confusion. It will stand thus:

5	represents	a
†	"	d
8	"	e
3	"	g
4	"	h
6	"	i
*	"	n
‡	"	o
(	"	r
;	"	t

"We have, therefore, no less than ten of the most important letters represented, and it will be unnecessary to proceed with the details of the solution. I have said enough to convince you that ciphers of this nature are readily soluble, and to give you some insight into the *rationale* of their development. But be assured that the specimen before us appertains to the very simplest species of cryptograph. It now only remains to give you the full translation of the characters upon the parchment, as unriddled. Here it is:

"'*A good glass in the bishop's hostel in the devil's seat forty-one degrees and thirteen minutes northeast and by north main branch seventh limb east side shoot from the left eye of the death's-head a bee line from the tree through the shot fifty feet out.*'"

"But," said I, "the enigma seems still in as bad a condition as ever. How is it possible to extort a meaning from all this jargon about 'devil's seats,' 'death's heads,' and 'bishop's hotels?'"

"I confess," replied Legrand, "that the matter still wears a serious aspect, when regarded with a casual glance. My first endeavor was to divide the sentence into the natural division intended by the cryptographist."

"You mean, to punctuate it?"

"Something of that kind."

"But how was it possible to effect this?"

"I reflected that it had been a *point* with the writer to run his words together without division, so as to increase the difficulty of solution. Now, a not over-acute man, in pursuing such an object would be nearly certain to overdo the matter. When, in the course of his composition, he arrived at a break in his subject which would naturally require a pause, or a point, he would be exceedingly apt to run his characters, at this place, more than usually close together. If you will observe the MS., in the present instance, you will easily detect five such cases of unusual crowding. Acting upon this hint, I made the division thus:

"'*A good glass in the Bishop's hostel in the Devil's seat—forty-one degrees and thirteen minutes—northeast and by north—main branch seventh limb east side—shoot from the left eye of the death's-head—a bee-line from the tree through the shot fifty feet out.*'"

"Even this division," said I, "leaves me still in the dark."

"It left me also in the dark," replied Legrand, "for a few days; during which I made diligent inquiry, in the neighborhood of Sullivan's Island, for any building which went by the name of the 'Bishop's Hotel;' for, of course, I dropped the obsolete word 'hostel.' Gaining no information on the subject, I was on the point of extending my sphere of search, and proceeding in a more systematic manner, when, one morning, it entered into my head, quite suddenly, that this 'Bishop's Hostel' might have some reference to an old family, of the name of Bessop, which, time out of mind, had held possession of an ancient manor-house, about four miles to the northward of the Island. I accordingly went over to the plantation, and re-instituted my inquiries among the older negroes of the place. At length one of the most aged of the women said that she had heard of such a place as *Bessop's Castle*, and thought that she could guide me to it, but that it was not a castle nor a tavern, but a high rock.

"I offered to pay her well for her trouble, and, after some demur, she consented to accompany me to the spot. We found it without much difficulty, when, dismissing her, I proceeded to examine the place. The 'castle' consisted of an irregular assemblage of cliffs and rocks—one of the latter being quite remarkable for its height as well as for its insulated and artificial appearance I clambered to its apex, and then felt much at a loss as to what should be next done.

"While I was busied in reflection, my eyes fell upon a narrow ledge in the eastern face of the rock, perhaps a yard below the summit upon which I stood. This ledge projected about eighteen inches, and was not more than a foot wide, while a niche in the cliff just above it, gave it a rude resemblance to one of the hollow-backed chairs used by our ancestors. I made no doubt that here was the 'devil's seat' alluded to in the MS., and now I seemed to grasp the full secret of the riddle.

"The 'good glass,' I knew, could have reference to nothing but a telescope; for the word 'glass' is rarely employed in any other sense by seamen. Now here, I at once saw, was a telescope to be used, and a definite point of view, *admitting no variation*, from which to use it. Nor did I hesitate to believe that the phrases, 'forty-one degrees and thirteen minutes,' and 'northeast and by north,' were intended as directions for the levelling of the glass. Greatly excited by these discoveries, I hurried home, procured a telescope, and returned to the rock.

"I let myself down to the ledge, and found that it was impossible to retain a seat upon it except in one particular position. This fact confirmed my preconceived idea. I proceeded to use the glass. Of course, the 'forty-one degrees and thirteen minutes' could allude to nothing but elevation above the visible horizon, since the horizontal direction was clearly indicated by the words, 'northeast and by north.' This latter direction I at once established by means of a pocket-compass; then, pointing the glass as nearly at an angle of forty-one degrees of elevation as I could do it by guess, I moved it cautiously up or down, until my attention was arrested by a circular rift or opening in the foliage of a large tree that overtopped its fellows in the distance. In the center of this rift I perceived a white spot, but could not, at first, distinguish what it was. Adjusting the focus of the telescope, I again looked, and now made it out to be a human skull.

"On this discovery I was so sanguine as to consider the enigma solved; for the phrase 'main branch, seventh limb, east side,' could refer only to the position of the skull upon the tree, while 'shoot from the left eye of the death's head' admitted, also, of but one interpretation, in regard to a search for buried treasure. I perceived that the design was to drop a bullet from the left eye of the skull, and that a bee-line, or, in other words, a straight line, drawn from the nearest point of the trunk through 'the shot,' (or the spot where the bullet fell,) and thence extended to a distance of fifty feet, would indicate a definite point—and beneath this point I thought it at least *possible* that a deposit of value lay concealed."

"All this," I said, "is exceedingly clear, and, although ingenious, still simple and explicit. When you left the Bishop's Hotel, what then?"

"Why, having carefully taken the bearings of the tree, I turned homewards. The instant that I left 'the devil's seat,' however, the circular rift vanished; nor could I get a glimpse of it afterwards, turn as I would. What seems to me the chief ingenuity in this whole business, is the fact (for repeated experiment has convinced me it is a fact) that the circular opening in question is visible from no other attainable point of view than that afforded by the narrow ledge upon the face of the rock.

"In this expedition to the 'Bishop's Hotel' I had been attended by Jupiter, who had, no doubt, observed, for some weeks past, the abstraction of my demeanor, and took especial care not to leave me alone. But, on the next day, getting up very early, I contrived to give him the slip, and went into the hills in search of the tree. After much toil I found it. When I came home at night my valet proposed to give me a flogging. With the rest of the adventure I believe you are as well acquainted as myself."

"I suppose," said I, "you missed the spot, in the first attempt at digging, through Jupiter's stupidity in letting the bug fall through the right instead of through the left eye of the skull."

"Precisely. This mistake made a difference of about two inches and a half in the 'shot'—that is to say, in the position of the peg nearest the tree; and had the treasure been *beneath* the 'shot,' the error would have been of little moment; but 'the shot,' together with the nearest point of the tree, were merely two points for the establishment of a line of direction; of course the error, however trivial in the beginning, increased as we proceeded with the line, and by the time we had gone fifty feet, threw us quite off the scent. But for my deep-seated impressions that treasure was here somewhere actually buried, we might have had all our labor in vain."

"But your grandiloquence, and your conduct in swinging the beetle—how excessively odd! I was sure you were mad. And why did you insist upon letting fall the bug, instead of a bullet, from the skull?"

"Why, to be frank, I felt somewhat annoyed by your evident suspicions touching my sanity, and so resolved to punish you quietly, in my own way, by a little bit of sober mystification. For this reason I swung the beetle,

and for this reason I let it fall it from the tree. An observation of yours about its great weight suggested the latter idea."

"Yes, I perceive; and now there is only one point which puzzles me. What are we to make of the skeletons found in the hole?"

"That is a question I am no more able to answer than yourself. There seems, however, only one plausible way of accounting for them—and yet it is dreadful to believe in such atrocity as my suggestion would imply. It is clear that Kidd—if Kidd indeed secreted this treasure, which I doubt not—it is clear that he must have had assistance in the labor. But this labor concluded, he may have thought it expedient to remove all participants in his secret. Perhaps a couple of blows with a mattock were sufficient, while his coadjutors were busy in the pit; perhaps it required a dozen—who shall tell?"

The Black Cat

[First published in *The Sunday Evening Post* on August 19, 1843, this horror story narrated by an unreliable narrator is one of Poe's darkest tales.]

For the most wild, yet most homely narrative which I am about to pen, I neither expect nor solicit belief. Mad indeed would I be to expect it, in a case where my very senses reject their own evidence. Yet, mad am I not—and very surely do I not dream. But tomorrow I die, and today I would unburthen my soul. My immediate purpose is to place before the world, plainly, succinctly, and without comment, a series of mere household events. In their consequences, these events have terrified—have tortured—have destroyed me. Yet I will not attempt to expound them. To me, they have presented little but Horror—to many they will seem less terrible than *baroques*. Hereafter, perhaps, some intellect may be found which will reduce my phantasm to the common-place—some intellect more calm, more logical, and far less excitable than my own, which will perceive, in the circumstances I detail with awe, nothing more than an ordinary succession of very natural causes and effects.

From my infancy I was noted for the docility and humanity of my disposition. My tenderness of heart was even so conspicuous as to make me the jest of my companions. I was especially fond of animals, and was indulged by my parents with a great variety of pets. With these I spent most of my time, and never was so happy as when feeding and caressing them. This peculiarity of character grew with my growth, and in my manhood, I derived from it one of my principal sources of pleasure. To those who have cherished an affection for a faithful and sagacious dog, I need hardly be at the trouble of explaining the nature or the intensity of the gratification thus derivable. There is something in the unselfish and self-sacrificing love of a brute, which goes directly to the heart of him who has had frequent occasion to test the paltry friendship and gossamer fidelity of mere *Man*.

I married early, and was happy to find in my wife a disposition not uncongenial with my own. Observing my partiality for domestic pets, she lost no opportunity of procuring those of the most agreeable kind. We had birds, gold-fish, a fine dog, rabbits, a small monkey, and *a cat*.

This latter was a remarkably large and beautiful animal, entirely black, and sagacious to an astonishing degree. In speaking of his intelligence, my wife, who at heart was not a little tinctured with superstition, made frequent allusion to the ancient popular notion, which regarded all black cats as witches in disguise. Not that she was ever *serious* upon this point—and I mention the matter at all for no better reason than that it happens, just now, to be remembered.

Pluto—this was the cat's name—was my favorite pet and playmate. I alone fed him, and he attended me wherever I went about the house. It was even with difficulty that I could prevent him from following me through the streets.

Our friendship lasted, in this manner, for several years, during which my general temperament and character—through the instrumentality of the Fiend Intemperance—had (I blush to confess it) experienced a radical alteration for the worse. I grew, day by day, more moody, more irritable, more regardless of the feelings of others. I suffered myself to use intemperate language to my wife. At length, I even offered her personal violence. My pets, of course, were made to feel the change in my disposition. I not only neglected, but ill-used them. For Pluto, however, I still retained sufficient regard to restrain me from maltreating him, as I made no scruple of maltreating the rabbits, the monkey, or even the dog, when by accident, or through affection, they came in my way. But my disease grew upon me—for what disease is like Alcohol!—and at length even Pluto, who was now becoming old, and consequently somewhat peevish—even Pluto began to experience the effects of my ill temper.

One night, returning home, much intoxicated, from one of my haunts about town, I fancied that the cat avoided my presence. I seized him; when, in his fright at my violence, he inflicted a slight wound upon my hand with his teeth. The fury of a demon instantly possessed me. I knew myself no longer. My original soul seemed, at once, to take its flight from my body and a more than fiendish malevolence, gin-nurtured, thrilled every fibre of my frame. I took from my waistcoat-pocket a pen-knife, opened it, grasped the poor beast by the throat, and deliberately cut one of its eyes from the socket! I blush, I burn, I shudder, while I pen the damnable atrocity.

When reason returned with the morning—when I had slept off the fumes of the night's debauch—I experienced a sentiment half of horror, half of remorse, for the crime of which I had been guilty; but it was, at best, a feeble and equivocal feeling, and the soul remained untouched. I again plunged into excess, and soon drowned in wine all memory of the deed.

In the meantime the cat slowly recovered. The socket of the lost eye presented, it is true, a frightful appearance, but he no longer appeared to suffer any pain. He went about the house as usual, but, as might be expected, fled in extreme terror at my approach. I had so much of my old heart left, as to be at first grieved by this evident dislike on the part of a creature which had once so loved me. But this feeling soon gave place to irritation. And then came, as if to my final and irrevocable overthrow, the spirit of PERVERSENESS. Of this spirit philosophy takes no account. Yet I am not more sure that my soul lives, than I am that perverseness is one of the primitive impulses of the human heart—one of the indivisible primary faculties, or sentiments, which give direction to the character of Man. Who has not, a hundred times, found himself committing a vile or a silly action, for no other reason than because he knows he should *not*? Have we not a perpetual inclination, in the teeth of our best judgment, to violate that which is *Law*, merely because we understand it to be such? This spirit of perverseness, I say, came to my final overthrow. It was this unfathomable longing of the soul *to vex itself*—to offer violence to its own nature—to do wrong for the wrong's sake only—that urged me to continue and finally to consummate the injury I had inflicted upon the unoffending brute. One morning, in cool blood, I slipped a noose about its neck and hung it to the limb of a tree;—hung it with the tears streaming from my eyes, and with the bitterest remorse at my heart;—hung it *because* I knew that it had loved me, and *because* I felt it had given me no reason of offence;—hung it *because* I knew that in so doing I was committing a sin—a deadly sin that would so jeopardize my immortal soul as to place it—if such a thing wore possible—even beyond the reach of the infinite mercy of the Most Merciful and Most Terrible God.

On the night of the day on which this cruel deed was done, I was aroused from sleep by the cry of fire. The curtains of my bed were in flames. The whole house was blazing. It was with great difficulty that my wife, a servant, and myself, made our escape from the conflagration. The destruction was complete. My entire worldly wealth was swallowed up, and I resigned myself thenceforward to despair.

I am above the weakness of seeking to establish a sequence of cause and effect, between the disaster and the atrocity. But I am detailing a chain of facts—and wish not to leave even a possible link imperfect. On the day succeeding the fire, I visited the ruins. The walls, with one exception, had fallen in. This exception was found in a compartment wall, not very thick, which stood about the middle of the house, and against which had rested the head of my bed. The plastering had here, in great measure, resisted the action of the fire—a fact which I attributed to its having been recently spread. About this wall a dense crowd were collected, and many persons seemed to be examining a particular portion of it with very minute and eager attention. The words "strange!" "singular!" and other similar expressions, excited my curiosity. I approached and saw, as if graven in *bas relief* upon the white surface, the figure of a gigantic *cat*. The impression was given with an accuracy truly marvelous. There was a rope about the animal's neck.

When I first beheld this apparition—for I could scarcely regard it as less—my wonder and my terror were extreme. But at length reflection came to my aid. The cat, I remembered, had been hung in a garden adjacent to the house. Upon the alarm of fire, this garden had been immediately filled by the crowd—by some one of whom the animal must have been cut from the tree and thrown, through an open window, into my chamber. This had probably been done with the view of arousing me from sleep. The falling of other walls had compressed the victim of my cruelty into the substance of the freshly-spread plaster; the lime of which, with the flames, and the *ammonia* from the carcass, had then accomplished the portraiture as I saw it.

Although I thus readily accounted to my reason, if not altogether to my conscience, for the startling fact just detailed, it did not the less fail to make a deep impression upon my fancy. For months I could not rid myself of the phantasm of the cat; and, during this period, there came back into my spirit a half-sentiment that seemed, but was not, remorse. I went so far as to regret the loss of the animal, and to look about me, among the vile haunts which I now habitually frequented, for another pet of the same species, and of somewhat similar appearance, with which to supply its place.

One night as I sat, half stupefied, in a den of more than infamy, my attention was suddenly drawn to some black object, reposing upon the head of one of the immense hogsheads of Gin, or of Rum, which constituted the chief furniture of the apartment. I had been looking steadily at the top of this hogshead for some minutes, and what now caused me surprise was the fact that I had not sooner perceived the object thereupon. I approached it, and touched it with my hand. It was a black cat—a very large one—fully as large as Pluto, and closely resembling him in every respect but one. Pluto had not a white hair upon any portion of his body; but this cat had a large, although indefinite splotch of white, covering nearly the whole region of the breast.

Upon my touching him, he immediately arose, purred loudly, rubbed against my hand, and appeared delighted with my notice. This, then, was the very creature of which I was in search. I at once offered to purchase it of the landlord; but this person made no claim to it—knew nothing of it—had never seen it before.

I continued my caresses, and, when I prepared to go home, the animal evinced a disposition to accompany me. I permitted it to do so; occasionally stooping and patting it as I proceeded. When it reached the house it domesticated itself at once, and became immediately a great favorite with my wife.

For my own part, I soon found a dislike to it arising within me. This was just the reverse of what I had anticipated; but—I know not how or why it was—its evident fondness for myself rather disgusted and annoyed. By slow degrees, these feelings of disgust and annoyance rose into the bitterness of hatred. I avoided the creature; a certain sense of shame, and the remembrance of my former deed of cruelty, preventing me from physically abusing it. I did not, for some weeks, strike, or otherwise violently ill use it; but gradually—very gradually—I came to look upon it with unutterable loathing, and to flee silently from its odious presence, as from the breath of a pestilence.

What added, no doubt, to my hatred of the beast, was the discovery, on the morning after I brought it home, that, like Pluto, it also had been deprived of one of its eyes. This circumstance, however, only endeared it to my wife, who, as I have already said, possessed, in a high degree, that humanity of feeling which had once been my distinguishing trait, and the source of many of my simplest and purest pleasures.

With my aversion to this cat, however, its partiality for myself seemed to increase. It followed my footsteps with a pertinacity which it would be difficult to make the reader comprehend. Whenever I sat, it would crouch beneath my chair, or spring upon my knees, covering me with its loathsome caresses. If I arose to walk it would get between my feet and thus nearly throw me down, or, fastening its long and sharp claws in my dress, clamber, in this manner, to my breast. At such times, although I longed to destroy it with a blow, I was yet withheld from so doing, partly by a memory of my former crime, but chiefly—let me confess it at once—by absolute *dread* of the beast.

This dread was not exactly a dread of physical evil—and yet I should be at a loss how otherwise to define it. I am almost ashamed to own—yes, even in this felon's cell, I am almost ashamed to own—that the terror and horror with which the animal inspired me, had been heightened by one of the merest chimaeras it would be possible to conceive. My wife had called my attention, more than once, to the character of the mark of white hair, of which I have spoken, and which constituted the sole visible difference between the strange beast and the one I had destroyed. The reader will remember that this mark, although large, had been originally very indefinite; but, by slow degrees—degrees nearly imperceptible, and which for a long time my Reason struggled to reject as fanciful—it had, at length, assumed a rigorous distinctness of outline. It was now the representation of an object that I shudder to name—and for this, above all, I loathed, and dreaded, and would have rid myself of the monster *had I dared*—it was now, I say, the image of a hideous—of a ghastly thing—of the GALLOWS!—oh, mournful and terrible engine of Horror and of Crime—of Agony and of Death!

And now was I indeed wretched beyond the wretchedness of mere Humanity. And *a brute beast* —whose fellow I had contemptuously destroyed—*a brute beast* to work out for *me*—for me a man, fashioned in the image of the High God—so much of insufferable wo! Alas! neither by day nor by night knew I the blessing of Rest any more! During the former the creature left me no moment alone; and, in the latter, I started, hourly, from dreams of unutterable fear, to find the hot breath of *the thing* upon my face, and its vast weight—an incarnate Nightmare that I had no power to shake off—incumbent eternally upon my *heart!*

Beneath the pressure of torments such as these, the feeble remnant of the good within me succumbed. Evil thoughts became my sole intimates—the darkest and most evil of thoughts. The moodiness of my usual temper increased to hatred of all things and of all mankind; while, from the sudden, frequent, and ungovernable outbursts of a fury to which I now blindly abandoned myself, my uncomplaining wife, alas! was the most usual and the most patient of sufferers.

One day she accompanied me, upon some household errand, into the cellar of the old building which our poverty compelled us to inhabit. The cat followed me down the steep stairs, and, nearly throwing me headlong, exasperated me to madness. Uplifting an axe, and forgetting, in my wrath, the childish dread which had hitherto stayed my hand, I aimed a blow at the animal which, of course, would have proved instantly fatal had it descended as I wished. But this blow was arrested by the hand of my wife. Goaded, by the interference, into a rage more than demoniacal, I withdrew my arm from her grasp and buried the axe in her brain. She fell dead upon the spot, without a groan.

This hideous murder accomplished, I set myself forthwith, and with entire deliberation, to the task of concealing the body. I knew that I could not remove it from the house, either by day or by night, without the risk of being observed by the neighbors. Many projects entered my mind. At one period I thought of cutting the corpse into minute fragments, and destroying them by fire. At another, I resolved to dig a grave for it in the floor of the cellar. Again, I deliberated about casting it in the well in the yard—about packing it in a box, as if merchandize, with the usual arrangements, and so getting a porter to take it from the house. Finally I hit upon what I considered a far better expedient than either of these. I determined to wall it up in the cellar—as the monks of the middle ages are recorded to have walled up their victims.

For a purpose such as this the cellar was well adapted. Its walls were loosely constructed, and had lately been plastered throughout with a rough plaster, which the dampness of the atmosphere had prevented from hardening. Moreover, in one of the walls was a projection, caused by a false chimney, or fireplace, that had been filled up, and made to resemble the red of the cellar. I made no doubt that I could readily displace the bricks at this point, insert the corpse, and wall the whole up as before, so that no eye could detect anything suspicious.

And in this calculation I was not deceived. By means of a crow-bar I easily dislodged the bricks, and, having carefully deposited the body against the inner wall, I propped it in that position, while, with little trouble, I re-laid the whole structure as it originally stood. Having procured mortar, sand, and hair, with every possible precaution, I prepared a plaster which could not be distinguished from the old, and with this I very carefully went over the new brickwork. When I had finished, I felt satisfied that all was right. The wall did not present the slightest appearance of having been disturbed. The rubbish on the floor was picked up with the minutest care. I looked around triumphantly, and said to myself—"Here at least, then, my labor has not been in vain."

My next step was to look for the beast which had been the cause of so much wretchedness; for I had, at length, firmly resolved to put it to death. Had I been able to meet with it, at the moment, there could have been no doubt of its fate; but it appeared that the crafty animal had been alarmed at the violence of my previous anger, and forebore to present itself in my present mood. It is impossible to describe, or to imagine, the deep, the blissful sense of relief which the absence of the detested creature occasioned in my bosom. It did not make its appearance during the night—and thus for one night at least, since its introduction into the house, I soundly and tranquilly slept; aye, *slept* even with the burden of murder upon my soul!

The second and the third day passed, and still my tormentor came not. Once again I breathed as a freeman. The monster, in terror, had fled the premises forever! I should behold it no more! My happiness was supreme! The guilt of my dark deed disturbed me but little. Some few inquiries had been made, but these had been readily answered. Even a search had been instituted—but of course nothing was to be discovered. I looked upon my future felicity as secured.

Upon the fourth day of the assassination, a party of the police came, very unexpectedly, into the house, and proceeded again to make rigorous investigation of the premises. Secure, however, in the inscrutability of my place of concealment, I felt no embarrassment whatever. The officers bade me accompany them in their search. They left no nook or corner unexplored. At length, for the third or fourth time, they descended into the cellar. I quivered not in a muscle. My heart beat calmly as that of one who slumbers in innocence. I walked the cellar from end to end. I folded my arms upon my bosom, and roamed easily to and fro. The police were thoroughly satisfied and prepared to depart. The glee at my heart was too strong to be restrained. I burned to say if but one word, by way of triumph, and to render doubly sure their assurance of my guiltlessness.

"Gentlemen," I said at last, as the party ascended the steps, "I delight to have allayed your suspicions. I wish you all health, and a little more courtesy. By the bye, gentlemen, this—this is a very well-constructed house." (In the rabid desire to say something easily, I scarcely knew what I uttered at all.)—"I may say an *excellently* well-constructed house. These walls—are you going, gentlemen?—these walls are solidly put together;" and here, through the mere phrenzy of bravado, I rapped heavily, with a cane which I held in my hand, upon that very portion of the brick-work behind which stood the corpse of the wife of my bosom.

But may God shield and deliver me from the fangs of the Arch-Fiend! No sooner had the reverberation of my blows sunk into silence, than I was answered by a voice from within the tomb!—by a cry, at first muffled and broken, like the sobbing of a child, and then quickly swelling into one long, loud, and continuous scream, utterly anomalous and inhuman—a howl—a wailing shriek, half of horror and half of triumph, such as might have arisen only out of hell, conjointly from the throats of the dammed in their agony and of the demons that exult in the damnation.

Of my own thoughts it is folly to speak. Swooning, I staggered to the opposite wall. For one instant the party upon the stairs remained motionless, through extremity of terror and of awe. In the next, a dozen stout arms were toiling at the wall. It fell bodily. The corpse, already greatly decayed and clotted with gore, stood erect before the eyes of the spectators. Upon its head, with red extended mouth and solitary eye of fire, sat the hideous beast whose craft had seduced me into murder, and whose informing voice had consigned me to the hangman. I had walled the monster up within the tomb!

The Premature Burial

[Written in the nineteenth century when the fear of being buried alive was rooted in the Western culture, this horror short story was first published in the *Philadelphia Dollar Newspaper* in 1844.]

There are certain themes of which the interest is all-absorbing, but which are too entirely horrible for the purposes of legitimate fiction. These the mere romanticist must eschew, if he do not wish to offend or to disgust. They are with propriety handled only when the severity and majesty of Truth sanctify and sustain them. We thrill, for example, with the most intense of "pleasurable pain" over the accounts of the Passage of the Beresina, of the Earthquake at Lisbon, of the Plague at London, of the Massacre of St. Bartholomew, or of the stifling of the hundred and twenty-three prisoners in the Black Hole at Calcutta. But, in these accounts, it is the fact—it is the reality—it is the history which excites. As inventions, we should regard them with simple abhorrence.

I have mentioned some few of the more prominent and august calamities on record; but in these it is the extent, not less than the character of the calamity, which so vividly impresses the fancy. I need not remind the reader that, from the long and weird catalogue of human miseries, I might have selected many individual instances more replete with essential suffering than any of these vast generalities of disaster. The true wretchedness, indeed—the ultimate woe—is particular, not diffuse.

That the ghastly extremes of agony are endured by man the unit, and never by man the mass—for this let us thank a merciful God!

To be buried while alive is, beyond question, the most terrific of these extremes which has ever fallen to the lot of mere mortality. That it has frequently, very frequently, so fallen will scarcely be denied by those who think. The boundaries which divide Life from Death are at best shadowy and vague. Who shall say where the one ends, and where the other begins? We know that there are diseases in which occur total cessations of all the apparent functions of vitality, and yet in which these cessations are merely suspensions, properly so called. They are only temporary pauses in the incomprehensible mechanism. A certain period elapses, and some unseen mysterious principle again sets in motion the magic pinions and the wizard wheels. The silver cord was not for ever loosed, nor the golden bowl irreparably broken. But where, meantime, was the soul?

Apart, however, from the inevitable conclusion, *a priori* that such causes must produce such effects; that the well-known occurrence of such cases of suspended animation must naturally give rise, now and then, to premature interments—apart from this consideration, we have the direct testimony of medical and ordinary experience to prove that a vast number of such interments have actually taken place. I might refer at once, if necessary to a hundred well-authenticated instances. One of very remarkable character, and of which the circumstances may be fresh in the memory of some of my readers, occurred, not very long ago, in the neighboring city of Baltimore, where it occasioned a painful, intense, and widely-extended excitement. The wife of one of the most respectable citizens—a lawyer of eminence and a member of Congress—was seized with a sudden and unaccountable illness, which completely baffled the skill of her physicians. After much suffering she died, or was supposed to die. No one suspected, indeed, or had reason to suspect, that she was not actually dead. She presented all the ordinary appearances of death. The face assumed the usual pinched and sunken outline. The lips were of the usual marble pallor. The eyes were lusterless. There was no warmth. Pulsation had ceased. For three days the body was preserved unburied, during which it had acquired a stony rigidity. The funeral, in short, was hastened, on account of the rapid advance of what was supposed to be decomposition.

The lady was deposited in her family vault, which, for three subsequent years, was undisturbed. At the expiration of this term it was opened for the reception of a sarcophagus;—but, alas! how fearful a shock awaited the husband, who, personally, threw open the door! As its portals swung outwardly back, some white-appareled object fell rattling within his arms. It was the skeleton of his wife in her yet unmolded shroud.

A careful investigation rendered it evident that she had revived within two days after her entombment; that her struggles within the coffin had caused it to fall from a ledge, or shelf to the floor, where it was so broken as to permit her escape. A lamp which had been accidentally left, full of oil, within the tomb, was found empty; it might have been exhausted, however, by evaporation. On the uppermost of the steps which led down into the dread chamber was a large fragment of the coffin, with which, it seemed, that she had endeavored to arrest attention by striking the iron door. While thus occupied, she probably swooned, or possibly died, through sheer terror; and in falling, her shroud became entangled in some ironwork which projected interiorly. Thus she remained, and thus she rotted, erect.

In the year 1810, a case of living inhumation happened in France, attended with circumstances which go far to warrant the assertion that truth is, indeed, stranger than fiction. The heroine of the story was a Mademoiselle Victorine Lafourcade, a young girl of illustrious family, of wealth, and of great personal beauty. Among her numerous suitors was Julien Bossuet, a poor *littérateur*, or journalist, of Paris. His talents and general amiability had recommended him to the notice of the heiress, by whom he seems to have been truly beloved; but her pride of birth decided her, finally, to reject him, and to wed a Monsieur Renelle, a banker and a diplomatist of some eminence. After marriage, however, this gentleman neglected, and, perhaps, even more positively ill-treated her. Having passed with him some wretched years, she died—at least her condition so closely resembled death as to deceive every one who saw her. She was buried—not in a vault, but in an ordinary grave in the village of her nativity. Filled with despair, and still inflamed by the memory of a profound attachment, the lover journeys from the capital to the remote province in which the village lies, with the romantic purpose of disinterring the corpse, and possessing himself of its luxuriant tresses. He reaches the grave. At midnight he unearths the coffin, opens it, and is in the act of detaching the hair, when he is arrested by the unclosing of the beloved eyes. In fact, the lady had been buried alive. Vitality had not altogether departed, and she was aroused by the caresses of her lover from the lethargy which had been mistaken for death. He bore her frantically to his lodgings in the village. He employed certain powerful restoratives suggested by no little medical learning. In fine, she revived. She recognized her preserver. She remained with him until, by slow degrees, she fully recovered her original health. Her woman's heart was not adamant, and this last lesson of love sufficed to soften it. She bestowed it upon Bossuet. She returned no more to her husband, but, concealing from him her resurrection, fled with her lover to America. Twenty years afterward, the two returned to France, in the persuasion that time had so greatly altered the lady's appearance that her friends would be unable to recognize her. They were mistaken, however, for, at the first meeting, Monsieur Renelle did actually recognize and make claim to his wife. This claim she resisted, and a judicial tribunal sustained her in her resistance, deciding that the peculiar circumstances, with the long lapse of years, had extinguished, not only equitably, but legally, the authority of the husband.

The *Chirurgical Journal* of Leipzig—a periodical of high authority and merit, which some American booksellers would do well to translate and republish, records in a late number a very distressing event of the character in question.

An officer of artillery, a man of gigantic stature and of robust health, being thrown from an unmanageable horse, received a very severe contusion upon the head, which rendered him insensible at once; the skull was slightly fractured, but no immediate danger was apprehended. Trepanning was accomplished successfully. He was bled, and many other of the ordinary means of relief were adopted. Gradually, however, he fell into a more and more hopeless state of stupor, and, finally, it was thought that he died.

The weather was warm, and he was buried with indecent haste in one of the public cemeteries. His funeral took place on Thursday. On the Sunday following, the grounds of the cemetery were, as usual, much thronged with visiters, and about noon an intense excitement was created by the declaration of a peasant that, while sitting upon the grave of the officer, he had distinctly felt a commotion of the earth, as if occasioned by some one struggling beneath. At first little attention was paid to the man's asseveration; but his evident terror, and the dogged obstinacy with which he persisted in his story, had at length their natural effects upon the crowd. Spades were hurriedly procured, and the grave, which was shamefully shallow, was in a few minutes so far thrown open that the head of its occupant appeared. He was then seemingly dead; but he sat nearly erect within his coffin, the lid of which, in his furious struggles, he had partially uplifted.

He was forthwith conveyed to the nearest hospital, and there pronounced to be still living, although in an asphytic condition. After some hours he revived, recognized individuals of his acquaintance, and, in broken sentences spoke of his agonies in the grave.

From what he related, it was clear that he must have been conscious of life for more than an hour, while inhumed, before lapsing into insensibility. The grave was carelessly and loosely filled with an exceedingly porous soil; and thus some air was necessarily admitted. He heard the footsteps of the crowd overhead, and endeavored to make himself heard in turn. It was the tumult within the grounds of the cemetery, he said, which appeared to awaken him from a deep sleep, but no sooner was he awake than he became fully aware of the awful horrors of his position.

This patient, it is recorded, was doing well, and seemed to be in a fair way of ultimate recovery, but fell a victim to the quackeries of medical experiment. The galvanic battery was applied, and he suddenly expired in one of those ecstatic paroxysms which, occasionally, it superinduces.

The mention of the galvanic battery, nevertheless, recalls to my memory a well-known and very extraordinary case in point, where its action proved the means of restoring to animation a young attorney of London, who had been interred for two days. This occurred in 1831, and created, at the time, a very profound sensation wherever it was made the subject of converse.

The patient, Mr. Edward Stapleton, had died, apparently of typhus fever, accompanied with some anomalous symptoms which had excited the curiosity of his medical attendants. Upon his seeming decease, his friends were requested to sanction a *post-mortem* examination, but declined to permit it. As often happens, when such refusals are made, the practitioners resolved to disinter the body and dissect it at leisure, in private. Arrangements were easily effected with some of the numerous corps of body-snatchers, with which London abounds; and, upon the third night after the funeral, the supposed corpse was unearthed from a grave eight feet deep, and deposited in the opening chamber of one of the private hospitals.

An incision of some extent had been actually made in the abdomen, when the fresh and undecayed appearance of the subject suggested an application of the battery. One experiment succeeded another, and the customary effects supervened, with nothing to characterize them in any respect, except, upon one or two occasions, a more than ordinary degree of life-likeness in the convulsive action.

It grew late. The day was about to dawn; and it was thought expedient, at length, to proceed at once to the dissection. A student, however, was especially desirous of testing a theory of his own, and insisted upon applying the battery to one of the pectoral muscles. A rough gash was made, and a wire hastily brought in contact, when the patient, with a hurried but quite unconvulsive movement, arose from the table, stepped into the middle of the floor, gazed about him uneasily for a few seconds, and then—spoke. What he said was unintelligible, but words were uttered; the syllabification was distinct. Having spoken, he fell heavily to the floor.

For some moments all were paralyzed with awe—but the urgency of the case soon restored them their presence of mind. It was seen that Mr. Stapleton was alive, although in a swoon. Upon exhibition of ether he revived and was rapidly restored to health, and to the society of his friends—from whom, however, all knowledge of his resuscitation was withheld, until a relapse was no longer to be apprehended. Their wonder—their rapturous astonishment—may be conceived.

The most thrilling peculiarity of this incident, nevertheless, is involved in what Mr. S. himself asserts. He declares that at no period was he altogether insensible—that, dully and confusedly, he was aware of everything which happened to him, from the moment in which he was pronounced *dead* by his physicians, to that in which he fell swooning to the floor of the hospital. "I am alive," were the uncomprehended words which, upon recognizing the locality of the dissecting-room, he had endeavored, in his extremity, to utter.

It were an easy matter to multiply such histories as these—but I forbear—for, indeed, we have no need of such to establish the fact that premature interments occur. When we reflect how very rarely, from the nature of the case, we have it in our power to detect them, we must admit that they may *frequently* occur without our cognizance. Scarcely, in truth, is a graveyard ever encroached upon, for any purpose, to any great extent, that skeletons are not found in postures which suggest the most fearful of suspicions.

Fearful indeed the suspicion—but more fearful the doom! It may be asserted, without hesitation, that *no* event is so terribly well adapted to inspire the supremeness of bodily and of mental distress, as is burial before death. The unendurable oppression of the lungs—the stifling fumes from the damp earth—the clinging to the death garments—the rigid embrace of the narrow house—the blackness of the absolute Night—the silence like a sea that overwhelms—the unseen but palpable presence of the Conqueror Worm—these things, with the thoughts of the air and grass above, with memory of dear friends who would fly to save us if but informed of our fate, and with consciousness that of this fate they can *never* be informed—that our hopeless portion is that of the really dead—these considerations, I say, carry into the heart, which still palpitates, a degree of appalling and intolerable horror from which the most daring imagination must recoil. We know of nothing so agonizing upon Earth—we can dream of nothing half so hideous in the realms of the nethermost Hell. And thus all narratives upon this topic have an interest profound; an interest, nevertheless, which, through the sacred awe of the topic itself, very properly and very peculiarly depends upon our conviction of the *truth* of the matter narrated. What I have now to tell is of my own actual knowledge—of my own positive and personal experience.

For several years I had been subject to attacks of the singular disorder which physicians have agreed to term catalepsy, in default of a more definitive title. Although both the immediate and the predisposing causes, and even the actual diagnosis, of this disease are still mysterious, its obvious and apparent character is sufficiently well understood. Its variations seem to be chiefly of degree. Sometimes the patient lies, for a day only, or even for a shorter period, in a species of exaggerated lethargy. He is senseless and externally motionless; but the pulsation of the heart is still faintly perceptible; some traces of warmth remain; a slight colour lingers within the center of the cheek; and, upon application of a mirror to the lips, we can detect a torpid, unequal, and vacillating action of the lungs. Then again the duration of the trance is for weeks—even for months; while the closest scrutiny, and the most rigorous medical tests, fail to establish any material distinction between the state of the sufferer and what we conceive of absolute death. Very usually he is saved from premature interment solely by the knowledge of his friends that he has been previously subject to catalepsy, by the consequent suspicion excited, and, above all, by the non-appearance of decay. The advances of the malady are, luckily, gradual. The first manifestations, although marked, are unequivocal. The fits grow successively more and more distinctive, and endure each for a longer term than the preceding. In this lies the principal security from inhumation. The unfortunate whose *first* attack should be of the extreme character which is occasionally seen, would almost inevitably be consigned alive to the tomb.

My own case differed in no important particular from those mentioned in medical books. Sometimes, without any apparent cause, I sank, little by little, into a condition of hemi-syncope, or half swoon; and, in this condition, without pain, without ability to stir, or, strictly speaking, to think, but with a dull lethargic consciousness of life and of the presence of those who surrounded my bed, I remained, until the crisis of the disease restored me, suddenly, to perfect sensation. At other times I was quickly and impetuously smitten. I grew sick, and numb, and chilly, and dizzy, and so fell prostrate at once. Then, for weeks, all was void, and black, and silent, and Nothing became the universe. Total annihilation could be no more. From these latter attacks I awoke, however, with a gradation slow in proportion to the suddenness of the seizure. Just as the day dawns to the friendless and houseless beggar who roams the streets throughout the long desolate winter night—just so tardily—just so wearily—just so cheerily came back the light of the Soul to me.

Apart from the tendency to trance, however, my general health appeared to be good; nor could I perceive that it was at all affected by the one prevalent malady—unless, indeed, an idiosyncrasy in my ordinary *sleep* may be looked upon as superinduced. Upon awaking from slumber, I could never gain, at once, thorough possession of my senses, and always remained, for many minutes, in much bewilderment and perplexity;—

the mental faculties in general, but the memory in especial, being in a condition of absolute abeyance.

In all that I endured there was no physical suffering but of moral distress an infinitude. My fancy grew charnel, I talked "of worms, of tombs, and epitaphs." I was lost in reveries of death, and the idea of premature burial held continual possession of my brain. The ghastly Danger to which I was subjected haunted me day and night. In the former, the torture of meditation was excessive—in the latter, supreme. When the grim Darkness overspread the Earth, then, with every horror of thought, I shook—shook as the quivering plumes upon the hearse. When Nature could endure wakefulness no longer, it was with a struggle that I consented to sleep—for I shuddered to reflect that, upon awaking, I might find myself the tenant of a grave. And when, finally, I sank into slumber, it was only to rush at once into a world of phantasms, above which, with vast, sable, overshadowing wing, hovered, predominant, the one sepulchral Idea.

From the innumerable images of gloom which thus oppressed me in dreams, I select for record but a solitary vision. Methought I was immersed in a cataleptic trance of more than usual duration and profundity. Suddenly there came an icy hand upon my forehead, and an impatient, gibbering voice whispered the word "Arise!" within my ear.

I sat erect. The darkness was total. I could not see the figure of him who had aroused me. I could call to mind neither the period at which I had fallen into the trance, nor the locality in which I then lay. While I remained motionless, and busied in endeavors to collect my thought, the cold hand grasped me fiercely by the wrist, shaking it petulantly, while the gibbering voice said again:

"Arise! did I not bid thee arise?"

"And who," I demanded, "art thou?"

"I have no name in the regions which I inhabit," replied the voice mournfully; "I was mortal, but am fiend. I was merciless, but am pitiful. Thou dost feel that I shudder. My teeth chatter as I speak, yet it is not with the chilliness of the night—of the night without end. But this hideousness is insufferable. How canst *thou* tranquilly sleep? I cannot rest for the cry of these great agonies. These sights are more than I can bear. Get thee up! Come with me into the outer Night, and let me unfold to thee the graves. Is not this a spectacle of woe?—Behold!"

I looked; and the unseen figure, which still grasped me by the wrist, had caused to be thrown open the graves of all mankind, and from each issued the faint phosphoric radiance of decay, so that I could see into the innermost recesses, and there view the shrouded bodies in their sad and solemn slumbers with the worm. But alas! the real sleepers were fewer, by many millions, than those who slumbered not at all; and there was a feeble struggling; and there was a general sad unrest; and from out the depths of the countless pits there came a melancholy rustling from the garments of the buried. And of those who seemed tranquilly to repose, I saw that a vast number had changed, in a greater or less degree, the rigid and uneasy position in which they had originally been entombed. And the voice again said to me as I gazed:

"Is it not—oh! is it *not* a pitiful sight?"—but, before I could find words to reply, the figure had ceased to grasp my wrist, the phosphoric lights expired, and the graves were closed with a sudden violence, while from out them arose a tumult of despairing cries, saying again: "Is it not—O, God, is it *not* a very pitiful sight?"

Phantasies such as these, presenting themselves at night, extended their terrific influence far into my waking hours. My nerves became thoroughly unstrung, and I fell a prey to perpetual horror. I hesitated to ride, or to walk, or to indulge in any exercise that would carry me from home. In fact, I no longer dared trust myself out of the immediate presence of those who were aware of my proneness to catalepsy, lest, falling into one of my usual fits, I should be buried before my real condition could be ascertained. I doubted the care, the fidelity of my dearest friends. I dreaded that, in some trance of more than customary duration, they might be prevailed upon to regard me as irrecoverable. I even went so far as to fear that, as I occasioned much trouble, they might be glad to consider any very protracted attack as sufficient excuse for getting rid of me altogether. It was in vain they endeavored to reassure me by the most solemn promises. I exacted the most sacred oaths, that under no circumstances they would bury me until decomposition had so materially advanced as to render farther preservation impossible. And, even then, my mortal terrors would listen to no reason—would accept no consolation. I entered into a series of elaborate precautions. Among other things, I had the family vault so remodeled as to admit of being readily opened from within. The slightest pressure upon a long lever that extended far into the tomb would cause the iron portal to fly back. There were arrangements also for the free admission of air and light, and convenient receptacles for food and water, within immediate reach of the coffin intended for my reception. This coffin was warmly and softly padded, and was provided with a lid, fashioned upon the principle of the vault door, with the addition of springs so contrived that the feeblest movement of the body would be sufficient to set it at liberty. Besides all this, there was suspended from the roof of the tomb, a large bell, the rope of which, it was designed, should extend through a hole in the coffin, and so be fastened to one of the hands of the corpse. But, alas, what avails the vigilance against the Destiny of man? Not even these well-contrived securities sufficed to save from the uttermost agonies of living inhumation, a wretch to these agonies foredoomed!

There arrived an epoch—as often before there had arrived—in which I found myself emerging from total unconsciousness into the first feeble and indefinite sense of existence. Slowly—with a tortoise gradation—approached the faint gray dawn of the psychal day. A torpid uneasiness. An apathetic endurance of dull pain. No care—no hope—no effort. Then, after a long interval, a ringing in the ears; then, after a lapse still longer, a prickling or tingling sensation in the extremities; then a seemingly eternal period of pleasurable quiescence, during which the awakening feelings are struggling into thought; then a brief re-sinking into nonentity; then a sudden recovery. At length the slight quivering of an eyelid, and immediately thereupon, an electric shock of a terror, deadly and indefinite, which sends the blood in torrents from the temples to the heart. And now the first positive effort to think. And now the first endeavor to remember. And now a partial and evanescent success. And now the memory has so far regained its dominion, that, in some measure, I am cognizant of my state. I feel that I am not awaking from ordinary sleep. I recollect that I have been subject to catalepsy. And now, at last, as if by the rush of an ocean, my shuddering spirit is overwhelmed by the one grim Danger—by the one spectral and ever-prevalent idea.

For some minutes after this fancy possessed me, I remained without motion. And why? I could not summon courage to move. I dared not make the effort which was to satisfy me of my fate—and yet there was something at my heart which whispered me *it was sure.* Despair—such as no other species of wretchedness ever calls into being—despair alone urged me, after long irresolution, to uplift the heavy lids of my eyes. I uplifted them. It was dark—all dark. I knew that the fit was over. I knew that the crisis of my disorder had long passed. I knew that I had now fully recovered the use of my visual faculties—and yet it was dark—all dark—the intense and utter raylessness of the Night that endureth for evermore.

I endeavored to shriek; and my lips and my parched tongue moved convulsively together in the attempt—but no voice issued from the cavernous lungs, which, oppressed as if by the weight of some incumbent mountain, gasped and palpitated, with the heart, at every elaborate and struggling inspiration.

The movement of the jaws, in this effort to cry aloud, showed me that they were bound up, as is usual with the dead. I felt, too, that I lay upon some hard substance, and by something similar my sides were also closely compressed. So far, I had not ventured to stir any of my limbs—but now I violently threw up my arms, which had been lying at length, with the wrists crossed. They struck a solid wooden substance, which extended above my person at an elevation of not more than six inches from my face. I could no longer doubt that I reposed within a coffin at last.

And now, amid all my infinite miseries, came sweetly the cherub Hope—for I thought of my precautions. I writhed, and made spasmodic exertions to force open the lid: it would not move. I felt my wrists for the bell-rope: it was not to be found. And now the Comforter fled for ever, and a still sterner Despair reigned triumphant; for I could not help perceiving the absence of the paddings which I had so carefully prepared—and then, too, there came suddenly to my nostrils the strong peculiar odor of moist earth. The conclusion was irresistible. I was *not* within the vault. I had fallen into a trance while absent from home—while among strangers—when, or how, I could not remember—and it was they who had buried me as a dog—nailed up in some common coffin—and thrust deep, deep, and for ever, into some ordinary and nameless *grave*.

As this awful conviction forced itself, thus, into the innermost chambers of my soul, I once again struggled to cry aloud. And in this second endeavor I succeeded. A long, wild, and continuous shriek, or yell of agony, resounded through the realms of the subterranean Night.

"Hillo! hillo, there!" said a gruff voice, in reply.

"What the devil's the matter now!" said a second.

"Get out o' that!" said a third.

Arthur Rackham

"What do you mean by yowling in that ere kind of style, like a cattymount?" said a fourth; and hereupon I was seized and shaken without ceremony, for several minutes, by a junto of very rough-looking individuals. They did not arouse me from my slumber—for I was wide awake when I screamed—but they restored me to the full possession of my memory.

This adventure occurred near Richmond, in Virginia. Accompanied by a friend, I had proceeded, upon a gunning expedition, some miles down the banks of the James River. Night approached, and we were overtaken by a storm. The cabin of a small sloop lying at anchor in the stream, and laden with garden mold, afforded us the only available shelter. We made the best of it, and passed the night on board. I slept in one of the only two berths in the vessel—and the berths of a sloop of sixty or twenty tons need scarcely be described. That which I occupied had no bedding of any kind. Its extreme width was eighteen inches. The distance of its bottom from the deck overhead was precisely the same. I found it a matter of exceeding difficulty to squeeze myself in. Nevertheless, I slept soundly, and the whole of my vision—for it was no dream, and no nightmare—arose naturally from the circumstances of my position—from my ordinary bias of thought—and from the difficulty, to which I have alluded, of collecting my senses, and especially of regaining my memory, for a long time after awaking from slumber. The men who shook me were the crew of the sloop, and some laborers engaged to unload it. From the load itself came the earthly smell. The bandage about the jaws was a silk handkerchief in which I had bound up my head, in default of my customary nightcap.

The tortures endured, however, were indubitably quite equal for the time, to those of actual sepulture. They were fearfully—they were inconceivably hideous; but out of Evil proceeded Good; for their very excess wrought in my spirit an inevitable revulsion. My soul acquired tone—acquired temper. I went abroad. I took vigorous exercise. I breathed the free air of Heaven. I thought upon other subjects than Death. I discarded my medical books. *Buchan* I burned. I read no *Night Thoughts*—no fustian about churchyards—no bugaboo tales—*such as this.* In short, I became a new man, and lived a man's life. From that memorable night, I dismissed forever my charnel apprehensions, and with them vanished the cataleptic disorder, of which, perhaps, they had been less the consequence than the cause.

There are moments when, even to the sober eye of Reason, the world of our sad Humanity may assume the semblance of a Hell—but the imagination of man is no Carathis, to explore with impunity its every cavern. Alas! the grim legion of sepulchral terrors cannot be regarded as altogether fanciful—but, like the Demons in whose company Afrasiab made his voyage down the Oxus, they must sleep, or they will devour us—they must be suffered to slumber, or we perish.

The Purloined Letter

[The third of Poe's three detective stories featuring the Parisian amateur detective C. Auguste Dupin, it was first published in December 1844 in the literary annual *The Gift: A Christmas and New Year's Present for 1845*. It is one of the early precursors of the modern detective story.]

Nil sapientiae odiosius acumine nimio.

—Seneca

At Paris, just after dark one gusty evening in the autumn of 18—, I was enjoying the twofold luxury of meditation and a meerschaum, in company with my friend C. Auguste Dupin, in his little back library, or book-closet, *au troisième, No.* 33, *Rue Dunôt, Faubourg St. Germain.* For one hour at least we had maintained a profound silence; while each, to any casual observer, might have seemed intently and exclusively occupied with the curling eddies of smoke that oppressed the atmosphere of the chamber. For myself, however, I was mentally discussing certain topics which had formed matter for conversation between us at an earlier period of the evening; I mean the affair of the Rue Morgue, and the mystery attending the murder of Marie Rogêt. I looked upon it, therefore, as something of a coincidence, when the door of our apartment was thrown open and admitted our old acquaintance, Monsieur G—, the Prefect of the Parisian police.

We gave him a hearty welcome; for there was nearly half as much of the entertaining as of the contemptible about the man, and we had not seen him for several years. We had been sitting in the dark, and Dupin now arose for the purpose of lighting a lamp, but sat down again, without doing so, upon G.'s saying that he had called to consult us, or rather to ask the opinion of my friend, about some official business which had occasioned a great deal of trouble.

"If it is any point requiring reflection," observed Dupin, as he forebore to enkindle the wick, "we shall examine it to better purpose in the dark."

"That is another of your odd notions," said the Prefect, who had a fashion of calling everything "odd" that was beyond his comprehension, and thus lived amid an absolute legion of "oddities."

"Very true," said Dupin, as he supplied his visiter with a pipe, and rolled towards him a comfortable chair.

"And what is the difficulty now?" I asked. "Nothing more in the assassination way, I hope?"

"Oh, no; nothing of that nature. The fact is, the business is *very* simple indeed, and I make no doubt that we can manage it sufficiently well ourselves; but then I thought Dupin would like to hear the details of it, because it is so excessively *odd*."

"Simple and odd," said Dupin.

"Why, yes; and not exactly that, either. The fact is, we have all been a good deal puzzled because the affair is so simple, and yet baffles us altogether."

"Perhaps it is the very simplicity of the thing which puts you at fault," said my friend.

"What nonsense you *do* talk!" replied the Prefect, laughing heartily.

"Perhaps the mystery is a little *too* plain," said Dupin.

"Oh, good heavens! who ever heard of such an idea?"

"A little *too* self-evident."

"Ha! ha! ha—ha! ha! ha!—ho! ho! ho!"—roared our visiter, profoundly amused, "oh, Dupin, you will be the death of me yet!"

"And what, after all, *is* the matter on hand?" I asked.

"Why, I will tell you," replied the Prefect, as he gave a long, steady and contemplative puff, and settled himself in his chair. "I will tell you in a few words; but, before I begin, let me caution you that this is an affair demanding the greatest secrecy, and that I should most probably lose the position I now hold, were it known that I confided it to any one."

"Proceed," said I.

"Or not," said Dupin.

"Well, then; I have received personal information, from a very high quarter, that a certain document of the last importance, has been purloined from the royal apartments. The individual who purloined it is known; this beyond a doubt; he was seen to take it. It is known, also, that it still remains in his possession."

"How is this known?" asked Dupin.

"It is clearly inferred," replied the Prefect, "from the nature of the document, and from the non-appearance of certain results which would at once arise from its passing *out* of the robber's possession—that is to say, from his employing it as he must design in the end to employ it."

"Be a little more explicit," I said.

"Well, I may venture so far as to say that the paper gives its holder a certain power in a certain quarter where such power is immensely valuable." The Prefect was fond of the cant of diplomacy.

"Still I do not quite understand," said Dupin.

"No? Well; the disclosure of the document to a third person, who shall be nameless, would bring in question the honor of a personage of most exalted station; and this fact gives the holder of the document an ascendancy over the illustrious personage whose honor and peace are so jeopardized."

"But this ascendancy," I interposed, "would depend upon the robber's knowledge of the loser's knowledge of the robber. Who would dare—"

"The thief," said G., "is the Minister D—, who dares all things, those unbecoming as well as those becoming a man. The method of the theft was not less ingenious than bold. The document in question—a letter, to be frank—had been received by the personage robbed while alone in the royal *boudoir.* During its perusal she was suddenly interrupted by the entrance of the other exalted personage from whom especially it was her wish to conceal it. After a hurried and vain endeavor to thrust it in a drawer, she was forced to place it, open as it was, upon a table. The address, however, was uppermost, and, the contents thus unexposed, the letter escaped notice. At this juncture enters the Minister D—. His lynx eye immediately perceives the paper, recognizes the handwriting of the address, observes the confusion of the personage addressed, and fathoms her secret. After some business transactions, hurried through in his ordinary manner, he produces a letter somewhat similar to the one in question, opens it, pretends to read it, and then places it in close juxtaposition to the other. Again he converses, for some fifteen minutes, upon the public affairs. At length, in taking leave, he takes also from the table the letter to which he had no claim. Its rightful owner saw, but, of course, dared not call attention to the act, in the presence of the third personage who stood at her elbow. The minister decamped; leaving his own letter—one of no importance—upon the table."

"Here, then," said Dupin to me, "you have precisely what you demand to make the ascendancy complete—the robber's knowledge of the loser's knowledge of the robber."

"Yes," replied the Prefect; "and the power thus attained has, for some months past, been wielded, for political purposes, to a very dangerous extent. The personage robbed is more thoroughly convinced, every day, of the necessity of reclaiming her letter. But this, of course, cannot be done openly. In fine, driven to despair, she has committed the matter to me."

"Than whom," said Dupin, amid a perfect whirlwind of smoke, "no more sagacious agent could, I suppose, be desired, or even imagined."

"You flatter me," replied the Prefect; "but it is possible that some such opinion may have been entertained."

"It is clear," said I, "as you observe, that the letter is still in possession of the minister; since it is this possession, and not any employment of the letter, which bestows the power. With the employment the power departs."

"True," said G.; "and upon this conviction I proceeded. My first care was to make thorough search of the minister's hotel; and here my chief embarrassment lay in the necessity of searching without his knowledge. Beyond all things, I have been warned of the danger which would result from giving him reason to suspect our design."

"But," said I, "you are quite *au fait* in these investigations. The Parisian police have done this thing often before."

"O yes; and for this reason I did not despair. The habits of the minister gave me, too, a great advantage. He is frequently absent from home all night. His servants are by no means numerous. They sleep at a distance from their master's apartment, and, being chiefly Neapolitans, are readily made drunk. I have keys, as you know, with which I can open any chamber or cabinet in Paris. For three months a night has not passed, during the greater part of which I have not been engaged, personally, in ransacking the D— Hotel. My honor is interested, and, to mention a great secret, the reward is enormous. So I did not abandon the search until I had become fully satisfied that the thief is a more astute man than myself. I fancy that I have investigated every nook and corner of the premises in which it is possible that the paper can be concealed."

"But is it not possible," I suggested, "that although the letter may be in possession of the minister, as it unquestionably is, he may have concealed it elsewhere than upon his own premises?"

"This is barely possible," said Dupin. "The present peculiar condition of affairs at court, and especially of those intrigues in which D— is known to be involved, would render the instant availability of the document—its susceptibility of being produced at a moment's notice—a point of nearly equal importance with its possession."

"Its susceptibility of being produced?" said I.

"That is to say, of being *destroyed*," said Dupin.

"True," I observed; "the paper is clearly then upon the premises. As for its being upon the person of the minister, we may consider that as out of the question."

"Entirely," said the Prefect. "He has been twice waylaid, as if by footpads, and his person rigorously searched under my own inspection."

"You might have spared yourself this trouble," said Dupin. "D—, I presume, is not altogether a fool, and, if not, must have anticipated these waylayings, as a matter of course."

"Not *altogether* a fool," said G., "but then he's a poet, which I take to be only one remove from a fool."

"True," said Dupin, after a long and thoughtful whiff from his meerschaum, "although I have been guilty of certain doggerel myself."

"Suppose you detail," said I, "the particulars of your search."

"Why the fact is, we took our time, and we searched *everywhere*. I have had long experience in these affairs. I took the entire building, room by room; devoting the nights of a whole week to each. We examined, first, the furniture of each apartment. We opened every possible drawer; and I presume you know that, to a properly trained police agent, such a thing as a *secret* drawer is impossible. Any man is a dolt who permits a 'secret' drawer to escape him in a search of this kind. The thing is so plain. There is a certain amount of bulk—of space—to be accounted for in every cabinet. Then we have accurate rules. The fiftieth part of a line could not escape us. After the cabinets we took the chairs. The cushions we probed with the fine long needles you have seen me employ. From the tables we removed the tops."

"Why so?"

"Sometimes the top of a table, or other similarly arranged piece of furniture, is removed by the person wishing to conceal an article; then the leg is excavated, the article deposited within the cavity, and the top replaced. The bottoms and tops of bedposts are employed in the same way."

"But could not the cavity be detected by sounding?" I asked.

"By no means, if, when the article is deposited, a sufficient wadding of cotton be placed around it. Besides, in our case, we were obliged to proceed without noise."

"But you could not have removed—you could not have taken to pieces *all* articles of furniture in which it would have been possible to make a deposit in the manner you mention. A letter may be compressed into a thin spiral roll, not differing much in shape or bulk from a large knitting needle, and in this form it might be inserted into the rung of a chair, for example. You did not take to pieces all the chairs?"

"Certainly not; but we did better—we examined the rungs of every chair in the hotel, and, indeed the jointings of every description of furniture, by the aid of a most powerful microscope. Had there been any traces of recent disturbance we should not have failed to detect it instantly. A single grain of gimlet-dust, for example, would have been as obvious as an apple. Any disorder in the gluing—any unusual gaping in the joints—would have sufficed to insure detection."

"I presume you looked to the mirrors, between the boards and the plates, and you probed the beds and the bed-clothes, as well as the curtains and carpets."

"That of course; and when we had absolutely completed every particle of the furniture in this way, then we examined the house itself. We divided its entire surface into compartments, which we numbered, so that none might be missed; then we scrutinized each individual square inch throughout the premises, including the two houses immediately adjoining, with the microscope, as before."

"The two houses adjoining!" I exclaimed; "you must have had a great deal of trouble."

"We had; but the reward offered is prodigious!"

"You include the *grounds* about the houses?"

"All the grounds are paved with brick. They gave us comparatively little trouble. We examined the moss between the bricks, and found it undisturbed."

"You looked among D—'s papers, of course, and into the books of the library?"

"Certainly; we opened every package and parcel; we not only opened every book, but we turned over every leaf in each volume, not contenting ourselves with a mere shake, according to the fashion of some of our police officers. We also measured the thickness of every book-*cover*, with the most accurate admeasurement, and applied to each the most jealous scrutiny of the microscope. Had any of the bindings been recently meddled with, it would have been utterly impossible that the fact should have escaped observation. Some five or six volumes, just from the hands of the binder, we carefully probed, longitudinally, with the needles."

"You explored the floors beneath the carpets?"

"Beyond doubt. We removed every carpet, and examined the boards with the microscope."

"And the paper on the walls?"

"Yes."

"You looked into the cellars?"

"We did."

"Then," I said, "you have been making a miscalculation, and the letter is *not* upon the premises, as you suppose."

"I fear you are right there," said the Prefect. "And now, Dupin, what would you advise me to do?"

"To make a thorough re-search of the premises."

"That is absolutely needless," replied G—. "I am not more sure that I breathe than I am that the letter is not at the Hotel."

"I have no better advice to give you," said Dupin. "You have, of course, an accurate description of the letter?"

"Oh yes!"—And here the Prefect, producing a memorandum book proceeded to read aloud a minute account of the internal, and especially of the external appearance of the missing document. Soon after finishing the perusal of this description, he took his departure, more entirely depressed in spirits than I had ever known the good gentleman before.

In about a month afterwards he paid us another visit, and found us occupied very nearly as before. He took a pipe and a chair and entered into some ordinary conversation. At length I said,—

"Well, but G—, what of the purloined letter? I presume you have at last made up your mind that there is no such thing as overreaching the Minister?"

"Confound him, say I—yes; I made the re-examination, however, as Dupin suggested—but it was all labor lost, as I knew it would be."

"How much was the reward offered, did you say?" asked Dupin.

"Why, a very great deal—a *very* liberal reward—I don't like to say how much, precisely; but one thing I *will* say, that I wouldn't mind giving my individual check for fifty thousand francs to any one who could obtain me that letter. The fact is, it is becoming of more and more importance every day; and the reward has been lately doubled. If it were trebled, however, I could do no more than I have done."

"Why, yes," said Dupin, drawlingly, between the whiffs of his meerschaum, "I really—think, G—, you have not exerted yourself—to the utmost in this matter. You might—do a little more, I think, eh?"

"How?—in what way?'

"Why—puff, puff—you might—puff, puff—employ counsel in the matter, eh?—puff, puff, puff. Do you remember the story they tell of Abernethy?"

"No; hang Abernethy!"

"To be sure! hang him and welcome. But, once upon a time, a certain rich miser conceived the design of sponging upon this Abernethy for a medical opinion. Getting up, for this purpose, an ordinary conversation in a private company, he insinuated his case to the physician, as that of an imaginary individual.

"'We will suppose,' said the miser, 'that his symptoms are such and such; now, doctor, what would you have directed him to take?'

"'Take!' said Abernethy, 'why, take *advice*, to be sure.'"

"But," said the Prefect, a little discomposed, "I am *perfectly* willing to take advice, and to pay for it. I would *really* give fifty thousand francs to any one who would aid me in the matter."

"In that case," replied Dupin, opening a drawer, and producing a cheque-book, "you may as well fill me up a cheque for the amount mentioned. When you have signed it, I will hand you the letter."

I was astounded. The Prefect appeared absolutely thunder-stricken. For some minutes he remained speechless and motionless, looking incredulously at my friend with open mouth, and eyes that seemed starting from their sockets; then, apparently recovering himself in some measure, he seized a pen, and after several pauses and vacant stares, finally filled up and signed a check for fifty thousand francs, and handed it across the table to Dupin. The latter examined it carefully and deposited it in his pocket-book; then, unlocking an *escritoire*, took thence a letter and gave it to the Prefect. This functionary grasped it in a perfect agony of joy, opened it with a trembling hand, cast a rapid glance at its contents, and then, scrambling and struggling to the door, rushed at length unceremoniously from the room and from the house, without having uttered a syllable since Dupin had requested him to fill up the cheque.

When he had gone, my friend entered into some explanations.

"The Parisian police," he said, "are exceedingly able in their way. They are persevering, ingenious, cunning, and thoroughly versed in the knowledge which their duties seem chiefly to demand. Thus, when G— detailed to us his mode of searching the premises at the Hotel D—, I felt entire confidence in his having made a satisfactory investigation—so far as his labors extended."

"So far as his labors extended?" said I.

"Yes," said Dupin. "The measures adopted were not only the best of their kind, but carried out to absolute perfection. Had the letter been deposited within the range of their search, these fellows would, beyond a question, have found it."

I merely laughed—but he seemed quite serious in all that he said.

"The measures, then," he continued, "were good in their kind, and well executed; their defect lay in their being inapplicable to the case, and to the man. A certain set of highly ingenious resources are, with the Prefect, a sort of Procrustean bed, to which he forcibly adapts his designs. But he perpetually errs by being too deep or too shallow, for the matter in hand; and many a schoolboy is a better reasoner than he. I knew one about eight years of age, whose success at guessing in the game of 'even and odd' attracted universal admiration. This game is simple, and is played with marbles. One player holds in his hand a number of these toys, and demands of another whether that number is even or odd. If the guess is right, the guesser wins one; if wrong, he loses one. The boy to whom I allude won all the marbles of the school. Of course he had some principle of guessing; and this lay in mere observation and admeasurement of the astuteness of his opponents. For example, an arrant simpleton is his opponent, and, holding up his closed hand, asks, 'Are they even or odd?' Our schoolboy replies, 'odd,' and loses; but upon the second trial he wins, for he then says to himself, 'the simpleton had them even upon the first trial, and his amount of cunning is just sufficient to make him have them odd upon the second; I will therefore guess odd;'—he guesses odd, and wins. Now, with a simpleton a degree above the first, he would have reasoned thus: 'This fellow finds that in the first instance I guessed odd, and, in the second, he will propose to himself, upon the first impulse, a simple variation from even to odd, as did the first simpleton; but then a second thought will suggest that this is too simple a variation, and finally he will decide upon putting it even as before. I will therefore guess even;'—he guesses even, and wins. Now this mode of reasoning in the schoolboy, whom his fellows termed 'lucky,'—what, in its last analysis, is it?"

"It is merely," I said, "an identification of the reasoner's intellect with that of his opponent."

"It is," said Dupin; "and, upon inquiring of the boy by what means he effected the *thorough* identification in which his success consisted, I received answer as follows: 'When I wish to find out how wise, or how stupid, or how good, or how wicked is any one, or what are his thoughts at the moment, I fashion the expression of my face, as accurately as possible, in accordance with the expression of his, and then wait to see what thoughts or sentiments arise in my mind or heart, as if to match or correspond with the expression.' This response of the schoolboy lies at the bottom of all the spurious profundity which has been attributed to Rochefoucault, to La Bougive, to Machiavelli, and to Campanella."

"And the identification," I said, "of the reasoner's intellect with that of his opponent, depends, if I understand you aright, upon the accuracy with which the opponent's intellect is admeasured."

"For its practical value it depends upon this," replied Dupin; "and the Prefect and his cohort fail so frequently, first, by default of this identification, and, secondly, by ill-admeasurement, or rather through non-admeasurement, of the intellect with which they are engaged. They consider only their *own* ideas of ingenuity; and, in searching for anything hidden, advert only to the modes in which *they* would have hidden it. They are right in this much—that their own ingenuity is a faithful representative of that of the *mass*; but when the cunning of the individual felon is diverse in character from their own, the felon foils them, of course. This always happens when it is above their own, and very usually when it is below. They have no variation of principle in their investigations; at best, when urged by some unusual emergency—by some extraordinary reward—they extend or exaggerate their old modes of *practice*, without touching their principles. What, for example, in this case of D—, has been done to vary the principle of action? What is all this boring, and probing, and sounding, and scrutinizing with the microscope and dividing the surface of the building into registered square inches—what is it all but an exaggeration of *the application* of the one principle or set of principles of search, which are based upon the one set of notions regarding human ingenuity, to which the Prefect, in the long routine of his duty, has been accustomed? Do you not see he has taken it for granted that *all* men proceed to conceal a letter,—not exactly in a gimlet hole bored in a chair-leg—but, at least, in *some* out-of-the-way hole or corner suggested by the same tenor of thought which would urge a man to secrete a letter in a gimlet-hole bored in a chair-leg? And do you not see also, that such *recherchés* nooks for concealment are adapted only for ordinary occasions, and would be adopted only by ordinary intellects; for, in all cases of concealment, a disposal of the article concealed—a disposal of it in this *recherché* manner—is, in the very first instance, presumable and presumed; and thus its discovery depends, not at all upon the acumen, but altogether upon the mere care, patience, and determination of the seekers; and where the case is of importance—or, what amounts to the same thing in the policial eyes, when the reward is of magnitude,—the qualities in question have *never* been known to fail. You will now understand what I meant in suggesting that, had the purloined letter been hidden any where within the limits of the Prefect's examination—in other words, had the principle of its concealment been comprehended within the principles of the Prefect—its discovery would have been a matter altogether beyond question. This functionary, however, has been thoroughly mystified; and the remote source of his defeat lies in the supposition that the Minister is a fool, because he has acquired renown as a poet. All fools are poets; this the Prefect *feels*; and he is merely guilty of a *non distributio medii* in thence inferring that all poets are fools."

"But is this really the poet?" I asked. "There are two brothers, I know; and both have attained reputation in letters. The Minister I believe has written learnedly on the Differential Calculus. He is a mathematician, and no poet."

"You are mistaken; I know him well; he is both. As poet *and* mathematician, he would reason well; as mere mathematician, he could not have reasoned at all, and thus would have been at the mercy of the Prefect."

"You surprise me," I said, "by these opinions, which have been contradicted by the voice of the world. You do not mean to set at naught the well-digested idea of centuries. The mathematical reason has long been regarded as *the* reason *par excellence.*"

"'*Il y a à parièr,*'" replied Dupin, quoting from Chamfort, "'*que toute idée publique, toute convention reçue est une sottise, car elle a convenue au plus grand nombre.*' The mathematicians, I grant you, have done their best to promulgate the popular error to which you allude, and which is none the less an error for its promulgation as truth. With an art worthy a better cause, for example, they have insinuated the term 'analysis' into application to algebra. The French are the originators of this particular deception; but if a term is of any importance—if words derive any value from applicability—then 'analysis' conveys 'algebra' about as much as, in Latin, '*ambitus*' implies 'ambition,' '*religio*' 'religion,' or '*homines honesti*,' a set of *honorable* men."

"You have a quarrel on hand, I see," said I, "with some of the algebraists of Paris; but proceed."

"I dispute the availability, and thus the value, of that reason which is cultivated in any especial form other than the abstractly logical. I dispute, in particular, the reason educed by mathematical study. The mathematics are the science of form and quantity; mathematical reasoning is merely logic applied to observation upon form and quantity. The great error lies in supposing that even the truths of what is called *pure* algebra, are abstract or general truths. And this error is so egregious that I am confounded at the universality with which it has been received. Mathematical axioms are *not* axioms of general truth. What is true of *relation*—of form and quantity—is often grossly false in regard to morals, for example. In this latter science it is very usually *un*true that the aggregated parts are equal to the whole. In chemistry also the axiom fails. In the consideration of motive it fails; for two motives, each of a given value, have not, necessarily, a value when united, equal to the sum of their values apart. There are numerous other mathematical truths which are only truths within the limits of *relation*. But the mathematician argues, from his *finite truths*, through habit, as if they were of an absolutely general applicability—as the world indeed imagines them to be. Bryant, in his very learned *Mythology*, mentions an analogous source of error, when he says that 'although the Pagan fables *are* not believed, yet we forget ourselves continually, and make inferences from them as existing realities.' With the algebraists, however, who are Pagans themselves, the 'Pagan fables' *are* believed, and the inferences are made, not so much through lapse of memory, as through an unaccountable addling of the brains. In short, I never yet encountered the mere mathematician who could be trusted out of equal roots, or one who did not clandestinely hold it as a point of his faith that $x^2 + px$ was absolutely and unconditionally equal to q. Say to one of these gentlemen, by way of experiment, if you please, that you believe occasions may occur where $x^2 + px$ is not altogether equal to q, and, having made him understand what you mean, get out of his reach as speedily as convenient, for, beyond doubt, he will endeavor to knock you down.

"I mean to say," continued Dupin, while I merely laughed at his last observations, "that if the Minister had been no more than a mathematician, the Prefect would have been under no necessity of giving me this check. I know him, however, as both mathematician and poet, and my measures were adapted to his capacity, with reference to the circumstances by which he was surrounded. I knew him as a courtier, too, and as a bold *intriguant*. Such a man, I considered, could not fail to be aware of the ordinary policial modes of action. He could not have failed to anticipate—and events have proved that he did not fail to anticipate—the waylayings to which he was subjected. He must have foreseen, I reflected, the secret investigations of his premises. His frequent absences from home at night, which were hailed by the Prefect as certain aids to his success, I regarded only as ruses, to afford opportunity for thorough search to the police, and thus the sooner to impress them with the conviction to which G—, in fact, did finally arrive—the conviction that the letter was not upon the premises. I felt, also, that the whole train of thought, which I was at some pains in detailing to you just now, concerning the invariable principle of policial action in searches for articles concealed—I felt that this whole train of thought would necessarily pass through the mind of the Minister. It would imperatively lead him to despise all the ordinary *nooks* of concealment. *He* could not, I reflected, be so weak as not to see that the most intricate and remote recess of his hotel would be as open as his commonest closets to the eyes, to the probes, to the gimlets, and to the microscopes of the Prefect. I saw, in fine, that he would be driven, as a matter of course, to *simplicity*, if not deliberately induced to it as a matter of choice. You will remember, perhaps, how desperately the Prefect laughed when I suggested, upon our first interview, that it was just possible this mystery troubled him so much on account of its being so *very* self-evident."

"Yes," said I, "I remember his merriment well. I really thought he would have fallen into convulsions."

"The material world," continued Dupin, "abounds with very strict analogies to the immaterial; and thus some colour of truth has been given to the rhetorical dogma, that metaphor, or simile, may be made to strengthen an argument, as well as to embellish a description. The principle of the *vis inertiæ*, for example, seems to be identical in physics and metaphysics. It is not more true in the former, that a large body is with more difficulty set in motion than a smaller one, and that its subsequent *momentum* is commensurate with this difficulty, than it is, in the latter, that intellects of the vaster capacity, while more forcible, more constant, and more eventful in their movements than those of inferior grade, are yet the less readily moved, and more embarrassed and full of hesitation in the first few steps of their progress. Again: have you ever noticed which of the street signs, over the shop-doors, are the most attractive of attention?"

"I have never given the matter a thought," I said.

"There is a game of puzzles," he resumed, "which is played upon a map. One party playing requires another to find a given word—the name of town, river, state or empire—any word, in short, upon the motley and perplexed surface of the chart. A novice in the game generally seeks to embarrass his opponents by giving them the most minutely lettered names; but the adept selects such words as stretch, in large characters, from one end of the chart to the other. These, like the over-largely lettered signs and placards of the street, escape observation by dint of being excessively obvious; and here the physical oversight is precisely analogous with the moral inapprehension by which the intellect suffers to pass unnoticed those considerations which are too obtrusively and too palpably self-evident. But this is a point, it appears, somewhat above or beneath the understanding of the Prefect. He never once thought it probable, or possible, that the Minister had deposited the letter immediately beneath the nose of the whole world, by way of best preventing any portion of that world from perceiving it.

"But the more I reflected upon the daring, dashing, and discriminating ingenuity of D—; upon the fact that the document must always have been *at hand*, if he intended to use it to good purpose; and upon the decisive evidence, obtained by the Prefect, that it was not hidden within the limits of that dignitary's ordinary search—the more satisfied I became that, to conceal this letter, the Minister had resorted to the comprehensive and sagacious expedient of not attempting to conceal it at all.

"Full of these ideas, I prepared myself with a pair of green spectacles, and called one fine morning, quite by accident, at the Ministerial hotel. I found D— at home, yawning, lounging, and dawdling, as usual, and pretending to be in the last extremity of *ennui*. He is, perhaps, the most really energetic human being now alive—but that is only when nobody sees him.

"To be even with him, I complained of my weak eyes, and lamented the necessity of the spectacles, under cover of which I cautiously and thoroughly surveyed the whole apartment, while seemingly intent only upon the conversation of my host.

"I paid especial attention to a large writing-table near which he sat, and upon which lay confusedly, some miscellaneous letters and other papers, with one or two musical instruments and a few books. Here, however, after a long and very deliberate scrutiny, I saw nothing to excite particular suspicion.

"At length my eyes, in going the circuit of the room, fell upon a trumpery fillagree card-rack of pasteboard, that hung dangling by a dirty blue ribbon, from a little brass knob just beneath the middle of the mantel-piece. In this rack, which had three or four compartments, were five or six visiting cards and a solitary letter. This last was much soiled and crumpled. It was torn nearly in two, across the middle—as if a design, in the first instance, to tear it entirely up as worthless, had been altered, or stayed, in the second. It had a large black seal, bearing the D— cipher *very* conspicuously, and was addressed, in a diminutive female hand, to

D—, the minister, himself. It was thrust carelessly, and even, as it seemed, contemptuously, into one of the uppermost divisions of the rack.

"No sooner had I glanced at this letter, than I concluded it to be that of which I was in search. To be sure, it was, to all appearance, radically different from the one of which the Prefect had read us so minute a description. Here the seal was large and black, with the D— cipher; there it was small and red, with the ducal arms of the S— family. Here, the address, to the Minister, diminutive and feminine; there the superscription, to a certain royal personage, was markedly bold and decided; the size alone formed a point of correspondence. But, then, the *radicalness* of these differences, which was excessive; the dirt; the soiled and torn condition of the paper, so inconsistent with the *true* methodical habits of D—, and so suggestive of a design to delude the beholder into an idea of the worthlessness of the document; these things, together with the hyper-obtrusive situation of this document, full in the view of every visiter, and thus exactly in accordance with the conclusions to which I had previously arrived; these things, I say, were strongly corroborative of suspicion, in one who came with the intention to suspect.

"I protracted my visit as long as possible, and, while I maintained a most animated discussion with the Minister upon a topic which I knew well had never failed to interest and excite him, I kept my attention really riveted upon the letter. In this examination, I committed to memory its external appearance and arrangement in the rack; and also fell, at length, upon a discovery which set at rest whatever trivial doubt I might have entertained. In scrutinizing the edges of the paper, I observed them to be more *chafed* than seemed necessary. They presented the *broken* appearance which is manifested when a stiff paper, having been once folded and pressed with a folder, is refolded in a reversed direction, in the same creases or edges which had formed the original fold. This discovery was sufficient. It was clear to me that the letter had been turned, as a glove, inside out, re-directed, and re-sealed. I bade the Minister good morning, and took my departure at once, leaving a gold snuff-box upon the table.

"The next morning I called for the snuff-box, when we resumed, quite eagerly, the conversation of the preceding day. While thus engaged, however, a loud report, as if of a pistol, was heard immediately beneath the windows of the hotel, and was succeeded by a series of fearful screams, and the shoutings of a terrified mob. D— rushed to a casement, threw it open, and looked out. In the meantime, I stepped to the card-rack, took the letter, put it in my pocket, and replaced it by a *facsimile*, (so far as regards externals,) which I had carefully prepared at my lodgings—imitating the D— cipher, very readily, by means of a seal formed of bread.

"The disturbance in the street had been occasioned by the frantic behaviour of a man with a musket. He had fired it among a crowd of women and children. It proved, however, to have been without ball, and the fellow was suffered to go his way as a lunatic or a drunkard. When he had gone, D— came from the window, whither I had followed him immediately upon securing the object in view. Soon afterwards I bade him farewell. The pretended lunatic was a man in my own pay."

"But what purpose had you," I asked, "in replacing the letter by a *facsimile*? Would it not have been better, at the first visit, to have seized it openly, and departed?"

"D—," replied Dupin, "is a desperate man, and a man of nerve. His hotel, too, is not without attendants devoted to his interests. Had I made the wild attempt you suggest, I might never have left the Ministerial presence alive. The good people of Paris might have heard of me no more. But I had an object apart from these considerations. You know my political prepossessions. In this matter, I act as a partisan of the lady concerned. For eighteen months the Minister has had her in his power. She has now him in hers—since, being unaware that the letter is not in his possession, he will proceed with his exactions as if it was. Thus will he inevitably commit himself, at once, to his political destruction. His downfall, too, will not be more precipitate than awkward. It is all very well to talk about the *facilis descensus Averni*; but in all kinds of climbing, as Catalani said of singing, it is far more easy to get up than to come down. In the present instance I have no sympathy—at least no pity—for him who descends. He is that *monstrum horrendum*, an unprincipled man of genius. I confess, however, that I should like very well to know the precise character of his thoughts, when, being defied by her whom the Prefect terms 'a certain personage,' he is reduced to opening the letter which I left for him in the card-rack."

"How? Did you put anything particular in it?"

"Why—it did not seem altogether right to leave the interior blank—that would have been insulting. D—, at Vienna once, did me an evil turn, which I told him, quite good-humoredly, that I should remember. So, as I knew he would feel some curiosity in regard to the identity of the person who had outwitted him, I thought it a pity not to give him a clue. He is well acquainted with my MS., and I just copied into the middle of the blank sheet the words—

> "'——Un dessein si funeste,
> S'il n'est digne d'Atrée, est digne de Thyeste.
> They are to be found in Crebillon's '*Atrée*.'"

The Thousand-and-Second Tale of Scheherazade

[Intended to be a humorous sequel to *One Thousand and One Nights*, the collection of Middle Eastern tales, this short story first appeared in the February issue of *Godey's Lady's Book* in 1845.]

Truth is stranger than fiction.

—Old Saying

Having had occasion, lately, in the course of some Oriental investigations, to consult the *Tellmenow Isitsöornot*, a work which (like the *Zohar* of Simeon Jochaides) is scarcely known at all, even in Europe; and which has never been quoted, to my knowledge, by any American—if we except, perhaps, the author of the *Curiosities of American Literature*;—having had occasion, I say, to turn over some pages of the first-mentioned very remarkable work, I was not a little astonished to discover that the literary world has hitherto been strangely in error respecting the fate of the vizier's daughter, Scheherazade, as that fate is depicted in the *Arabian Nights*; and that the denouement there given, if not altogether inaccurate, as far as it goes, is at least to blame in not having gone very much farther.

For full information on this interesting topic, I must refer the inquisitive reader to the *Isitsöornot* itself, but in the meantime, I shall be pardoned for giving a summary of what I there discovered.

It will be remembered, that, in the usual version of the tales, a certain monarch having good cause to be jealous of his queen, not only puts her to death, but makes a vow, by his beard and the prophet, to espouse each night the most beautiful maiden in his dominions, and the next morning to deliver her up to the executioner.

Having fulfilled this vow for many years to the letter, and with a religious punctuality and method that conferred great credit upon him as a man of devout feeling and excellent sense, he was interrupted one afternoon (no doubt at his prayers) by a visit from his grand vizier, to whose daughter, it appears, there had occurred an idea.

Her name was Scheherazade, and her idea was, that she would either redeem the land from the depopulating tax upon its beauty, or perish, after the approved fashion of all heroines, in the attempt.

Accordingly, and although we do not find it to be leap-year (which makes the sacrifice more meritorious), she deputes her father, the grand vizier, to make an offer to the king of her hand. This hand the king eagerly accepts—(he had intended to take it at all events, and had put off the matter from day to day, only through fear of the vizier)—but, in accepting it now, he gives all parties very distinctly to understand, that, grand vizier or no grand vizier, he has not the slightest design of giving up one iota of his vow or of his privileges. When, therefore, the fair Scheherazade insisted upon marrying the king, and did actually marry him despite her father's excellent advice not to do anything of the kind—when she would and did marry him, I say, will I, nill I, it was with her beautiful black eyes as thoroughly open as the nature of the case would allow.

It seems, however, that this politic damsel (who had been reading Machiavelli, beyond doubt), had a very ingenious little plot in her mind. On the night of the wedding, she contrived, upon I forget what specious pretence, to have her sister occupy a couch sufficiently near that of the royal pair to admit of easy conversation from bed to bed; and, a little before cock-crowing, she took care to awaken the good monarch, her husband (who bore her none the worse will because he intended to wring her neck on the morrow)—she managed to awaken him, I say, (although on account of a capital conscience and an easy digestion, he slept well) by the profound interest of a story (about a rat and a black cat, I think) which she was narrating (all in an undertone, of course) to her sister. When the day broke, it so happened that this history was not altogether finished, and that Scheherazade, in the nature of things could not finish it just then, since it was high time for her to get up and be bowstrung—a thing very little more pleasant than hanging, only a trifle more genteel!

The king's curiosity, however, prevailing, I am sorry to say, even over his sound religious principles, induced him for this once to postpone the fulfilment of his vow until next morning, for the purpose and with the hope of hearing that night how it fared in the end with the black cat (a black cat, I think it was) and the rat.

The night having arrived, however, the lady Scheherazade not only put the finishing stroke to the black cat and the rat (the rat was blue) but before she well knew what she was about, found herself deep in the intricacies of a narration, having reference (if I am not altogether mistaken) to a pink horse (with green wings) that went, in a violent manner, by clockwork, and was wound up with an indigo key. With this history the king was even more profoundly interested than with the other—and, as the day broke before its conclusion (notwithstanding all the queen's endeavors to get through with it in time for the bowstringing), there was again no resource but to postpone that ceremony as before, for twenty-four hours. The next night there happened a similar accident with a similar result; and then the next—and then again the next; so that, in the end, the good monarch, having been unavoidably deprived of all opportunity to keep his vow during a period of no less than one thousand and one nights, either forgets it altogether by the expiration of this time, or gets himself absolved of it in the regular way, or (what is more probable) breaks it outright, as well as the head of his father confessor. At all events, Scheherazade, who, being lineally descended from Eve, fell heir, perhaps, to the whole seven baskets of talk, which the latter lady, we all know, picked up from under the trees in the garden of Eden—Scheherazade, I say, finally triumphed, and the tariff upon beauty was repealed.

Now, this conclusion (which is that of the story as we have it upon record) is, no doubt, excessively proper and pleasant—but alas! like a great many pleasant things, is more pleasant than true, and I am indebted altogether to the *Isitsöornot* for the means of correcting the error. "*Le mieux*," says a French proverb, "*est l'ennemi du bien*," and, in mentioning that Scheherazade had inherited the seven baskets of talk, I should have added that she put them out at compound interest until they amounted to seventy-seven.

"My dear sister," said she, on the thousand-and-second night, (I quote the language of the *Isitsöornot* at this point, *verbatim*), "my dear sister," said she, "now that all this little difficulty about the bowstring has blown over, and that this odious tax is so happily repealed, I feel that I have been guilty of great indiscretion in withholding from you and the king (who I am sorry to say, snores—a thing no gentleman would do) the full conclusion of Sinbad the sailor. This person went through numerous other and more interesting adventures than those which I related; but the truth is, I felt sleepy on the particular night of their narration, and so was seduced into cutting them short—a grievous piece of misconduct, for which I only trust that Allah will forgive me. But even yet it is not too late to remedy my great neglect—and as soon as I have given the king a pinch or two in order to wake him up so far that he may stop making that horrible noise, I will forthwith entertain you (and him if he pleases) with the sequel of this very remarkable story."

Hereupon the sister of Scheherazade, as I have it from the *Isitsöornot*, expressed no very particular intensity of gratification; but the king, having been sufficiently pinched, at length ceased snoring, and finally said, "Hum!" and then "Hoo!" when the queen, understanding these words (which are no doubt Arabic) to signify that he was all attention, and would do his best not to snore any more—the queen, I say, having arranged these matters to her satisfaction, re-entered thus, at once, into the history of Sinbad the sailor:

"'At length, in my old age,' (these are the words of Sinbad himself, as retailed by Scheherazade)—'at length, in my old age, and after enjoying many years of tranquility at home, I became once more possessed of a desire of visiting foreign countries; and one day, without acquainting any of my family with my design, I packed up some bundles of such merchandise as was most precious and least bulky, and, engaged a porter to carry them, went with him down to the sea-shore, to await the arrival of any chance vessel that might convey me out of the kingdom into some region which I had not as yet explored.

"'Having deposited the packages upon the sands, we sat down beneath some trees, and looked out into the ocean in the hope of perceiving a ship, but during several hours we saw none whatever. At length I fancied that I could hear a singular buzzing or humming sound; and the porter, after listening awhile, declared that he also could distinguish it. Presently it grew louder, and then still louder, so that we could have no doubt that the object which caused it was approaching us. At length, on the edge of the horizon, we discovered a black speck, which rapidly increased in size until we made it out to be a vast monster, swimming with a great part of its body above the surface of the sea. It came toward us with inconceivable swiftness, throwing up huge waves of foam around its breast, and illuminating all that part of the sea through which it passed, with a long line of fire that extended far off into the distance.

"'As the thing drew near we saw it very distinctly. Its length was equal to that of three of the loftiest trees that grow, and it was as wide as the great hall of audience in your palace, O most sublime and munificent of the Caliphs. Its body, which was unlike that of ordinary fishes, was as solid as a rock, and of a jetty blackness throughout all that portion of it which floated above the water, with the exception of a narrow blood-red streak that completely begirdled it. The belly, which floated beneath the surface, and of which we could get only a glimpse now and then as the monster rose and fell with the billows, was entirely covered with metallic scales, of a colour like that of the moon in misty weather. The back was flat and nearly white, and from it there extended upwards of six spines, about half the length of the whole body.

"'The horrible creature had no mouth that we could perceive, but, as if to make up for this deficiency, it was provided with at least four score of eyes, that protruded from their sockets like those of the green dragon-fly, and were arranged all around the body in two rows, one above the other, and parallel to the blood-red streak, which seemed to answer the purpose of an eyebrow. Two or three of these dreadful eyes were much larger than the others, and had the appearance of solid gold.

"'Although this beast approached us, as I have before said, with the greatest rapidity, it must have been moved altogether by necromancy—for it had neither fins like a fish nor web-feet like a duck, nor wings like the seashell which is blown along in the manner of a vessel; nor yet did it writhe itself forward as do the eels. Its head and its tail were shaped precisely alike, only, not far from the latter, were two small holes that served for nostrils, and through which the monster puffed out its thick breath with prodigious violence, and with a shrieking, disagreeable noise.

"'Our terror at beholding this hideous thing was very great, but it was even surpassed by our astonishment, when upon getting a nearer look, we perceived upon the creature's back a vast number of animals about the size and shape of men, and altogether much resembling them, except that they wore no garments (as men do), being supplied (by nature, no doubt) with an ugly uncomfortable covering, a good deal like cloth, but fitting so tight to the skin, as to render the poor wretches laughably awkward, and put them apparently to severe pain. On the very tips of their heads were certain square-looking boxes, which, at first sight, I thought might have been intended to answer as turbans, but I soon discovered that they were excessively heavy and solid, and I therefore concluded they were contrivances designed, by their great weight, to keep the heads of the animals steady and safe upon their shoulders. Around the necks of the creatures were fastened black collars, (badges of servitude, no doubt,) such as we keep on our dogs, only much wider and infinitely stiffer, so that it was quite impossible for these poor victims to move their heads in any direction without moving the body at the same time; and thus they were doomed to perpetual contemplation of their noses—a view puggish and snubby in a wonderful, if not positively in an awful degree.

"'When the monster had nearly reached the shore where we stood, it suddenly pushed out one of its eyes to a great extent, and emitted from it a terrible flash of fire, accompanied by a dense cloud of smoke, and a noise that I can compare to nothing but thunder. As the smoke cleared away, we saw one of the odd man-animals standing near the head of the large beast with a trumpet in his hand, through which (putting it to his mouth) he presently addressed us in loud, harsh, and disagreeable accents, that, perhaps, we should have mistaken for language, had they not come altogether through the nose.

"'Being thus evidently spoken to, I was at a loss how to reply, as I could in no manner understand what was said; and in this difficulty I turned to the porter, who was near swooning through affright, and demanded of him his opinion as to what species of monster it was, what it wanted, and what kind of creatures those were that so swarmed upon its back. To this the porter replied, as well as he could for trepidation, that he had once before heard of this sea-beast; that it was a cruel demon, with bowels of sulphur and blood of fire, created by evil genii as the means of inflicting misery upon mankind; that the things upon its back were vermin, such as sometimes infest cats and dogs, only a little larger and more savage; and that these vermin had their uses, however evil—for, through the torture they caused the beast by their nibbling and stingings, it was goaded into that degree of wrath which was requisite to make it roar and commit ill, and so fulfil the vengeful and malicious designs of the wicked genii.

"This account determined me to take to my heels, and, without once even looking behind me, I ran at full speed up into the hills, while the porter ran equally fast, although nearly in an opposite direction, so that, by these means, he finally made his escape with my bundles, of which I have no doubt he took excellent care—although this is a point I cannot determine, as I do not remember that I ever beheld him again.

"'For myself, I was so hotly pursued by a swarm of the men-vermin (who had come to the shore in boats) that I was very soon overtaken, bound hand and foot, and conveyed to the beast, which immediately swam out again into the middle of the sea.

"'I now bitterly repented my folly in quitting a comfortable home to peril my life in such adventures as this; but regret being useless, I made the best of my condition, and exerted myself to secure the goodwill of the man-animal that owned the trumpet, and who appeared to exercise authority over his fellows. I succeeded so well in this endeavor that, in a few days, the creature bestowed upon me various tokens of his favor, and in the end even went to the trouble of teaching me the rudiments of what it was vain enough to denominate its language; so that, at length, I was enabled to converse with it readily, and came to make it comprehend the ardent desire I had of seeing the world.

"'*Washish squashish squeak*, *Sinbad*, *hey-diddle diddle*, *grunt unt grumble*, *hiss*, *fiss*, *whiss*,' said he to me, one day after dinner—but I beg a thousand pardons, I had forgotten that your majesty is not conversant with the dialect of the Cock-neighs (so the man-animals were called; I presume because their language formed the connecting link between that of the horse and that of the rooster). With your permission, I will translate. '*Washish squashish*,' and so forth:—that is to say, 'I am happy to find, my dear Sinbad, that you are really a very excellent fellow; we are now about doing a thing which is called circumnavigating the globe; and since you are so desirous of seeing the world, I will strain a point and give you a free passage upon back of the beast.'"

When the Lady Scheherazade had proceeded thus far, relates the *Isitsöornot*, the king turned over from his left side to his right, and said:

"It is, in fact, *very* surprising, my dear queen, that you omitted, hitherto, these latter adventures of Sinbad. Do you know I think them exceedingly entertaining and strange?"

The king having thus expressed himself, we are told, the fair Scheherazade resumed her history in the following words:

"Sinbad went on in this manner with his narrative to the caliph—'I thanked the man-animal for its kindness, and soon found myself very much at home on the beast, which swam at a prodigious rate through the ocean; although the surface of the latter is, in that part of the world, by no means flat, but round like a pomegranate, so that we went—so to say—either uphill or downhill all the time.'"

"That I think, was very singular," interrupted the king.

"Nevertheless, it is quite true," replied Scheherazade.

"I have my doubts," rejoined the king; "but, pray, be so good as to go on with the story."

"I will," said the queen. "'The beast,' continued Sinbad to the caliph, 'swam, as I have related, uphill and downhill until, at length, we arrived at an island, many hundreds of miles in circumference, but which, nevertheless, had been built in the middle of the sea by a colony of little things like caterpillars.'"*

"Hum!" said the king.

"'Leaving this island,' said Sinbad—(for Scheherazade, it must be understood, took no notice of her husband's ill-mannered ejaculation)—'leaving this island, we came to another where the forests were of solid stone, and so hard that they shivered to pieces the finest-tempered axes with which we endeavored to cut them down.'"†

---

* The coralites.

† "One of the most remarkable natural curiosities in Texas is a petrified forest, near the head of Pasigno river. It consists of several hundred trees, in an erect position, all turned to stone. Some trees, now growing, are partly petrified. This is a startling fact for natural philosophers, and must cause them to modify the existing theory of petrification."—*Kennedy.*

This account, at first discredited, has since been corroborated by the discovery of a completely petrified forest, near the head waters of the Chayenne, or Chienne river, which has its source in the Black Hills of the rocky chain.

There is scarcely, perhaps, a spectacle on the surface of the globe more remarkable, either in a geological or picturesque point of view than that presented

"Hum!" said the king, again; but Scheherazade, paying him no attention, continued in the language of Sinbad.

"'Passing beyond this last island, we reached a country where there was a cave that ran to the distance of thirty or forty miles within the bowels of the earth, and that contained a greater number of far more spacious and more magnificent palaces than are to be found in all Damascus and Bagdad. From the roofs of these palaces there hung myriads of gems, like diamonds, but larger than men; and in among the streets of towers and pyramids and temples, there flowed immense rivers as black as ebony, and swarming with fish that had no eyes.'"*

"Hum!" said the king.

"'We then swam into a region of the sea where we found a lofty mountain, down whose sides there streamed torrents of melted metal, some of which were twelve miles wide and sixty miles long†; while from an abyss on the summit, issued so vast a quantity of ashes that the sun

---

by the petrified forest, near Cairo. The traveler, having passed the tombs of the caliphs, just beyond the gates of the city, proceeds to the southward, nearly at right angles to the road across the desert to Suez, and after having travelled some ten miles up a low barren valley, covered with sand, gravel, and sea-shells, fresh as if the tide had retired but yesterday, crosses a low range of sandhills, which has for some distance run parallel to his path. The scene now presented to him is beyond conception singular and desolate. A mass of fragments of trees, all converted into stone, and when struck by his horse's hoof ringing like cast iron, is seen to extend itself for miles and miles around him, in the form of a decayed and prostrate forest. The wood is of a dark brown hue, but retains its form in perfection, the pieces being from one to fifteen feet in length, and from half a foot to three feet in thickness, strewed so closely together, as far as the eye can reach, that an Egyptian donkey can scarcely thread its way through amongst them, and so natural that, were it in Scotland or Ireland, it might pass without remark for some enormous drained bog, on which the exhumed trees lay rotting in the sun. The roots and rudiments of the branches are, in many cases, nearly perfect, and in some the worm-holes eaten under the bark are readily recognizable. The most delicate of the sap vessels, and all the finer portions of the center of the wood, are perfectly entire, and bear to be examined with the strongest magnifiers. The whole are so thoroughly silicified as to scratch glass and are capable of receiving the highest polish.—*Asiatic Magazine.*

* The Mammoth Cave of Kentucky.

† In Iceland, 1783.

was entirely blotted out from the heavens, and it became darker than the darkest midnight; so that when we were even at the distance of a hundred and fifty miles from the mountain, it was impossible to see the whitest object, however close we held it to our eyes.'"*

"Hum!" said the king.

"'After quitting this coast, the beast continued his voyage until we met with a land in which the nature of things seemed reversed—for we here saw a great lake, at the bottom of which, more than a hundred feet beneath the surface of the water, there flourished in full leaf a forest of tall and luxuriant trees.'"†

"Hoo!" said the king.

"'Some hundred miles farther on brought us to a climate where the atmosphere was so dense as to sustain iron or steel, just as our own does feather.'"‡

"Fiddle de dee," said the king.

"'Proceeding still in the same direction, we presently arrived at the most magnificent region in the whole world. Through it there meandered a glorious river for several thousands of miles. This river was of unspeakable depth, and of a transparency richer than that of amber. It was from three to six miles in width; and its banks which arose on either side to twelve hundred feet in perpendicular height, were crowned with ever-blossoming trees and perpetual sweet-scented flowers, that made the

* "During the eruption of Hecla, in 1766, clouds of this kind produced such a degree of darkness that, at Glaumba, which is more than fifty leagues from the mountain, people could only find their way by groping. During the eruption of Vesuvius, in 1794, at Caserta, four leagues distant, people could only walk by the light of torches. On the first of May, 1812, a cloud of volcanic ashes and sand, coming from a volcano in the island of St. Vincent, covered the whole of Barbadoes, spreading over it so intense a darkness that, at midday, in the open air, one could not perceive the trees or other objects near him, or even a white handkerchief placed at the distance of six inches from the eye."—*Murray*, p. 215, *Phil. edit.*

† In the year 1790, in the Caraccas during an earthquake, a portion of the granite soil sank and left a lake eight hundred yards in diameter, and from eighty to a hundred feet deep. It was a part of the forest of Aripao which sank, and the trees remained green for several months under the water."—*Murray*, p. 221

‡ The hardest steel ever manufactured may, under the action of a blowpipe, be reduced to an impalpable powder, which will float readily in the atmospheric air.

whole territory one gorgeous garden; but the name of this luxuriant land was the Kingdom of Horror, and to enter it was inevitable death.'"*

"Humph!" said the king.

"'We left this kingdom in great haste, and, after some days, came to another, where we were astonished to perceive myriads of monstrous animals with horns resembling scythes upon their heads. These hideous beasts dig for themselves vast caverns in the soil, of a funnel shape, and line the sides of them with rocks, so disposed one upon the other that they fall instantly, when trodden upon by other animals, thus precipitating them into the monster's dens, where their blood is immediately sucked, and their carcasses afterwards hurled contemptuously out to an immense distance from the caverns of death.'"†

"Pooh!" said the king.

"'Continuing our progress, we perceived a district with vegetables that grew not upon any soil but in the air.‡ There were others that sprang from the substance of other vegetables;§ others that derived their substance from the bodies of living animals;¶ and then again, there were others that glowed

---

* The region of the Niger. See Simmond's *Colonial Magazine.*

† The *Myrmeleon*—lion-ant. The term "monster" is equally applicable to small abnormal things and to great, while such epithets as "vast" are merely comparative. The cavern of the myrmeleon is *vast* in comparison with the hole of the common red ant. A grain of silex is also a "rock."

‡ The *Epidendron,* Flos Aeris, of the family of the *Orchideae,* grows with merely the surface of its roots attached to a tree or other object, from which it derives no nutriment—subsisting altogether upon air.

§ The *Parasites,* such as the wonderful *Rafflesia Arnaldii.*

¶ *Schouw* advocates a class of plants that grow upon living animals—the *Plantae Epizoae.* Of this class are the *Fuci* and *Algae.*

Mr. J. B. Williams, of Salem, Mass., presented the "National Institute" with an insect from New Zealand, with the following description: "'*The Hotte,*' a decided caterpillar, or worm, is found gnawing at the root of the *Rota* tree, with a plant growing out of its head. This most peculiar and extraordinary insect travels up both the *Rota* and *Ferriri* trees, and entering into the top, eats its way, perforating the trunk of the trees until it reaches the root, and dies, or remains dormant, and the plant propagates out of its head; the body remains perfect and entire, of a harder substance than when alive. From this insect the natives make a colouring for tattooing.

all over with intense fire;* others that moved from place to place at pleasure,† and what was still more wonderful, we discovered flowers that lived and breathed and moved their limbs at will and had, moreover, the detestable passion of mankind for enslaving other creatures, and confining them in horrid and solitary prisons until the fulfillment of appointed tasks."'‡

"Pshaw!" said the king.

"'Quitting this land, we soon arrived at another in which the bees and the birds are mathematicians of such genius and erudition, that they give daily instructions in the science of geometry to the wise men of the empire. The king of the place having offered a reward for the solution of two very difficult problems, they were solved upon the spot—the one by the bees, and the other by the birds; but the king keeping their solution a secret, it was only after the most profound researches and labor, and the writing of an infinity of big books, during a long series of years, that the men-mathematicians at length arrived at the identical solutions which had been given upon the spot by the bees and by the birds."'§

---

* In mines and natural caves we find a species of cryptogamous *fungus* that emits an intense phosphorescence.

† The orchis, scabius and valisneria.

‡ "The corolla of this flower (*Aristolochia Clematitis*), which is tubular, but terminating upwards in a ligulate limb, is inflated into a globular figure at the base. The tubular part is internally beset with stiff hairs, pointing downwards. The globular part contains the pistil, which consists merely of a germen and stigma, together with the surrounding stamens. But the stamens, being shorter than the germen, cannot discharge the pollen so as to throw it upon the stigma, as the flower stands always upright till after impregnation. And hence, without some additional and peculiar aid, the pollen must necessarily fan down to the bottom of the flower. Now, the aid that nature has furnished in this case, is that of the *Tiputa Pennicornis*, a small insect, which entering the tube of the corrolla in quest of honey, descends to the bottom, and rummages about till it becomes quite covered with pollen; but not being able to force its way out again, owing to the downward position of the hairs, which converge to a point like the wires of a mouse-trap, and being somewhat impatient of its confinement it brushes backwards and forwards, trying every corner, till, after repeatedly traversing the stigma, it covers it with pollen sufficient for its impregnation, in consequence of which the flower soon begins to droop, and the hairs to shrink to the sides of the tube, effecting an easy passage for the escape of the insect."—*Rev. P. Keith—System of Physiological Botany.*

§ The bees—ever since bees were—have been constructing their cells with

"Oh my!" said the king.

"'We had scarcely lost sight of this empire when we found ourselves close upon another, from whose shores there flew over our heads a flock of fowls a mile in breadth, and two hundred and forty miles long; so that, although they flew a mile during every minute, it required no less than four hours for the whole flock to pass over us—in which there were several millions of millions of fowl.'"*

"Oh fy!" said the king.

"'No sooner had we got rid of these birds, which occasioned us great annoyance, than we were terrified by the appearance of a fowl of another kind, and infinitely larger than even the rocs which I met in my former voyages; for it was bigger than the biggest of the domes on your seraglio, oh, most Munificent of Caliphs. This terrible fowl had no head that we could perceive, but was fashioned entirely of belly, which was of a prodigious fatness and roundness, of a soft-looking substance, smooth, shining and striped with various colours. In its talons, the monster was bearing away to his eyrie in the heavens, a house from which it had knocked off the roof, and in the interior of which we distinctly saw human beings, who,

---

just such sides, in just such number, and at just such inclinations, as it has been demonstrated (in a problem involving the profoundest mathematical principles) are the very sides, in the very number, and at the very angles, which will afford the creatures the most room that is compatible with the greatest stability of structure.

During the latter part of the last century, the question arose among mathematicians—"to determine the best form that can be given to the sails of a windmill, according to their varying distances from the revolving vanes, and likewise from the centers of the revolution." This is an excessively complex problem, for it is, in other words, to find the best possible position at an infinity of varied distances and at an infinity of points on the arm. There were a thousand futile attempts to answer the query on the part of the most illustrious mathematicians, and when at length, an undeniable solution was discovered, men found that the wings of a bird had given it with absolute precision ever since the first bird had traversed the air.

* He observed a flock of pigeons passing betwixt Frankfort and the Indian territory, one mile at least in breadth; it took up four hours in passing, which, at the rate of one mile per minute, gives a length of 240 miles; and, supposing three pigeons to each square yard, gives 2,230,272,000 Pigeons.—*Travels in Canada and the United States, by Lieut. F. Hall.*

beyond doubt, were in a state of frightful despair at the horrible fate which awaited them. We shouted with all our might, in the hope of frightening the bird into letting go of its prey, but it merely gave a snort or puff, as if of rage and then let fall upon our heads a heavy sack which proved to be filled with sand!'"

"Stuff!" said the king.

"'It was just after this adventure that we encountered a continent of immense extent and prodigious solidity, but which, nevertheless, was supported entirely upon the back of a sky-blue cow that had no fewer than four hundred horns.'"*

"*That*, now, I believe," said the king, "because I have read something of the kind before, in a book."

"'We passed immediately beneath this continent, (swimming in between the legs of the cow), and, after some hours, found ourselves in a wonderful country indeed, which, I was informed by the man-animal, was his own native land, inhabited by things of his own species. This elevated the man-animal very much in my esteem, and in fact, I now began to feel ashamed of the contemptuous familiarity with which I had treated him; for I found that the man-animals in general were a nation of the most powerful magicians, who lived with worms in their brain,† which, no doubt, served to stimulate them by their painful writhings and wrigglings to the most miraculous efforts of imagination!'"

"Nonsense!" said the king.

"'Among the magicians, were domesticated several animals of very singular kinds; for example, there was a huge horse whose bones were iron and whose blood was boiling water. In place of corn, he had black stones for his usual food; and yet, in spite of so hard a diet, he was so strong and swift that he would drag a load more weighty than the grandest temple in this city, at a rate surpassing that of the flight of most birds.'"‡

---

* The earth is upheld by a cow of a blue colour, having horns four hundred in number."—*Sale's Koran.*

† "The *Entozoa*, or intestinal worms, have repeatedly been observed in the muscles, and in the cerebral substance of men."—*See Wyatt's Physiology*, p. 143.

‡ On the Great Western Railway, between London and Exeter, a speed of 71 miles per hour has been attained. A train weighing 90 tons was whirled from Paddington to Didcot (53 miles) in 51 minutes.

"Twattle!" said the king.

"'I saw, also, among these people a hen without feathers, but bigger than a camel; instead of flesh and bone she had iron and brick; her blood, like that of the horse, (to whom, in fact, she was nearly related,) was boiling water; and like him she ate nothing but wood or black stones. This hen brought forth very frequently, a hundred chickens in the day; and, after birth, they took up their residence for several weeks within the stomach of their mother.'"*

"Fa! Lal!" said the king.

"'One of this nation of mighty conjurors created a man out of brass and wood, and leather, and endowed him with such ingenuity that he would have beaten at chess, all the race of mankind with the exception of the great Caliph, Haroun Alraschid.† Another of these magi constructed (of like material) a creature that put to shame even the genius of him who made it; for so great were its reasoning powers that, in a second, it performed calculations of so vast an extent that they would have required the united labor of fifty thousand fleshy men for a year.‡ But a still more wonderful conjuror fashioned for himself a mighty thing that was neither man nor beast, but which had brains of lead, intermixed with a black matter like pitch, and fingers that it employed with such incredible speed and dexterity that it would have had no trouble in writing out twenty thousand copies of the Koran in an hour, and this with so exquisite a precision, that in all the copies there should not be found one to vary from another by the breadth of the finest hair. This thing was of prodigious strength, so that it erected or overthrew the mightiest empires at a breath; but its powers were exercised equally for evil and for good.'"

"Ridiculous!" said the king.

"'Among this nation of necromancers there was also one who had in his veins the blood of the salamanders; for he made no scruple of sitting down to smoke his chibouc in a red-hot oven until his dinner was thoroughly roasted upon its floor.§ Another had the faculty of converting

---

* The *Eccalobeion*

† Maelzel's Automaton Chess-player.

‡ Babbage's Calculating Machine.

§ *Chabert*, and since him, a hundred others.

the common metals into gold, without even looking at them during the process.* Another had such a delicacy of touch that he made a wire so fine as to be invisible.† Another had such quickness of perception that he counted all the separate motions of an elastic body, while it was springing backward and forward at the rate of nine hundred millions of times in a second.'"‡

"Absurd!" said the king.

"'Another of these magicians, by means of a fluid that nobody ever yet saw, could make the corpses of his friends brandish their arms, kick out their legs, fight, or even get up and dance at his will.§ Another had cultivated his voice to so great an extent that he could have made himself heard from one end of the world to the other.¶ Another had so long an arm that he could sit down in Damascus and indite a letter at Bagdad—or indeed at any distance whatsoever.** Another commanded the lightning to come down to him out of the heavens, and it came at his call; and served him for a plaything when it came. Another took two loud sounds and out of them made a silence. Another constructed a deep darkness out of two brilliant lights.†† Another

---

* The Electrotype.

† *Wollaston* made of platinum for the field of views in a telescope a wire one eighteen-thousandth part of an inch in thickness. It could be seen only by means of the microscope.

‡ Newton demonstrated that the retina beneath the influence of the violet ray of the spectrum, vibrated 900,000,000 of times in a second.

§ The Voltaic pile.

¶ The Electro Telegraph Printing Apparatus.

** The Electro telegraph transmits intelligence instantaneously—at least at so far as regards any distance upon the earth.

†† Common experiments in Natural Philosophy. If two red rays from two luminous points be admitted into a dark chamber so as to fall on a white surface, and differ in their length by 0.0000258 of an inch, their intensity is doubled. So also if the difference in length be any whole-number multiple of that fraction. A multiple by 2 1/4, 3 1/4, &c., gives an intensity equal to one ray only; but a multiple by 2 1/2, 3 1/2, &c., gives the result of total darkness. In violet rays similar effects arise when the difference in length is 0.0000157 of an inch; and with all other rays the results are the same—the difference varying with a uniform increase from the violet to the red.

"Analogous experiments in respect to sound produce analogous results."

made ice in a red-hot furnace.* Another directed the sun to paint his portrait, and the sun did.† Another took this luminary with the moon and the planets, and having first weighed them with scrupulous accuracy, probed into their depths and found out the solidity of the substance of which they were made. But the whole nation is, indeed, of so surprising a necromantic ability, that not even their infants, nor their commonest cats and dogs have any difficulty in seeing objects that do not exist at all, or that for twenty millions of years before the birth of the nation itself had been blotted out from the face of creation.'"‡

"Preposterous!" said the king.

"'The wives and daughters of these incomparably great and wise magi,'" continued Scheherazade, without being in any manner disturbed by these frequent and most ungentlemanly interruptions on the part of her husband—"'the wives and daughters of these eminent conjurers are everything that is accomplished and refined; and would be everything

---

* Place a platina crucible over a spirit lamp, and keep it a red heat; pour in some sulphuric acid, which, though the most volatile of bodies at a common temperature, will be found to become completely fixed in a hot crucible, and not a drop evaporates—being surrounded by an atmosphere of its own, it does not, in fact, touch the sides. A few drops of water are now introduced, when the acid, immediately coming in contact with the heated sides of the crucible, flies off in sulphurous acid vapor, and so rapid is its progress, that the caloric of the water passes off with it, which falls a lump of ice to the bottom; by taking advantage of the moment before it is allowed to remelt, it may be turned out a lump of ice from a red-hot vessel.

† The Daguerreotype.

‡ Although light travels 167,000 miles in a second, the distance of 61 Cygni (the only star whose distance is ascertained) is so inconceivably great, that its rays would require more than ten years to reach the earth. For stars beyond this, 20—or even 1000 years—would be a moderate estimate. Thus, if they had been annihilated 20, or 1000 years ago, we might still see them today by the light which *started* from their surfaces 20 or 1000 years in the past time. That many which we see daily are really extinct, is not impossible—not even improbable.

The elder Herschel maintains that the light of the faintest nebulae seen through his great telescope, must have taken 3,000,000 years in reaching the earth. Some, made visible by Lord Ross' instrument must, then, have required at least 20,000,000.

that is interesting and beautiful, but for an unhappy fatality that besets them, and from which not even the miraculous powers of their husbands and fathers has, hitherto, been adequate to save. Some fatalities come in certain shapes, and some in others—but this of which I speak has come in the shape of a crotchet.'"

"A what?" said the king.

"'A crotchet'" said Scheherazade. "'One of the evil genii, who are perpetually upon the watch to inflict ill, has put it into the heads of these accomplished ladies that the thing which we describe as personal beauty consists altogether in the protuberance of the region which lies not very far below the small of the back. Perfection of loveliness, they say, is in the direct ratio of the extent of this lump. Having been long possessed of this idea, and bolsters being cheap in that country, the days have long gone by since it was possible to distinguish a woman from a dromedary—'"

"Stop!" said the king—"I can't stand that, and I won't. You have already given me a dreadful headache with your lies. The day, too, I perceive, is beginning to break. How long have we been married?—my conscience is getting to be troublesome again. And then that dromedary touch—do you take me for a fool? Upon the whole, you might as well get up and be throttled."

These words, as I learn from the *Isitsöornot*, both grieved and astonished Scheherazade; but, as she knew the king to be a man of scrupulous integrity, and quite unlikely to forfeit his word, she submitted to her fate with a good grace. She derived, however, great consolation, (during the tightening of the bowstring,) from the reflection that much of the history remained still untold, and that the petulance of her brute of a husband had reaped for him a most righteous reward, in depriving him of many inconceivable adventures.

The Oval Portrait

[One of Poe's shortest stories, this tale of bereavement revolves around the baffling relationship between art and life. It was first published as a longer version in *Graham's Magazine* with the title 'Life in Death' in April 1842. This shorter version, renamed 'The Oval Portrait', appeared in the April 26, 1845, edition of the *Broadway Journal.* The story is narrated by an injured narrator.]

The château into which my valet had ventured to make forcible entrance, rather than permit me, in my desperately wounded condition, to pass a night in the open air, was one of those piles of commingled gloom and grandeur which have so long frowned among the Appennines, not less in fact than in the fancy of Mrs. Radcliffe. To all appearance it had been temporarily and very lately abandoned. We established ourselves in one of the smallest and least sumptuously furnished apartments. It lay in a remote turret of the building. Its decorations were rich, yet tattered and antique. Its walls were hung with tapestry and bedecked with manifold and multiform armorial trophies, together with an unusually great number of very spirited modern paintings in frames of rich golden arabesque. In these paintings, which depended from the walls not only in their main surfaces, but in very many nooks which the bizarre architecture of the château rendered necessary—in these paintings my incipient delirium, perhaps, had caused me to take deep interest; so that I bade Pedro to close the heavy shutters of the room—since it was already night—to light the tongues of a tall candelabrum which stood by the head of my bed—and to throw open far and wide the fringed curtains of black velvet which enveloped the bed itself. I wished all this done that I might resign myself, if not to sleep, at least alternately to the contemplation of these pictures, and the perusal of a small volume which had been found upon the pillow, and which purported to criticize and describe them.

Long, long I read, and devoutly, devotedly I gazed. Rapidly and gloriously the hours flew by and the deep midnight came. The position of the candelabrum displeased me, and outreaching my hand with difficulty, rather than disturb my slumbering valet, I placed it so as to throw its rays more fully upon the book.

But the action produced an effect altogether unanticipated. The rays of the numerous candles (for there were many) now fell within a niche of the room which had hitherto been thrown into deep shade by one of the bedposts. I thus saw in vivid light a picture all unnoticed before. It was the portrait of a young girl just ripening into womanhood. I glanced at the painting hurriedly, and then closed my eyes. Why I did this was not at first apparent even to my own perception. But while my lids remained thus shut, I ran over in my mind my reason for so shutting them. It was an impulsive movement to gain time for thought—to make sure that my vision had not deceived me—to calm and subdue my fancy for a more sober and more certain gaze. In a very few moments I again looked fixedly at the painting.

That I now saw aright I could not and would not doubt; for the first flashing of the candles upon that canvas had seemed to dissipate the dreamy stupor which was stealing over my senses, and to startle me at once into waking life.

The portrait, I have already said, was that of a young girl. It was a mere head and shoulders, done in what is technically termed a vignette manner; much in the style of the favorite heads of Sully. The arms, the bosom, and even the ends of the radiant hair melted imperceptibly into the vague yet deep shadow which formed the background of the whole. The frame was oval, richly gilded and filigreed in *Moresque*. As a thing of art nothing could be more admirable than the painting itself. But it could have been neither the execution of the work, nor the immortal beauty of the countenance, which had so suddenly and so vehemently moved me. Least of all, could it have been that my fancy, shaken from its half slumber, had mistaken the head for that of a living person. I saw at once that the peculiarities of the design, of the vignetting, and of the frame, must have instantly dispelled such idea—must have prevented even its momentary entertainment. Thinking earnestly upon these points, I remained, for an hour perhaps, half sitting, half reclining, with my vision riveted upon the portrait. At length, satisfied with the true secret of its effect, I fell back within the bed. I had found the spell of the picture in an absolute *life-likeliness* of expression, which, at first startling, finally confounded, subdued, and appalled me. With deep and reverent awe I replaced the candelabrum in its former position. The cause of my deep agitation being thus shut from view, I sought eagerly the volume which discussed the paintings and their histories. Turning to the number which designated the oval portrait, I there read the vague and quaint words which follow:

"She was a maiden of rarest beauty, and not more lovely than full of glee. And evil was the hour when she saw, and loved, and wedded the painter. He, passionate, studious, austere, and having already a bride in his Art; she a maiden of rarest beauty, and not more lovely than full of glee; all light and smiles, and frolicsome as the young fawn; loving and cherishing all things; hating only the Art which was her rival; dreading only the palette and brushes and other untoward instruments which deprived her of the countenance of her lover. It was thus a terrible thing for this lady to hear the painter speak of his desire to portray even his young bride. But she was humble and obedient, and sat meekly for many weeks in the dark, high turret-chamber where the light dripped upon the pale canvas only from overhead. But he, the painter, took glory in his work, which went on from hour to hour, and from day to day. And he was a passionate, and wild, and moody man, who became lost in reveries; so that he *would* not see that the light which fell so ghastly in that lone turret withered the health and the spirits of his bride, who pined visibly to all but him. Yet she smiled on and still on, uncomplainingly, because she saw that the painter (who had high renown) took a fervid and burning pleasure in his task, and wrought day and night to depict her who so loved him, yet who grew daily more dispirited and weak. And in sooth some who beheld the portrait spoke of its resemblance in low words, as of a mighty marvel, and a proof not less of the power of the painter than of his deep love for her whom he depicted so surpassingly well. But at length, as the labor drew nearer to its conclusion, there were admitted none into the turret; for the painter had grown wild with the ardour of his work, and turned his eyes from the canvas rarely, even to regard the countenance of his wife. And he *would* not see that the tints which he spread upon the canvas were drawn from the cheeks of her who sat beside him. And when many weeks had passed, and but little remained to do, save one brush upon the mouth and one tint upon the eye, the spirit of the lady again flickered up as the flame within the socket of the lamp. And then the brush was given, and then the tint was placed; and, for one moment, the painter stood entranced before the work which he had wrought; but in the next, while he yet gazed, he grew tremulous and very pallid, and aghast, and crying with a loud voice, 'This is indeed *Life* itself!' turned suddenly to regard his beloved:—*She was dead!*"

Some Words with a Mummy

[A satire on the interest in Egyptology during those times, this grotesque short story first appeared in April 1845 in *The American Review: A Whig Journal*.]

The *symposium* of the preceding evening had been a little too much for my nerves. I had a wretched headache, and was desperately drowsy. Instead of going out therefore to spend the evening as I had proposed, it occurred to me that I could not do a wiser thing than just eat a mouthful of supper and go immediately to bed.

A *light* supper of course. I am exceedingly fond of Welsh rabbit. More than a pound at once, however, may not at all times be advisable. Still, there can be no material objection to two. And really between two and three, there is merely a single unit of difference. I ventured, perhaps, upon four. My wife will have it five;—but, clearly, she has confounded two very distinct affairs. The abstract number, five, I am willing to admit; but, concretely, it has reference to bottles of Brown Stout, without which, in the way of condiment, Welsh rabbit is to be eschewed.

Having thus concluded a frugal meal, and donned my night-cap, with the serene hope of enjoying it till noon the next day, I placed my head upon the pillow, and, through the aid of a capital conscience, fell into a profound slumber forthwith.

But when were the hopes of humanity fulfilled? I could not have completed my third snore when there came a furious ringing at the street-door bell, and then an impatient thumping at the knocker, which awakened me at once. In a minute afterward, and while I was still rubbing my eyes, my wife thrust in my face a note, from my old friend, Doctor Ponnonner. It ran thus:

> Come to me, by all means, my dear good friend, as soon as you receive this. Come and help us to rejoice. At last, by long persevering diplomacy, I have gained the assent of the Directors of the City Museum, to my examination of the Mummy—you know the one I mean. I have permission to unswathe it and open it, if desirable. A few friends only will be present—you, of course. The Mummy is now at my house, and we shall begin to unroll it at eleven tonight.
>
> Yours ever,
>
> PONNONNER

By the time I had reached the "Ponnonner," it struck me that I was as wide awake as a man need be. I leaped out of bed in an ecstasy, overthrowing all in my way; dressed myself with a rapidity truly marvelous; and set off, at the top of my speed, for the Doctor's.

There I found a very eager company assembled. They had been awaiting me with much impatience; the Mummy was extended upon the dining-table; and the moment I entered its examination was commenced.

It was one of a pair brought, several years previously, by Captain Arthur Sabretash, a cousin of Ponnonner's, from a tomb near Eleithias, in the Lybian mountains, a considerable distance above Thebes on the Nile. The grottoes at this point, although less magnificent than the Theban sepulchres, are of higher interest, on account of affording more numerous illustrations of the private life of the Egyptians. The chamber from which our specimen was taken, was said to be very rich in such illustrations; the walls being completely covered with fresco paintings and bas-reliefs, while statues, vases, and Mosaic work of rich patterns, indicated the vast wealth of the deceased.

The treasure had been deposited in the Museum precisely in the same condition in which Captain Sabretash had found it;—that is to say, the coffin had not been disturbed. For eight years it had thus stood, subject only externally to public inspection. We had now, therefore, the complete Mummy at our disposal; and to those who are aware how very rarely the unransacked antique reaches our shores, it will be evident, at once that we had great reason to congratulate ourselves upon our good fortune.

Approaching the table, I saw on it a large box, or case, nearly seven feet long, and perhaps three feet wide, by two feet and a half deep. It was oblong—not coffin-shaped. The material was at first supposed to be the wood of the sycamore (*platanus*), but, upon cutting into it, we found it to be pasteboard, or, more properly, *papier maché*, composed of papyrus. It was thickly ornamented with paintings, representing funeral scenes, and other mournful subjects—interspersed among which, in every variety of position, were certain series of hieroglyphical characters, intended, no doubt, for the name of the departed. By good luck, Mr. Gliddon formed one of our party; and he had no difficulty in translating the letters, which were simply phonetic, and represented the word, *Allamistakeo.*

We had some difficulty in getting this case open without injury; but having at length accomplished the task, we came to a second, coffin-shaped, and very considerably less in size than the exterior one, but resembling it precisely in every other respect. The interval between the two was filled with resin, which had, in some degree, defaced the colours of the interior box.

Upon opening this latter (which we did quite easily), we arrived at a third case, also coffin-shaped, and varying from the second one in no particular, except in that of its material, which was cedar, and still emitted the peculiar and highly aromatic odor of that wood. Between the second and the third case there was no interval—the one fitting accurately within the other.

Removing the third case, we discovered and took out the body itself. We had expected to find it, as usual, enveloped in frequent rolls, or bandages, of linen; but, in place of these, we found a sort of sheath, made of papyrus, and coated with a layer of plaster, thickly gilt and painted. The paintings represented subjects connected with the various supposed duties of the soul, and its presentation to different divinities, with numerous identical human figures, intended, very probably, as portraits of the persons embalmed. Extending from head to foot was a columnar, or perpendicular, inscription, in phonetic hieroglyphics, giving again his name and titles, and the names and titles of his relations.

Around the neck thus ensheathed, was a collar of cylindrical glass beads, diverse in colour, and so arranged as to form images of deities, of the scarabæus, etc., with the winged globe. Around the small of the waist was a similar collar or belt.

Stripping off the papyrus, we found the flesh in excellent preservation, with no perceptible odor. The colour was reddish. The skin was hard, smooth, and glossy. The teeth and hair were in good condition. The eyes (it seemed) had been removed, and glass ones substituted, which were very beautiful and wonderfully life-like, with the exception of somewhat too determined a stare. The fingers and the nails were brilliantly gilded.

Mr. Gliddon was of opinion, from the redness of the epidermis, that the embalmment had been effected altogether by asphaltum; but, on scraping the surface with a steel instrument, and throwing into the fire some of the powder thus obtained, the flavor of camphor and other sweet-scented gums became apparent.

We searched the corpse very carefully for the usual openings through which the entrails are extracted, but, to our surprise, we could discover none. No member of the party was at that period aware that entire or unopened mummies are not infrequently met. The brain it was customary to withdraw through the nose; the intestines through an incision in the side; the body was then shaved, washed, and salted; then laid aside for several weeks, when the operation of embalming, properly so called, began.

As no trace of an opening could be found, Doctor Ponnonner was preparing his instruments for dissection, when I observed that it was then past two o'clock. Hereupon it was agreed to postpone the internal examination until the next evening; and we were about to separate for the present, when someone suggested an experiment or two with the Voltaic pile.

The application of electricity to a Mummy three or four thousand years old at the least, was an idea, if not very sage, still sufficiently original, and we all caught it at once. About one-tenth in earnest and nine-tenths in jest, we arranged a battery in the Doctor's study, and conveyed thither the Egyptian.

It was only after much trouble that we succeeded in laying bare some portions of the temporal muscle which appeared of less stony rigidity than other parts of the frame, but which, as we had anticipated, of course, gave no indication of galvanic susceptibility when brought in contact with the wire. This, the first trial, indeed, seemed decisive, and, with a hearty laugh at our own absurdity, we were bidding each other good night, when my eyes, happening to fall upon those of the Mummy, were there immediately riveted in amazement. My brief glance, in fact, had sufficed to assure me that the orbs which we had all supposed to be glass, and which were originally noticeable for a certain wild stare, were now so far covered by the lids, that only a small portion of the *tunica albuginea* remained visible.

With a shout I called attention to the fact, and it became immediately obvious to all.

I cannot say that I was *alarmed* at the phenomenon, because "alarmed" is, in my case, not exactly the word. It is possible, however, that, but for the Brown Stout, I might have been a little nervous. As for the rest of the company, they really made no attempt at concealing the downright fright which possessed them. Doctor Ponnonner was a man to be pitied. Mr. Gliddon, by some peculiar process, rendered himself invisible. Mr. Silk Buckingham, I fancy, will scarcely be so bold as to deny that he made his way, upon all fours, under the table.

After the first shock of astonishment, however, we resolved, as a matter of course, upon further experiment forthwith. Our operations were now directed against the great toe of the right foot. We made an incision over the outside of the exterior *os sesamoideum pollicis pedis,* and thus got at the root of the *abductor* muscle. Readjusting the battery, we now applied the fluid to the bisected nerves—when, with a movement of exceeding life-likeness, the Mummy first drew up its right knee so as to bring it nearly in contact with the abdomen, and then, straightening the limb with inconceivable force, bestowed a kick upon Doctor Ponnonner, which had the effect of discharging that gentleman, like an arrow from a catapult, through a window into the street below.

We rushed out *en masse* to bring in the mangled remains of the victim, but had the happiness to meet him upon the staircase, coming up in an unaccountable hurry, brimful of the most ardent philosophy, and more than ever impressed with the necessity of prosecuting our experiment with vigor and with zeal.

It was by his advice, accordingly, that we made, upon the spot, a profound incision into the tip of the subject's nose, while the Doctor himself, laying violent hands upon it, pulled it into vehement contact with the wire.

Morally and physically—figuratively and literally—was the effect electric. In the first place, the corpse opened its eyes and winked very rapidly for several minutes, as does Mr. Barnes in the pantomime, in the second place, it sneezed; in the third, it sat upon end; in the fourth, it shook its fist in Doctor Ponnonner's face; in the fifth, turning to Messieurs Gliddon and Buckingham, it addressed them, in very capital Egyptian, thus:

"I must say, gentlemen, that I am as much surprised as I am mortified at your behaviour. Of Doctor Ponnonner nothing better was to be expected. He is a poor little fat fool who *knows* no better. I pity and forgive him. But you, Mr. Gliddon—and you, Silk—who have traveled and resided in Egypt until one might imagine you to the manner born—you, I say who have been so much among us that you speak Egyptian fully as well, I think, as you write your mother tongue—you, whom I have always been led to regard as the firm friend of the mummies—I really did anticipate more gentlemanly conduct from *you*. What am I to think of your standing quietly by and seeing me thus unhandsomely used? What am I to suppose by your permitting Tom, Dick, and Harry to strip me of my coffins, and my clothes, in this wretchedly cold climate? In what light (to come to the point) am I to regard your aiding and abetting that miserable little villain, Doctor Ponnonner, in pulling me by the nose?"

It will be taken for granted, no doubt, that upon hearing this speech under the circumstances, we all either made for the door, or fell into violent hysterics, or went off in a general swoon. One of these three things was, I say, to be expected. Indeed each and all of these lines of conduct might have been very plausibly pursued. And, upon my word, I am at a loss to know how or why it was that we pursued neither the one nor the other. But, perhaps, the true reason is to be sought in the spirit of the age, which proceeds by the rule of contraries altogether, and is now usually admitted as the solution of everything in the way of paradox and impossibility. Or, perhaps, after all, it was only the Mummy's exceedingly natural and matter-of-course air that divested his words of the terrible. However this may be, the facts are clear, and no member of our party betrayed any very particular trepidation, or seemed to consider that anything had gone very especially wrong.

For my part I was convinced it was all right, and merely stepped aside, out of the range of the Egyptian's fist. Doctor Ponnonner thrust his hands into his breeches' pockets, looked hard at the Mummy, and grew excessively red in the face. Mr. Glidden stroked his whiskers and drew up the collar of his shirt. Mr. Buckingham hung down his head, and put his right thumb into the left corner of his mouth.

The Egyptian regarded him with a severe countenance for some minutes and at length, with a sneer, said:

"Why don't you speak, Mr. Buckingham? Did you hear what I asked you, or not? *Do* take your thumb out of your mouth!"

Mr. Buckingham, hereupon, gave a slight start, took his right thumb out of the left corner of his mouth, and, by way of indemnification inserted his left thumb in the right corner of the aperture above-mentioned.

Not being able to get an answer from Mr. B., the figure turned peevishly to Mr. Gliddon, and, in a peremptory tone, demanded in general terms what we all meant.

Mr. Gliddon replied at great length, in phonetics; and but for the deficiency of American printing-offices in hieroglyphical type, it would afford me much pleasure to record here, in the original, the whole of his very excellent speech.

I may as well take this occasion to remark, that all the subsequent conversation in which the Mummy took a part, was carried on in primitive Egyptian, through the medium (so far as concerned myself and other untraveled members of the company)—through the medium, I say, of Messieurs Gliddon and Buckingham, as interpreters. These gentlemen spoke the mother tongue of the Mummy with inimitable fluency and grace; but I could not help observing that (owing, no doubt, to the introduction of images entirely modern, and, of course, entirely novel to the stranger) the two travelers were reduced, occasionally, to the employment of sensible forms for the purpose of conveying a particular meaning. Mr. Gliddon, at one period, for example, could not make the Egyptian comprehend the term "politics," until he sketched upon the wall, with a bit of charcoal a little carbuncle-nosed gentleman, out at elbows, standing upon a stump, with his left leg drawn back, right arm thrown forward, with his fist shut, the eyes rolled up toward Heaven, and the mouth open at an angle of ninety degrees. Just in the same way Mr. Buckingham failed to convey the absolutely modern idea "wig," until (at Doctor Ponnonner's suggestion) he grew very pale in the face, and consented to take off his own.

It will be readily understood that Mr. Gliddon's discourse turned chiefly upon the vast benefits accruing to science from the unrolling and disemboweling of mummies; apologizing, upon this score, for any disturbance that might have been occasioned *him*, in particular, the individual Mummy called Allamistakeo; and concluding with a mere hint (for it could scarcely be considered more) that, as these little matters were now explained, it might be as well to proceed with the investigation intended. Here Doctor Ponnonner made ready his instruments.

In regard to the latter suggestions of the orator, it appears that Allamistakeo had certain scruples of conscience, the nature of which I did not distinctly learn; but he expressed himself satisfied with the apologies tendered, and, getting down from the table, shook hands with the company all round.

When this ceremony was at an end, we immediately busied ourselves in repairing the damages which our subject had sustained from the scalpel. We sewed up the wound in his temple, bandaged his foot, and applied a square inch of black plaster to the tip of his nose.

It was now observed that the Count (this was the title, it seems, of Allamistakeo) had a slight fit of shivering—no doubt from the cold. The Doctor immediately repaired to his wardrobe, and soon returned with a black dress coat, made in Jennings' best manner, a pair of sky-blue plaid pantaloons with straps, a pink gingham *chemise*, a flapped vest of brocade, a white sack overcoat, a walking cane with a hook, a hat with no brim, patent-leather boots, straw-coloured kid gloves, an eye-glass, a pair of whiskers, and a waterfall cravat. Owing to the disparity of size between the Count and the doctor (the proportion being as two to one), there was some little difficulty in adjusting these habiliments upon the person of the Egyptian; but when all was arranged, he might have been said to be dressed. Mr. Gliddon, therefore, gave him his arm, and led him to a comfortable chair by the fire, while the Doctor rang the bell upon the spot and ordered a supply of cigars and wine.

The conversation soon grew animated. Much curiosity was, of course, expressed in regard to the somewhat remarkable fact of Allamistakeo's still remaining alive.

"I should have thought," observed Mr. Buckingham, "that it is high time you were dead."

"Why," replied the Count, very much astonished, "I am little more than seven hundred years old! My father lived a thousand, and was by no means in his dotage when he died."

Here ensued a brisk series of questions and computations, by means of which it became evident that the antiquity of the Mummy had been grossly misjudged. It had been five thousand and fifty years and some months since he had been consigned to the catacombs at Eleithias.

"But my remark," resumed Mr. Buckingham, "had no reference to your age at the period of interment (I am willing to grant, in fact, that you are still a young man), and my illusion was to the immensity of time during which, by your own showing, you must have been done up in asphaltum."

"In what?" said the Count.

"In asphaltum," persisted Mr. B.

"Ah, yes; I have some faint notion of what you mean; it might be made to answer, no doubt—but in my time we employed scarcely anything else than the Bichloride of Mercury."

"But what we are especially at a loss to understand," said Doctor Ponnonner, "is how it happens that, having been dead and buried in Egypt five thousand years ago, you are here today all alive and looking so delightfully well."

"Had I been, as you say, *dead*," replied the Count, "it is more than probable that dead, I should still be; for I perceive you are yet in the infancy of Galvanism, and cannot accomplish with it what was a common thing among us in the old days. But the fact is, I fell into catalepsy, and it was considered by my best friends that I was either dead or should be; they accordingly embalmed me at once—I presume you are aware of the chief principle of the embalming process?"

"Why not altogether."

"Ah, I perceive—a deplorable condition of ignorance! Well I cannot enter into details just now: but it is necessary to explain that to embalm (properly speaking), in Egypt, was to arrest indefinitely *all* the animal functions subjected to the process. I use the word 'animal' in its widest sense, as including the physical not more than the moral and *vital* being. I repeat that the leading principle of embalmment consisted, with us, in the immediately arresting, and holding in perpetual *abeyance*, *all* the animal functions subjected to the process. To be brief, in whatever condition the individual was, at the period of embalmment, in that condition he remained. Now, as it is my good fortune to be of the blood of the Scarabæus, I was embalmed alive, as you see me at present."

"The blood of the Scarabæus!" exclaimed Doctor Ponnonner.

"Yes. The Scarabæus was the *insignium*, or the 'arms,' of a very distinguished and very rare patrician family. To be 'of the blood of the Scarabæus,' is merely to be one of that family of which the Scarabæus is the *insignium*. I speak figuratively."

"But what has this to do with you being alive?"

"Why, it is the general custom in Egypt to deprive a corpse, before embalmment, of its bowels and brains; the race of the Scarabæi alone did not coincide with the custom. Had I not been a Scarabæus, therefore, I should have been without bowels and brains; and without either it is inconvenient to live."

"I perceive that," said Mr. Buckingham, "and I presume that all the *entire* mummies that come to hand are of the race of Scarabæi."

"Beyond doubt."

"I thought," said Mr. Gliddon very meekly, "that the Scarabæus was one of the Egyptian gods."

"One of the Egyptian *what?*" exclaimed the Mummy, starting to its feet.

"Gods!" repeated the traveler.

"Mr. Gliddon, I really am astonished to hear you talk in this style," said the Count, resuming his chair. "No nation upon the face of the earth has ever acknowledged more than *one god*. The Scarabæus, the Ibis, etc., were with us (as similar creatures have been with others) the symbols, or *media*, through which we offered worship to the Creator too august to be more directly approached."

There was here a pause. At length the colloquy was renewed by Doctor Ponnonner.

"It is not improbable, then, from what you have explained," said he, "that among the catacombs near the Nile, there may exist other mummies of the Scarabæus tribe, in a condition of vitality?"

"There can be no question of it," replied the Count; "all the Scarabæi embalmed accidentally while alive, are alive now. Even some of those *purposely* so embalmed, may have been overlooked by their executors, and still remain in the tombs."

"Will you be kind enough to explain," I said, "what you mean by 'purposely so embalmed'?"

"With great pleasure!" answered the Mummy, after surveying me leisurely through his eye-glass—for it was the first time I had ventured to address him a direct question.

"With great pleasure," he said. "The usual duration of man's life, in my time, was about eight hundred years. Few men died, unless by most extraordinary accident, before the age of six hundred; few lived longer than a decade of centuries; but eight were considered the natural term. After the discovery of the embalming principle, as I have already described it to you, it occurred to our philosophers that a laudable curiosity might be gratified, and, at the same time, the interests of science much advanced, by living this natural term in instalments. In the case of history, indeed, experience demonstrated that something of this kind was indispensable. An historian, for example, having attained the age of five hundred, would write a book with great labor and then get himself carefully embalmed; leaving instructions to his executors *pro tem.*, that they should cause him to be revivified after the lapse of a certain period—say five or six hundred years. Resuming existence at the expiration of this term, he would invariably find his great work converted into a species of haphazard note-book—that is to say, into a kind of literary arena for the conflicting guesses, riddles, and personal squabbles of whole herds of exasperated commentators. These guesses, etc., which passed under the name of annotations, or emendations, were found so completely to have enveloped, distorted, and overwhelmed the text, that the author had to go about with a lantern to discover his own book. When discovered, it was never worth the trouble of the search. After re-writing it throughout, it was regarded as the bounden duty of the historian to set himself to work immediately in correcting, from his own private knowledge and experience, the traditions of the day concerning the epoch at which he had originally lived. Now this process of rescription and personal rectification, pursued by various individual sages from time to time, had the effect of preventing our history from degenerating into absolute fable."

"I beg your pardon," said Doctor Ponnonner at this point, laying his hand gently upon the arm of the Egyptian—"I beg your pardon, sir, but may I presume to interrupt you for one moment?"

"By all means, *sir*," replied the Count, drawing up.

"I merely wished to ask you a question," said the Doctor. "You mentioned the historian's personal correction of *traditions* respecting his own epoch. Pray, sir, upon an average what proportion of these Kabbala were usually found to be right?"

"The Kabbala, as you properly term them, sir, were generally discovered to be precisely on a par with the facts recorded in the un-rewritten histories themselves;—that is to say, not one individual iota of either was ever known, under any circumstances, to be not totally and radically wrong."

"But since it is quite clear," resumed the Doctor, "that at least five thousand years have elapsed since your entombment, I take it for granted that your histories at that period, if not your traditions were sufficiently explicit on that one topic of universal interest, the Creation, which took place, as I presume you are aware, only about ten centuries before."

"Sir!" said the Count Allamistakeo.

The Doctor repeated his remarks, but it was only after much additional explanation that the foreigner could be made to comprehend them. The latter at length said, hesitatingly:

"The ideas you have suggested are to me, I confess, utterly novel. During my time I never knew any one to entertain so singular a fancy as that the universe (or this world if you will have it so) ever had a beginning at all. I remember once, and once only, hearing something remotely hinted, by a man of many speculations, concerning the origin *of the human race;* and by this individual, the very word *Adam* (or Red Earth), which you make use of, was employed. He employed it, however, in a generical sense, with reference to the spontaneous germination from rank soil (just as a thousand of the lower *genera* of creatures are germinated)—the spontaneous germination, I say, of five vast hordes of men, simultaneously upspringing in five distinct and nearly equal divisions of the globe."

Here, in general, the company shrugged their shoulders, and one or two of us touched our foreheads with a very significant air. Mr. Silk Buckingham, first glancing slightly at the occiput and then at the sinciput of Allamistakeo, spoke as follows:

"The long duration of human life in your time, together with the occasional practice of passing it, as you have explained, in instalments, must have had, indeed, a strong tendency to the general development and conglomeration of knowledge. I presume, therefore, that we are to attribute the marked inferiority of the old Egyptians in all particulars of science, when compared with the moderns, and more especially with the Yankees, altogether to the superior solidity of the Egyptian skull."

"I confess again," replied the Count, with much suavity, "that I am somewhat at a loss to comprehend you; pray, to what particulars of science do you allude?"

Here our whole party, joining voices, detailed, at great length, the assumptions of phrenology and the marvels of animal magnetism.

Having heard us to an end, the Count proceeded to relate a few anecdotes, which rendered it evident that prototypes of Gall and Spurzheim had flourished and faded in Egypt so long ago as to have been nearly forgotten, and that the manoeuvres of Mesmer were really very contemptible tricks when put in collation with the positive miracles of the Theban *savans*, who created lice and a great many other similar things.

I here asked the Count if his people were able to calculate eclipses. He smiled rather contemptuously, and said they were.

This put me a little out, but I began to make other inquiries in regard to his astronomical knowledge, when a member of the company, who had never as yet opened his mouth, whispered in my ear that, for information on this head, I had better consult Ptolemy (whoever Ptolemy is) as well as one Plutarch *de facie lunae*.

I then questioned the Mummy about burning-glasses and lenses, and, in general, about the manufacture of glass; but I had not made an end of my queries before the silent member again touched me quietly on the elbow, and begged me for God's sake to take a peep at Diodorus Siculus. As for the Count, he merely asked me, in the way of reply, if we moderns possessed any such microscopes as would enable us to cut cameos in the style of the Egyptians. While I was thinking how I should answer this question, little Doctor Ponnonner committed himself in a very extraordinary way.

"Look at our architecture!" he exclaimed, greatly to the indignation of both the travelers, who pinched him black and blue to no purpose.

"Look," he cried with enthusiasm, "at the Bowling-Green Fountain in New York! or if this be too vast a contemplation, regard for a moment the Capitol at Washington, D. C.!"—and the good little medical man went on to detail very minutely, the proportions of the fabric to which he referred. He explained that the portico alone was adorned with no less than four and twenty columns, five feet in diameter, and ten feet apart.

The Count said that he regretted not being able to remember, just at that moment, the precise dimensions of any one of the principal buildings of the city of Aznac, whose foundations were laid in the night of Time, but the ruins of which were still standing, at the epoch of his entombment, in a vast plain of sand to the westward of Thebes. He recollected, however, (talking of the porticoes) that one affixed to an inferior palace in a kind of suburb called Carnac, consisted of a hundred and forty-four columns, thirty-seven feet in circumference, and twenty-five feet apart. The approach to this portico, from the Nile, was through an avenue two miles long, composed of sphynxes, statues, and obelisks, twenty, sixty, and a hundred feet in height. The palace itself (as well as he could remember) was, in one direction, two miles long, and might have been, altogether, about seven in circuit. Its walls were richly painted all over, within and without, with hieroglyphics. He would not pretend to *assert* that even fifty or sixty of the Doctor's Capitols might have been built within these walls, but he was by no means sure that two or three hundred of them might not have been squeezed in with some trouble. That palace at Carnac was an insignificant little building after all. He (the Count), however, could not conscientiously refuse to admit the ingenuity, magnificence, and superiority of the Fountain at the Bowling-Green, as described by the Doctor. Nothing like it, he was forced to allow, had ever been seen in Egypt or elsewhere.

I here asked the Count what he had to say to our railroads.

"Nothing," he replied, "in particular." They were rather slight, rather ill-conceived, and clumsily put together. They could not be compared, of course, with the vast, level, direct, iron-grooved causeways upon which the Egyptians conveyed entire temples and solid obelisks of a hundred and fifty feet in altitude.

I spoke of our gigantic mechanical forces.

He agreed that we knew something in that way, but inquired how I should have gone to work in getting up the imposts on the lintels of even the little palace at Carnac.

This question I concluded not to hear, and demanded if he had any idea of Artesian wells; but he simply raised his eyebrows; while Mr. Gliddon winked at me very hard and said, in a low tone, that one had been recently discovered by the engineers employed to bore for water in the Great Oasis.

I then mentioned our steel; but the foreigner elevated his nose, and asked me if our steel could have executed the sharp carved work seen on the obelisks, and which was wrought altogether by edge-tools of copper.

This disconcerted us so greatly that we thought it advisable to vary the attack to Metaphysics. We sent for a copy of a book called the *Dial*, and read out of it a chapter or two about something that is not very clear, but which the Bostonians call the Great Movement of Progress.

The Count merely said that Great Movements were awfully common things in his day, and as for Progress, it was at one time quite a nuisance, but it never progressed.

We then spoke of the great beauty and importance of Democracy, and were at much trouble in impressing the Count with a due sense of the advantages we enjoyed in living where there was suffrage *ad libitum*, and no king.

He listened with marked interest, and in fact seemed not a little amused. When we had done, he said that, a great while ago, there had occurred something of a very similar sort. Thirteen Egyptian provinces determined all at once to be free, and to set a magnificent example to the rest of mankind. They assembled their wise men, and concocted the most ingenious constitution it is possible to conceive. For a while they managed remarkably well; only their habit of bragging was prodigious. The thing ended, however, in the consolidation of the thirteen states, with some fifteen or twenty others, in the most odious and insupportable despotism that was ever heard of upon the face of the Earth.

I asked what was the name of the usurping tyrant.

As well as the Count could recollect, it was *Mob*.

Not knowing what to say to this, I raised my voice, and deplored the Egyptian ignorance of steam.

The Count looked at me with much astonishment, but made no answer. The silent gentleman, however, gave me a violent nudge in the ribs with his elbows—told me I had sufficiently exposed myself for once—and demanded if I was really such a fool as not to know that the modern steam engine is derived from the invention of Hero, through Solomon de Caus.

We were now in imminent danger of being discomfited; but, as good luck would have it, Doctor Ponnonner, having rallied, returned to our rescue, and inquired if the people of Egypt would seriously pretend to rival the moderns in the all-important particular of dress.

The Count, at this, glanced downward to the straps of his pantaloons, and then taking hold of the end of one of his coat-tails, held it up close to his eyes for some minutes. Letting it fall, at last, his mouth extended itself very gradually from ear to ear; but I do not remember that he said anything in the way of reply.

Hereupon we recovered our spirits, and the Doctor, approaching the Mummy with great dignity, desired it to say candidly, upon its honor as a gentleman, if the Egyptians had comprehended, at *any* period, the manufacture of either Ponnonner's lozenges or Brandreth's pills.

We looked, with profound anxiety, for an answer;—but in vain. It was not forthcoming. The Egyptian blushed and hung down his head. Never was triumph more consummate; never was defeat borne with so ill a grace. Indeed, I could not endure the spectacle of the poor Mummy's mortification. I reached my hat, bowed to him stiffly, and took leave.

Upon getting home I found it past four o'clock, and went immediately to bed. It is now ten a.m. I have been up since seven, penning these memoranda for the benefit of my family and of mankind. The former I shall behold no more. My wife is a shrew. The truth is, I am heartily sick of this life and of the nineteenth century in general. I am convinced that everything is going wrong. Besides, I am anxious to know who will be President in 2045. As soon, therefore, as I shave and swallow a cup of coffee, I shall just step over to Ponnonner's and get embalmed for a couple of hundred years.

The Imp of the Perverse

[Based on the metaphor of the Imp of Perverse, it explores the self-destructive impulses of the narrator. It was first published in *Graham's Magazine* in July 1845.]

In the consideration of the faculties and impulses—of the *prima mobilia* of the human soul, the phrenologists have failed to make room for a propensity which, although obviously existing as a radical, primitive, irreducible sentiment, has been equally overlooked by all the moralists who have preceded them. In the pure arrogance of the reason, we have all overlooked it. We have suffered its existence to escape our senses, solely through want of belief—of faith; whether it be faith in Revelation, or faith in the Kabbala. The idea of it has never occurred to us, simply because of its supererogation. We saw no *need* of the impulse—for the propensity. We could not perceive its necessity. We could not understand, that is to say, we could not have understood, had the notion of this *primum mobile* ever obtruded itself; we could not have understood in what manner it might be made to further the objects of humanity, either temporal or eternal. It cannot be denied that phrenology and, in great measure, all metaphysicianism have been concocted *a priori*. The intellectual or logical man, rather than the understanding or observant man, set himself to imagine designs—to dictate purposes to God. Having thus fathomed, to his satisfaction, the intentions of Jehovah, out of these intentions he built his innumerable systems of mind. In the matter of phrenology, for example, we first determined, naturally enough, that it was the design of the Deity that man should eat. We then assigned to man an organ of alimentiveness, and this organ is the scourge with which the Deity compels man, willy-nilly, into eating. Secondly, having settled it to be God's will that man should continue his species, we discovered an organ of amativeness, forthwith. And so with combativeness, with ideality, with causality, with constructiveness—so, in short, with every organ, whether representing a propensity, a moral sentiment, or a faculty of the pure intellect. And in these arrangements of the *principia* of human action, the Spurzheimites, whether right or wrong, in part, or upon the whole, have but followed, in principle, the footsteps of their predecessors, deducing and establishing everything from the preconceived destiny of man, and upon the ground of the objects of his Creator.

It would have been wiser, it would have been safer, to classify (if classify we must) upon the basis of what man usually or occasionally did, and was always occasionally doing, rather than upon the basis of what we took it for granted the Deity intended him to do. If we cannot comprehend God in His visible works, how then in His inconceivable thoughts, that call the works into being? If we cannot understand Him in His objective creatures, how then in His substantive moods and phases of creation?

Induction, *a posteriori*, would have brought phrenology to admit, as an innate and primitive principle of human action, a paradoxical something, which we may call *perverseness*, for want of a more characteristic term. In the sense I intend, it is, in fact, a *mobile* without motive, a motive not *motivirt.* Through its promptings we act without comprehensible object; or, if this shall be understood as a contradiction in terms, we may so far modify the proposition as to say, that through its promptings we act, for the reason that we should *not.* In theory, no reason can be more unreasonable, but, in fact, there is none more strong. With certain minds, under certain conditions, it becomes absolutely irresistible. I am not more certain that I breathe, than that the assurance of the wrong or error of any action is often the one unconquerable *force* which impels us, and alone impels us to its prosecution. Nor will this overwhelming tendency to do wrong for the wrong's sake, admit of analysis, or resolution into ulterior elements. It is a radical, a primitive impulse—elementary. It will be said, I am aware, that when we persist in acts because we feel we should *not* persist in them, our conduct is but a modification of that which ordinarily springs from the *combativeness* of phrenology. But a glance will show the fallacy of this idea. The phrenological combativeness has for its essence, the necessity of self-defence. It is our safeguard against injury. Its principle regards our well-being; and thus the desire to be well is excited simultaneously with its development. It follows, that the desire to be well must be excited simultaneously with any principle which shall be merely a modification of combativeness, but in the case of that something which I term *perverseness*, the desire to be well is not only not aroused, but a strongly antagonistical sentiment exists.

An appeal to one's own heart is, after all, the best reply to the sophistry just noticed. No one who trustingly consults and thoroughly questions his own soul, will be disposed to deny the entire radicalness of the propensity in question. It is not more incomprehensible than distinctive. There lives no man who at some period has not been tormented, for example, by an earnest desire to tantalize a listener by circumlocution. The speaker is aware that he displeases; he has every intention to please, he is usually curt, precise, and clear, the most laconic and luminous language is struggling for utterance upon his tongue, it is only with difficulty that he restrains himself from giving it flow; he dreads and deprecates the anger of him whom he addresses; yet, the thought strikes him, that by certain involutions and parentheses this anger may be engendered. That single thought is enough. The impulse increases to a wish, the wish to a desire, the desire to an uncontrollable longing, and the longing (to the deep regret and mortification of the speaker, and in defiance of all consequences) is indulged.

We have a task before us which must be speedily performed. We know that it will be ruinous to make delay. The most important crisis of our life calls, trumpet-tongued, for immediate energy and action. We glow, we are consumed with eagerness to commence the work, with the anticipation of whose glorious result our whole souls are on fire. It must, it shall be undertaken today, and yet we put it off until tomorrow; and why? There is no answer, except that we feel *perverse*, using the word with no comprehension of the principle. Tomorrow arrives, and with it a more impatient anxiety to do our duty, but with this very increase of anxiety arrives, also, a nameless, a positively fearful, because unfathomable, craving for delay. This craving gathers strength as the moments fly. The last hour for action is at hand. We tremble with the violence of the conflict within us—of the definite with the indefinite—of the substance with the shadow. But, if the contest has proceeded thus far, it is the shadow which prevails—we struggle in vain. The clock strikes, and is the knell of our welfare. At the same time, it is the chanticleer-note to the ghost that has so long overawed us. It flies—it disappears—we are free. The old energy returns. We will labor *now*. Alas, it is *too* late!

We stand upon the brink of a precipice. We peer into the abyss—we grow sick and dizzy. Our first impulse is to shrink from the danger. Unaccountably we remain. By slow degrees our sickness and dizziness and horror become merged in a cloud of unnamable feeling. By gradations, still more imperceptible, this cloud assumes shape, as did the vapor from the bottle out of which arose the genius in the *Arabian Nights*. But out of this *our* cloud upon the precipice's edge, there grows into palpability, a shape, far more terrible than any genius or any demon of a tale, and yet it is but a thought, although a fearful one, and one which chills the very marrow of our bones with the fierceness of the delight of its horror. It is merely the idea of what would be our sensations during the sweeping precipitancy of a fall from such a height. And this fall—this rushing annihilation—for the very reason that it involves that one most ghastly and loathsome of all the most ghastly and loathsome images of death and suffering which have ever presented themselves to our imagination—for this very cause do we now the most vividly desire it. And because our reason violently deters us from the brink, *therefore* do we the most impetuously approach it. There is no passion in nature so demoniacally impatient, as that of him who, shuddering upon the edge of a precipice, thus meditates a plunge. To indulge, for a moment, in any attempt at *thought*, is to be inevitably lost; for reflection but urges us to forbear, and *therefore* it is, I say, that we *cannot*. If there be no friendly arm to check us, or if we fail in a sudden effort to prostrate ourselves backward from the abyss, we plunge, and are destroyed.

Examine these similar actions as we will, we shall find them resulting solely from the spirit of the *Perverse*. We perpetrate them because we feel that we should *not*. Beyond or behind this there is no intelligible principle; and we might, indeed, deem this perverseness a direct instigation of the Arch-Fiend, were it not occasionally known to operate in furtherance of good.

I have said thus much, that in some measure I may answer your question, that I may explain to you why I am here, that I may assign to you something that shall have at least the faint aspect of a cause for my wearing these fetters, and for my tenanting this cell of the condemned. Had I not been thus prolix, you might either have misunderstood me altogether, or, with the rabble, have fancied me mad. As it is, you will easily perceive that I am one of the many uncounted victims of the Imp of the Perverse.

It is impossible that any deed could have been wrought with a more thorough deliberation. For weeks, for months, I pondered upon the means of the murder. I rejected a thousand schemes, because their accomplishment involved a *chance* of detection. At length, in reading some French memoirs, I found an account of a nearly fatal illness that occurred to Madame Pilau, through the agency of a candle accidentally poisoned. The idea struck my fancy at once. I knew my victim's habit of reading in bed. I knew, too, that his apartment was narrow and ill-ventilated. But I need not vex you with impertinent details. I need not describe the easy artifices by which I substituted, in his bedroom candle-stand, a wax-light of my own making for the one which I there found. The next morning he was discovered dead in his bed, and the Coroner's verdict was—"Death by the visitation of God."

Having inherited his estate, all went well with me for years. The idea of detection never once entered my brain. Of the remains of the fatal taper I had myself carefully disposed. I had left no shadow of a clew by which it would be possible to convict, or even to suspect, me of the crime. It is inconceivable how rich a sentiment of satisfaction arose in my bosom as I reflected upon my absolute security. For a very long period of time I was accustomed to revel in this sentiment. It afforded me more real delight than all the mere worldly advantages accruing from my sin. But there arrived at length an epoch, from which the pleasurable feeling grew, by scarcely perceptible gradations, into a haunting and harassing thought. It harassed because it haunted. I could scarcely get rid of it for an instant. It is quite a common thing to be thus annoyed with the ringing in our ears, or rather in our memories, of the burthen of some ordinary song, or some unimpressive snatches from an opera. Nor will we be the less tormented if the song in itself be good, or the opera air meritorious. In this manner, at last, I would perpetually catch myself pondering upon my security, and repeating, in a low undertone, the phrase, "I am safe."

One day, whilst sauntering along the streets, I arrested myself in the act of murmuring, half aloud, these customary syllables. In a fit of petulance, I remodeled them thus: "I am safe—I am safe—yes—if I be not fool enough to make open confession!"

A Rackham

No sooner had I spoken these words, than I felt an icy chill creep to my heart. I had had some experience in these fits of perversity (whose nature I have been at some trouble to explain), and I remembered well that in no instance I had successfully resisted their attacks. And now my own casual self-suggestion, that I might possibly be fool enough to confess the murder of which I had been guilty, confronted me, as if the very ghost of him whom I had murdered—and beckoned me on to death.

At first, I made an effort to shake off this nightmare of the soul. I walked vigorously—faster—still faster—at length I ran. I felt a maddening desire to shriek aloud. Every succeeding wave of thought overwhelmed me with new terror, for, alas! I well, too well, understood that to *think*, in my situation, was to be lost. I still quickened my pace. I bounded like a madman through the crowded thoroughfares. At length, the populace took the alarm and pursued me. I felt *then* the consummation of my fate. Could I have torn out my tongue, I would have done it, but a rough voice resounded in my ears—a rougher grasp seized me by the shoulder. I turned—I gasped for breath. For a moment I experienced all the pangs of suffocation; I became blind, and deaf, and giddy; and then some invisible fiend, I thought, struck me with his broad palm upon the back. The long-imprisoned secret burst forth from my soul.

They say that I spoke with a distinct enunciation, but with marked emphasis and passionate hurry, as if in dread of interruption before concluding the brief, but pregnant sentences that consigned me to the hangman and to hell.

Having related all that was necessary for the fullest judicial conviction, I fell prostrate in a swoon.

But why shall I say more? Today I wear these chains, and am *here*! Tomorrow I shall be fetterless!—*but where?*

The Facts in the Case of M. Valdemar

[Published simultaneously in the December 20, 1845, issue of the *Broadway Journal* and the December 1845 issue of *American Reviewer: A Whig Journal* (wherein it was titled 'The Facts of M. Valdemar's Case'), this is a tale of suspense, horror and, to a certain degree, hoax.]

Of course I shall not pretend to consider it any matter for wonder, that the extraordinary case of M. Valdemar has excited discussion. It would have been a miracle had it not—especially under the circumstances. Through the desire of all parties concerned, to keep the affair from the public, at least for the present, or until we had farther opportunities for investigation—through our endeavors to effect this—a garbled or exaggerated account made its way into society, and became the source of many unpleasant misrepresentations, and, very naturally, of a great deal of disbelief.

It is now rendered necessary that I give the *facts*—as far as I comprehend them myself. They are, succinctly, these:

My attention, for the last three years, had been repeatedly drawn to the subject of Mesmerism; and, about nine months ago it occurred to me, quite suddenly, that in the series of experiments made hitherto, there had been a very remarkable and most unaccountable omission:—no person had as yet been mesmerized *in articulo mortis.* It remained to be seen, first, whether, in such condition, there existed in the patient any susceptibility to the magnetic influence; secondly, whether, if any existed, it was impaired or increased by the condition; thirdly, to what extent, or for how long a period, the encroachments of Death might be arrested by the process. There were other points to be ascertained, but these most excited my curiosity—the last in especial, from the immensely important character of its consequences.

In looking around me for some subject by whose means I might test these particulars, I was brought to think of my friend, M. Ernest Valdemar, the well-known compiler of the *Bibliotheca Forensica*, and author (under the *nom de plume* of Issachar Marx) of the Polish versions of *Wallenstein* and *Gargantua*. M. Valdemar, who has resided principally at Harlem, N.Y., since the year 1839, is (or was) particularly noticeable for the extreme spareness of his person—his lower limbs much resembling those of John Randolph; and, also, for the whiteness of his whiskers, in violent contrast to the blackness of his hair—the latter, in consequence, being very generally mistaken for a wig. His temperament was markedly nervous, and rendered him a good subject for mesmeric experiment. On two or three occasions I had put him to sleep with little difficulty, but was disappointed in other results which his peculiar constitution had naturally led me to anticipate. His will was at no period positively, or thoroughly, under my control, and in regard to *clairvoyance*, I could accomplish with him nothing to be relied upon. I always attributed my failure at these points to the disordered state of his health. For some months previous to my becoming acquainted with him, his physicians had declared him in a confirmed phthisis. It was his custom, indeed, to speak calmly of his approaching dissolution, as of a matter neither to be avoided nor regretted.

When the ideas to which I have alluded first occurred to me, it was of course very natural that I should think of M. Valdemar. I knew the steady philosophy of the man too well to apprehend any scruples from *him*; and he had no relatives in America who would be likely to interfere. I spoke to him frankly upon the subject; and, to my surprise, his interest seemed vividly excited. I say to my surprise, for, although he had always yielded his person freely to my experiments, he had never before given me any tokens of sympathy with what I did. His disease was of that character which would admit of exact calculation in respect to the epoch of its termination in death; and it was finally arranged between us that he would send for me about twenty-four hours before the period announced by his physicians as that of his decease.

It is now rather more than seven months since I received, from M. Valdemar himself, the subjoined note:

> My Dear P—,
> You may as well come *now*. D— and F— are agreed that I cannot hold out beyond tomorrow midnight; and I think they have hit the time very nearly.
> Valdemar

I received this note within half an hour after it was written, and in fifteen minutes more I was in the dying man's chamber. I had not seen him for ten days, and was appalled by the fearful alteration which the brief interval had wrought in him. His face wore a leaden hue; the eyes were utterly lusterless; and the emaciation was so extreme that the skin had been broken through by the cheek-bones. His expectoration was excessive. The pulse was barely perceptible. He retained, nevertheless, in a very remarkable manner, both his mental power and a certain degree of physical strength. He spoke with distinctness—took some palliative medicines without aid—and, when I entered the room, was occupied in penciling memoranda in a pocket-book. He was propped up in the bed by pillows. Doctors D— and F— were in attendance.

After pressing Valdemar's hand, I took these gentlemen aside, and obtained from them a minute account of the patient's condition. The left lung had been for eighteen months in a semi-osseous or cartilaginous state, and was, of course, entirely useless for all purposes of vitality. The right, in its upper portion, was also partially, if not thoroughly, ossified, while the lower region was merely a mass of purulent tubercles, running one into another. Several extensive perforations existed; and, at one point, permanent adhesion to the ribs had taken place. These appearances in the right lobe were of comparatively recent date. The ossification had proceeded with very unusual rapidity; no sign of it had been discovered a month before, and the adhesion had only been observed during the three previous days. Independently of the phthisis, the patient was suspected of aneurism of the aorta; but on this point the osseous symptoms rendered an exact diagnosis impossible. It was the opinion of both physicians that M. Valdemar would die about midnight on the morrow (Sunday). It was then seven o'clock on Saturday evening.

On quitting the invalid's bedside to hold conversation with myself, Doctors D— and F— had bidden him a final farewell. It had not been their intention to return; but, at my request, they agreed to look in upon the patient about ten the next night.

When they had gone, I spoke freely with M. Valdemar on the subject of his approaching dissolution, as well as, more particularly, of the experiment proposed. He still professed himself quite willing and even anxious to have it made, and urged me to commence it at once. A male and a female nurse were in attendance; but I did not feel myself altogether at liberty to engage in a task of this character with no more reliable witnesses than these people, in case of sudden accident, might prove. I therefore postponed operations until about eight the next night, when the arrival of a medical student with whom I had some acquaintance, (Mr. Theodore L—l,) relieved me from farther embarrassment. It had been my design, originally, to wait for the physicians; but I was induced to proceed, first, by the urgent entreaties of M. Valdemar, and secondly, by my conviction that I had not a moment to lose, as he was evidently sinking fast.

Mr. L—l was so kind as to accede to my desire that he would take notes of all that occurred, and it is from his memoranda that what I now have to relate is, for the most part, either condensed or copied *verbatim*.

It wanted about five minutes of eight when, taking the patient's hand, I begged him to state, as distinctly as he could, to Mr. L—1, whether he (M. Valdemar) was entirely willing that I should make the experiment of mesmerizing him in his then condition.

He replied feebly, yet quite audibly, "Yes, I wish to be mesmerized," adding immediately afterwards, "I fear you have deferred it too long."

While he spoke thus, I commenced the passes which I had already found most effectual in subduing him. He was evidently influenced with the first lateral stroke of my hand across his forehead; but although I exerted all my powers, no further perceptible effect was induced until some minutes after ten o'clock, when Doctors D— and F— called, according to appointment. I explained to them, in a few words, what I designed, and as they opposed no objection, saying that the patient was already in the death agony, I proceeded without hesitation—exchanging, however, the lateral passes for downward ones, and directing my gaze entirely into the right eye of the sufferer.

By this time his pulse was imperceptible and his breathing was stertorous, and at intervals of half a minute.

This condition was nearly unaltered for a quarter of an hour. At the expiration of this period, however, a natural although a very deep sigh escaped the bosom of the dying man, and the stertorous breathing ceased—that is to say, its stertorousness was no longer apparent; the intervals were undiminished. The patient's extremities were of an icy coldness.

At five minutes before eleven I perceived unequivocal signs of the mesmeric influence. The glassy roll of the eye was changed for that expression of uneasy *inward* examination which is never seen except in cases of sleep-waking, and which it is quite impossible to mistake. With a few rapid lateral passes I made the lids quiver, as in incipient sleep, and with a few more I closed them altogether. I was not satisfied, however, with this, but continued the manipulations vigorously, and with the fullest exertion of the will, until I had completely stiffened the limbs of the slumberer, after placing them in a seemingly easy position. The legs were at full length; the arms were nearly so, and reposed on the bed at a moderate distance from the loins. The head was very slightly elevated.

When I had accomplished this, it was fully midnight, and I requested the gentlemen present to examine M. Valdemar's condition. After a few experiments, they admitted him to be an unusually perfect state of mesmeric trance. The curiosity of both the physicians was greatly excited. Dr. D— resolved at once to remain with the patient all night, while Dr. F— took leave with a promise to return at daybreak. Mr. L—l and the nurses remained.

We left M. Valdemar entirely undisturbed until about three o'clock in the morning, when I approached him and found him in precisely the same condition as when Dr. F— went away—that is to say, he lay in the same position; the pulse was imperceptible; the breathing was gentle (scarcely noticeable, unless through the application of a mirror to the lips); the eyes were closed naturally; and the limbs were as rigid and as cold as marble. Still, the general appearance was certainly not that of death.

As I approached M. Valdemar I made a kind of half effort to influence his right arm into pursuit of my own, as I passed the latter gently to and fro above his person. In such experiments with this patient, I had never perfectly succeeded before, and assuredly I had little thought of succeeding now; but to my astonishment, his arm very readily, although feebly, followed every direction I assigned it with mine. I determined to hazard a few words of conversation.

"M. Valdemar," I said, "are you asleep?" He made no answer, but I perceived a tremor about the lips, and was thus induced to repeat the question, again and again. At its third repetition, his whole frame was agitated by a very slight shivering; the eyelids unclosed themselves so far as to display a white line of the ball; the lips moved sluggishly, and from between them, in a barely audible whisper, issued the words:

"Yes;—asleep now. Do not wake me!—let me die so!"

I here felt the limbs and found them as rigid as ever. The right arm, as before, obeyed the direction of my hand. I questioned the sleep-waker again:

"Do you still feel pain in the breast, M. Valdemar?"

The answer now was immediate, but even less audible than before: "No pain—I am dying."

I did not think it advisable to disturb him farther just then, and nothing more was said or done until the arrival of Dr. F—, who came a little before sunrise, and expressed unbounded astonishment at finding the patient still alive. After feeling the pulse and applying a mirror to the lips, he requested me to speak to the sleep-waker again. I did so, saying:

"M. Valdemar, do you still sleep?"

As before, some minutes elapsed ere a reply was made; and during the interval the dying man seemed to be collecting his energies to speak. At my fourth repetition of the question, he said very faintly, almost inaudibly:

"Yes; still asleep—dying."

It was now the opinion, or rather the wish, of the physicians, that M. Valdemar should be suffered to remain undisturbed in his present apparently tranquil condition, until death should supervene—and this, it was generally agreed, must now take place within a few minutes. I concluded, however, to speak to him once more, and merely repeated my previous question.

While I spoke, there came a marked change over the countenance of the sleep-waker. The eyes rolled themselves slowly open, the pupils disappearing upwardly; the skin generally assumed a cadaverous hue, resembling not so much parchment as white paper; and the circular hectic spots which, hitherto, had been strongly defined in the center of each cheek, *went out* at once. I use this expression, because the suddenness of their departure put me in mind of nothing so much as the extinguishment of a candle by a puff of the breath. The upper lip, at the same time, writhed itself away from the teeth, which it had previously covered completely; while the lower jaw fell with an audible jerk, leaving the mouth widely extended, and disclosing in full view the swollen and blackened tongue. I presume that no member of the party then present had been unaccustomed to death-bed horrors; but so hideous beyond conception was the appearance of M. Valdemar at this moment, that there was a general shrinking back from the region of the bed.

I now feel that I have reached a point of this narrative at which every reader will be startled into positive disbelief. It is my business, however, simply to proceed.

There was no longer the faintest sign of vitality in M. Valdemar; and concluding him to be dead, we were consigning him to the charge of the nurses, when a strong vibratory motion was observable in the tongue. This continued for perhaps a minute. At the expiration of this period, there issued from the distended and motionless jaws a voice—such as it would be madness in me to attempt describing. There are, indeed, two or three epithets which might be considered as applicable to it in part; I might say, for example, that the sound was harsh, and broken and hollow; but the hideous whole is indescribable, for the simple reason that no similar sounds have ever jarred upon the ear of humanity. There were two particulars, nevertheless, which I thought then, and still think, might fairly be stated as characteristic of the intonation—as well adapted to convey some idea of its unearthly peculiarity. In the first place, the voice seemed to reach our ears—at least mine—from a vast distance, or from some deep cavern within the earth. In the second place, it impressed me (I fear, indeed, that it will be impossible to make myself comprehended) as gelatinous or glutinous matters impress the sense of touch.

I have spoken both of "sound" and of "voice." I mean to say that the sound was one of distinct—of even wonderfully, thrillingly distinct—syllabification. M. Valdemar *spoke*—obviously in reply to the question I had propounded to him a few minutes before. I had asked him, it will be remembered, if he still slept. He now said:

"Yes;—no;—I *have been* sleeping—and now—now—I *am dead*."

No person present even affected to deny, or attempted to repress, the unutterable, shuddering horror which these few words, thus uttered, were so well calculated to convey. Mr. L—l (the student) swooned.

The nurses immediately left the chamber, and could not be induced to return. My own impressions I would not pretend to render intelligible to the reader. For nearly an hour, we busied ourselves, silently—without the utterance of a word—in endeavors to revive Mr. L—l. When he came to himself, we addressed ourselves again to an investigation of M. Valdemar's condition.

It remained in all respects as I have last described it, with the exception that the mirror no longer afforded evidence of respiration. An attempt to draw blood from the arm failed. I should mention, too, that this limb was no farther subject to my will. I endeavored in vain to make it follow the direction of my hand. The only real indication, indeed, of the mesmeric influence, was now found in the vibratory movement of the tongue, whenever I addressed M. Valdemar a question. He seemed to be making an effort to reply, but had no longer sufficient volition. To queries put to him by any other person than myself he seemed utterly insensible—although I endeavored to place each member of the company in mesmeric *rapport* with him. I believe that I have now related all that is necessary to an understanding of the sleep-waker's state at this epoch. Other nurses were procured; and at ten o'clock I left the house in company with the two physicians and Mr. L—l.

In the afternoon we all called again to see the patient. His condition remained precisely the same. We had now some discussion as to the propriety and feasibility of awakening him; but we had little difficulty in agreeing that no good purpose would be served by so doing. It was evident that, so far, death (or what is usually termed death) had been arrested by the mesmeric process. It seemed clear to us all that to awaken M. Valdemar would be merely to insure his instant, or at least his speedy dissolution.

From this period until the close of last week—*an interval of nearly seven months*—we continued to make daily calls at M. Valdemar's house, accompanied, now and then, by medical and other friends. All this time the sleep-waker remained *exactly* as I have last described him. The nurses' attentions were continual.

It was on Friday last that we finally resolved to make the experiment of awakening or attempting to awaken him; and it is the (perhaps) unfortunate result of this latter experiment which has given rise to so much discussion in private circles—to so much of what I cannot help thinking unwarranted popular feeling.

For the purpose of relieving M. Valdemar from the mesmeric trance, I made use of the customary passes. These, for a time, were unsuccessful. The first indication of revival was afforded by a partial descent of the iris. It was observed, as especially remarkable, that this lowering of the pupil was accompanied by the profuse outflowing of a yellowish ichor (from beneath the lids) of a pungent and highly offensive odor.

It was now suggested that I should attempt to influence the patient's arm, as heretofore. I made the attempt and failed. Dr. F— then intimated a desire to have me put a question. I did so, as follows:

"M. Valdemar, can you explain to us what are your feelings or wishes now?"

There was an instant return of the hectic circles on the cheeks; the tongue quivered, or rather rolled violently in the mouth (although the jaws and lips remained rigid as before); and at length the same hideous voice which I have already described, broke forth:

"For God's sake!—quick!—quick!—put me to sleep—or, quick!—waken me!—quick!—*I say to you that I am dead!*"

I was thoroughly unnerved, and for an instant remained undecided what to do. At first I made an endeavor to re-compose the patient; but, failing in this through total abeyance of the will, I retraced my steps and as earnestly struggled to awaken him. In this attempt I soon saw that I should be successful—or at least I soon fancied that my success would be complete—and I am sure that all in the room were prepared to see the patient awaken.

For what really occurred, however, it is quite impossible that any human being could have been prepared.

As I rapidly made the mesmeric passes, amid ejaculations of "dead! dead!" absolutely *bursting* from the tongue and not from the lips of the sufferer, his whole frame at once—within the space of a single minute, or even less, shrunk—crumbled—absolutely *rotted* away beneath my hands. Upon the bed, before that whole company, there lay a nearly liquid mass of loathsome—of detestable putridity.

The Cask of Amontillado

[This tale of mystery was first published in the November 1846 issue of the *Godey's Lady's Book*.]

The thousand injuries of Fortunato I had borne as I best could; but when he ventured upon insult, I vowed revenge. You, who so well know the nature of my soul, will not suppose, however, that I gave utterance to a threat. *At length* I would be avenged; this was a point definitively settled—but the very definitiveness with which it was resolved, precluded the idea of risk. I must not only punish, but punish with impunity. A wrong is unredressed when retribution overtakes its redresser. It is equally unredressed when the avenger fails to make himself felt as such to him who has done the wrong.

It must be understood, that neither by word nor deed had I given Fortunato cause to doubt my good will. I continued, as was my wont, to smile in his face, and he did not perceive that my smile *now* was at the thought of his immolation.

He had a weak point—this Fortunato—although in other regards he was a man to be respected and even feared. He prided himself on his connoisseurship in wine. Few Italians have the true virtuoso spirit. For the most part their enthusiasm is adopted to suit the time and opportunity—to practice imposture upon the British and Austrian *millionaires*. In painting and gemmary, Fortunato, like his countrymen, was a quack—but in the matter of old wines he was sincere. In this respect I did not differ from him materially: I was skilful in the Italian vintages myself, and bought largely whenever I could.

It was about dusk, one evening during the supreme madness of the carnival season, that I encountered my friend. He accosted me with excessive warmth, for he had been drinking much. The man wore motley. He had on a tight-fitting parti-striped dress, and his head was surmounted by the conical cap and bells. I was so pleased to see him that I thought I should never have done wringing his hand.

I said to him—"My dear Fortunato, you are luckily met. How remarkably well you are looking today! But I have received a pipe of what passes for Amontillado, and I have my doubts."

"How?" said he. "Amontillado? A pipe? Impossible! And in the middle of the carnival!"

"I have my doubts," I replied; "and I was silly enough to pay the full Amontillado price without consulting you in the matter. You were not to be found, and I was fearful of losing a bargain."

"Amontillado!"

"I have my doubts."

"Amontillado!"

"And I must satisfy them."

"Amontillado!"

"As you are engaged, I am on my way to Luchesi. If anyone has a critical turn, it is he. He will tell me—"

"Luchesi cannot tell Amontillado from Sherry."

"And yet some fools will have it that his taste is a match for your own."

"Come, let us go."

"Whither?"

"To your vaults."

"My friend, no; I will not impose upon your good nature. I perceive you have an engagement. Luchesi—"

"I have no engagement;—come."

"My friend, no. It is not the engagement, but the severe cold with which I perceive you are afflicted. The vaults are insufferably damp. They are encrusted with niter."

"Let us go, nevertheless. The cold is merely nothing. Amontillado! You have been imposed upon. And as for Luchesi, he cannot distinguish Sherry from Amontillado."

Thus speaking, Fortunato possessed himself of my arm. Putting on a mask of black silk, and drawing a *roquelaire* closely about my person, I suffered him to hurry me to my palazzo.

There were no attendants at home; they had absconded to make merry in honor of the time. I had told them that I should not return until the morning, and had given them explicit orders not to stir from the house. These orders were sufficient, I well knew, to insure their immediate disappearance, one and all, as soon as my back was turned.

I took from their sconces two flambeaux, and giving one to Fortunato, bowed him through several suites of rooms to the archway that led into the vaults. I passed down a long and winding staircase, requesting him to be cautious as he followed. We came at length to the foot of the descent, and stood together on the damp ground of the catacombs of the Montresors.

The gait of my friend was unsteady, and the bells upon his cap jingled as he strode.

"The pipe," said he.

"It is farther on," said I; "but observe the white web-work which gleams from these cavern walls."

He turned towards me, and looked into my eyes with two filmy orbs that distilled the rheum of intoxication.

"Niter?" he asked, at length.

"Niter," I replied. "How long have you had that cough?"

"Ugh! ugh! ugh!—ugh! ugh! ugh!—ugh! ugh! ugh!—ugh! ugh! ugh!—ugh! ugh! ugh!"

My poor friend found it impossible to reply for many minutes.

"It is nothing," he said, at last.

"Come," I said, with decision, "we will go back; your health is precious. You are rich, respected, admired, beloved; you are happy, as once I was. You are a man to be missed. For me it is no matter. We will go back; you will be ill, and I cannot be responsible. Besides, there is Luchesi—"

"Enough," he said; "the cough is a mere nothing; it will not kill me. I shall not die of a cough."

"True—true," I replied; "and, indeed, I had no intention of alarming you unnecessarily—but you should use all proper caution. A draught of this Medoc will defend us from the damps."

Here I knocked off the neck of a bottle which I drew from a long row of its fellows that lay upon the mold.

"Drink," I said, presenting him the wine.

He raised it to his lips with a leer. He paused and nodded to me familiarly, while his bells jingled.

"I drink," he said, "to the buried that repose around us."

"And I to your long life."

He again took my arm, and we proceeded.

"These vaults," he said, "are extensive."

"The Montresors," I replied, "were a great and numerous family."

"I forget your arms."

"A huge human foot d'or, in a field azure; the foot crushes a serpent rampant whose fangs are embedded in the heel."

"And the motto?"

"*Nemo me impune lacessit.*"

"Good!" he said.

The wine sparkled in his eyes and the bells jingled. My own fancy grew warm with the Medoc. We had passed through walls of piled bones, with casks and puncheons intermingling, into the inmost recesses of the catacombs. I paused again, and this time I made bold to seize Fortunato by an arm above the elbow.

"The niter!" I said: "see, it increases. It hangs like moss upon the vaults. We are below the river's bed. The drops of moisture trickle among the bones. Come, we will go back ere it is too late. Your cough—"

"It is nothing," he said; "let us go on. But first, another draught of the Medoc."

I broke and reached him a flaçon of De Grâve. He emptied it at a breath. His eyes flashed with a fierce light. He laughed and threw the bottle upwards with a gesticulation I did not understand.

I looked at him in surprise. He repeated the movement—a grotesque one.

"You do not comprehend?" he said.

"Not I," I replied.

"Then you are not of the brotherhood."

"How?"

"You are not of the masons."

"Yes, yes," I said, "yes, yes."

"You? Impossible! A mason?"

"A mason," I replied.

"A sign," he said, 'a sign.'

"It is this," I answered, producing from beneath the folds of my *roquelaire* a trowel.

"You jest," he exclaimed, recoiling a few paces. "But let us proceed to the Amontillado."

"Be it so," I said, replacing the tool beneath the cloak, and again offering him my arm. He leaned upon it heavily. We continued our route in search of the Amontillado. We passed through a range of low arches, descended, passed on, and descending again, arrived at a deep crypt, in which the foulness of the air caused our flambeaux rather to glow than flame.

At the most remote end of the crypt there appeared another less spacious. Its walls had been lined with human remains, piled to the vault overhead, in the fashion of the great catacombs of Paris. Three sides of this interior crypt were still ornamented in this manner. From the fourth the bones had been thrown down, and lay promiscuously upon the earth, forming at one point a mound of some size. Within the wall thus exposed by the displacing of the bones, we perceived a still interior recess, in depth about four feet, in width three, in height six or seven. It seemed to have been constructed for no especial use in itself, but formed merely the interval between two of the colossal supports of the roof of the catacombs, and was backed by one of their circumscribing walls of solid granite.

It was in vain that Fortunato, uplifting his dull torch, endeavored to pry into the depths of the recess. Its termination the feeble light did not enable us to see.

"Proceed," I said; "herein is the Amontillado. As for Luchesi—"

"He is an ignoramus," interrupted my friend, as he stepped unsteadily forward, while I followed immediately at his heels. In an instant he had reached the extremity of the niche, and finding his progress arrested by the rock, stood stupidly bewildered. A moment more and I had fettered him to the granite. In its surface were two iron staples, distant from each other about two feet, horizontally. From one of these depended a short chain, from the other a padlock. Throwing the links about his waist, it was but the work of a few seconds to secure it. He was too much astounded to resist. Withdrawing the key I stepped back from the recess.

"Pass your hand," I said, "over the wall; you cannot help feeling the niter. Indeed it is *very* damp. Once more let me *implore* you to return. No?

Then I must positively leave you. But I must first render you all the little attentions in my power."

"The Amontillado!" ejaculated my friend, not yet recovered from his astonishment.

"True," I replied; "the Amontillado."

As I said these words I busied myself among the pile of bones of which I have before spoken. Throwing them aside, I soon uncovered a quantity of building stone and mortar. With these materials and with the aid of my trowel, I began vigorously to wall up the entrance of the niche.

I had scarcely laid the first tier of my masonry when I discovered that the intoxication of Fortunato had in a great measure worn off. The earliest indication I had of this was a low moaning cry from the depth of the recess. It was *not* the cry of a drunken man. There was then a long and obstinate silence. I laid the second tier, and the third, and the fourth; and then I heard the furious vibrations of the chain. The noise lasted for several minutes, during which, that I might hearken to it with the more satisfaction, I ceased my labors and sat down upon the bones. When at last the clanking subsided, I resumed the trowel, and finished without interruption the fifth, the sixth, and the seventh tier. The wall was now nearly upon a level with my breast. I again paused, and holding the flambeaux over the mason-work, threw a few feeble rays upon the figure within.

A succession of loud and shrill screams, bursting suddenly from the throat of the chained form, seemed to thrust me violently back. For a brief moment I hesitated, I trembled. Unsheathing my rapier, I began to grope with it about the recess: but the thought of an instant reassured me. I placed my hand upon the solid fabric of the catacombs, and felt satisfied. I reapproached the wall. I replied to the yells of him who clamoured. I re-echoed, I aided, I surpassed them in volume and in strength. I did this, and the clamourer grew still.

It was now midnight, and my task was drawing to a close. I had completed the eighth, the ninth, and the tenth tier. I had finished a portion of the last and the eleventh; there remained but a single stone to be fitted and plastered in. I struggled with its weight; I placed it partially in its destined position. But now there came from out the niche a low laugh that erected the hairs upon my head. It was succeeded by a sad voice, which I had difficulty in recognizing as that of the noble Fortunato. The voice said—

"Ha! ha! ha!—he! he!—a very good joke indeed—an excellent jest. We will have many a rich laugh about it at the palazzo—he! he! he!—over our wine—he! he! he!"

"The Amontillado!" I said.

"He! he! he!—he! he! he!—yes, the Amontillado. But is it not getting late? Will not they be awaiting us at the palazzo, the Lady Fortunato and the rest? Let us be gone."

"Yes," I said, "let us be gone."

"*For the love of God, Montresor!*"

"Yes," I said, "for the love of God!"

But to these words I hearkened in vain for a reply. I grew impatient. I called aloud—

"Fortunato!"

No answer. I called again—

"Fortunato!"

No answer still. I thrust a torch through the remaining aperture and let it fall within. There came forth in return only a jingling of the bells. My heart grew sick; it was the dampness of the catacombs that made it so. I hastened to make an end of my labor. I forced the last stone into its position; I plastered it up. Against the new masonry I re-erected the old rampart of bones. For the half of a century no mortal has disturbed them. *In pace requiescat!*

Essays
&
Criticism

Letter to B——

[First published as 'Letters to Mr. — ——' in *Poems* (1831). Revised and published as 'Letter to B——' in the July 1836 issue of the *Southern Literary Messenger*.]

It has been said that a good critique on a poem may be written by one who is no poet himself. This, according to *your* idea and *mine* of poetry, I feel to be false—the less poetical the critic, the less just the critique, and the converse. On this account, and because there are but few B——'s in the world, I would be as much ashamed of the world's good opinion as proud of your own. Another than yourself might here observe, "Shakespeare is in possession of the world's good opinion, and yet Shakespeare is the greatest of poets. It appears then that the world judge correctly, why should you be ashamed of their favorable judgment?" The difficulty lies in the interpretation of the word "judgment" or "opinion." The opinion is the world's, truly, but it may be called theirs as a man would call a book his, having bought it; he did not write the book, but it is his; they did not originate the opinion, but it is theirs. A fool, for example, thinks Shakespeare a great poet—yet the fool has never read Shakespeare. But the fool's neighbor, who is a step higher on the Andes of the mind, whose head (that is to say his more exalted thought) is too far above the fool to be seen or understood, but whose feet (by which I mean his every-day actions) are sufficiently near to be discerned, and by means of which that superiority is ascertained, which *but* for them would never have been discovered—this neighbor asserts that Shakespeare is a great poet—the fool believes him, and it is henceforward his *opinion.*

This neighbor's own opinion has, in like manner, been adopted from one above *him*, and so, ascendingly, to a few gifted individuals, who kneel around the summit, beholding, face to face, the master spirit who stands upon the pinnacle.

***

You are aware of the great barrier in the path of an American writer. He is read, if at all, in preference to the combined and established wit of the world. I say established; for it is with literature as with law or empire—an established name is an estate in tenure, or a throne in possession. Besides, one might suppose that books, like their authors, improve by travel—their having crossed the sea is, with us, so great a distinction. Our antiquaries abandon time for distance; our very fops glance from the binding to the bottom of the title-page, where the mystic characters which spell London, Paris, or Genoa, are precisely so many letters of recommendation.

***

I mentioned just now a vulgar error as regards criticism. I think the notion that no poet can form a correct estimate of his own writings is another. I remarked before, that in proportion to the poetical talent, would be the justice of a critique upon poetry. Therefore, a bad poet would, I grant, make a false critique, and his self-love would infallibly bias his little judgment in his favor; but a poet, who is indeed a poet, could not, I think, fail of making a just critique. Whatever should be deducted on the score of self-love, might be replaced on account of his intimate acquaintance with the subject; in short, we have more instances of false criticism than of just, where one's own writings are the test, simply because we have more bad poets than good. There are of course many objections to what I say: Milton is a great example of the contrary; but his opinion with respect to the 'Paradise Regained', is by no means fairly ascertained. By what trivial circumstances men are often led to assert what they do not really believe! Perhaps an inadvertent word has descended to posterity. But, in fact, the 'Paradise Regained' is little, if at all, inferior to the Paradise Lost, and is only supposed so to be, because men do not like epics, whatever they may say to the contrary, and reading those of Milton in their natural order, are too much wearied with the first to derive any pleasure from the second.

I dare say Milton preferred 'Comus' to either—if so—justly.

***

As I am speaking of poetry, it will not be amiss to touch slightly upon the most singular heresy in its modern history—the heresy of what is called very foolishly, the Lake School. Some years ago I might have been induced, by an occasion like the present, to attempt a formal refutation of their doctrine; at present it would be a work of supererogation. The wise must bow to the wisdom of such men as Coleridge and Southey, but being wise, have laughed at poetical theories so prosaically exemplified.

Aristotle, with singular assurance, has declared poetry the most philosophical of all writing—but it required a Wordsworth to pronounce it the most metaphysical. He seems to think that the end of poetry is, or should be, instruction—yet it is a truism that the end of our existence is happiness; if so, the end of every separate part of our existence—every thing connected with our existence should be still happiness. Therefore the end of instruction should be happiness; and happiness is another name for pleasure;—therefore the end of instruction should be pleasure: yet we see the above mentioned opinion implies precisely the reverse.

To proceed: *ceteris paribus*, he who pleases, is of more importance to his fellow men than he who instructs, since utility is happiness, and pleasure is the end already obtained which instruction is merely the means of obtaining.

I see no reason, then, why our metaphysical poets should plume themselves so much on the utility of their works, unless indeed they refer to instruction with eternity in view; in which case, sincere respect for their piety would not allow me to express my contempt for their judgment; contempt which it would be difficult to conceal, since their writings are professedly to be understood by the few, and it is the many who stand in need of salvation. In such case I should no doubt be tempted to think of the devil in 'Melmoth', who labors indefatigably through three octavo volumes, to accomplish the destruction of one or two souls, while any common devil would have demolished one or two thousand.

***

Against the subtleties which would make poetry a study—not a passion—it becomes the metaphysician to reason—but the poet to protest. Yet Wordsworth and Coleridge are men in years; the one imbued in contemplation from his childhood, the other a giant in intellect and learning. The diffidence, then, with which I venture to dispute their authority, would be overwhelming, did I not feel, from the bottom of my heart, that learning has little to do with the imagination—intellect with the passions—or age with poetry.

***

"Trifles, like straws, upon the surface flow,
He who would search for pearls must dive below,"

are lines which have done much mischief. As regards the greater truths, men oftener err by seeking them at the bottom than at the top; the depth lies in the huge abysses where wisdom is sought—not in the palpable palaces where she is found. The ancients were not always right in hiding the goddess in a well: witness the light which Bacon has thrown upon philosophy; witness the principles of our divine faith—that moral mechanism by which the simplicity of a child may overbalance the wisdom of a man.

We see an instance of Coleridge's liability to err, in his *Biographia Literaria*—professedly his literary life and opinions, but, in fact, a treatise *de omni scibili et quibusdam aliis.* He goes wrong by reason of his very profundity, and of his error we have a natural type in the contemplation of a star. He who regards it directly and intensely sees, it is true, the star, but it is the star without a ray—while he who surveys it less inquisitively is conscious of all for which the star is useful to us below—its brilliancy and its beauty.

***

As to Wordsworth, I have no faith in him. That he had, in youth, the feelings of a poet I believe—for there are glimpses of extreme delicacy in his writings—(and delicacy is the poet's own kingdom—his *El Dorado*)—

but they have the appearance of a better day recollected; and glimpses, at best, are little evidence of present poetic fire—we know that a few straggling flowers spring up daily in the crevices of the glacier.

He was to blame in wearing away his youth in contemplation with the end of poetizing in his manhood. With the increase of his judgment the light which should make it apparent has faded away. His judgment consequently is too correct. This may not be understood—but the old Goths of Germany would have understood it, who used to debate matters of importance to their State twice, once when drunk, and once when sober—sober that they might not be deficient in formality—drunk lest they should be destitute of vigor.

The long wordy discussions by which he tries to reason us into admiration of his poetry, speak very little in his favor: they are full of such assertions as this—(I have opened one of his volumes at random) "Of genius the only proof is the act of doing well what is worthy to be done, and what was never done before"—indeed! then it follows that in doing what is *un*worthy to be done, or what *has* been done before, no genius can be evinced: yet the picking of pockets is an unworthy act, pockets have been picked time immemorial, and Barrington, the pick-pocket, in point of genius, would have thought hard of a comparison with William Wordsworth, the poet.

Again—in estimating the merit of certain poems, whether they be Ossian's or M'Pherson's, can surely be of little consequence, yet, in order to prove their worthlessness, Mr. W. has expended many pages in the controversy. *Tantæne animis?* Can great minds descend to such absurdity? But worse still: that he may bear down every argument in favor of these poems, he triumphantly drags forward a passage, in his abomination of which he expects the reader to sympathize. It is the beginning of the epic poem *Temora.* "The blue waves of Ullin roll in light; the green hills are covered with day; trees shake their dusky heads in the breeze." And this—this gorgeous, yet simple imagery, where all is alive and panting with immortality—this, William Wordsworth, the author of 'Peter Bell', has *selected* for his contempt. We shall see what better he, in his own person, has to offer. Imprimis:

> "And now she's at the pony's head,
> And now she's at the pony's tail,

On that side now, and now on this,
And almost stifled her with bliss—
A few sad tears does Betty shed,
She pats the pony where or when
She knows not: happy Betty Foy!
O Johnny! never mind the Doctor!"
Secondly:
"The dew was falling fast, the—stars began to
blink,
I heard a voice, it said—drink, pretty creature,
drink;
And looking o'er the hedge, be—fore me I espied
A snow-white mountain lamb with a—maiden at
its side,
No other sheep were near, the lamb was all alone,
And by a slender cord was—tether'd to a stone."

Now we have no doubt this is all true; we *will* believe it, indeed we will, Mr. W. Is it sympathy for the sheep you wish to excite? I love a sheep from the bottom of my heart.

***

But there *are* occasions, dear B——, there are occasions when even Wordsworth is reasonable. Even Stamboul, it is said, shall have an end, and the most unlucky blunders must come to a conclusion. Here is an extract from his preface—

"Those who have been accustomed to the phraseology of modern writers, if they persist in reading this book to a conclusion (*impossible!*) will, no doubt, have to struggle with feelings of awkwardness; (ha! ha! ha!) they will look round for poetry (ha! ha! ha! ha!) and will be induced to inquire by what species of courtesy these attempts have been permitted to assume that title." Ha! ha! ha! ha! ha!

Yet let not Mr. W. despair; he has given immortality to a wagon, and the bee Sophocles has transmitted to eternity a sore toe, and dignified a tragedy with a chorus of turkeys.

***

Of Coleridge, I cannot speak but with reverence. His towering intellect! his gigantic power! He is one more evidence of the fact "que la plupart des sectes ont raison dans une bonne partie de ce qu'elles avancent, mais non pas en ce qu'elles nient." He has imprisoned his own conceptions by the barrier he has erected against those of others. It is lamentable to think that such a mind should be buried in metaphysics, and, like the Nyctanthes, waste its perfume upon the night alone. In reading his poetry I tremble—like one who stands upon a volcano, conscious, from the very darkness bursting from the crater, of the fire and the light that are weltering below.

***

What is Poetry?—Poetry! that Proteus-like idea, with as many appellations as the nine-titled Corcyra! Give me, I demanded of a scholar some time ago, give me a definition of poetry? "Très-volontiers," and he proceeded to his library, brought me a Dr. Johnson, and overwhelmed me with a definition. Shade of the immortal Shakespeare! I imagined to myself the scowl of your spiritual eye upon the profanity of that scurrilous Ursa Major. Think of poetry, dear B——, think of poetry, and then think of—Dr. Samuel Johnson! Think of all that is airy and fairy-like, and then of all that is hideous and unwieldy; think of his huge bulk, the Elephant! and then—and then think of the Tempest—the Midsummer Night's Dream—Prospero—Oberon—and Titania!

***

A poem, in my opinion, is opposed to a work of science by having, for its *immediate* object, pleasure, not truth; to romance, by having for its object an *indefinite* instead of a *definite* pleasure, being a poem only so far as this object is attained; romance presenting perceptible images with definite, poetry with *in*definite sensations, to which end music is an *essential*, since the comprehension of sweet sound is our most indefinite conception. Music, when combined with a pleasurable idea, is poetry;

music without the idea is simply music; the idea without the music is prose from its very definitiveness.

What was meant by the invective against him who had no music in his soul?

***

To sum up this long rigmarole, I have, dear B——, what you no doubt perceive, for the metaphysical poets, *as* poets, the most sovereign contempt. That they have followers proves nothing—

No Indian prince has to his palace
More followers than a thief to the gallows.

Maelzel's Chess-Player

[First published in the April 1836 issue of the *Southern Literary Messenger*.]

Perhaps no exhibition of the kind has ever elicited so general attention as the Chess-Player of Maelzel. Wherever seen it has been an object of intense curiosity, to all persons who think. Yet the question of its *modus operandi* is still undetermined. Nothing has been written on this topic which can be considered as decisive—and accordingly we find every where men of mechanical genius, of great general acuteness, and discriminative understanding, who make no scruple in pronouncing the Automaton a *pure machine*, unconnected with human agency in its movements, and consequently, beyond all comparison, the most astonishing of the inventions of mankind. And such it would undoubtedly be, were they right in their supposition. Assuming this hypothesis, it would be grossly absurd to compare with the Chess-Player, any similar thing of either modern or ancient days. Yet there have been many and wonderful automata. In Brewster's Letters on Natural Magic, we have an account of the most remarkable. Among these may be mentioned, as having beyond doubt existed, firstly, the coach invented by M. Camus for the amusement of Louis XIV when a child. A table, about four feet square, was introduced, into the room appropriated for the exhibition. Upon this table was placed a carriage, six inches in length, made of wood, and drawn by two horses of the same material. One window being down, a lady was seen on the back seat. A coachman held the reins on the box, and a footman and page were in their places behind. M. Camus now touched a spring; whereupon the coachman smacked his whip, and the horses proceeded in a natural manner, along the edge of the table, drawing after them the carriage. Having gone as far as possible in this direction, a sudden turn was made to the left, and the vehicle was driven at right angles to its former course, and still closely along the edge of the table. In this way the coach proceeded until it arrived opposite the chair of the young prince. It then stopped, the page descended and opened the door, the lady alighted, and presented a petition to her sovereign. She then re-entered. The page put up the steps, closed the door, and resumed his station. The coachman whipped his horses, and the carriage was driven back to its original position.

The magician of M. Maillardet is also worthy of notice. We copy the following account of it from the *Letters* before mentioned of Dr. B., who derived his information principally from the Edinburgh Encyclopædia.

"One of the most popular pieces of mechanism which we have seen, is the Magician constructed by M. Maillardet, for the purpose of answering certain given questions. A figure, dressed like a magician, appears seated at the bottom of a wall, holding a wand in one hand, and a book in the other. A number of questions, ready prepared, are inscribed on oval medallions, and the spectator takes any of these he chooses, and to which he wishes an answer, and having placed it in a drawer ready to receive it, the drawer shuts with a spring till the answer is returned. The magician then arises from his seat, bows his head, describes circles with his wand, and consulting the book as if in deep thought, he lifts it towards his face. Having thus appeared to ponder over the proposed question, he raises his wand, and striking with it the wall above his head, two folding doors fly open, and display an appropriate answer to the question. The doors again close, the magician resumes his original position, and the drawer opens to return the medallion. There are twenty of these medallions, all containing different questions, to which the magician returns the most suitable and striking answers. The medallions are thin plates of brass, of an elliptical form, exactly resembling each other. Some of the medallions have a question inscribed on each side, both of which the magician answered in succession. If the drawer is shut without a medallion being put into it, the magician rises, consults his book, shakes his head, and resumes his seat. The folding doors remain shut, and the drawer is returned empty. If two medallions are put into the drawer together, an answer is returned only to the lower one. When the machinery is wound up, the movements continue about an hour, during which time about fifty questions may be answered. The inventor stated that the means by which the different medallions acted upon the machinery, so as to produce the proper answers to the questions which they contained, were extremely simple."

The duck of Vaucanson was still more remarkable. It was *of* the size of life, and so perfect an imitation of the living animal that all the spectators were deceived. It executed, says Brewster, all the natural movements and gestures, it ate and drank with avidity, performed all the quick motions of the head and throat which are peculiar to the duck, and like it muddled the water which it drank with its bill. It produced also the sound of quacking in the most natural manner. In the anatomical structure the artist exhibited the highest skill. Every bone in the real duck had its representative in the automaton, and its wings were anatomically exact. Every cavity, apophysis, and curvature was imitated, and each bone executed its proper movements. When corn was thrown down before it, the duck stretched out its neck to pick it up, swallowed, and digested it.*

But if these machines were ingenious, what shall we think of the calculating machine of Mr. Babbage? What shall we think of an engine of wood and metal which can not only compute astronomical and navigation tables to any given extent, but render the exactitude of its operations mathematically certain through its power of correcting its possible errors? What shall we think of a machine which can not only accomplish all this, but actually print off its elaborate results, when obtained, without the slightest intervention of the intellect of man? It will, perhaps, be said, in reply, that a machine such as we have described is altogether above comparison with the Chess-Player of Maelzel. By no means—it is altogether beneath it—that is to say provided we assume (what should never for a moment be assumed) that the Chess-Player is a *pure machine*, and performs its operations without any immediate human agency. Arithmetical or algebraical calculations are, from their very nature, fixed and determinate. Certain *data* being given, certain results necessarily and inevitably follow. These results have dependence upon nothing, and are influenced by nothing but the *data* originally given. And the question to be solved proceeds, or should

* Under the head *Androides* in the Edinburgh Encyclopedia may be found a full account of the principal automata of ancient and modern times.

proceed, to its final determination, by a succession of unerring steps liable to no change, and subject to no modification. This being the case, we can without difficulty conceive the *possibility* of so arranging a piece of mechanism, that upon starting it in accordance with the *data* of the question to be solved, it should continue its movements regularly, progressively, and undeviatingly towards the required solution, since these movements, however complex, are never imagined to be otherwise than finite and determinate. But the case is widely different with the Chess-Player. With him there is no determinate progression. No one move in chess necessarily follows upon any one other. From no particular disposition of the men at one period of a game can we predicate their disposition at a different period. Let us place the *first move* in a game of chess, in juxta-position with the *data* of an algebraical question, and their great difference will be immediately perceived. From the latter—from the *data*—the second step of the question, dependent thereupon, inevitably follows. It is modelled by the *data*. It must be *thus* and not otherwise. But from the first move in the game of chess no especial second move follows of necessity. In the algebraical question, as it proceeds towards solution, the *certainty* of its operations remains altogether unimpaired. The second step having been a consequence of the *data*, the third step is equally a consequence of the second, the fourth of the third, the fifth of the fourth, and so on, *and not possibly otherwise*, to the end. But in proportion to the progress made in a game of chess, is the *uncertainty* of each ensuing move. A few moves having been made, *no* step is certain. Different spectators of the game would advise different moves. All is then dependent upon the variable judgment of the players. Now even granting (what should not be granted) that the movements of the Automaton Chess-Player were in themselves determinate, they would be necessarily interrupted and disarranged by the indeterminate will of his antagonist. There is then no analogy whatever between the operations of the Chess-Player, and those of the calculating machine of Mr. Babbage, and if we choose to call the former a *pure machine* we must be prepared to admit that it is, beyond all comparison, the most wonderful of the inventions of mankind. Its original projector, however, Baron Kempelen, had no scruple in declaring it to be a "very ordinary piece of mechanism—a *bagatelle* whose effects appeared so marvellous only from the boldness of the conception, and the fortunate choice of the methods adopted for promoting the illusion." But it is needless to dwell upon this point. It is quite certain that the operations of the Automaton are regulated by *mind,* and by nothing else. Indeed this matter is susceptible of a mathematical demonstration, *a priori.* The only question then is of the *manner* in which human agency is brought to bear. Before entering upon this subject it would be as well to give a brief history and description of the Chess-Player for the benefit of such of our readers as may never have had an opportunity of witnessing Mr. Maelzel's exhibition.

The Automaton Chess-Player was invented in 1769, by Baron Kempelen, a nobleman of Presburg in Hungary, who afterwards disposed of it, together with the secret of its operations, to its present possessor. Soon after its completion it was exhibited in Presburg, Paris, Vienna, and other continental cities. In 1783 and 1784, it was taken to London by Mr. Maelzel. Of late years it has visited the principal towns in the United States. Wherever seen, the most intense curiosity was excited by its appearance, and numerous have been the attempts, by men of all classes, to fathom the mystery of its evolutions. The cut above gives a tolerable representation of the figure as seen by the citizens of Richmond a few weeks ago. The right arm, however, should lie more at length upon the box, a chess-board should appear upon it, and the cushion should not be seen while the pipe is held. Some immaterial alterations have been made in the costume of the player since it came into the possession of Maelzel—the plume, for example, was not originally worn.

At the hour appointed for exhibition, a curtain is withdrawn, or folding doors are thrown open, and the machine rolled to within about twelve feet of the nearest of the spectators, between whom and it (the machine) a rope is stretched. A figure is seen habited as a Turk, and seated, with its legs crossed, at a large box apparently of maple wood, which serves it as a table. The exhibiter will, if requested, roll the machine to any portion of the room, suffer it to remain altogether on any designated spot, or even shift its location repeatedly during the progress of a game. The bottom of the box is elevated considerably above the floor by means of the castors or brazen rollers on which it moves, a clear view of the surface immediately beneath the Automaton being thus afforded to the spectators. The chair on which the figure sits is affixed permanently to the box. On the top of this latter is a chess-board, also permanently affixed. The right arm of the Chess-Player is extended at full length before him, at right angles with his body, and lying, in an apparently careless position, by the side of the board. The back of the hand is upwards. The board itself is eighteen inches square. The left arm of the figure is bent at the elbow, and in the left hand is a pipe. A green drapery conceals the back of the Turk, and falls partially over the front of both shoulders. To judge from the external appearance of the box, it is divided into five compartments—three cupboards of equal dimensions, and two drawers occupying that portion of the chest lying beneath the cupboards. The foregoing observations apply to the appearance of the Automaton upon its first introduction into the presence of the spectators.

Maelzel now informs the company that he will disclose to their view the mechanism of the machine. Taking from his pocket a bunch of keys he unlocks with one of them, door marked 1 in the cut above, and throws the cupboard fully open to the inspection of all present. Its whole interior is apparently filled with wheels, pinions, levers, and other machinery, crowded very closely together, so that the eye can penetrate but a little distance into the mass. Leaving this door open to its full extent, he goes now round to the back of the box, and raising the drapery of the figure, opens another door situated precisely in the rear of the one first opened. Holding a lighted candle at this door, and shifting the position of the whole machine repeatedly at the same time, a bright light is thrown entirely through the cupboard, which is now clearly seen to be full, completely full, of machinery. The spectators being satisfied of this fact, Maelzel closes the back door, locks it, takes the key from the lock, lets fall the drapery of the figure, and comes round to the front. The door marked 1, it will be remembered, is still open. The exhibiter now proceeds to open the drawer which lies beneath the cupboards at the bottom of the box—for although there are apparently two drawers, there is really only one—the two handles and two key holes being intended merely for ornament. Having opened this drawer to its full extent, a small cushion, and a set of chessmen, fixed in a frame work made to support them perpendicularly, are discovered. Leaving this drawer, as well as cupboard No. 1 open, Maelzel now unlocks door No. 2, and door No. 3, which are discovered to be folding doors, opening into one and the same compartment. To the right of this compartment, however, (that is to say the spectators' right) a small division, six inches wide, and filled with machinery, is partitioned off. The main compartment itself (in speaking of that portion of the box visible upon opening doors 2 and 3, we shall always call it the main compartment) is lined with dark cloth and contains no machinery whatever beyond two pieces of steel, quadrant-shaped, and situated one in each of the rear top corners of the compartment. A small protuberance about eight inches square, and also covered with dark cloth, lies on the floor of the compartment near the rear corner on the spectators' left hand. Leaving doors No. 2 and No. 3 open as well as the drawer, and door No. 1, the exhibiter now goes round to the back of the main compartment, and, unlocking another door there, displays clearly all the interior of the main compartment, by introducing a candle behind it and within it. The whole box being thus apparently disclosed to the scrutiny of the company, Maelzel, still leaving the doors and drawer open, rolls the Automaton entirely round, and exposes the back of the Turk by lifting up the drapery. A door about ten inches square is thrown open in the loins of the figure, and a smaller one also in the left thigh. The interior of the figure, as seen through these apertures, appears to be crowded with machinery. In general, every spectator is now thoroughly satisfied of having beheld and completely scrutinized, at one and the same time, every individual portion of the Automaton, and the idea of any person being concealed in the interior, during so complete an exhibition of that interior, if ever entertained, is immediately dismissed as preposterous in the extreme.

M. Maelzel, having rolled the machine back into its original position, now informs the company that the Automaton will play a game of chess with any one disposed to encounter him. This challenge being accepted, a small table is prepared for the antagonist, and placed close by the rope, but on the spectators' side of it, and so situated as not to prevent the company from obtaining a full view of the Automaton. From a drawer in this table is taken a set of chess-men, and Maelzel arranges them generally, but not always, with his own hands, on the chess-board, which consists merely of the usual number of squares painted upon the table. The antagonist having taken his seat, the exhibiter approaches the drawer of the box, and takes therefrom the cushion, which, after removing the pipe from the hand of the Automaton, he places under its left arm as a support. Then taking also from the drawer the Automaton's set of chess-men, he arranges them upon the chess-board before the figure. He now proceeds to close the doors and to lock them—leaving the bunch of keys in door No. 1. He also closes the drawer, and, finally, winds up the machine, by applying a key to an aperture in the left end (the spectators' left) of the box. The game now commences—the Automaton taking the first move. The duration of the contest is usually limited to half an hour, but if it be not finished at the expiration of this period, and the antagonist still contend that he can beat the Automaton, M. Maelzel has seldom any objection to continue it. Not to weary the company, is the ostensible, and no doubt the real object of the limitation. It will of course be understood that when a move is made at his own table, by the antagonist, the corresponding move is made at the box of the Automaton, by Maelzel himself, who then acts as the representative of the antagonist. On the other hand, when the Turk moves, the corresponding move is made at the table of the antagonist, also by M. Maelzel, who then acts as the representative of the Automaton. In this manner it is necessary that the exhibiter should often pass from one table to the other. He also frequently goes in rear of the figure to remove the chess-men which it has taken, and which it deposits, when taken, on the box to the left (to its own left) of the board. When the Automaton hesitates in relation to its move, the exhibiter is occasionally seen to place himself very near its right side, and to lay his hand, now and then, in a careless manner upon the box. He has also a peculiar shuffle with his feet, calculated to induce suspicion of collusion with the machine in minds which are more cunning than sagacious. These peculiarities are, no doubt, mere mannerisms of M. Maelzel, or, if he is aware of them at all, he puts them in practice with a view of exciting in the spectators a false idea of pure mechanism in the Automaton.

The Turk plays with his left hand. All the movements of the arm are at right angles. In this manner, the hand (which is gloved and bent in a natural way,) being brought directly above the piece to be moved, descends finally upon it, the fingers receiving it, in most cases, without difficulty. Occasionally, however, when the piece is not precisely in its proper situation, the Automaton fails in his attempt at seizing it. When this occurs, no second effort is made, but the arm continues its movement in the direction originally intended, precisely as if the piece were in the fingers. Having thus designated the spot whither the move should have been made, the arm returns to its cushion, and Maelzel performs the evolution which the Automaton pointed out. At every movement of the figure machinery is heard in motion. During the progress of the game, the figure now and then rolls its eyes, as if surveying the board, moves its head, and pronounces the word *echec* (check) when necessary.* If a false move be made by his antagonist, he raps briskly on the box with the fingers of his right hand, shakes his head roughly, and replacing the piece falsely moved, in its former situation, assumes the next move himself. Upon beating the game, he waves his head with an air of triumph, looks round complacently upon the spectators, and drawing his left arm farther back than usual, suffers his fingers alone to rest upon the cushion. In general, the Turk is victorious—once or twice he has been beaten. The game being ended, Maelzel will again, if desired, exhibit the mechanism of the box, in the same manner as before. The machine is then rolled back, and a curtain hides it from the view of the company.

There have been many attempts at solving the mystery of the Automaton. The most general opinion in relation to it, an opinion too not unfrequently adopted by men who should have known better, was, as we have before said, that no immediate human agency was employed—in other words, that the machine was purely a machine and nothing else. Many, however maintained that the exhibiter himself regulated the movements of the figure by mechanical means operating through the feet of the box. Others again, spoke confidently of a magnet. Of the first of these opinions we shall say nothing at present more than we have already said. In relation to the second it is only necessary to repeat what we have before stated, that the machine is rolled about on castors, and will, at the request of a spectator, be moved to and fro to any portion of the room, even during the progress of a game. The supposition of the magnet is also untenable—for if a magnet were the agent, any other magnet in the pocket of a spectator would disarrange the entire mechanism. The exhibiter, however, will suffer the most powerful loadstone to remain even upon the box during the whole of the exhibition.

The first attempt at a written explanation of the secret, at least the first attempt of which we ourselves have any knowledge, was made in a large pamphlet printed at Paris in 1785. The author's hypothesis amounted to this—that a dwarf actuated the machine. This dwarf he

* The making the Turk pronounce the word *echec*, is an improvement by M. Maelzel. When in possession of Baron Kempelen, the figure indicated a check by rapping on the box with his right hand.

supposed to conceal himself during the opening of the box by thrusting his legs into two hollow cylinders, which were represented to be (but which are not) among the machinery in the cupboard No. 1, while his body was out of the box entirely, and covered by the drapery of the Turk. When the doors were shut, the dwarf was enabled to bring his body within the box—the noise produced by some portion of the machinery allowing him to do so unheard, and also to close the door by which he entered. The interior of the Automaton being then exhibited, and no person discovered, the spectators, says the author of this pamphlet, are satisfied that no one is within any portion of the machine. This whole hypothesis was too obviously absurd to require comment, or refutation, and accordingly we find that it attracted very little attention.

In 1789 a book was published at Dresden by M. I. F. Freyhere in which another endeavor was made to unravel the mystery. Mr. Freyhere's book was a pretty large one, and copiously illustrated by coloured engravings. His supposition was that "a well-taught boy very thin and tall of his age (sufficiently so that he could be concealed in a drawer almost immediately under the chess-board") played the game of chess and effected all the evolutions of the Automaton. This idea, although even more silly than that of the Parisian author, met with a better reception, and was in some measure believed to be the true solution of the wonder, until the inventor put an end to the discussion by suffering a close examination of the top of the box.

These bizarre attempts at explanation were followed by others equally bizarre. Of late years however, an anonymous writer, by a course of reasoning exceedingly unphilosophical, has contrived to blunder upon a plausible solution—although we cannot consider it altogether the true one. His Essay was first published in a Baltimore weekly paper, was illustrated by cuts, and was entitled "An attempt to analyze the Automaton Chess-Player of M. Maelzel." This Essay we suppose to have been the original of the *pamphlet* to which Sir David Brewster alludes in his letters on Natural Magic, and which he has no hesitation in declaring a thorough and satisfactory explanation. The *results* of the analysis are undoubtedly, in the main, just; but we can only account for Brewster's pronouncing the Essay a thorough and satisfactory explanation, by supposing him to have bestowed upon it a very cursory and inattentive perusal. In the compendium of the Essay, made use of in the Letters on

Natural Magic, it is quite impossible to arrive at any distinct conclusion in regard to the adequacy or inadequacy of the analysis, on account of the gross misarrangement and deficiency of the letters of reference employed. The same fault is to be found in the "Attempt &c," as we originally saw it. The solution consists in a series of minute explanations, (accompanied by wood-cuts, the whole occupying many pages) in which the object is to show the *possibility* of *so shifting the partitions* of the box, as to allow a human being, concealed in the interior, to move portions of his body from one part of the box to another, during the exhibition of the mechanism—thus eluding the scrutiny of the spectators. There can be no doubt, as we have before observed, and as we will presently endeavor to show, that the principle, or rather the result, of this solution is the true one. Some person *is* concealed in the box during the whole time of exhibiting the interior. We object, however, to the whole verbose description of the *manner* in which the partitions are shifted, to accommodate the movements of the person concealed. We object to it as a mere theory assumed in the first place, and to which circumstances are afterwards made to adapt themselves. It was not, and could not have been, arrived at by any inductive reasoning. In whatever way the shifting is managed, it is of course concealed at every step from observation. To show that certain movements might possibly be effected in a certain way, is very far from showing that they are actually so effected. There may be an infinity of other methods by which the same results may be obtained. The probability of the one assumed proving the correct one is then as unity to infinity. But, in reality, this particular point, the shifting of the partitions, is of no consequence whatever. It was altogether unnecessary to devote seven or eight pages for the purpose of proving what no one in his senses would deny—viz: that the wonderful mechanical genius of Baron Kempelen could invent the necessary means for shutting a door or slipping aside a pannel, with a human agent too at his service in actual contact with the pannel or the door, and the whole operations carried on, as the author of the Essay himself shows, and as we shall attempt to show more fully hereafter, entirely out of reach of the observation of the spectators.

In attempting ourselves an explanation of the Automaton, we will, in the first place, endeavor to show how its operations are effected, and afterwards describe, as briefly as possible, the nature of the *observations* from which we have deduced our result.

It will be necessary for a proper understanding of the subject, that we repeat here in a few words, the routine adopted by the exhibiter in disclosing the interior of the box—a routine from which he *never* deviates in any material particular. In the first place he opens the door No. 1. Leaving this open, he goes round to the rear of the box, and opens a door precisely at the back of door No. 1. To this back door he holds a lighted candle. He then *closes the back door*, locks it, and, coming round to the front, opens the drawer to its full extent. This done, he opens the doors No. 2 and No. 3, (the folding doors) and displays the interior of the main compartment. Leaving open the main compartment, the drawer, and the front door of cupboard No. 1, he now goes to the rear again, and throws open the back door of the main compartment. In shutting up the box no particular order is observed, except that the folding doors are always closed before the drawer.

Now, let us suppose that when the machine is first rolled into the presence of the spectators, a man is already within it. His body is situated behind the dense machinery in cupboard No. 1, (the rear portion of which machinery is so contrived as to slip *en masse*, from the main compartment to the cupboard No. 1, as occasion may require,) and his legs lie at full length in the main compartment. When Maelzel opens the door No. 1, the man within is not in any danger of discovery, for the keenest eye cannot penetrate more than about two inches into the darkness within. But the case is otherwise when the back door of the cupboard No. 1, is opened. A bright light then pervades the cupboard, and the body of the man would be discovered if it were there. But it is not. The putting the key in the lock of the back door was a signal on hearing which the person concealed brought his body forward to an angle as acute as possible—throwing it altogether, or nearly so, into the main compartment. This, however, is a painful position, and cannot be long maintained. Accordingly we find that Maelzel *closes the back door.* This being done, there is no reason why the body of the man may not resume its former situation—for the cupboard is again so dark as to defy scrutiny. The drawer is now opened, and the legs of the person within drop down behind it in the space it formerly occupied.*

* Sir David Brewster supposes that there is always a large space behind this drawer even when shut—in other words that the drawer is a "false drawer,"

There is, consequently, now no longer any part of the man in the main compartment—his body being behind the machinery in cupboard No. 1, and his legs in the space occupied by the drawer. The exhibiter, therefore, finds himself at liberty to display the main compartment. This he does—opening both its back and front doors—and no person is discovered. The spectators are now satisfied that the whole of the box is exposed to view—and exposed too, all portions of it at one and the same time. But of course this is not the case. They neither see the space behind the drawer, nor the interior of cupboard No. 1—the front door of which latter the exhibiter virtually shuts in shutting its back door. Maelzel, having now rolled the machine around, lifted up the drapery of the Turk, opened the doors in his back and thigh, and shown his trunk to be full of machinery, brings the whole back into its original position, and closes the doors. The man within is now at liberty to move about. He gets up into the body of the Turk just so high as to bring his eyes above the level of the chess-board. It is very probable that he seats himself upon the little square block or protuberance which is seen in a corner of the main compartment when the doors are open. In this position he sees the chess-board through the bosom of the Turk which is of gauze. Bringing his right arm across his breast he actuates the little machinery necessary to guide the left arm and the fingers of the figure. This machinery is situated just beneath the left shoulder of the Turk, and is consequently easily reached by the right hand of the man concealed, if we suppose his right arm brought across the breast. The motions of the head and eyes, and of the right arm of the figure, as well as the sound *echec* are produced by other mechanism in the interior, and actuated at will by the man within. The whole of this mechanism—that is to say all the mechanism essential to the machine—is most probably contained within the little cupboard (of about six inches in breadth) partitioned off at the right (the spectators' right) of the main compartment.

In this analysis of the operations of the Automaton, we have purposely avoided any allusion to the manner in which the partitions are shifted,

---

and does not extend to the back of the box. But the idea is altogether untenable. So common-place a trick would be immediately discovered—especially as the drawer is always opened to its fun extent, and an opportunity thus afforded of comparing its depth with that of the box.

and it will now be readily comprehended that this point is a matter of no importance, since, by mechanism within the ability of any common carpenter, it might be effected in an infinity of different ways, and since we have shown that, however performed, it is performed out of the view of the spectators. Our result is founded upon the following *observations* taken during frequent visits to the exhibition of Maelzel.*

1. The moves of the Turk are not made at regular intervals of time, but accommodate themselves to the moves of the antagonist—although this point (of regularity) so important in all kinds of mechanical contrivance, might have been readily brought about by limiting the time allowed for the moves of the antagonist. For example, if this limit were three minutes, the moves of the Automaton might be made at any given intervals longer than three minutes. The fact then of irregularity, when regularity might have been so easily attained, goes to prove that regularity is unimportant to the action of the Automaton—in other words, that the Automaton is not *a pure machine.*
2. When the Automaton is about to move a piece, a distinct motion is observable just beneath the left shoulder, and which motion agitates in a slight degree, the drapery covering the front of the left shoulder. This motion invariably precedes, by about two seconds, the movement of the arm itself—and the arm never, in any instance, moves without this preparatory motion in the shoulder. Now let the antagonist move a piece, and let the corresponding move be made by Maelzel, as usual, upon the board of the Automaton. Then let the antagonist narrowly watch the Automaton, until he detect the preparatory motion in the shoulder. Immediately upon detecting this motion, and before the arm itself begins to move, let him withdraw his piece, as if perceiving an error in his manœuvre. It will then be seen that the movement of the arm, which, in all

* Some of these *observations* are intended merely to prove that the machine must be regulated *by mind*, and it may be thought a work of supererogation to advance farther arguments in support of what has been already fully decided. But our object is to convince, in especial, certain of our friends upon whom a train of suggestive reasoning will have more influence than the most positive *a priori* demonstration.

other cases, immediately succeeds the motion in the shoulder, is withheld—is not made—although Maelzel has not yet performed, on the board of the Automaton, any move corresponding to the withdrawal of the antagonist. In this case, that the Automaton was about to move is evident—and that he did not move, was an effect plainly produced by the withdrawal of the antagonist, and without any intervention of Maelzel.

This fact fully proves, 1—that the intervention of Maelzel, in performing the moves of the antagonist on the board of the Automaton, is not essential to the movements of the Automaton, 2—that its movements are regulated by *mind*—by some person who sees the board of the antagonist, 3—that its movements are not regulated by the mind of Maelzel, whose back was turned towards the antagonist at the withdrawal of his move.

3. The Automaton does not invariably win the game. Were the machine a pure machine this would not be the case—it would always win. The *principle* being discovered by which a machine can be made to *play* a game of chess, an extension of the same principle would enable it to *win* a game—a farther extension would enable it to *win all* games—that is, to beat any possible game of an antagonist. A little consideration will convince any one that the difficulty of making a machine beat all games, is not in the least degree greater, as regards the principle of the operations necessary, than that of making it beat a single game. If then we regard the Chess-Player as a machine, we must suppose, (what is highly improbable,) that its inventor preferred leaving it incomplete to perfecting it—a supposition rendered still more absurd, when we reflect that the leaving it incomplete would afford an argument against the possibility of its being a pure machine—the very argument we now adduce.
4. When the situation of the game is difficult or complex, we never perceive the Turk either shake his head or roll his eyes. It is only when his next move is obvious, or when the game is so circumstanced that to a man in the Automaton's place there would be no necessity for reflection. Now these peculiar movements of the head and eyes are movements customary with persons engaged in meditation, and the ingenious Baron Kempelen would have

adapted these movements (were the machine a pure machine) to occasions proper for their display—that is, to occasions of complexity. But the reverse is seen to be the case, and this reverse applies precisely to our supposition of a man in the interior. When engaged in meditation about the game he has no time to think of setting in motion the mechanism of the Automaton by which are moved the head and the eyes. When the game, however, is obvious, he has time to look about him, and, accordingly, we see the head shake and the eyes roll.

5. When the machine is rolled round to allow the spectators an examination of the back of the Turk, and when his drapery is lifted up and the doors in the trunk and thigh thrown open, the interior of the trunk is seen to be crowded with machinery. In scrutinizing this machinery while the Automaton was in motion, that is to say while the whole machine was moving on the castors, it appeared to us that certain portions of the mechanism changed their shape and position in a degree too great to be accounted for by the simple laws of perspective; and subsequent examinations convinced us that these undue alterations were attributable to mirrors in the interior of the trunk. The introduction of mirrors among the machinery could not have been intended to influence, in any degree, the machinery itself. Their operation, whatever that operation should prove to be, must necessarily have reference to the eye of the spectator. We at once concluded that these mirrors were so placed to multiply to the vision some few pieces of machinery within the trunk so as to give it the appearance of being crowded with mechanism. Now the direct inference from this is that the machine is not a pure machine. For if it were, the inventor, so far from wishing its mechanism to appear complex, and using deception for the purpose of giving it this appearance, would have been especially desirous of convincing those who witnessed his exhibition, of the *simplicity* of the means by which results so wonderful were brought about.
6. The external appearance, and, especially, the deportment of the Turk, are, when we consider them as imitations of *life,* but very indifferent imitations. The countenance evinces no ingenuity, and is surpassed, in its resemblance to the human face, by the very

commonest of wax-works. The eyes roll unnaturally in the head, without any corresponding motions of the lids or brows. The arm, particularly, performs its operations in an exceedingly stiff, awkward, jerking, and rectangular manner. Now, all this is the result either of inability in Maelzel to do better, or of intentional neglect—accidental neglect being out of the question, when we consider that the whole time of the ingenious proprietor is occupied in the improvement of his machines. Most assuredly we must not refer the unlife-like appearances to inability—for all the rest of Maelzel's automata are evidence of his full ability to copy the motions and peculiarities of life with the most wonderful exactitude. The rope-dancers, for example, are inimitable. When the clown laughs, his lips, his eyes, his eye-brows, and eye-lids—indeed, all the features of his countenance—are imbued with their appropriate expressions. In both him and his companion, every gesture is so entirely easy, and free from the semblance of artificiality, that, were it not for the diminutiveness of their size, and the fact of their being passed from one spectator to another previous to their exhibition on the rope, it would be difficult to convince any assemblage of persons that these wooden automata were not living creatures. We cannot, therefore, doubt Mr. Maelzel's ability, and we must necessarily suppose that he intentionally suffered his Chess-Player to remain the same artificial and unnatural figure which Baron Kempelen (no doubt also through design) originally made it. What this design was it is not difficult to conceive. Were the Automaton life-like in its motions, the spectator would be more apt to attribute its operations to their true cause, (that is, to human agency within) than he is now, when the awkward and rectangular manœuvres convey the idea of pure and unaided mechanism.

7. When, a short time previous to the commencement of the game, the Automaton is wound up by the exhibiter as usual, an ear in any degree accustomed to the sounds produced in winding up a system of machinery, will not fail to discover, instantaneously, that the axis turned by the key in the box of the Chess-Player, cannot possibly be connected with either a weight, a spring, or any system of machinery whatever. The inference here is the same as in our

last observation. The winding up is inessential to the operations of the Automaton, and is performed with the design of exciting in the spectators the false idea of mechanism.

8. When the question is demanded explicitly of Maelzel—"Is the Automaton a pure machine or not?" his reply is invariably the same—"I will say nothing about it." Now the notoriety of the Automaton, and the great curiosity it has every where excited, are owing more especially to the prevalent opinion that it *is* a pure machine, than to any other circumstance. Of course, then, it is the interest of the proprietor to represent it as a pure machine. And what more obvious, and more effectual method could there be of impressing the spectators with this desired idea, than a positive and explicit declaration to that effect? On the other hand, what more obvious and effectual method could there be of exciting a disbelief in the Automaton's being a pure machine, than by withholding such explicit declaration? For, people will naturally reason thus,—It is Maelzel's interest to represent this thing a pure machine—he refuses to do so, directly, in words, although he does not scruple, and is evidently anxious to do so, indirectly by actions—were it actually what he wishes to represent it by actions, he would gladly avail himself of the more direct testimony of words—the inference is, that a consciousness of its *not* being a pure machine, is the reason of his silence—his actions cannot implicate him in a falsehood—his words may.

9. When, in exhibiting the interior of the box, Maelzel has thrown open the door No. 1, and also the door immediately behind it, he holds a lighted candle at the back door (as mentioned above) and moves the entire machine to and fro with a view of convincing the company that the cupboard No. 1 is entirely filled with machinery. When the machine is thus moved about, it will be apparent to any careful observer, that whereas that portion of the machinery near the front door No. 1, is perfectly steady and unwavering, the portion farther within fluctuates, in a very slight degree, with the movements of the machine. This circumstance first aroused in us the suspicion that the more remote portion of the machinery was so arranged as to be easily slipped, *en masse*, from its position when occasion should require it. This occasion we have already stated to

occur when the man concealed within brings his body into an erect position upon the closing of the back door.

10. Sir David Brewster states the figure of the Turk to be of the size of life—but in fact it is far above the ordinary size. Nothing is more easy than to err in our notions of magnitude. The body of the Automaton is generally insulated, and, having no means of immediately comparing it with any human form, we suffer ourselves to consider it as of ordinary dimensions. This mistake may, however, be corrected by observing the Chess-Player when, as is sometimes the case, the exhibiter approaches it. Mr. Maelzel, to be sure, is not very tall, but upon drawing near the machine, his head will be found at least eighteen inches below the head of the Turk, although the latter, it will be remembered, is in a sitting position.

11. The box behind which the Automaton is placed, is precisely three feet six inches long, two feet four inches deep, and two feet six inches high. These dimensions are fully sufficient for the accommodation of a man very much above the common size—and the main compartment alone is capable of holding any ordinary man in the position we have mentioned as assumed by the person concealed. As these are facts, which any one who doubts them may prove by actual calculation, we deem it unnecessary to dwell upon them. We will only suggest that, although the top of the box is apparently a board of about three inches in thickness, the spectator may satisfy himself by stooping and looking up at it when the main compartment is open, that it is in reality very thin. The height of the drawer also will be misconceived by those who examine it in a cursory manner. There is a space of about three inches between the top of the drawer as seen from the exterior, and the bottom of the cupboard—a space which must be included in the height of the drawer. These contrivances to make the room within the box appear less than it actually is, are referrible to a design on the part of the inventor, to impress the company again with a false idea, viz. that no human being can be accommodated within the box.

12. The interior of the main compartment is lined throughout with *cloth*. This cloth we suppose to have a twofold object. A portion of it may form, when tightly stretched, the only partitions which there is any necessity for removing during the changes of the man's position,

viz: the partition between the rear of the main compartment and the rear of the cupboard No. 1, and the partition between the main compartment, and the space behind the drawer when open. If we imagine this to be the case, the difficulty of shifting the partitions vanishes at once, if indeed any such difficulty could be supposed under any circumstances to exist. The second object of the cloth is to deaden and render indistinct all sounds occasioned by the movements of the person within.

13. The antagonist (as we have before observed) is not suffered to play at the board of the Automaton, but is seated at some distance from the machine. The reason which, most probably, would be assigned for this circumstance, if the question were demanded, is, that were the antagonist otherwise situated, his person would intervene between the machine and the spectators, and preclude the latter from a distinct view. But this difficulty might be easily obviated, either by elevating the seats of the company, or by turning the end of the box towards them during the game. The true cause of the restriction is, perhaps, very different. Were the antagonist seated in contact with the box, the secret would be liable to discovery, by his detecting, with the aid of a quick car, the breathings of the man concealed.
14. Although M. Maelzel, in disclosing the interior of the machine, sometimes slightly deviates from the *routine* which we have pointed out, yet *never* in any instance does he *so* deviate from it as to interfere with our solution. For example, he has been known to open, first of all, the drawer—but he never opens the main compartment without first closing the back door of cupboard No. 1—he never opens the main compartment without first pulling out the drawer—he never shuts the drawer without first shutting the main compartment—he never opens the back door of cupboard No. 1 while the main compartment is open—and the game of chess is never commenced until the whole machine is closed. Now, if it were observed that *never, in any single instance*, did M. Maelzel differ from the routine we have pointed out as necessary to our solution, it would be one of the strongest possible arguments in corroboration of it—but the argument becomes infinitely strengthened if we duly consider the circumstance that he *does occasionally* deviate from the routine, but never does *so* deviate as to falsify the solution.

15. There are six candles on the board of the Automaton during exhibition. The question naturally arises—"Why are so many employed, when a single candle, or, at farthest, two, would have been amply sufficient to afford the spectators a clear view of the board, in a room otherwise so well lit up as the exhibition room always is—when, moreover, if we suppose the machine a *pure machine*, there can be no necessity for so much light, or indeed any light at all, to enable *it* to perform its operations—and when, especially, only a single candle is placed upon the table of the antagonist?" The first and most obvious inference is, that so strong a light is requisite to enable the man within to see through the transparent material (probably fine gauze) of which the breast of the Turk is composed. But when we consider the *arrangement* of the candles, another reason immediately presents itself. There are six lights (as we have said before) in all. Three of these are on each side of the figure. Those most remote from the spectators are the longest—those in the middle are about two inches shorter—and those nearest the company about two inches shorter still—and the candles on one side differ in height from the candles respectively opposite on the other, by a ratio different from two inches—that is to say, the longest candle on one side is about three inches shorter than the longest candle on the other, and so on. Thus it will be seen that no two of the candles are of the same height, and thus also the difficulty of ascertaining the *material* of the breast of the figure (against which the light is especially directed) is greatly augmented by the dazzling effect of the complicated crossings of the rays—crossings which are brought about by placing the centres of radiation all upon different levels.

16. While the Chess-Player was in possession of Baron Kempelen, it was more than once observed, first, that an Italian in the suite of the Baron was never visible during the playing of a game at chess by the Turk, and, secondly, that the Italian being taken seriously ill, the exhibition was suspended until his recovery. This Italian professed a *total* ignorance of the game of chess, although all others of the suite played well. Similar observations have been made since the Automaton has been purchased by Maelzel. There is a man, *Schlumberger*, who attends him wherever he goes, but

who has no ostensible occupation other than that of assisting in the packing and unpacking of the automata. This man is about the medium size, and has a remarkable stoop in the shoulders. Whether he professes to play chess or not, we are not informed. It is quite certain, however, that he is never to be seen during the exhibition of the Chess-Player, although frequently visible just before and just after the exhibition. Moreover, some years ago Maelzel visited Richmond with his automata, and exhibited them, we believe, in the house now occupied by M. Bossieux as a Dancing Academy. *Schlumberger* was suddenly taken ill, and during his illness there was no exhibition of the Chess-Player. These facts are well known to many of our citizens. The reason assigned for the suspension of the Chess-Player's performances, was *not* the illness of *Schlumberger*. The inferences from all this we leave, without farther comment, to the reader.

17. The Turk plays with his *left* arm. A circumstance so remarkable cannot be accidental. Brewster takes no notice of it whatever, beyond a mere statement, we believe, that such is the fact. The early writers of treatises on the Automaton, seem not to have observed the matter at all, and have no reference to it. The author of the pamphlet alluded to by Brewster, mentions it, but acknowledges his inability to account for it. Yet it is obviously from such prominent discrepancies or incongruities as this that deductions are to be made (if made at all) which shall lead us to the truth.

The circumstance of the Automaton's playing with his left hand cannot have connexion with the operations of the machine, considered merely as such. Any mechanical arrangement which would cause the figure to move, in any given manner, the left arm—could, if reversed, cause it to move, in the same manner, the right. But these principles cannot be extended to the human organization, wherein there is a marked and radical difference in the construction, and, at all events, in the powers, of the right and left arms. Reflecting upon this latter fact, we naturally refer the incongruity noticeable in the Chess-Player to this peculiarity in the human organization. If so, we must imagine some *reversion*—for the Chess-Player plays precisely as a man *would not.* These ideas, once entertained, are sufficient of themselves, to suggest the notion of a man in the interior. A few more imperceptible steps lead us, finally, to the result. The Automaton plays with his left arm, because under no other circumstances could the man within play with his right—a *desideratum* of course. Let us, for example, imagine the Automaton to play with his right arm. To reach the machinery which moves the arm, and which we have before explained to lie just beneath the shoulder, it would be necessary for the man within either to use his right arm in an exceedingly painful and awkward position, (viz. brought up close to his body and tightly compressed between his body and the side of the Automaton,) or else to use his left arm brought across his breast. In neither case could he act with the requisite ease or precision. On the contrary, the Automaton playing, as it actually does, with the left arm, all difficulties vanish. The right arm of the man within is brought across his breast, and his right fingers act, without any constraint, upon the machinery in the shoulder of the figure.

We do not believe that any reasonable objections can be urged against this solution of the Automaton Chess-Player.

The Philosophy of Furniture

[This humorous and unusual essay was first published in the May 1840 issue of *Burton's Gentleman's Magazine*. This is the slightly revised version which appeared as 'House Furniture' on May 3, 1845, in the *Broadway Journal*.]

In the internal decoration, if not in the external architecture of their residences, the English are supreme. The Italians have but little sentiment beyond marbles and colours. In France *meliora probant, deteriora sequuntur*—the people are too much a race of gad-abouts to maintain those household proprieties of which, indeed, they have a delicate appreciation, or at least the elements of a proper sense. The Chinese and most of the eastern races have a warm but inappropriate fancy. The Scotch are *poor* decorists. The Dutch have, perhaps, an indeterminate idea that a curtain is not a cabbage. In Spain they are *all* curtains—a nation of hangmen. The Russians do not furnish. The Hottentots and Kickapoos are very well in their way. The Yankees alone are preposterous.

How this happens it is not difficult to see. We have no aristocracy of blood, and having therefore as a natural, and indeed as an inevitable thing, fashioned for ourselves an aristocracy of dollars, the *display of wealth* has here to take the place and perform the office of the heraldic display in monarchical countries. By a transition readily understood, and which might have been as readily foreseen, we have been brought to merge in simple *show* our notions of taste itself.

To speak less abstractly. In England, for example, no mere parade of costly appurtenances would be so likely as with us, to create an impression of the beautiful in respect to the appurtenances themselves—or of taste as regards the proprietor:—this for the reason, first, that wealth is not, in England, the loftiest object of ambition as constituting a nobility; and secondly, that there the true nobility of blood, confining itself within the strict limits of legitimate taste, rather avoids than affects that mere costliness in which a *parvenu* rivalry may at any time be successfully attempted. The people *will* imitate the nobles, and the result is a thorough diffusion of the proper feeling. But in America the coins current being the sole arms of the aristocracy, their display may be said, in general, to be the sole means of the aristocratic distinction; and the populace, looking always upward for models, are insensibly led to confound the two entirely separate ideas of magnificence and beauty. In short, the cost of an article of furniture has at length come to be, with us, nearly the sole test of its merit in a decorative point of view—and this test, once established, has led the way to many analogous errors, readily traceable to the one primitive folly.

There could be nothing more directly offensive to the eyc of an artist than the interior of what is termed in the United States—that is to say in Appallachia—a well-furnished apartment. Its most usual defect is a want of keeping. We speak of the keeping of a room as we would of the keeping of a picture—for both the picture and the room are amenable to those undeviating principles which regulate all varieties of art; and very nearly the same laws by which we decide on the higher merits of a painting, suffice for decision on the adjustment of a chamber.

A want of keeping is observable sometimes in the character of the several pieces of furniture, but generally in their colours or modes of adaptation to use. *Very* often the eye is offended by their inartistical arrangement. Straight lines are too prevalent—too uninterruptedly continued—or clumsily interrupted at right angles. If curved lines occur, they are repeated into unpleasant uniformity. By undue precision the appearance of many a fine apartment is utterly spoiled.

Curtains are rarely well disposed, or well chosen, in respect to other decorations. With formal furniture curtains are out of place; and an extensive volume of drapery of any kind is, under any circumstances, irreconcilable with good taste: the proper quantum, as well as the proper adjustment, depending upon the character of the general effect.

Carpets are better understood of late than of ancient days, but we still very frequently err in their patterns and colours. The soul of the apartment is the carpet. From it are deduced not only the hues but the forms of all objects incumbent. A judge at common law may be an ordinary man; a good judge of a carpet *must be* a genius. Yet we have heard discoursing of carpets, with the air "*d'un mouton qui réve*," fellows who should not and who could not be entrusted with the management of their own *moustaches*. Every one knows that a large floor *may* have a covering of large figures, and that a small one *must* have a covering of small—yet this is not all the knowledge in the world. As regards texture the Saxony is alone admissible. Brussels is the preter-pluperfect tense of fashion, and Turkey is taste in its dying agonies. Touching pattern—a carpet should *not* be bedizzened out like a Riccaree Indian—all red chalk, yellow ochre, and cock's feathers. In brief—distinct grounds, and vivid circular or cycloid figures, *of no meaning*, are here Median laws. The abomination of flowers, or representations of well-known objects of any kind, should not be endured within the limits of Christendom. Indeed, whether on carpets, or curtains, or tapestry, or ottoman-coverings, all upholstery of this nature should be rigidly Arabesque. As for those antique floor-cloths still occasionally seen in the dwellings of the rabble—cloths of huge, sprawling, and radiating devices, stripe-interspersed, and glorious with all hues, among which no ground is intelligible—these are but the wicked invention of a race of time-servers and money-lovers—children of Baal and worshippers of Mammon—Benthams, who to spare thought and economize fancy, first cruelly invented the Kaleidoscope, and then established joint-stock companies to twirl it by steam.

Glare is a leading error in the philosophy of American household decoration—an error easily recognized as deduced from the perversion of taste just specified. We are violently enamoured of gas and of glass. The former is totally inadmissible within doors. Its harsh and unsteady light offends. No one having both brains and eyes will use it. A mild, or what artists term a cool light, with its consequent warm shadows, will do wonders for even an ill-furnished apartment. Never was a more lovely thought than that of the astral lamp. We mean, of course, the astral lamp proper—the lamp of Argand, with its original plain ground glass shade, and its tempered and uniform moonlight rays. The cut glass shade is a weak invention of the enemy. The eagerness with which we have adopted it, partly on account of its *flashiness*, but principally on account of its *greater cost*, is a good commentary on the proposition with which we began. It is not too much to say that the deliberate employer of a cut glass shade, is either radically deficient in taste, or blindly subservient to the caprices of fashion. The light proceeding from one of these gaudy abominations is unequal, broken, and painful. It alone is sufficient to mar a world of good effect in the furniture subjected to its influence. Female loveliness, in especial, is more than one half disenchanted beneath its evil eye.

In the matter of glass, generally, we proceed upon false principles. Its leading feature is *glitter*—and in that one word how much of all that is detestable do we express! Flickering, unquiet lights, are *sometimes* pleasing—to children and idiots always so—but in the embellishment of a room they should be scrupulously avoided. In truth, even strong *steady* lights are inadmissible. The huge and unmeaning glass chandeliers, prism-cut, gas-lighted, and without shade, which dangle in our most fashionable drawing rooms, may be cited as the quintessence of all that is false in taste or preposterous in folly.

The rage for *glitter*—because its idea has become, as we before observed, confounded with that of magnificence in the abstract—has led us, also, to the exaggerated employment of mirrors. We line our dwellings with great British plates, and then imagine we have done a fine thing. Now the slightest thought will be sufficient to convince any one who has an eye at all, of the ill effect of numerous looking-glasses, and especially of large ones. Regarded apart from its reflection, the mirror presents a continuous, flat, colourless, unrelieved surface—a thing always and obviously unpleasant. Considered as a reflector, it is potent in producing a monstrous and odious uniformity:—and the evil is here aggravated, not in merely direct proportion with the augmentation of its sources, but in a ratio constantly increasing. In fact, a room with four or five mirrors arranged at random, is, for all purposes of artistic show, a room of no shape at all. If we add to this evil, the attendant glitter upon glitter, we have a perfect farrago of discordant and displeasing effects. The veriest bumpkin, on entering an apartment so bedizzened, would be instantly aware of something wrong, although he might be altogether unable to assign a cause for his dissatisfaction. But let the same person be led into a room tastefully furnished, and he would be startled into an exclamation of pleasure and surprise.

It is an evil growing out of our republican institutions, that here a man of large purse has usually a very little soul which he keeps in it. The corruption of taste is a portion or a pendant of the dollar-manufacture. As we grow rich our ideas grow rusty. It is, therefore, not among *our* aristocracy that we must look (if at all, in Appallachia) for the spirituality of a British *boudoir.* But we have seen apartments in the tenure of Americans of modern means—which, in negative merit at least, might vie with any of the *or-molu'd* cabinets of our friends across the water. Even *now*, there is present to our mind's eye a small and not ostentatious chamber with whose decorations no fault can be found. The proprietor lies asleep on a sofa—the weather is cool—the time is near midnight—we will make a sketch of the room during his slumber.

It is oblong—some thirty feet in length and twenty-five in breadth—a shape affording the best (ordinary) opportunities for the adjustment of furniture. It has but one door—by no means a wide one—which is at one end of the parallelogram, and but two windows, which are at the other. These latter are large, reaching down to the floor—have deep recesses, and open on an Italian *veranda.* Their panes are of a crimson-tinted glass, set in rose-wood framings, more massive than usual. They are curtained within the recess, by a thick silver tissue adapted to the shape of the window, and hanging loosely in small volumes. Without the recess are curtains of an exceedingly rich crimson silk, fringed with a deep network of gold, and lined with the silver tissue, which is the material of the exterior blind. There are no cornices; but the folds of the whole fabric (which are sharp rather than massive, and have an airy appearance) issue from beneath a broad entablature of rich gilt work, which encircles the room at the junction of the ceiling and walls. The drapery is thrown open also, or closed, by means of a thick rope of gold loosely enveloping it, and resolving itself readily into a knot;—no pins or other such devices are apparent. The colours of the curtains and their fringe—the tints of crimson and gold—appear everywhere in profusion, and determine the *character* of the room. The carpet, of Saxony material, is quite half an inch thick, and is of the same crimson ground, relieved simply by the appearance of a gold cord (like that festooning the curtains) slightly relieved above the surface of the *ground*, and thrown upon it in such a manner as to form a succession of short irregular curves—one occasionally overlaying the other. The walls are papered with a glossy paper of a silver grey tint, spotted with small Arabesque devices of a fainter hue of the prevalent crimson. Many paintings relieve the expanse of the paper. These are chiefly landscapes of an imaginative cast—such as the fairy grottoes of Stanfield, or the lake of the Dismal Swamp, of Chapman. There are, nevertheless, three or four female heads, of an ethereal beauty—portraits in the manner of Sully. The tone of each picture is warm, but dark. There are no "brilliant effects." *Repose* speaks in all. Not one is of small size. Diminutive paintings give that *spotty* look to a room, which is the blemish of so many a fine work of Art overtouched. The frames are broad but not deep, and richly carved, without being *dulled* or filigreed. They have the whole lustre of burnished gold. They lie flat on the walls, and do not hang off with cords. The designs themselves are often seen to better advantage in this latter position, but the general appearance of the chamber is injured. But one mirror, and this not a very large one, is visible. In shape it is nearly circular—and it is hung so that a reflection of the person can be obtained from it in none of the ordinary sitting-places of the room. Two large low sofas of rose-wood and crimson silk, gold-flowered, form the only seats with the exception of two light conversation chairs, also of rose-wood. There is a piano-forte (rose-wood also), without cover, and thrown open. An octagonal table, formed altogether of the richest gold-threaded marble, is placed near one of the sofas. This is also without cover—the drapery of the curtains has been thought sufficient. Four large and gorgeous Sèvres vases, in which bloom a profusion of sweet and vivid flowers, occupy the slightly rounded angles of the room. A tall candelabrum, bearing a small antique lamp with highly perfumed oil, is standing near the head of my sleeping friend. Some light and graceful hanging shelves, with golden edges and crimson silk cords with gold tassels, sustain two or three hundred magnificently bound books. Beyond these things, there is no furniture, if we except an Argand lamp, with a plain crimson-tinted ground glass-shade, which depends from the lofty vaulted ceiling by a single slender gold chain, and throws a tranquil but magical radiance over all.

Review of Twice-Told Tales

[Published in *Graham's Magazine* in April and May 1842. Revised and printed as 'Tale-Writing — Nathaniel Hawthorne' in *Godey's Lady's Book* in November 1847.]

TALE-WRITING — NATHANIEL HAWTHORNE

TWICE-TOLD TALES. By Nathaniel Hawthorne. James Munroe & Co., Boston, 1842.

In the preface to my sketches of New York Literati, while speaking of the broad distinction between the seeming public and real private opinion respecting our authors, I thus alluded to Nathaniel Hawthorne:—

"For example, Mr. Hawthorne, the author of 'Twice-Told Tales,' is scarcely recognized by the press or by the public, and when noticed at all, is noticed merely to be damned by faint praise. Now, my own opinion of him is, that although his walk is limited and he is fairly to be charged with mannerism, treating all subjects in a similar tone of dreamy *innuendo*, yet in this walk he evinces extraordinary genius, having no rival either in America or elsewhere; and this opinion I have never heard gainsaid by any one literary person in the country. That this opinion, however, is a spoken and not a written one, is referable to the facts, first, that Mr. Hawthorne is a poor man, and, secondly, that he is *not* an ubiquitous quack."

The reputation of the author of "Twice-Told Tales" has been confined, indeed, until very lately, to literary society; and I have not been wrong, perhaps, in citing him as *the* example, *par excellence*, in this country, of the privately-admired and publicly-unappreciated man of genius. Within the last year or two, it is true, an occasional critic has been urged, by honest indignation, into very warm approval. Mr. Webber, for instance, (than whom no one has a keener relish for that kind of writing which Mr. Hawthorne has best illustrated,) gave us, in a late number of "The American Review," a cordial and certainly a full tribute to his talents; and since the issue of the "Mosses from an Old Manse," criticisms of similar tone have been by no means infrequent in our more authoritative journals. I can call to mind few reviews of Hawthorne published *before* the "Mosses." One I remember in "Arcturus" (edited by Matthews and Duyckinck) for May, 1841; another in the "American Monthly" (edited by Hoffman and Herbert) for March, 1838; a third in the ninety-sixth number of the "North American Review." These criticisms, however, seemed to have little effect on the popular taste—at least, if we are to form any idea of the popular taste by reference to its expression in the newspapers, or by the sale of the author's book. It was never the fashion (until lately) to speak of him in any summary of our best authors. The daily critics would say, on such occasions, "Is there not Irving and Cooper, and Bryant and Paulding, and—Smith?" or, "Have we not Halleck and Dana, and Longfellow and—Thompson?" or, "Can we not point triumphantly to our own Sprague, Willis, Channing, Bancroft, Prescott and—Jenkins?" but these unanswerable queries were never wound up by the name of Hawthorne.

Beyond doubt, this inappreciation of him on the part of the public arose chiefly from the two causes to which I have referred—from the facts that he is neither a man of wealth nor a quack;—but these are insufficient to account for the whole effect. No small portion of it is attributable to the very marked idiosyncrasy of Mr. Hawthorne himself. In one sense, and in great measure, to be peculiar is to be original, and than the true originality there is no higher literary virtue. This true or commendable originality, however, implies not the uniform, but the continuous peculiarity—a peculiarity springing from ever-active vigor of fancy—better still if from ever-present force of imagination, giving its own hue, its own character to everything it touches, and, especially, *self impelled to touch everything.*

It is often said, inconsiderately, that very original writers always fail in popularity—that such and such persons are too original to be comprehended by the mass. "Too peculiar," should be the phrase, "too idiosyncratic." It is, in fact, the excitable, undisciplined and child-like popular mind which most keenly feels the original. The criticism of the conservatives, of the hackneys, of the cultivated old clergymen of the "North American Review," is precisely the criticism which condemns and alone condemns it. "It becometh not a divine," saith Lord Coke, "to be of a fiery and salamandrine spirit." Their conscience allowing them to move nothing themselves, these dignitaries have a holy horror of being moved. "Give us *quietude*," they say. Opening their mouths with proper caution, they sigh forth the word "*Repose.*" And this is, indeed, the one thing they should be permitted to enjoy, if only upon the Christian principle of give and take.

The fact is, that if Mr. Hawthorne were really original, he could not fail of making himself felt by the public. But the fact is, he is *not* original in any sense. Those who speak of him as original, mean nothing more than that he differs in his manner or tone, and in his choice of subjects, from any author of their acquaintance—their acquaintance not extending to the German Tieck, whose manner, in *some* of his works, is absolutely identical with that *habitual* to Hawthorne. But it is clear that the element of the literary originality is novelty. The element of its appreciation by the reader is the reader's sense of the new. Whatever gives him a new and insomuch a pleasurable emotion, he considers original, and whoever frequently gives him such emotion, he considers an original writer. In a word, it is by the sum total of these emotions that he decides upon the writer's claim to originality. I may observe here, however, that there is clearly a point at which even novelty itself would cease to produce the legitimate originality, if we judge this originality, as we should, by the effect designed: this point is that at which *novelty becomes nothing novel*; and here the artist, *to preserve his originality*, will subside into the common-place. No one, I think, has noticed that, merely through inattention to this matter, Moore has comparatively failed in his "Lalla Rookh." Few readers, and indeed few critics, have commended this poem for originality—and, in fact, the effect, originality, is not produced by it—yet no work of equal size so abounds in the happiest originalities, individually considered. They are so excessive as, in the end, to deaden in the reader all capacity for their appreciation.

These points properly understood, it will be seen that the critic (unacquainted with Tieck) who reads a single tale or essay by Hawthorne, may be justified in thinking him original; but the tone, or manner, or choice of subject, which induces in this critic the sense of the new, will—if not in a second tale, at least in a third and all subsequent ones—not only fail of inducing it, but bring about an exactly antagonistic impression. In concluding a volume, and more especially in concluding all the volumes of the author, the critic will abandon his first design of calling him "original," and content himself with styling him "peculiar."

With the vague opinion that to be original is to be popular, I could, indeed, agree, were I to adopt an understanding of originality which, to my surprise, I have known adopted by many who have a right to be called critical. They have limited, in a love for mere words, the literary to the metaphysical originality. They regard as original in letters, only such combinations of thought, of incident, and so forth, as are, in fact, absolutely novel. It is clear, however, not only that it is the novelty of *effect* alone which is worth consideration, but that this effect is *best* wrought, for the end of all fictitious composition, pleasure, by shunning rather than by seeking the absolute novelty of combination. Originality, thus understood, tasks and startles the intellect, and so brings into undue action the faculties to which, in the lighter literature, we least appeal. And thus understood, it cannot fail to prove unpopular with the masses, who, seeking in this literature amusement, are positively offended by instruction. But the true originality—true in respect of its purposes—is that which, in bringing out the half-formed, the reluctant, or the unexpressed fancies of mankind, or in exciting the more delicate pulses of the heart's passion, or in giving birth to some universal sentiment or instinct in embryo, thus combines with the pleasurable effect of *apparent* novelty, a real egotistic delight. The reader, in the case first supposed, (that of the absolute novelty,) is excited, but embarrassed, disturbed, in some degree even pained at his own want of perception, at his own folly in not having himself hit upon the idea. In the second case, his pleasure is doubled. He is filled with an intrinsic and extrinsic delight. He feels and intensely enjoys the seeming novelty of the thought, enjoys it as really novel, as absolutely original with the writer—*and himself.* They two, he fancies, have, alone of all men, thought thus. They two have, together, created this thing. Henceforward there is a bond of sympathy between them, a sympathy which irradiates every subsequent page of the book.

There is a species of writing which, with some difficulty, may be admitted as a lower degree of what I have called the true original. In its perusal, we say to ourselves, not "how original this is!" nor "here is an idea which I and the author have alone entertained," but "here is a charmingly obvious fancy," or sometimes even, "here is a thought which I am not sure has ever occurred to myself, but which, of course, has occurred to all the rest of the world." This kind of composition (which still appertains to a high order) is usually designated as "the natural." It has little external resemblance, but strong internal affinity to the true original, if, indeed, as I have suggested, it is not of this latter an inferior degree. It is best exemplified, among English writers, in Addison, Irving and *Hawthorne*. The "ease" which is so often spoken of as its distinguishing feature, it has been the fashion to regard as ease in appearance alone, as a point of really difficult attainment. This idea, however, must be received with some reservation. The natural style is difficult only to those who should never intermeddle with it—to the unnatural. It is but the result of writing with the understanding, or with the instinct, that the *tone*, in composition, should be that which, at any given point or upon any given topic, would be the tone of the great mass of humanity. The author who, after the manner of the North Americans, is merely at *all* times *quiet*, is, of course, upon *most* occasions, merely silly or stupid, and has no more right to be thought "easy" or "natural" than has a cockney exquisite or the sleeping beauty in the wax-works.

The "peculiarity" or sameness, or monotone of Hawthorne, would, in its mere character of "peculiarity," and without reference to what *is* the peculiarity, suffice to deprive him of all chance of popular appreciation. But at his failure to be appreciated, we can, *of course*, no longer wonder, when we find him monotonous at decidedly the worst of all possible points—at that point which, having the least concern with Nature, is the farthest removed from the popular intellect, from the popular sentiment and from the popular taste. I allude to the strain of allegory which completely overwhelms the greater number of his subjects, and which in some measure interferes with the direct conduct of absolutely all.

In defence of allegory, (however, or for whatever object, employed,) there is scarcely one respectable word to be said. Its best appeals are made to the fancy—that is to say, to our sense of adaptation, not of matters proper, but of matters improper for the purpose, of the real with the unreal; having never more of intelligible connection than has something with nothing, never half so much of effective affinity as has the substance for the shadow. The deepest emotion aroused within us by the happiest allegory, *as* allegory, is a very, very imperfectly satisfied sense of the writer's ingenuity in overcoming a difficulty we should have preferred his not having attempted to overcome. The fallacy of the idea that allegory, in any of its moods, can be made to enforce a truth—that metaphor, for example, may illustrate as well as embellish an argument—could be promptly demonstrated: the converse of the supposed fact might be shown, indeed, with very little trouble—but these are topics foreign to my present purpose. One thing is clear, that if allegory ever establishes a fact, it is by dint of over-turning a fiction. Where the suggested meaning runs through the obvious one in a *very* profound undercurrent, so as never to interfere with the upper one without our own volition, so as never to show itself unless *called* to the surface, there only, for the proper uses of fictitious narrative, is it available at all. Under the best circumstances, it must always interfere with that unity of effect which, to the artist, is worth all the allegory in the world. Its vital injury, however, is rendered to the most vitally important point in fiction—that of earnestness or verisimilitude. That "The Pilgrim's Progress" is a ludicrously over-rated book, owing its seeming popularity to one or two of those accidents in critical literature which by the critical are sufficiently well understood, is a matter upon which no two thinking people disagree; but the pleasure derivable from it, in any sense, will be found in the direct ratio of the reader's capacity to smother its true purpose, in the direct ratio of his ability to keep the allegory out of sight, or of his *in*ability to comprehend it. Of allegory properly handled, judiciously subdued, seen only as a shadow or by suggestive glimpses, and making its nearest approach to truth in a not obtrusive and therefore not unpleasant *appositeness*, the "Undine" of De La Motte Fouqué is the best, and undoubtedly a very remarkable specimen.

The obvious causes, however, which have prevented Mr. Hawthorne's *popularity*, do not suffice to condemn him in the eyes of the few who belong properly to books, and to whom books, perhaps, do not quite so properly belong. These few estimate an author, not as do the public, altogether by what he does, but in great measure—indeed, even in the greatest measure—by what he evinces a capability of doing. In this view, Hawthorne stands among literary people in America much in the same light as did Coleridge in England. The few, also, through a certain warping of the taste, which long pondering upon books as books merely never fails to induce, are not in condition to view the errors of a scholar as errors altogether. At any time these gentlemen are prone to think the public not right rather than an educated author wrong. But the simple truth is, that the writer who aims at impressing the people, is *always* wrong when he fails in forcing that people to receive the impression. How far Mr. Hawthorne has addressed the people at all, is, of course, not a question for me to decide. His books afford strong internal evidence of having been written to himself and his particular friends alone.

There has long existed in literature a fatal and unfounded prejudice, which it will be the office of this age to overthrow—the idea that the mere bulk of a work must enter largely into our estimate of its merit. I do not suppose even the weakest of the Quarterly reviewers weak enough to maintain that in a book's size or mass, abstractly considered, there is anything which especially calls for our admiration. A mountain, simply through the sensation of physical magnitude which it conveys, does, indeed, affect us with a sense of the sublime, but we cannot admit any such influence in the contemplation even of "The Columbiad." The Quarterlies themselves will not admit it. And yet, what else are we to understand by their continual prating about "sustained effort?" Granted that this sustained effort has accomplished an epic—let us then admire the effort (if this be a thing admirable), but certainly not the epic on the effort's account. Common sense, in the time to come, may possibly insist upon measuring a work of art rather by the object it fulfills, by the impression it makes, than by the time it took to fulfil the object, or by the extent of "sustained effort" which became necessary to produce the impression. The fact is, that perseverance is one thing and genius quite another; nor can all the transcendentalists in Heathendom confound them.

Full of its bulky ideas, the last number of the "North American Review," in what it imagines a criticism on Simms, "honestly avows that it has little opinion of the mere tale;" and the honesty of the avowal is in no slight degree guaranteed by the fact that this Review has never yet been known to put forth an opinion which was *not* a very little one indeed.

The tale proper affords the fairest field which can be afforded by the wide domains of mere prose, for the exercise of the highest genius. Were I bidden to say how this genius could be most advantageously employed for the best display of its powers, I should answer, without hesitation, "in the composition of a rhymed poem not to exceed in length what might be perused in an hour." Within this limit alone can the noblest order of poetry exist. I have discussed this topic elsewhere, and need here repeat only that the phrase "a long poem" embodies a paradox. A poem must intensely excite Excitement is its province, its essentiality. Its value is in the ratio of its (elevating) excitement. But all excitement is, from a psychal necessity, transient. It cannot be sustained through a poem of great length. In the course of an hour's reading, at most, it flags, fails; and then the poem is, in effect, no longer such. Men admire, but are wearied with the "Paradise Lost;" for platitude follows platitude, *inevitably*, at regular interspaces (the depressions between the waves of excitement), until the poem (which, properly considered, is but a succession of brief poems), having been brought to an end, we discover that the sums of our pleasure and of displeasure have been very nearly equal. The absolute, ultimate or aggregate effect of any epic under the sun is, for these reasons, a nullity. "The Iliad," in its form of epic, has but an imaginary existence; granting it real, however, I can only say of it that it is based on a primitive sense of Art. Of the modern epic nothing can be so well said as that it is a blindfold imitation of a "come-by-chance." By and by these propositions will be understood as self-evident, and in the meantime will not be essentially damaged as truths by being generally condemned as falsities.

A poem *too* brief, on the other hand, may produce a sharp or vivid, but never a profound or enduring impression. Without a certain continuity, without a certain duration or repetition of the cause, the soul is seldom moved to the effect. There must be the dropping of the water on the rock. There must be the pressing steadily down of the stamp upon the wax. De Béranger has wrought brilliant things, pungent and spirit-stirring, but most of them are too immassive to have *momentum*, and, as so many feathers of fancy, have been blown aloft only to be whistled down the wind. Brevity, indeed, may degenerate into epigrammatism, but this danger does not prevent extreme length from being the one unpardonable sin.

Were I called upon, however, to designate that class of composition which, next to such a poem as I have suggested, should best fulfil the demands and serve the purposes of ambitious genius, should offer it the most advantageous field of exertion, and afford it the fairest opportunity of display, I should speak at once of the brief prose tale. History, philosophy, and other matters of that kind, we leave out of the question of course. *Of course*, I say, and in spite of the graybeards. These graver topics, to the end of time, will be best illustrated by what a discriminating world, turning up its nose at the drab pamphlets, has agreed to understand as *talent*. The ordinary novel is objectionable, from its length, for reasons analogous to those which render length objectionable in the poem. As the novel cannot be read at one sitting, it cannot avail itself of the immense benefit of *totality*. Worldly interests, intervening during the pauses of perusal, modify, counteract and annul the impressions intended. But simple cessation in reading would, of itself, be sufficient to destroy the true unity. In the brief tale, however, the author is enabled to carry out his full design without interruption. During the hour of perusal, the soul of the reader is at the writer's control.

A skilful artist has constructed a tale. He has not fashioned his thoughts to accommodate his incidents, but having deliberately conceived a certain *single effect* to be wrought, he then invents such incidents, he then combines such events, and discusses them in such tone as may best serve him in establishing this preconceived effect. If his very first sentence tend not to the outbringing of this effect, then in his very first step has he committed a blunder. In the whole composition there should be no word written of which the tendency, direct or indirect, is not to the one pre-established design. And by such means, with such care and skill, a picture is at length painted which leaves in the mind of him who contemplates it with a kindred art, a sense of the fullest satisfaction. The idea of the tale, its thesis, has been presented unblemished, because undisturbed—an end absolutely demanded, yet, in the novel altogether unattainable.

Of skillfully-constructed tales—I speak now without reference to other points, some of them more important than construction—there are very few American specimens. I am acquainted with no better one, upon the whole, than the "Murder Will Out" of Mr. Simms, and this has some glaring defects. The "Tales of a Traveler," by Irving, are graceful and impressive narratives—"The Young Italian" is especially good—but there is not one of the series which can be commended as a whole. In many of them the interest is subdivided and frittered away, and their conclusions are insufficiently *climatic*. In the higher requisites of composition, John Neal's magazine stories excel—I mean in vigor of thought, picturesque combination of incident, and so forth—but they ramble too much, and invariably break down just before coming to an end, as if the writer had received a sudden and irresistible summons to dinner, and thought it incumbent upon him to make a finish of his story before going. One of the happiest and best-sustained tales I have seen, is "Jack Long; or, The Shot in the Eye," by Charles W. Webber, the assistant editor of Mr. Colton's "American Review." But in general skill of construction, the tales of Willis, I think, surpass those of any American writer—with the exception of Mr. Hawthorne.

I must defer to the better opportunity of a volume now in hand, a full discussion of his individual pieces, and hasten to conclude this paper with a summary of his merits and demerits.

He is peculiar and not original—unless in those detailed fancies and detached thoughts which his want of general originality will deprive of the appreciation due to them, in preventing them forever reaching the *public eye*. He is infinitely too fond of allegory, and can never hope for popularity so long as he persists in it. This he will not do, for allegory is at war with the whole tone of his nature, which disports itself never so well as when escaping from the mysticism of his Goodman Browns and White Old Maids into the hearty, genial, but still Indian-summer sunshine of his Wakefields and Little Annie's Rambles. Indeed, *his* spirit of "metaphor runmad" is clearly imbibed from the phalanx and phalanstery atmosphere in which he has been so long struggling for breath. He has not half the material for the exclusiveness of authorship that he possesses for its universality. He has the purest style, the finest taste, the most available scholarship, the most delicate humor, the most touching pathos, the most radiant imagination, the most consummate ingenuity; and with these varied good qualities he has done *well* as a mystic. But is there any one of these qualities which should prevent his doing doubly as well in a career of honest, upright, sensible, prehensible and comprehensible things? Let him mend his pen, get a bottle of visible ink, come out from the Old Manse, cut Mr. Alcott, hang (if possible) the editor of "The Dial," and throw out of the window to the pigs all his odd numbers of "The North American Review."

Morning on the Wissahiccon

[First published in *The Opal: A Pure Gift for the Holy Days*, an annual gift book, in 1844.]

The natural scenery of America has often been contrasted, in its general features as well as in detail, with the landscape of the Old World—more especially of Europe—and not deeper has been the enthusiasm, than wide the dissension, of the supporters of each region. The discussion is one not likely to be soon closed, for, although much has been said on both sides, a word more yet remains to be said.

The most conspicuous of the British tourists who have attempted a comparison, seem to regard our northern and eastern seaboard, comparatively speaking, as all of America, at least, as all of the United States, worthy consideration. They say little, because they have seen less, of the gorgeous interior scenery of some of our western and southern districts—of the vast valley of Louisiana, for example—a realization of the wildest dreams of paradise. For the most part, these travelers content themselves with a hasty inspection of the natural *lions* of the land—the Hudson, Niagara, the Catskills, Harper's Ferry, the lakes of New York, the Ohio, the prairies, and the Mississippi. These, indeed, are objects well worthy the contemplation even of him who has just clambered by the castellated Rhine, or roamed

By the blue rushing of the arrowy Rhone;

but these are not *all* of which we can boast; and, indeed, I will be so hardy as to assert that there are innumerable quiet, obscure, and scarcely explored nooks, within the limits of the United States, that, by the true artist, or cultivated lover of the grand and beautiful amid the works of God, will be preferred to each and to all of the chronicled and better accredited scenes to which I have referred.

In fact, the real Edens of the land lie far away from the track of our own most deliberate tourists—how very far, then, beyond the reach of the foreigner, who, having made with his publisher at home arrangements for a certain amount of comment upon America, to be furnished in a stipulated period, can hope to fulfil his agreement in no other manner than by steaming it, memorandum-book in hand, through only the most beaten thoroughfares of the country!

I mentioned, just above, the valley of Louisiana. Of all extensive areas of natural loveliness, this is perhaps the most lovely. No fiction has approached it. The most gorgeous imagination might derive suggestions from its exuberant beauty. And *beauty* is, indeed, its sole character. It has little, or rather nothing, of the sublime. Gentle undulations of soil, interwreathed with fantastic crystallic streams, banked by flowery slopes, and backed by a forest vegetation, gigantic, glossy, multicoloured, sparkling with gay birds and burthened with perfume—these features make up, in the vale of Louisiana, the most voluptuous natural scenery upon earth.

But, even of this delicious region, the sweeter portions are reached only by the bypaths. Indeed, in America generally, the traveler who would behold the finest landscapes, must seek them not by the railroad, nor by the steamboat, not by the stage-coach, nor in his private carriage, not yet even on horseback—but on foot. He must walk, he must leap ravines, he must risk his neck among precipices, or he must leave unseen the truest, the richest, and most unspeakable glories of the land.

Now in the greater portion of Europe no such necessity exists. In England it exists not at all. The merest dandy of a tourist may there visit every nook worth visiting without detriment to his silk stockings; so thoroughly known are all points of interest, and so well-arranged are the means of attaining them. This consideration has never been allowed its due weight, in comparisons of the natural scenery of the Old and New Worlds. The entire loveliness of the former is collated with only the most noted, and with by no means the most eminent items in the general loveliness of the latter.

River scenery has, unquestionably, within itself, all the main elements of beauty, and, time out of mind, has been the favorite theme of the poet. But much of this fame is attributable to the predominance of travel in fluvial over that in mountainous districts. In the same way, large rivers, because usually highways, have, in all countries, absorbed an undue share of admiration. They are more observed, and, consequently, made more the subject of discourse, than less important, but often more interesting streams.

A singular exemplification of my remarks upon this head may be found in the Wissahiccon, a brook (for more it can scarcely be called), which empties itself into the Schuylkill, about six miles westward of Philadelphia. Now the Wissahiccon is of so remarkable a loveliness that, were it flowing in England, it would be the theme of every bard, and the common topic of every tongue, if, indeed, its banks were not parceled off in lots, at an exorbitant price, as building-sites for the villas of the opulent. Yet it is only within a very few years that any one has more than heard of the Wissahiccon, while the broader and more navigable water into which it flows, has been long celebrated as one of the finest specimens of American river scenery. The Schuylkill, whose beauties have been much exaggerated, and whose banks, at least in the neighborhood of Philadelphia, are marshy like those of the Delaware, is not at all comparable, as an object of picturesque interest, with the more humble and less notorious rivulet of which we speak.

It was not until Fanny Kemble, in her droll book about the United States, pointed out to the Philadelphians the rare loveliness of a stream which lay at their own doors, that this loveliness was more than suspected by a few adventurous pedestrians of the vicinity. But, the "Journal" having opened all eyes, the Wissahiccon, to a certain extent, rolled at once into notoriety. I say "to a certain extent," for, in fact, the true beauty of the stream lies far above the *route* of the Philadelphian picturesque-hunters, who rarely proceed farther than a mile or two above the mouth of the rivulet—for the very excellent reason that here the carriage-road stops. I would advise the adventurer who would behold its finest points to take the Ridge Road, running westwardly from the city, and, having reached the second lane beyond the sixth mile-stone, to follow this lane to its termination. He will thus strike the Wissahiccon, at one of its best reaches, and, in a skiff, or by clambering along its banks, he can go up or down the stream, as best suits his fancy, and in either direction will meet his reward.

I have already said, or should have said, that the brook is narrow. Its banks are generally, indeed almost universally, precipitous, and consist of high hills, clothed with noble shrubbery near the water, and crowned at a greater elevation, with some of the most magnificent forest trees of America, among which stands conspicuous the *liriodendron tulipiferum*. The immediate shores, however, are of granite, sharply defined or moss-covered, against which the pellucid water lolls in its gentle flow, as the blue waves of the Mediterranean upon the steps of her palaces of marble. Occasionally in front of the cliffs, extends a small definite *plateau* of richly herbaged land, affording the most picturesque position for a cottage and garden which the richest imagination could conceive. The windings of the stream are many and abrupt, as is usually the case where banks are precipitous, and thus the impression conveyed to the voyager's eye, as he proceeds, is that of an endless succession of infinitely varied small lakes, or, more properly speaking, tarns. The Wissahiccon, however, should be visited, not like "fair Melrose," by moonlight, or even in cloudy weather, but amid the brightest glare of a noonday sun; for the narrowness of the gorge through which it flows, the height of the hills on either hand, and the density of the foliage, conspire to produce a gloominess, if not an absolute dreariness of effect, which, unless relieved by a bright general light, detracts from the mere beauty of the scene.

Not long ago I visited the stream by the route described, and spent the better part of a sultry day in floating in a skiff upon its bosom. The heat gradually overcame me, and, resigning myself to the influence of the scenes and of the weather, and of the gentle moving current, I sank into a half slumber, during which my imagination reveled in visions of the Wissahiccon of ancient days—of the "good old days" when the Demon of the Engine was not, when picnics were undreamed of, when "water privileges" were neither bought nor sold, and when the red man trod alone, with the elk, upon the ridges that now towered above. And, while gradually these conceits took possession of my mind, the lazy brook had borne me, inch by inch, around one promontory and within full view of another that bounded the prospect at the distance of forty or fifty yards. It was a steep rocky cliff, abutting far into the stream, and presenting much more of the Salvator character than any portion of the shore hitherto passed. What I saw upon this cliff, although surely an object of very extraordinary nature, the place and season considered, at first neither startled nor amazed me—so thoroughly and appropriately did it chime in with the half-slumberous fancies that enwrapped me. I saw, or dreamed that I saw, standing upon the extreme verge of the precipice, with neck outstretched, with ears erect, and the whole attitude indicative of profound and melancholy inquisitiveness, one of the oldest and boldest of those identical elks which had been coupled with the red men of my vision.

I say that, for a few moments, this apparition neither startled nor amazed me. During this interval my whole soul was bound up in intense sympathy alone. I fancied the elk repining, not less than wondering, at the manifest alterations for the worse, wrought upon the brook and its vicinage, even within the last few years, by the stern hand of the utilitarian. But a slight movement of the animal's head at once dispelled the dreaminess which invested me, and aroused me to a full sense of novelty of the adventure. I arose upon one knee within the skiff, and, while I hesitated whether to stop my career, or let myself float nearer to the object of my wonder, I heard the words "hist! hist!" ejaculated quickly but cautiously, from the shrubbery overhead. In an instant afterwards, a negro emerged from the thicket, putting aside the bushes with care, and treading stealthily. He bore in one hand a quantity of salt, and, holding it towards the elk, gently yet steadily approached. The noble animal, although a little fluttered, made no attempt at escape. The negro advanced; offered the salt; and spoke a few words of encouragement or conciliation. Presently, the elk bowed and stamped, and then lay quietly down and was secured with a halter.

Thus ended my romance of the elk. It was a *pet* of great age and very domestic habits, and belonged to an English family occupying a villa in the vicinity.

Some Secrets of the Magazine Prison-House

[Published in the February 15, 1845, issue of the *Broadway Journal.*]

The want of an International Copy-Right Law, by rendering it nearly impossible to obtain anything from the booksellers in the way of remuneration for literary labor, has had the effect of forcing many of our very best writers into the service of the Magazines and Reviews, which with a pertinacity that does them credit, keep up in a certain or uncertain degree the good old saying, that even in the thankless field of Letters the laborer is worthy of his hire. How—by dint of what dogged instinct of the honest and proper, these journals have contrived to persist in their paying practices, in the very teeth of the opposition got up by the Fosters and Leonard Scotts, who furnish for eight dollars any four of the British periodicals for a year, is a point we have had much difficulty in settling to our satisfaction, and we have been forced to settle it, at last, upon no more reasonable ground than that of a still lingering *esprit de patrie.* That Magazines can live, and not only live but thrive, and not only thrive but afford to disburse money for original contributions, are facts which can only be solved, under the circumstances, by the really fanciful but still agreeable supposition, that there is somewhere still existing an ember not altogether quenched among the fires of good feeling for letters and literary men, that once animated the American bosom.

It would *not do* (perhaps this is the idea) to let our poor devil authors absolutely starve, while we grow fat, in a literary sense, on the good things of which we unblushingly pick the pocket of all Europe: it would not be exactly the thing *comme il faut*, to permit a positive atrocity of this kind and hence we have Magazines, and hence we have a portion of the public who subscribe to these Magazines (through sheer pity), and hence we have Magazine publishers (who sometimes take upon themselves the duplicate title of "editor *and* proprietor")—publishers, we say, who, under certain conditions of good conduct, occasional puffs, and decent subserviency at all times, make it a point of conscience to encourage the poor devil author with a dollar or two, more or less as he behaves himself properly and abstains from the indecent habit of turning up his nose.

We hope, however, that we are not so prejudiced or so vindictive as to insinuate that what certainly does look like illiberality on the part of them (the Magazine publishers) is really an illiberality chargeable to *them*. In fact, it will be seen at once, that what we have said has a tendency directly the reverse of any such accusation. These publishers pay *something*—other publishers nothing at all. Here certainly is a difference—although a mathematician might contend that the difference might be infinitesimally small. Still, these Magazine editors and proprietors *pay* (that is the word), and with your true poor-devil author the smallest favors are sure to be thankfully received. No: the illiberality lies at the door of the demagogue-ridden public, who suffer their anointed delegates (or perhaps arointed—which is it?) to insult the common sense of them (the public) by making orations in our national halls on the beauty and conveniency of robbing the Literary Europe on the highway, and on the gross absurdity in especial of admitting so unprincipled a principle, that a man has any right and title either to his own brains or to the flimsy material that he chooses to spin out of them, like a confounded caterpillar as he is. If anything of this gossamer character stands in need of protection, why we have our hands full at once with the silk-worms and the *morus multicaulis*.

But if we cannot, under the circumstances, complain of the absolute illiberality of the Magazine publishers (since pay they do), there is at least one particular in which we have against them good grounds of accusation. Why (since pay they must) do they not pay with a good grace, and *promptly*. Were we in an ill humor at this moment, we could a tale unfold which would erect the hair on the head of Shylock. A young author, struggling with Despair itself in the shape of a ghastly poverty, which has no alleviation—no sympathy from an every-day world, that cannot understand his necessities, and that would pretend not to understand them if it comprehended them ever so well—this young author is politely requested to compose an article, for which he will "be handsomely paid." Enraptured, he neglects perhaps for a month the sole employment which affords him the chance of a livelihood, and having starved through the month (he and his family) completes at length the month of starvation and the article, and despatches the latter (with a broad hint about the former) to the pursy "editor" and bottle-nosed "proprietor" who has condescended to honor him (the poor devil) with his patronage. A month (starving still), and no reply. Another month—still none. Two months more—still none. A second letter, modestly hinting that the article may not have reached its destination—still no reply. At the expiration of six additional months, personal application is made at the "editor and proprietor's" office. Call again. The poor devil goes out, and does not fail to call again. Still call again;—and call again is the word for three or four months more. His patience exhausted, the article is demanded. No—he can't have it (the truth is, it was too good to be given up so easily) "it is in print," and "contributions of this character are never paid for (it is a *rule* we have) under six months after publication. Call in six months after the issue of your affair, and your money is ready for you—for we are business men, ourselves—prompt." With this the poor devil is satisfied, and makes up his mind that the "editor and proprietor" is a gentleman, and that of course he (the poor devil) will wait as requested. And it is supposable that he would have waited if he could—but Death in the meantime would not. He dies, and by the good luck of his decease (which came by starvation) the fat "editor and proprietor" is fat henceforward and for ever to the amount of five and twenty dollars, very cleverly saved, to be spent generously in canvas-backs and champagne.

There are two things which we hope the reader will not do, as he runs over this article: first, we hope that he will not believe that we write from any personal experience of our own, for we have only the reports of actual sufferers to depend upon, and second, that he will not make any personal application of our remarks to any Magazine publisher now living, it being well known that they are all as remarkable for their generosity and urbanity, as for their intelligence, and appreciation of Genius.

The Philosophy of Composition

[First published in the *Graham's Magazine* in April 1846.]

Charles Dickens, in a note now lying before me, alluding to an examination I once made of the mechanism of "Barnaby Rudge," says—"By the way, are you aware that Godwin wrote his 'Caleb Williams' backwards? He first involved his hero in a web of difficulties, forming the second volume, and then, for the first, cast about him for some mode of accounting for what had been done."

I cannot think this the *precise* mode of procedure on the part of Godwin—and indeed what he himself acknowledges, is not altogether in accordance with Mr. Dickens' idea—but the author of "Caleb Williams" was too good an artist not to perceive the advantage derivable from at least a somewhat similar process. Nothing is more clear than that every plot, worth the name, must be elaborated to its *dénouement* before any thing be attempted with the pen. It is only with the *dénouement* constantly in view that we can give a plot its indispensable air of consequence, or causation, by making the incidents, and especially the tone at all points, tend to the development of the intention.

There is a radical error, I think, in the usual mode of constructing a story. Either history affords a thesis—or one is suggested by an incident of the day—or, at best, the author sets himself to work in the combination of striking events to form merely the basis of his narrative—designing, generally, to fill in with description, dialogue, or autorial comment, whatever crevices of fact, or action, may, from page to page, render themselves apparent.

I prefer commencing with the consideration of an *effect*. Keeping originality *always* in view—for he is false to himself who ventures to dispense with so obvious and so easily attainable a source of interest—I say to myself, in the first place, "Of the innumerable effects, or impressions, of which the heart, the intellect, or (more generally) the soul is susceptible, what one shall I, on the present occasion, select?" Having chosen a novel, first, and secondly a vivid effect, I consider whether it can best be wrought by incident or tone—whether by ordinary incidents and peculiar tone, or the converse, or by peculiarity both of incident and tone—afterward looking about me (or rather within) for such combinations of event, or tone, as shall best aid me in the construction of the effect.

I have often thought how interesting a magazine paper might be written by any author who would—that is to say, who could—detail, step by step, the processes by which any one of his compositions attained its ultimate point of completion. Why such a paper has never been given to the world, I am much at a loss to say—but, perhaps, the autorial vanity has had more to do with the omission than any one other cause. Most writers—poets in especial—prefer having it understood that they compose by a species of fine frenzy—an ecstatic intuition—and would positively shudder at letting the public take a peep behind the scenes, at the elaborate and vacillating crudities of thought—at the true purposes seized only at the last moment—at the innumerable glimpses of idea that arrived not at the maturity of full view—at the fully matured fancies discarded in despair as unmanageable—at the cautious selections and rejections—at the painful erasures and interpolations—in a word, at the wheels and pinions—the tackle for scene-shifting—the step-ladders and demon-traps—the cock's feathers, the red paint and the black patches, which, in ninety-nine cases out of the hundred, constitute the properties of the literary *histrio*.

I am aware, on the other hand, that the case is by no means common, in which an author is at all in condition to retrace the steps by which his conclusions have been attained. In general, suggestions, having arisen pell-mell, are pursued and forgotten in a similar manner.

For my own part, I have neither sympathy with the repugnance alluded to, nor, at any time, the least difficulty in recalling to mind the progressive steps of any of my compositions; and, since the interest of an analysis, or reconstruction, such as I have considered a *desideratum*, is quite independent of any real or fancied interest in the thing analyzed, it will not be regarded as a breach of decorum on my part to show the *modus operandi* by which some one of my own works was put together. I select "The Raven," as most generally known. It is my design to render it manifest that no one point in its composition is referrible either to accident or intuition—that the work proceeded, step by step, to its completion with the precision and rigid consequence of a mathematical problem.

Let us dismiss, as irrelevant to the poem, *per se,* the circumstance—or say the necessity—which, in the first place, gave rise to the intention of composing *a* poem that should suit at once the popular and the critical taste.

We commence, then, with this intention.

The initial consideration was that of extent. If any literary work is too long to be read at one sitting, we must be content to dispense with the immensely important effect derivable from unity of impression—for, if two sittings be required, the affairs of the world interfere, and every thing like totality is at once destroyed. But since, *ceteris paribus*, no poet can afford to dispense with *any thing* that may advance his design, it but remains to be seen whether there is, in extent, any advantage to counterbalance the loss of unity which attends it. Here I say no, at once. What we term a long poem is, in fact, merely a succession of brief ones—that is to say, of brief poetical effects. It is needless to demonstrate that a poem is such, only inasmuch as it intensely excites, by elevating, the soul; and all intense excitements are, through a psychal necessity, brief. For this reason, at least one half of the "Paradise Lost" is essentially prose—a succession of poetical excitements interspersed, *inevitably*, with corresponding depressions—the whole being deprived, through the extremeness of its length, of the vastly important artistic element, totality, or unity, of effect.

It appears evident, then, that there is a distinct limit, as regards length, to all works of literary art—the limit of a single sitting—and that, although in certain classes of prose composition, such as "Robinson Crusoe" (demanding no unity), this limit may be advantageously overpassed, it can never properly be overpassed in a poem. Within this limit, the extent of a poem may be made to bear mathematical relation to its merit—in other words, to the excitement or elevation—again in other words, to the degree of the true poetical effect which it is capable of inducing; for it is clear that the brevity must be in direct ratio of the intensity of the intended effect:—

this, with one proviso—that a certain degree of duration is absolutely requisite for the production of any effect at all.

Holding in view these considerations, as well as that degree of excitement which I deemed not above the popular, while not below the critical, taste, I reached at once what I conceived the proper *length* for my intended poem—a length of about one hundred lines. It is, in fact, a hundred and eight.

My next thought concerned the choice of an impression, or effect, to be conveyed: and here I may as well observe that, throughout the construction, I kept steadily in view the design of rendering the work *universally* appreciable. I should be carried too far out of my immediate topic were I to demonstrate a point upon which I have repeatedly insisted, and which, with the poetical, stands not in the slightest need of demonstration—the point, I mean, that Beauty is the sole legitimate province of the poem. A few words, however, in elucidation of my real meaning, which some of my friends have evinced a disposition to misrepresent. That pleasure which is at once the most intense, the most elevating, and the most pure, is, I believe, found in the contemplation of the beautiful. When, indeed, men speak of Beauty, they mean, precisely, not a quality, as is supposed, but an effect—they refer, in short, just to that intense and pure elevation of *soul—not* of intellect, or of heart—upon which I have commented, and which is experienced in consequence of contemplating "the beautiful." Now I designate Beauty as the province of the poem, merely because it is an obvious rule of Art that effects should be made to spring from direct causes—that objects should be attained through means best adapted for their attainment—no one as yet having been weak enough to deny that the peculiar elevation alluded to, is *most readily* attained in the poem. Now the object, Truth, or the satisfaction of the intellect, and the object Passion, or the excitement of the heart, are, although attainable, to a certain extent, in poetry, far more readily attainable in prose. Truth, in fact, demands a precision, and Passion, a *homeliness* (the truly passionate will comprehend me) which are absolutely antagonistic to that Beauty which, I maintain, is the excitement, or pleasurable elevation, of the soul. It by no means follows from any thing here said, that passion, or even truth, may not be introduced, and even profitably introduced, into a poem—for they may serve in elucidation, or aid the general effect, as do discords in music, by contrast—but the true artist will always contrive, first, to tone them into proper subservience to the predominant aim, and, secondly, to enveil them, as far as possible, in that Beauty which is the atmosphere and the essence of the poem.

Regarding, then, Beauty as my province, my next question referred to the *tone* of its highest manifestation—and all experience has shown that this tone is one of *sadness*. Beauty of whatever kind, in its supreme development, invariably excites the sensitive soul to tears. Melancholy is thus the most legitimate of all the poetical tones.

The length, the province, and the tone, being thus determined, I betook myself to ordinary induction, with the view of obtaining some artistic piquancy which might serve me as a key-note in the construction of the poem—some pivot upon which the whole structure might turn. In carefully thinking over all the usual artistic effects—or more properly *points*, in the theatrical sense—I did not fail to perceive immediately that no one had been so universally employed as that of the *refrain*. The universality of its employment sufficed to assure me of its intrinsic value, and spared me the necessity of submitting it to analysis. I considered it, however, with regard to its susceptibility of improvement, and soon saw it to be in a primitive condition. As commonly used, the *refrain,* or burden, not only is limited to lyric verse, but depends for its impression upon the force of monotone—both in sound and thought. The pleasure is deduced solely from the sense of identity—of repetition. I resolved to diversify, and so vastly heighten, the effect, by adhering, in general, to the monotone of sound, while I continually varied that of thought: that is to say, I determined to produce continuously novel effects, by the variation *of the application* of the *refrain*—the *refrain* itself remaining, for the most part, unvaried.

These points being settled, I next bethought me of the *nature* of my *refrain*. Since its application was to be repeatedly varied, it was clear that the *refrain* itself must be brief, for there would have been an insurmountable difficulty in frequent variations of application in any sentence of length. In proportion to the brevity of the sentence, would, of course, be the facility of the variation. This led me at once to a single word as the best *refrain*.

The question now arose as to the *character* of the word. Having made up my mind to a *refrain,* the division of the poem into stanzas was, of course, a corollary: the *refrain* forming the close to each stanza. That such a close, to have force, must be sonorous and susceptible of protracted emphasis, admitted no doubt: and these considerations inevitably led me to the long *o* as the most sonorous vowel, in connection with *r* as the most producible consonant.

The sound of the *refrain* being thus determined, it became necessary to select a word embodying this sound, and at the same time in the fullest possible keeping with that melancholy which I had predetermined as the tone of the poem. In such a search it would have been absolutely impossible to overlook the word "Nevermore." In fact, it was the very first which presented itself.

The next *desideratum* was a pretext for the continuous use of the one word "nevermore." In observing the difficulty which I at once found in inventing a sufficiently plausible reason for its continuous repetition, I did not fail to perceive that this difficulty arose solely from the pre-assumption that the word was to be so continuously or monotonously spoken by *a human* being—I did not fail to perceive, in short, that the difficulty lay in the reconciliation of this monotony with the exercise of reason on the part of the creature repeating the word. Here, then, immediately arose the idea of a *non*-reasoning creature capable of speech; and, very naturally, a parrot, in the first instance, suggested itself, but was superseded forthwith by a Raven, as equally capable of speech, and infinitely more in keeping with the intended *tone.*

I had now gone so far as the conception of a Raven—the bird of ill omen—monotonously repeating the one word, "Nevermore," at the conclusion of each stanza, in a poem of melancholy tone, and in length about one hundred lines. Now, never losing sight of the object *supremeness,* or perfection, at all points, I asked myself—"Of all melancholy topics, what, according to the *universal* understanding of mankind, is the *most* melancholy?" Death—was the obvious reply. "And when," I said, "is this most melancholy of topics most poetical?" From what I have already explained at some length, the answer, here also, is obvious—"When it most closely allies itself to *Beauty*: the death, then, of a beautiful woman is, unquestionably, the most poetical topic in the world—and equally is it beyond doubt that the lips best suited for such topic are those of a bereaved lover."

I had now to combine the two ideas, of a lover lamenting his deceased mistress and a Raven continuously repeating the word "Nevermore"—I had to combine these, bearing in mind my design of varying, at every turn, the *application* of the word repeated; but the only intelligible mode of such combination is that of imagining the Raven employing the word in answer to the queries of the lover. And here it was that I saw at once the opportunity afforded for the effect on which I had been depending—that is to say, the effect of the *variation of application.* I saw that I could make the first query propounded by the lover—the first query to which the Raven should reply "Nevermore"—that I could make this first query a commonplace one—the second less so—the third still less, and so on—until at length the lover, startled from his original *nonchalance* by the melancholy character of the word itself—by its frequent repetition—and by a consideration of the ominous reputation of the fowl that uttered it—is at length excited to superstition, and wildly propounds queries of a far different character—queries whose solution he has passionately at heart—propounds them half in superstition and half in that species of despair which delights in self-torture—propounds them not altogether because he believes in the prophetic or demoniac character of the bird (which, reason assures him, is merely repeating a lesson learned by rote) but because he experiences a phrenzied pleasure in so modeling his questions as to receive from the *expected* "Nevermore" the most delicious because the most intolerable of sorrow. Perceiving the opportunity thus afforded me—or, more strictly, thus forced upon me in the progress of the construction—I first established in mind the climax, or concluding query—that to which "Nevermore" should be in the last place an answer—that in reply to which this word "Nevermore" should involve the utmost conceivable amount of sorrow and despair.

Here then the poem may be said to have its beginning—at the end, where all works of art should begin—for it was here, at this point of my preconsiderations, that I first put pen to paper in the composition of the stanza:

"Prophet," said I, "thing of evil! prophet still if bird
    or devil!
By that heaven that bends above us—by that God
    we both adore,
Tell this soul with sorrow laden, if within the
    distant Aidenn,

It shall clasp a sainted maiden whom the angels
    name Lenore—
Clasp a rare and radiant maiden whom the angels
    name Lenore."
                Quoth the Raven "Nevermore."

I composed this stanza, at this point, first that, by establishing the climax, I might the better vary and graduate, as regards seriousness and importance, the preceding queries of the lover—and, secondly, that I might definitely settle the rhythm, the metre, and the length and general arrangement of the stanza—as well as graduate the stanzas which were to precede, so that none of them might surpass this in rhythmical effect. Had I been able, in the subsequent composition, to construct more vigorous stanzas, I should, without scruple, have purposely enfeebled them, so as not to interfere with the climacteric effect.

And here I may as well say a few words of the versification. My first object (as usual) was originality. The extent to which this has been neglected, in versification, is one of the most unaccountable things in the world. Admitting that there is little possibility of variety in mere *rhythm*, it is still clear that the possible varieties of metre and stanza are absolutely infinite—and yet, *for centuries, no man, in verse, has ever done, or ever seemed to think of doing, an original thing.* The fact is, originality (unless in minds of very unusual force) is by no means a matter, as some suppose, of impulse or intuition. In general, to be found, it must be elaborately sought, and although a positive merit of the highest class, demands in its attainment less of invention than negation.

Of course, I pretend to no originality in either the rhythm or metre of the "Raven." The former is trochaic—the latter is octametre acatalectic, alternating with heptameter catalectic repeated in the *refrain* of the fifth verse, and terminating with tetrameter catalectic. Less pedantically—the feet employed throughout (trochees) consist of a long syllable followed by a short: the first line of the stanza consists of eight of these feet—the second of seven and a half (in effect two-thirds)—the third of eight—the fourth of seven and a half—the fifth the same—the sixth three and a half. Now, each of these lines, taken individually, has been employed before, and what originality the "Raven" has, is in their *combination into stanza;* nothing even remotely approaching this combination has ever been attempted. The effect of this originality of combination is aided by other unusual, and some altogether novel effects, arising from an extension of the application of the principles of rhyme and alliteration.

The next point to be considered was the mode of bringing together the lover and the Raven—and the first branch of this consideration was the *locale*. For this the most natural suggestion might seem to be a forest, or the fields—but it has always appeared to me that a close *circumscription of space* is absolutely necessary to the effect of insulated incident:—it has the force of a frame to a picture. It has an indisputable moral power in keeping concentrated the attention, and, of course, must not be confounded with mere unity of place.

I determined, then, to place the lover in his chamber—in a chamber rendered sacred to him by memories of her who had frequented it. The room is represented as richly furnished—this in mere pursuance of the ideas I have already explained on the subject of Beauty, as the sole true poetical thesis.

The *locale* being thus determined, I had now to introduce the bird—and the thought of introducing him through the window, was inevitable. The idea of making the lover suppose, in the first instance, that the flapping of the wings of the bird against the shutter, is a "tapping" at the door, originated in a wish to increase, by prolonging, the reader's curiosity, and in a desire to admit the incidental effect arising from the lover's throwing open the door, finding all dark, and thence adopting the half-fancy that it was the spirit of his mistress that knocked.

I made the night tempestuous, first, to account for the Raven's seeking admission, and secondly, for the effect of contrast with the (physical) serenity within the chamber.

I made the bird alight on the bust of Pallas, also for the effect of contrast between the marble and the plumage—it being understood that the bust was absolutely *suggested* by the bird—the bust of *Pallas* being chosen, first, as most in keeping with the scholarship of the lover, and, secondly, for the sonorousness of the word, Pallas, itself.

About the middle of the poem, also, I have availed myself of the force of contrast, with a view of deepening the ultimate impression. For example, an air of the fantastic—approaching as nearly to the ludicrous as was admissible—is given to the Raven's entrance. He comes in "with many a flirt and flutter."

Not the *least obeisance made he*—not a moment
stopped or stayed he,
But with mien of lord or lady, perched above my
chamber door.

In the two stanzas which follow, the design is more obviously carried out:—

Then this ebony bird beguiling my sad fancy into
smiling
By the *grave and stern decorum of the countenance it
wore,*
"Though thy *crest be shorn and shaven* thou," I said,
"art sure no craven,
Ghastly grim and ancient Raven wandering from
the nightly shore—
Tell me what thy lordly name is on the Night's
Plutonian shore!"
Quoth the Raven "Nevermore."

Much I marvelled *this ungainly fowl* to hear discourse
so plainly,
Though its answer little meaning—little relevancy
bore;
For we cannot help agreeing that no living human
being
*Ever yet was blessed with seeing bird above his chamber
door—*
*Bird or beast upon the sculptured bust above his chamber
door,*
With such name as "Nevermore."

The effect of the *dénouement* being thus provided for, I immediately drop the fantastic for a tone of the most profound seriousness:—this tone commencing in the stanza directly following the one last quoted, with the line,

But the Raven, sitting lonely on that placid bust,
spoke only, etc.

From this epoch the lover no longer jests—no longer sees any thing even of the fantastic in the Raven's demeanor. He speaks of him as a "grim, ungainly, ghastly, gaunt, and ominous bird of yore," and feels the "fiery eyes" burning into his "bosom's core." This revolution of thought, or fancy, on the lover's part, is intended to induce a similar one on the part of the reader—to bring the mind into a proper frame for the *dénouement*—which is now brought about as rapidly and as *directly* as possible.

With the *dénouement* proper—with the Raven's reply, "Nevermore," to the lover's final demand if he shall meet his mistress in another world—the poem, in its obvious phase, that of a simple narrative, may be said to have its completion. So far, every thing is within the limits of the accountable—of the real. A raven, having learned by rote the single word "Nevermore," and having escaped from the custody of its owner, is driven, at midnight, through the violence of a storm, to seek admission at a window from which a light still gleams—the chamber-window of a student, occupied half in poring over a volume, half in dreaming of a beloved mistress deceased. The casement being thrown open at the fluttering of the bird's wings, the bird itself perches on the most convenient seat out of the immediate reach of the student, who, amused by the incident and the oddity of the visiter's demeanor, demands of it, in jest and without looking for a reply, its name. The raven addressed, answers with its customary word, "Nevermore"—a word which finds immediate echo in the melancholy heart of the student, who, giving utterance aloud to certain thoughts suggested by the occasion, is again startled by the fowl's repetition of "Nevermore." The student now guesses the state of the case, but is impelled, as I have before explained, by the human thirst for self-torture, and in part by superstition, to propound such queries to the bird as will bring him, the lover, the most of the luxury of sorrow, through the anticipated answer "Nevermore." With the indulgence, to the utmost extreme, of this self-torture, the narration, in what I have termed its first or obvious phase, has a natural termination, and so far there has been no overstepping of the limits of the real.

But in subjects so handled, however skilfully, or with however vivid an array of incident, there is always a certain hardness or nakedness, which repels the artistical eye. Two things are invariably required—first, some amount of complexity, or more properly, adaptation; and, secondly, some amount of suggestiveness—some under-current, however indefinite, of meaning. It is this latter, in especial, which imparts to a work of art so much of that *richness* (to borrow from colloquy a forcible term) which we are too fond of confounding with *the ideal.* It is the *excess* of the suggested meaning—it is the rendering this the upper instead of the under-current of the theme—which turns into prose (and that of the very flattest kind) the so called poetry of the so called transcendentalists.

Holding these opinions, I added the two concluding stanzas of the poem—their suggestiveness being thus made to pervade all the narrative which has preceded them. The under-current of meaning is rendered first apparent in the lines—

"Take thy beak from out *my heart*, and take thy form
from off my door!"
Quoth the Raven "Nevermore!"

It will be observed that the words, "from out my heart," involve the first metaphorical expression in the poem. They, with the answer, "Nevermore," dispose the mind to seek a moral in all that has been previously narrated. The reader begins now to regard the Raven as emblematical—but it is not until the very last line of the very last stanza, that the intention of making him emblematical of *Mournful and Never-ending Remembrance* is permitted distinctly to be seen:

And the Raven, never flitting, still is sitting, still is
sitting,
On the pallid bust of Pallas just above my chamber
door;
And his eyes have all the seeming of a demon's that
is dreaming,
And the lamplight o'er him streaming throws his
shadow on the floor;
And my soul *from out that shadow* that lies floating
on the floor
Shall be lifted—nevermore.

The Poetic Principle

[First appeared posthumously in the August 31, 1850, issue of the *Home Journal.* This is the version published in the Griswold edition of *The Works of Late Edgar Allan Poe* (1850).]

In speaking of the Poetic Principle, I have no design to be either thorough or profound. While discussing, very much at random, the essentiality of what we call Poetry, my principal purpose will be to cite for consideration, some few of those minor English or American poems which best suit my own taste, or which, upon my own fancy, have left the most definite impression. By "minor poems" I mean, of course, poems of little length. And here, in the beginning, permit me to say a few words in regard to a somewhat peculiar principle, which, whether rightfully or wrongfully, has always had its influence in my own critical estimate of the poem. I hold that a long poem does not exist. I maintain that the phrase, "a long poem," is simply a flat contradiction in terms.

I need scarcely observe that a poem deserves its title only inasmuch as it excites, by elevating the soul. The value of the poem is in the ratio of this elevating excitement. But all excitements are, through a psychal necessity, transient. That degree of excitement which would entitle a poem to be so called at all, cannot be sustained throughout a composition of any great length. After the lapse of half an hour, at the very utmost, it flags—fails—a revulsion ensues—and then the poem is, in effect, and in fact, no longer such.

There are, no doubt, many who have found difficulty in reconciling the critical dictum that the "Paradise Lost" is to be devoutly admired throughout, with the absolute impossibility of maintaining for it, during perusal, the amount of enthusiasm which that critical dictum would demand. This great work, in fact, is to be regarded as poetical, only when, losing sight of that vital requisite in all works of Art, Unity, we view it merely as a series of minor poems. If, to preserve its Unity—its totality of effect or impression—we read it (as would be necessary) at a single sitting, the result is but a constant alternation of excitement and depression. After a passage of what we feel to be true poetry, there follows, inevitably, a passage of platitude which no critical pre-judgment can force us to admire; but if, upon completing the work, we read it again, omitting the first book—that is to say, commencing with the second—we shall be surprised at now finding that admirable which we before condemned—that damnable which we had previously so much admired. It follows from all this that the ultimate, aggregate, or absolute effect of even the best epic under the sun, is a nullity:—and this is precisely the fact.

In regard to the Iliad, we have, if not positive proof, at least very good reason for believing it intended as a series of lyrics; but, granting the epic intention, I can say only that the work is based in an imperfect sense of art. The modern epic is, of the supposititious ancient model, but an inconsiderate and blindfold imitation. But the day of these artistic anomalies is over. If, at any time, any very long poem *were* popular in reality, which I doubt, it is at least clear that no very long poem will ever be popular again.

That the extent of a poetical work is, *ceteris paribus,* the measure of its merit, seems undoubtedly, when we thus state it, a proposition sufficiently absurd—yet we are indebted for it to the Quarterly Reviews. Surely there can be nothing in mere *size,* abstractly considered—there can be nothing in mere *bulk*, so far as a volume is concerned, which has so continuously elicited admiration from these saturnine pamphlets! A mountain, to be sure, by the mere sentiment of physical magnitude which it conveys, *does* impress us with a sense of the sublime—but no man is impressed after *this* fashion by the material grandeur of even "The Columbiad." Even the Quarterlies have not instructed us to be so impressed by it. As *yet,* they have not *insisted* on our estimating Lamartine by the cubic foot, or Pollock by the pound—but what else are we to *infer* from their continual prating about "sustained effort?" If, by "sustained effort," any little gentleman has accomplished an epic, let us frankly commend him for the effort—if this indeed be a thing commendable—but let us forbear praising the epic on the effort's account. It is to be hoped that common sense, in the time to come, will prefer deciding upon a work of Art, rather by the impression it makes—by the effect it produces—than by the time it took to impress the effect, or by the amount of "sustained effort" which had been found necessary in effecting the impression. The fact is, that perseverance is one thing and genius quite another—nor can all the Quarterlies in Christendom confound them. By-and-by, this proposition, with many which I have been just urging, will be received as self-evident. In the meantime, by being generally condemned as falsities, they will not be essentially damaged as truths.

On the other hand, it is clear that a poem may be improperly brief. Undue brevity degenerates into mere epigrammatism. A *very* short poem, while now and then producing a brilliant or vivid, never produces a profound or enduring effect. There must be the steady pressing down of the stamp upon the wax. De Béranger has wrought innumerable things, pungent and spirit-stirring; but, in general, they have been too imponderous to stamp themselves deeply into the public attention; and thus, as so many feathers of fancy, have been blown aloft only to be whistled down the wind.

A remarkable instance of the effect of undue brevity in depressing a poem—in keeping it out of the popular view—is afforded by the following exquisite little Serenade:

I arise from dreams of thee
    In the first sweet sleep of night,
When the winds are breathing low,
    And the stars are shining bright.
I arise from dreams of thee,
    And a spirit in my feet
Has led me—who knows how?—
    To thy chamber-window, sweet!

The wandering airs they faint
    On the dark, the silent stream—
The champak odors fail
    Like sweet thoughts in a dream;

The nightingale's complaint,
    It dies upon her heart,
As I must die on thine,
    O, beloved as thou art!

O, lift me from the grass!
    I die, I faint, I fail!
Let thy love in kisses rain
    On my lips and eyelids pale.
My cheek is cold and white, alas!
    My heart beats loud and fast:
Oh! press it close to thine again,
    Where it will break at last!

Very few, perhaps, are familiar with these lines—yet no less a poet than Shelley is their author. Their warm, yet delicate and ethereal imagination will be appreciated by all—but by none so thoroughly as by him who has himself arisen from sweet dreams of one beloved, to bathe in the aromatic air of a southern midsummer night.

One of the finest poems by Willis—the very best, in my opinion, which he has ever written—has, no doubt, through this same defect of undue brevity, been kept back from its proper position, not less in the critical than in the popular view.

The shadows lay along Broadway,
    'Twas near the twilight-tide—
And slowly there a lady fair
    Was walking in her pride.
Alone walk'd she; but, viewlessly,
    Walk'd spirits at her side.

Peace charm'd the street beneath her feet,
    And Honor charm'd the air;
And all astir looked kind on her,
    And called her good as fair—
For all God ever gave to her
    She kept with chary care.

She kept with care her beauties rare
    From lovers warm and true—
For her heart was cold to all but gold,
    And the rich came not to woo—
But honor'd well are charms to sell
    If priests the selling do.

Now walking there was one more fair—
    A slight girl, lily-pale;
And she had unseen company
    To make the spirit quail—
'Twixt Want and Scorn she walk'd forlorn,
    And nothing could avail.

No mercy now can clear her brow
    For this world's peace to pray;
For, as love's wild prayer dissolved in air,
    Her woman's heart gave way!—
But the sin forgiven by Christ in Heaven
    By man is cursed alway!

In this composition we find it difficult to recognize the Willis who has written so many mere "verses of society." The lines are not only richly ideal, but full of energy; while they breathe an earnestness—an evident sincerity of sentiment—for which we look in vain throughout all the other works of this author.

While the epic mania—while the idea that, to merit in poetry, prolixity is indispensable—has, for some years past, been gradually dying out of the public mind, by mere dint of its own absurdity—we find it succeeded by a heresy too palpably false to be long tolerated, but one which, in the brief period it has already endured, may be said to have accomplished more in the corruption of our Poetical Literature than all its other enemies combined. I allude to the heresy of *The Didactic.* It has been assumed, tacitly and avowedly, directly and indirectly, that the ultimate object of all Poetry is Truth. Every poem, it is said, should inculcate a moral; and by this moral is the poetical merit of the work to be adjudged. We Americans especially have patronized this happy idea; and we Bostonians, very especially, have developed it in full. We have taken it into our heads that to write a poem simply for the poem's sake, and to acknowledge such to have been our design, would be to confess ourselves radically wanting in the true poetic dignity and force:—but the simple fact is, that, would we but permit ourselves to look into our own souls, we should immediately there discover that under the sun there neither exists nor *can* exist any work more thoroughly dignified—more supremely noble than this very poem—this poem *per se*—this poem which is a poem and nothing more, this poem written solely for the poem's sake.

With as deep a reverence for the True as ever inspired the bosom of man, I would nevertheless, limit, in some measure, its modes of inculcation. I would limit to enforce them. I would not enfeeble them by dissipation. The demands of Truth are severe. She has no sympathy with the myrtles. All *that* which is so indispensable in Song, is precisely all *that* with which *she* has nothing whatever to do. It is but making her a flaunting paradox, to wreathe her in gems and flowers. In enforcing a truth, we need severity rather than efflorescence of language. We must be simple, precise, terse. We must be cool, calm, unimpassioned. In a word, we must be in that mood which, as nearly as possible, is the exact converse of the poetical. *He* must be blind indeed who does not perceive the radical and chasmal differences between the truthful and the poetical modes of inculcation. He must be theory-mad beyond redemption who, in spite of these differences, shall still persist in attempting to reconcile the obstinate oils and waters of Poetry and Truth.

Dividing the world of mind into its three most immediately obvious distinctions, we have the Pure Intellect, Taste, and the Moral Sense. I place Taste in the middle, because it is just this position which, in the mind, it occupies. It holds intimate relations with either extreme; but from the Moral Sense is separated by so faint a difference that Aristotle has not hesitated to place some of its operations among the virtues themselves. Nevertheless, we find the *offices* of the trio marked with a sufficient distinction. Just as the Intellect concerns itself with Truth, so Taste informs us of the Beautiful while the Moral Sense is regardful of Duty. Of this latter, while Conscience teaches the obligation, and Reason the expediency, Taste contents herself with displaying the charms:—waging war upon Vice solely on the ground of her deformity—her disproportion—her animosity to the fitting, to the appropriate, to the harmonious—in a word, to Beauty.

An immortal instinct, deep within the spirit of man, is thus, plainly, a sense of the Beautiful. This it is which administers to his delight in the manifold forms, and sounds, and odors, and sentiments amid which he exists. And just as the lily is repeated in the lake, or the eyes of Amaryllis in the mirror, so is the mere oral or written repetition of these forms, and sounds, and colours, and odors, and sentiments, a duplicate source of delight. But this mere repetition is not poetry. He who shall simply sing, with however glowing enthusiasm, or with however vivid a truth of description, of the sights, and sounds, and odors, and colours, and sentiments, which greet *him* in common with all mankind—he, I say, has yet failed to prove his divine title. There is still a something in the distance which he has been unable to attain. We have still a thirst unquenchable, to allay which he has not shown us the crystal springs. This thirst belongs to the immortality of Man. It is at once a consequence and an indication of his perennial existence. It is the desire of the moth for the star. It is no mere appreciation of the Beauty before us—but a wild effort to reach the Beauty above. Inspired by an ecstatic prescience of the glories beyond the grave, we struggle, by multiform combinations among the things and thoughts of Time, to attain a portion of that Loveliness whose very elements, perhaps, appertain to eternity alone. And thus when by Poetry—or when by Music, the most entrancing of the Poetic moods—we find ourselves melted into tears—we weep then—not as the Abbaté Gravina supposes—through excess of pleasure, but through a certain, petulant, impatient sorrow at our inability to grasp *now*, wholly, here on earth, at once and for ever, those divine and rapturous joys of which *through* the poem, or *through* the music, we attain to but brief and indeterminate glimpses.

The struggle to apprehend the supernal Loveliness—this struggle, on the part of souls fittingly constituted—has given to the world all *that* which it (the world) has ever been enabled at once to understand and *to feel* as poetic.

The Poetic Sentiment, of course, may develope itself in various modes—in Painting, in Sculpture, in Architecture, in the Dance—very especially in Music—and very peculiarly, and with a wide field, in the composition of the Landscape Garden. Our present theme, however, has regard only to its manifestation in words. And here let me speak briefly on the topic of rhythm. Contenting myself with the certainty that Music, in its various modes of metre, rhythm, and rhyme, is of so vast a moment in Poetry as never to be wisely rejected—is so vitally important an adjunct, that he is simply silly who declines its assistance, I will not now pause to maintain its absolute essentiality. It is in Music, perhaps, that the soul most nearly attains the great end for which, when inspired by the Poetic Sentiment, it struggles—the creation of supernal Beauty. It *may* be, indeed, that here this sublime end is, now and then, attained *in fact.* We are often made to feel, with a shivering delight, that from an earthly harp are stricken notes which *cannot* have been unfamiliar to the angels. And thus there can be little doubt that in the union of Poetry with Music in its popular sense, we shall find the widest field for the Poetic development. The old Bards and Minnesingers had advantages which we do not possess—and Thomas Moore, singing his own songs, was, in the most legitimate manner, perfecting them as poems.

To recapitulate, then:—I would define, in brief, the Poetry of words as *The Rhythmical Creation of Beauty. Its* sole arbiter is Taste. With the Intellect or with the Conscience, it has only collateral relations. Unless incidentally, it has no concern whatever either with Duty or with Truth.

A few words, however, in explanation. *That* pleasure which is at once the most pure, the most elevating, and the most intense, is derived, I maintain, from the contemplation of the Beautiful. In the contemplation of Beauty we alone find it possible to attain that pleasurable elevation, or excitement, *of the soul*, which we recognise as the Poetic Sentiment, and which is so easily distinguished from Truth, which is the satisfaction of the Reason, or from Passion, which is the excitement of the heart. I make Beauty, therefore—using the word as inclusive of the sublime—I make Beauty the province of the poem, simply because it is an obvious rule of Art that effects should be made to spring as directly as possible from their causes:—no one as yet having been weak enough to deny that the peculiar elevation in question is at least *most readily* attainable in the poem. It by no means follows, however, that the incitements of Passion, or the precepts of Duty, or even the lessons of Truth, may not be introduced into a poem, and with advantage; for they may subserve, incidentally, in various ways, the general purposes of the work:—but the true artist will always contrive to tone them down in proper subjection to that *Beauty* which is the atmosphere and the real essence of the poem.

I cannot better introduce the few poems which I shall present for your consideration, than by the citation of the Pröem to Mr. Longfellow's "Waif":

The day is done, and the darkness
    Falls from the wings of Night,
As a feather is wafted downward
    From an Eagle in his flight.

I see the lights of the village
    Gleam through the rain and the mist,
And a feeling of sadness comes o'er me,
    That my soul cannot resist;

A feeling of sadness and longing,
    That is not akin to pain,
And resembles sorrow only
    As the mist resembles the rain.

Come, read to me some poem,
    Some simple and heartfelt lay,
That shall soothe this restless feeling,
    And banish the thoughts of day.

Not from the grand old masters,
    Not from the bards sublime,
Whose distant footsteps echo
    Through the corridors of time.

For, like strains of martial music,
    Their mighty thoughts suggest
Life's endless toil and endeavor;
    And tonight I long for rest.

Read from some humbler poet,
    Whose songs gushed from his heart,
As showers from the clouds of summer,
    Or tears from the eyelids start;

Who through long days of labor,
    And nights devoid of ease,

Still heard in his soul the music
    Of wonderful melodies.

Such songs have power to quiet
    The restless pulse of care,
And come like the benediction
    That follows after prayer.

Then read from the treasured volume
    The poem of thy choice,
And lend to the rhyme of the poet
    The beauty of thy voice.

And the night shall be filled with music,
    And the cares that infest the day,
Shall fold their tents, like the Arabs,
    And as silently steal away.

With no great range of imagination, these lines have been justly admired for their delicacy of expression. Some of the images are very effective. Nothing can be better than—

——————the bards sublime,
    Whose distant footsteps echo
Down the corridors of Time.

The idea of the last quatrain is also very effective. The poem, on the whole, however, is chiefly to be admired for the graceful *insouciance* of its metre, so well in accordance with the character of the sentiments, and especially for the *ease* of the general manner. This "ease," or naturalness, in a literary style, it has long been the fashion to regard as ease in appearance alone—as a point of really difficult attainment. But not so:—a natural manner is difficult only to him who should never meddle with it—to the unnatural. It is but the result of writing with the understanding, or with the instinct, that *the tone,* in composition, should always be that which the mass of mankind would adopt—and must perpetually vary, of course, with the occasion. The author who, after the fashion of "The North American Review," should be, upon *all* occasions, merely "quiet," must necessarily upon *many* occasions, be simply silly, or stupid; and has no more right to be considered "easy," or "natural," than a Cockney exquisite, or than the sleeping Beauty in the wax-works.

Among the minor poems of Bryant, none has so much impressed me as the one which he entitles "June." I quote only a portion of it:

There, through the long, long summer hours,
    The golden light should lie,
And thick young herbs and groups of flowers
    Stand in their beauty by.
The oriole should build and tell
His love-tale, close beside my cell;
    The idle butterfly
Should rest him there, and there be heard
The housewife-bee and humming bird.

And what, if cheerful shouts at noon,
    Come, from the village sent,
Or songs of maids, beneath the moon,
    With fairy laughter blent?
And what if, in the evening light,
Betrothed lovers walk in sight
    Of my low monument?
I would the lovely scene around
Might know no sadder sight nor sound.

I know, I know I should not see
    The season's glorious show,
Nor would its brightness shine for me,
    Nor its wild music flow;
But if, around my place of sleep,
The friends I love should come to weep,
    They might not haste to go.
Soft airs, and song, and light, and bloom
Should keep them lingering by my tomb.

These to their soften'd hearts should bear
    The thought of what has been,
And speak of one who cannot share
    The gladness of the scene;
Whose part, in all the pomp that fills
The circuit of the summer hills,
    Is—that his grave is green;
And deeply would their hearts rejoice
To hear again his living voice.

The rhythmical flow, here, is even voluptuous—nothing could be more melodious. The poem has always affected me in a remarkable manner. The intense melancholy which seems to well up, perforce, to the surface of all the poet's cheerful sayings about his grave, we find thrilling us to the soul—while there is the truest poetic elevation in the thrill. The impression left is one of a pleasurable sadness. And if, in the remaining compositions which I shall introduce to you, there be more or less of a similar tone always apparent, let me remind you that (how or why we know not) this certain taint of sadness is inseparably connected with all the higher manifestations of true Beauty. It is, nevertheless,

A feeling of sadness and longing
    That is not akin to pain,
And resembles sorrow only
    As the mist resembles the rain.

The taint of which I speak is clearly perceptible even in a poem so full of brilliancy and spirit as "The Health" of Edward Coote Pinkney:—

I fill this cup to one made up
    Of loveliness alone,
A woman, of her gentle sex
    The seeming paragon;
To whom the better elements
    And kindly stars have given
A form so fair, that, like the air,
    'Tis less of earth than heaven.

Her every tone is music's own,
    Like those of morning birds,
And something more than melody
    Dwells ever in her words;
The coinage of her heart are they,
    And from her lips each flows
As one may see the burden'd bee
    Forth issue from the rose.

Affections are as thoughts to her,
    The measures of her hours;
Her feelings have the flagrancy,
    The freshness of young flowers;
And lovely passions, changing oft,
    So fill her, she appears
The image of themselves by turns,—
    The idol of past years!
Of her bright face one glance will trace
    A picture on the brain,
And of her voice in echoing hearts
    A sound must long remain;
But memory, such as mine of her,
    So very much endears,
When death is nigh my latest sigh
    Will not be life's, but hers.

I fill'd this cup to one made up
    Of loveliness alone,
A woman, of her gentle sex
    The seeming paragon—
Her health! and would on earth there stood,
    Some more of such a frame,
That life might be all poetry,
    And weariness a name.

It was the misfortune of Mr. Pinkney to have been born too far south. Had he been a New Englander, it is probable that he would have been ranked as the first of American lyrists, by that magnanimous cabal which has so long controlled the destinies of American Letters, in conducting the thing called "The North American Review." The poem just cited is especially beautiful; but the poetic elevation which it induces, we must refer chiefly to our sympathy in the poet's enthusiasm. We pardon his hyperboles for the evident earnestness with which they are uttered.

It was by no means my design, however, to expatiate upon the *merits* of what I should read you. These will necessarily speak for themselves. Boccalini, in his "Advertisements from Parnassus," tells us that Zoilus once presented Apollo a very caustic criticism upon a very admirable book:—whereupon the god asked him for the beauties of the work. He replied that he only busied himself about the errors. On hearing this, Apollo, handing him a sack of unwinnowed wheat, bade him pick out *all the chaff* for his reward.

Now this fable answers very well as a hit at the critics—but I am by no means sure that the god was in the right. I am by no means certain that the true limits of the critical duty are not grossly misunderstood. Excellence, in a poem especially, may be considered in the light of an axiom, which need only be properly *put*, to become self-evident. It is *not* excellence if it require to be demonstrated as such:—and thus, to point out too particularly the merits of a work of Art, is to admit that they are *not* merits altogether.

Among the "Melodies" of Thomas Moore, is one whose distinguished character as a poem proper, seems to have been singularly left out of view. I allude to his lines beginning—"Come, rest in this bosom." The intense energy of their expression is not surpassed by anything in Byron. There are two of the lines in which a sentiment is conveyed that embodies the *all in all* of the divine passion of Love—a sentiment which, perhaps, has found its echo in more, and in more passionate, human hearts than any other single sentiment ever embodied in words:

> Come, rest in this bosom, my own stricken deer,
> Though the herd have fled from thee, thy home is
>   still here;
> Here still is the smile, that no cloud can o'ercast,
> And a heart and a hand all thy own to the last.

Oh! what was love made for, if 'tis not the same
Through joy and through torment, through glory
and shame?
I know not, I ask not, if guilt's in that heart,
I but know that I love thee, whatever thou art.

Thou hast call'd me thy Angel in moments of bliss,
And thy Angel I'll be, 'mid the horrors of this,—
Through the furnace, unshrinking, thy steps to
pursue,
And shield thee, and save thee,—or perish there
too!

It has been the fashion of late days, to deny Moore Imagination, while granting him Fancy—a distinction originating with Coleridge—than whom no man more fully comprehended the great powers of Moore. The fact is, that the fancy of this poet so far predominates over all his other faculties, and over the fancy of all other men, as to have induced, very naturally, the idea that he is fanciful *only*. But never was there a greater mistake. Never was a grosser wrong done the fame of a true poet. In the compass of the English language I can call to mind no poem more profoundly—more weirdly *imaginative*, in the best sense, than the lines commencing—"I would I were by that dim lake"—which are the composition of Thomas Moore. I regret that I am unable to remember them.

One of the noblest—and, speaking of Fancy, one of the most singularly fanciful of modern poets, was Thomas Hood. His "Fair Ines" had always, for me, an inexpressible charm:

O saw ye not fair Ines?
She's gone into the West,
To dazzle when the sun is down,
And rob the world of rest:
She took our daylight with her,
The smiles that we love best,
With morning blushes on her cheek,
And pearls upon her breast.

O turn again, fair Ines,
    Before the fall of night,
For fear the moon should shine alone,
    And stars unrivall'd bright;
And blessed will the lover be
    That walks beneath their light,
And breathes the love against thy cheek
    I dare not even write!

Would I had been, fair Ines,
    That gallant cavalier,
Who rode so gaily by thy side,
    And whisper'd thee so near!
Were there no bonny dames at home,
    Or no true lovers here,
That he should cross the seas to win
    The dearest of the dear?

I saw thee, lovely Ines,
    Descend along the shore,
With bands of noble gentlemen,
    And banners waved before;
And gentle youth and maidens gay,
    And snowy plumes they wore;
It would have been a beauteous dream,
    —If it had been no more!

Alas, alas, fair Ines,
    She went away with song,
With music waiting on her steps,
    And shoutings of the throng;
But some were sad and felt no mirth,
    But only Music's wrong,
In sounds that sang Farewell, Farewell,
    To her you've loved so long.

Farewell, farewell, fair Ines,
    That vessel never bore
So fair a lady on its deck,
    Nor danced so light before,—
Alas for pleasure on the sea,
    And sorrow on the shore!
The smile that blest one lover's heart
    Has broken many more!

"The Haunted House," by the same author, is one of the truest poems ever written—one of the *truest*—one of the most unexceptionable—one of the most thoroughly artistic, both in its theme and in its execution. It is, moreover, powerfully ideal—imaginative. I regret that its length renders it unsuitable for the purposes of this Lecture. In place of it, permit me to offer the universally appreciated "Bridge of Sighs."

One more Unfortunate,
Weary of breath,
Rashly importunate,
Gone to her death!

Take her up tenderly,
Lift her with care;—
Fashion'd so slenderly,
Young, and so fair!

Look at her garments
Clinging like cerements;
Whilst the wave constantly
Drips from her clothing;
Take her up instantly,
Loving, not loathing.

Touch her not scornfully;
Think of her mournfully,
Gently and humanly;
Not of the stains of her,

All that remains of her
Now, is pure womanly.

Make no deep scrutiny
Into her mutiny
Rash and undutiful;
Past all dishonor,
Death has left on her
Only the beautiful.

Still, for all slips of hers,
One of Eve's family—
Wipe those poor lips of hers
Oozing so clammily,
Loop up her tresses
Escaped from the comb,
Her fair auburn tresses;
Whilst wonderment guesses
Where was her home?

Who was her father?
Who was her mother?
Had she a sister?
Had she a brother?
Or was there a dearer one
Still, and a nearer one
Yet, than all other?

Alas! for the rarity
Of Christian charity
Under the sun!
Oh! it was pitiful!
Near a whole city full,
Home she had none.

Sisterly, brotherly,
Fatherly, motherly,

Feelings had changed:
Love, by harsh evidence,
Thrown from its eminence;
Even God's providence
Seeming estranged.
Where the lamps quiver
Sor far in the river,
With many a light
From window and casement
From garret to basement,
She stood, with amazement,
Houseless by night.

The bleak wind of March
Made her tremble and shiver;
But not the dark arch,
Or the black flowing river:
Mad from life's history,
Glad to death's mystery,
Swift to be hurl'd—
Anywhere, anywhere
Out of the world!

In she plunged boldly,
No matter how coldly
The rough river ran—
Over the brink of it,
Picture it—think of it,
Dissolute Man!
Lave in it, drink of it
Then, if you can!

Take her up tenderly,
Lift her with care;
Fashion'd so slenderly,
Young, and so fair!
Ere her limbs frigidly

Stiffen too rigidly,
Decently,—kindly,—
Smooth, and compose them;
And her eyes, close them,
Staring so blindly!
Dreadfully staring
Through muddy impurity,
As when with the daring
Last look of despairing
Fixed on futurity.

Perishing gloomily,
Spurred by contumely,
Cold inhumanity,
Burning insanity,
Into her rest,—
Cross her hands humbly,
As if praying dumbly,
Over her breast!
Owning her weakness,
Her evil behaviour,
And leaving, with meekness,
Her sins to her Savior!

The vigor of this poem is no less remarkable than its pathos. The versification, although carrying the fanciful to the very verge of the fantastic, is nevertheless admirably adapted to the wild insanity which is the thesis of the poem.

Among the minor poems of Lord Byron, is one which has never received from the critics the praise which it undoubtedly deserves:

Though the day of my destiny's over,
    And the star of my fate hath declined,
Thy soft heart refused to discover
    The faults which so many could find;
Though thy soul with my grief was acquainted,
    It shrunk not to share it with me,

And the love which my spirit hath painted
    It never hath found but in *thee.*

Then when nature around me is smiling,
    The last smile which answers to mine,
I do not believe it beguiling,
    Because it reminds me of thine;
And when winds are at war with the ocean,
    As the breasts I believed in with me,
If their billows excite an emotion,
    It is that they bear me from *thee.*

Though the rock of my last hope is shivered,
    And its fragments are sunk in the wave,
Though I feel that my soul is delivered
    To pain—it shall not be its slave.
There is many a pang to pursue me:
    They may crush, but they shall not contemn—
They may torture, but shall not subdue me—
    'Tis of *thee* that I think—not of them.

Though human, thou didst not deceive me,
    Though woman, thou didst not forsake,
Though loved, thou forborest to grieve me,
    Though slandered, thou never couldst shake,—
Though trusted, thou didst not disclaim me,
    Though parted, it was not to fly,
Though watchful, 'twas not to defame me,
    Nor mute, that the world might belie.

Yet I blame not the world, nor despise it,
    Nor the war of the many with one—
If my soul was not fitted to prize it,
    'Twas folly not sooner to shun:
And if dearly that error hath cost me,
    And more than I once could foresee,

I have found that whatever it lost me,
　　It could not deprive me of *thee.*

From the wreck of the past, which hath perished,
　　Thus much I at least may recall,
It hath taught me that which I most cherished
　　Deserved to be dearest of all:
In the desert a fountain is springing,
　　In the wide waste there still is a tree,
And a bird in the solitude singing,
　　Which speaks to my spirit of *thee.*

Although the rhythm, here, is one of the most difficult, the versification could scarcely be improved. No nobler *theme* ever engaged the pen of poet. It is the soul-elevating idea, that no man can consider himself entitled to complain of Fate while, in his adversity, he still retains the unwavering love of woman.

From Alfred Tennyson—although in perfect sincerity I regard him as the noblest poet that ever lived—I have left myself time to cite only a very brief specimen. I call him, and *think* him the noblest of poets—*not* because the impressions he produces are, at *all* times, the most profound—*not* because the poetical excitement which he induces is, at *all* times, the most intense—but because it *is*, at all times, the most ethereal—in other words, the most elevating and most pure. No poet is so little of the earth, earthy. What I am about to read is from his last long poem, "The Princess":

　　Tears, idle tears, I know not what they mean,
Tears from the depth of some divine despair
Rise in the heart, and gather to the eyes,
In looking on the happy Autumn-fields,
And thinking of the days that are no more.

　　Fresh as the first beam glittering on a sail,
That brings our friends up from the underworld,
Sad as the last which reddens over one

That sinks with all we love below the verge;
So sad, so fresh, the days that are no more.

Ah, sad and strange as in dark summer dawns
The earliest pipe of half-awaken'd birds
To dying ears, when unto dying eyes
The casement slowly grows a glimmering square;
So sad, so strange, the days that are no more.

Dear as remember'd kisses after death,
And sweet as those by hopeless fancy feign'd
On lips that are for others; deep as love,
Deep as first love, and wild with all regret;
O Death in Life, the days that are no more.

Thus, although in a very cursory and imperfect manner, I have endeavored to convey to you my conception of the Poetic Principle. It has been my purpose to suggest that, while this Principle itself is, strictly and simply, the Human Aspiration for Supernal Beauty, the manifestation of the Principle is always found in *an elevating excitement of the Soul*, quite independent of that passion which is the intoxication of the Heart—or of that Truth which is the satisfaction of the Reason. For, in regard to Passion, alas! its tendency is to degrade, rather than to elevate the Soul. Love, on the contrary—Love—the true, the divine Eros—the Uranian, as distinguished from the Dionæan Venus—is unquestionably the purest and truest of all poetical themes. And in regard to Truth—if, to be sure, through the attainment of a truth, we are led to perceive a harmony where none was apparent before, we experience, at once, the true poetical effect—but this effect is referable to the harmony alone, and not in the least degree to the truth which merely served to render the harmony manifest.

We shall reach, however, more immediately a distinct conception of what the true Poetry is, by mere reference to a few of the simple elements which induce in the Poet himself the true poetical effect. He recognizes the ambrosia which nourishes his soul, in the bright orbs that shine in Heaven—in the volutes of the flower—in the clustering of low shrubberies—in the waving of the grain-fields—in the slanting of tall, Eastern trees—in the blue distance of mountains—in the grouping of clouds—in the twinkling of half-hidden brooks—in the gleaming of silver rivers—in the repose of sequestered lakes—in the star-mirroring depths of lonely wells. He perceives it in the songs of birds—in the harp of Æolus—in the sighing of the night-wind—in the repining voice of the forest—in the surf that complains to the shore—in the fresh breath of the woods—in the scent of the violet—in the voluptuous perfume of the hyacinth—in the suggestive odor that comes to him, at eventide, from far-distant, undiscovered islands, over dim oceans, illimitable and unexplored. He owns it in all noble thoughts—in all unworldly motives—in all holy impulses—in all chivalrous, generous, and self-sacrificing deeds. He feels it in the beauty of woman—in the grace of her step—in the luster of her eye—in the melody of her voice—in her soft laughter—in her sigh—in the harmony of the rustling of her robes. He deeply feels it in her winning endearments—in her burning enthusiasms—in her gentle charities—in her meek and devotional endurances—but above all—ah, far above all—he kneels to it—he worships it in the faith, in the purity, in the strength, in the altogether divine majesty—of her *love.*

Let me conclude—by the recitation of yet another brief poem—one very different in character from any that I have before quoted. It is by Motherwell, and is called "The Song of the Cavalier." With our modern and altogether rational ideas of the absurdity and impiety of warfare, we are not precisely in that frame of mind best adapted to sympathize with the sentiments, and thus to appreciate the real excellence of the poem. To do this fully, we must identify ourselves, in fancy, with the soul of the old cavalier.

Then mounte! then mounte, brave gallants, all,
    And don your helmes amaine:
Deathe's couriers, Fame and Honor, call
    Us to the field againe.
No shrewish teares shall fill our eye
    When the sword-hilt's in our hand,—
Heart-whole we'll part, and no whit sighe
    For the fayrest of the land;
Let piping swaine, and craven wight,
    Thus weepe and puling crye,
Our business is like men to fight,
    And hero-like to die!

Letters

Poe to J. P. Kennedy

Dear Sir,—Your kind invitation to dinner today has wounded me to the quick. I cannot come—and for reasons of the most humiliating nature—my personal appearance. You may conceive my deep mortification in making this disclosure to you—but it was necessary. If you will be my friend so far as to loan me $20, I will call on you tomorrow—otherwise it will be impossible, and I must submit to my fate.

Sincerely Yours,
E. A. Poe.

J. P. Kennedy Esq.,
Sunday 15th.

Poe to J. P. Kennedy

RICHMOND, JAN. 22, 1836.

DEAR SIR,—Although I have never yet acknowledged the receipt of your letter of advice some months ago, it was not without great influence upon me. I have since then, fought the enemy manfully, and am now, in every respect, comfortable and happy. I know you will be pleased to hear this. My health is better than for years past, my mind is fully occupied, my pecuniary difficulties have vanished, I have a fair prospect of future success—in a word all is right. I shall never forget to whom all this happiness is in a great degree to be attributed. I know that without your timely aid I should have sunk under my trials. Mrs White is very liberal, and besides my salary of $520 pays me liberally for extra work, so that I have nearly $800. Next year, that is, at the commencement of the second volume, I am to get $1000. Besides this, I receive, from publishers, nearly all new publications. My friends in Richmond have received me with open arms, and my reputation is extending—especially in the South. Contrast all this with those circumstances of absolute despair in which you found me, and you will see how great reason I have to be grateful to God—and to yourself.

Some matters in relation to the death of Mrs Catherine Clemm, who resided at Mount Prospect, four miles from Baltimore, render it necessary for me to apply to an attorney, and I have thought it probable you would be kind enough to advise me . . . I should be glad to have your opinion in regard to my Editorial course in the Messenger. How do you like my Critical Notices? I have understood (from the Preface to your 3rd Edition of Horse-Shoe), that you are engaged in another work. If so, can you not send me a copy in advance of the publication? Remember me to your family, and believe me with the highest respect & esteem

Yours very truly
EDGAR ALLAN POE.

Poe to Thomas W. White

BALTIMORE, May 30, 1835.

MR. T. W. WHITE.

DEAR SIR,—I duly recd, through Mr. Kennedy your favour of the 20th enclosing $5; and an order for $4.94. I assure you it was very welcome. Miscarriages of double letters are by no means unfrequent just now, but yours, at least, came safely to hand. Had I reflected a moment I should have acknowledged the rect before. I suppose you have heard about—— Gwynn Jones of this place, late Editor of the Gazette. He was detected in purloining letters from the office to which the Clerks were in the habit of admitting him familiarly. He acknowledged the theft of more than $2000 in this way at different times. He probably took even more than that, and I am quite sure that on the part of the Clerks themselves advantage was taken of his arrest to embezzle double that sum. I have been a loser myself to a small amount.

I have not seen Mr. Kennedy for some days, having been too unwell to go abroad. When I saw him last he assured me his book would reach Richd in time for your next number, and under this assurance, I thought it useless to make such extracts from the book as I wished—thinking you could please yourself in this matter. I cannot imagine what delays its publication, for it has been for some time ready for issue. In regard to my critique I seriously feel ashamed of what I have written. I fully intended to have given the work a thorough review, and examine it in detail. Ill health alone prevented me from so doing. At the time I wrote the hasty sketch I sent you I was so ill as to be hardly able to see the paper on which I wrote, and finished in a state of complete exhaustion. I have therefore, not done anything like justice to the book, and I am vexed about the matter, for Mr. K. has proved himself a kind friend to me in every respect, and I am sincerely grateful to him for many acts of generosity and attention.

I read the article in the Compiler relating to the "Confessions of a Poet" but there is no necessity of giving it a reply. The book is silly enough of itself, without the aid of any controversy concerning it. In your private ear however I may say a word or two. The writer "I" founds his opinion that I have not read the book simply upon one fact—that I disagree with him concerning it. I have looked over his article two or three times attentively and can see no other reason adduced by him. If this is a good reason, one way, it is equally good another—ergo—*He* has not read the book because he disagrees with me. Neither of us having read it then, it is better to say no more about it.

But seriously—I *have* read it from beginning to end and was very much amused at it. My opinion concerning it is pretty much the opinion of the press at large. I have heard no person offer one serious word in its defence.

My notice of your Messenger in the Republican was I am afraid too brief for your views. But I could command no greater space in its editorial columns. I have often wondered at your preferring to insert such notices in the *Republican.* It is a paper by no means in the hands of the first people here. Would not the American suit as well? Its columns are equally at your service. Did you notice the alteration I made in the name of the authority of the lines to Mr. Wilde? They were written by Mrs. Dr. Buckler of this city—not Buckley.

You ask me if I am perfectly satisfied with your course. I reply that I am—entirely. My poor services are not worth what you give me for them.

The high compliment of Judge Tucker is rendered doubly flattering to me by my knowledge of his literary character.

Very sincerely yours
EDGAR A. POE.

Poe to Philip P. Cooke

PHILADELPHIA, September 21, 1839.

MY DEAR SIR,—I received your letter this morning—and read it with more pleasure than I can well express. You wrong me, indeed, in supposing that I meant one word of mere flattery in what I said. I have an inveterate habit of speaking the truth—and had I not valued your opinion more highly than that of any man in America I should not have written you as I did.

I say that I read your letter with delight. In fact I am aware of no delight greater than that of feeling one's self appreciated (in such wild matters as "Ligeia") by those in whose judgment one has faith. You read my most intimate spirit "like a book," and with the single exception of D'Israeli, I have had communication with no other person who does. Willis had a glimpse of it—Judge Tucker saw about one half way through—but your ideas are the very echo of my own. I am very far from meaning to flatter—I am flattered and honored. Beside me is now lying a letter from Washington Irving in which he speaks with enthusiasm of a late tale of mine, "The Fall of the House of Usher,"—and in which he promises to make his opinion public, upon the first opportunity,—but from the bottom of my heart I assure you, I regard his best word as but dust in the balance when weighed with those discriminating opinions of your own, which teach me that you feel and perceive.

Touching "Ligeia" you are right—all right—throughout. The *gradual* perception of the fact that Ligeia lives again in the person of Rowena is a far loftier and more thrilling idea than the one I have embodied. It offers in my opinion, the widest possible scope to the imagination—it might be rendered even sublime. And this idea was mine—had I never written before I should have adopted it—but then there is "Morella." Do you remember there the *gradual* conviction on the part of the parent that the spirit of the first Morella tenants the person of the second? It was necessary, since "Morella" was written, to modify "Ligeia." I was forced to be content with a sudden half-consciousness, on the part of the narrator, that Ligeia stood before him. One point I have not fully carried out—I should have intimated that the *will* did not perfect its intention—there should have been a relapse—a final one—and Ligeia (who had only succeeded in so much as to convey an idea of the truth to the narrator) should be at length entombed as Rowena—the bodily alterations having gradually faded away.

But since "Morella" is upon record I will suffer "Ligeia" to remain as it is. Your word that it is "intelligible" suffices—and your commentary sustains your word. As for the mob—let them talk on. I should be grieved if I thought they comprehended me here. The "saith Verulam" shall be put right—your "impertinence" is quite pertinent.

I send the "Gentleman's Magazine" (July, August, September). Do not think of subscribing. The criticisms are not worth your notice. Of course I pay no attention to them—for there are two of us. It is not pleasant to be taxed with the twaddle of other people, or to let other people be taxed with ours. Therefore, for the present, I remain upon my oars—merely penning an occasional paragraph, without care. The critiques, such as they are, are all mine in the July number, and all mine in the August and September, with the exception of the three first in each—which are by Burton. As soon as Fate allows I will have a Magazine of my own—and will endeavor to kick up a dust. Do you ever see the "Pittsburg Examiner" (a New Monthly)? I wrote a Review of "Tortesa," at some length in the July number. In the October number of the "Gentleman's Magazine," I will have "William Wilson" from "The Gift" for 1840. This tale I think you will like—it is perhaps the best, although not the last, I have done. During the autumn I will publish all in two volumes—now I have done with my egotism.

It makes me laugh to hear you speaking about "romantic young persons" as of a race with whom, for the future, you have nothing to do.

You need not attempt to shake off or to banter off Romance. It is an evil you will never get rid of to the end of your days. It is a part of yourself—a portion of your soul. Age will only mellow it a little, and give it a holier tone. I will give your contributions a hearty welcome, and the choicest position in the magazine.

Sincerely yours,
EDGAR A. POE.

Poe to R. W. Griswold

PHILADELPHIA, March 29, 1841.

R. W. GRISWOLD, Esq.

MY DEAR SIR,—On the other leaf I send such poems as I think my best, from which you can select any which please your fancy. I should be proud to see one or two of them in your book. The one called "The Haunted Palace" is that of which I spoke in reference to Professor Longfellow's plagiarism. I first published the "H. P." in Brooks' "Museum," a monthly journal at Baltimore, now dead. Afterwards, I embodied it in a tale called "The House of Usher," in Burton's Magazine. Here it was, I suppose, that Professor Longfellow saw it; for, about six weeks afterwards, there appeared in the "Southern Literary Messenger" a poem by him called "The Beleaguered City," which may now be found in his volume. The identity in title is striking; for by "The Haunted Palace" I mean to imply a mind haunted by phantoms—a disordered brain—and by the "Beleaguered City," Prof. L. means just the same. But the whole tournure of the poem is based upon mine, as you will see at once. Its allegorical conduct, the style of its versification and expression—all are mine. As I understood you to say that you meant to preface each set of poems by some biographical notice, I have ventured to send you the above memoranda—the particulars of which (in a case where an author is so little known as myself) might not be easily obtained elsewhere. "The Coliseum" was the prize poem alluded to.

With high respect, I am your obedient servant,

EDGAR A. POE.

Poe to Griswold

NEW YORK, JAN. 16, 1845.

DEAR GRISWOLD,—If you will permit me to call you so—your letter occasioned me first pain and then pleasure: pain, because it gave me to see that I had lost, through my own folly, an honorable friend:—pleasure, because I saw in it a hope of reconciliation. I have been aware, for several weeks, that my reasons for speaking of your book as I did, (of yourself I have always spoken kindly,) were based in the malignant slanders of a mischief-maker by profession. Still, as I supposed you irreparably offended, I could make no advances when we met at the "Tribune" office, although I longed to do so. I know of nothing which would give me more sincere pleasure than your accepting these apologies, and meeting me as a friend. If you can do this, and forget the past, let me know where I shall call on you—or come and see me at the "Mirror" office, any morning about ten. We can then talk over the other matters, which, to me at least, are far less important than your good will.

Sincerely yours,
EDGAR A. POE.

Poe to Fitz-Greene Halleck

PHILADELPHIA, JUNE 24, 1841.

DEAR SIR,—Mr. George Graham, of this city, and myself, design to establish a Monthly Magazine, upon certain conditions—one of which is the procuring your assistance in the enterprise. Will you pardon me for saying a few words upon the subject?

I need not call your attention to the signs of the times in respect to Magazine literature. You will admit the tendency of the age in this direction. The brief, the terse, and the easily circulated will take place of the diffuse, the ponderous, and the inaccessible. Even our Reviews are found too massive for the taste of the day—I do not mean for the taste of the merely uneducated, but also for that of the few. In the meantime the finest minds of Europe are beginning to lend their spirit to Magazines. In this country, unhappily, we have no journal of the class, which can either afford to compensate the highest talent, or which is, in all respects, a fitting vehicle for its thoughts. In the supply of this deficiency there would be a point gained; and the project of which I speak has originated in the hope of supplying it.

Mr. Graham is a lawyer, but for some time past, has been occupied in publishing. His experience of the periodical business is great. He is a gentleman of high social standing, and possessed of ample pecuniary means. Together, we would enter the field with a full understanding of the difficulties to be encountered, and, I trust, with ability to meet them.

The work will be an octavo of 90 pages. The paper will be excellent—superior to that of the N. A. Review. The type will be new (always new) clear and bold, with distinct face. The matter will be disposed in single column. The printing will be done upon a hand-press in the best manner. There will be a broad margin. We shall have no engravings, except occasional wood-cuts (by the best artists) when demanded in obvious illustration of the text; and, when so required, they will be worked in with the type—not upon separate pages as in "Arcturus." The stitching will be done in the French style, permitting the book to lie fully open. Upon the cover, and throughout, the endeavour will be to preserve the greatest purity of taste, consistent with decision and force. The price will be $5.

The chief feature of the literary department will be that of contributions from the more distinguished pens (of America) *exclusively*. Or, if this plan cannot be wholly carried out, we purpose, at least, to procure the constant aid of some five or six of the most distinguished, and to admit few articles from other sources—none which are not of a high order of excellence. We shall endeavor to procure the services of yourself, Mr. Bryant, Mr. Longfellow, Mr. Irving, Mr. Cooper, Mr. Paulding, Mr. Kennedy, Mr. Willis, and perhaps one or two others. In fact, as before said, our success in making these engagements is a condition, without which the Magazine will not go into operation; and my immediate object in addressing you now is to ascertain how far I may depend upon yourself for assistance.

It would be desirable that you agree to furnish one paper each month—either a complete poem, or a portion of one—and of such length as you deem proper. The terms will be left entirely to your own decision. The services specified will be paid as you may suggest—in advance if necessary. It would be advisable that an agreement be made for one year, during which you should be pledged to write for no other (American) Magazine. The journal will be commenced on the first of January, 1842, and (should we be so fortunate as to obtain your consent to our proposal) it would be proper that we should have in hand by the first of December next, at least two papers from each contributor.

With this letter I despatch one of similar tenor to each of the gentlemen above named. If you cannot make it convenient to give me an unconditional reply, will you be kind enough to say whether you will write for us upon condition that we are able to engage others — specifying what others?

With high respect — yr ob. st,
EDGAR A. POE.

Poe to Griswold

c.1849

Dear Griswold,—Your uniform kindness leads me to hope that you will attend to this little matter of Mrs. L_____, to whom I truly think you have done less than justice. I am ashamed to ask favors of you, to whom I am so much indebted, but I have promised Mrs. L_____ this. They lied to you, (if they told—what he says you told him,) upon the subject of my forgotten Lecture on the American Poets, and I take this opportunity to say that what I have always held in conversations about you, and what I believe to be entirely true, as far as it goes, is contained in my notice of your "Female Poets of America," in the forthcoming "Southern Literary Messenger." By glancing at what I have published about you, (Aut. in Graham, 1841; Review in Pioneer, 1843; Notice in B. Journal, 1845; Letter in Int., 1847; and the Review of your Female Poets,) you will see that I have never hazarded my own reputation by a disrespectful word of you, though there were, as I long ago explained, in consequence of _____'s false imputation of that beastly article to you, some absurd jokes at your expense in the Lecture at Philadelphia. Come up and see me: the cars pass within a few rods of the New York Hotel, where I have called two or three times without finding you in.

Yours truly,
Poe.

Poe to Evert A. Duyckinck

FORDHAM, MARCH 8, 1849

DEAR SIR,—If you have looked over the Von Kempelen article which I left with your brother, you will have fully perceived its drift. I mean it as a kind of "exercise," or experiment, in the plausible or verisimilar style. Of course, there is not one word of truth in it, from beginning to end. I thought that such a style, applied to the gold-excitement, could not fail of effect. My sincere opinion is that nine persons out of ten (even among the best-informed) *will* believe the quiz (provided the design does not leak out before publication) and that thus, acting as a sudden, although of course a very temporary, *check* to the gold-fever, it will create a stir to some purpose.

I had prepared the hoax for a Boston weekly called "The Flag" where it will be quite thrown away. The proprietor will give me $15 for it on presentation to his agent here; and my object in referring the article to you is simply to see if you could not venture to take it for the "World." If so, I am willing to take for it $10—or, in fact, whatever you think you can afford.

I believe the quiz is the first deliberate literary attempt of the kind on record. In the story of Mrs Veal, we are permitted, now and then, to perceive a tone of banter. In "Robinson Crusoe" the design was far more to please, or excite, than to deceive by verisimilitude, in which particular merely, Sir. Ed. Seaward's narrative is the more skilful book. In my "Valdemar Case" (which was credited by many) I had not the slightest idea that any person should credit it as anything more than a "Magazine-paper"—but here the whole strength is laid out in verisimilitude.

I am very much obliged to you for your reprint of "Ulalume."

Truly Yours,
EDGAR A. POE.

EVERT A. DUYCKINCK, Esq.

P. S. If you feel the least shy about the article, make no hesitation in returning it, of course:—for I willingly admit that it is not a paper which every editor would like to "take the responsibility" of printing—although merely as a contribution with a known name:—but if you decline the quiz, please do not let out the secret.

Poe to ———— (G. W. Eveleth)

4TH OF JANUARY, 1848.

GOOD FRIEND,—Your last, dated July 26th, ends with—"Write, will you not?" I have been living ever since in a constant state of intention to write, and finally concluded not to write at all, until I could say something definite about the Stylus and other matters. You perceive that I now send you a Prospectus. But before I speak farther on this topic, let me succinctly reply to various points in your letter.

1. "Hawthorne" is out. How do you like it?

2. "The Rationale of Verse" was found to come down too heavily (as I forewarned you it did) upon some of poor Colton's friends in Frogpondium—the "pundits," you know; so I gave him "a song" for it and took it back. The song was "Ulalume—a Ballad," published in the December number of the *American Review.* I enclose it, as copied by the *Home Journal* (Willis's paper), with the editor's remarks. Please let me know how you like "Ulalume." As for the "Rat. of Verse," I sold it to "Graham" at a round advance on Colton's price, and in Graham's hands it is still—but not to remain even there; for I mean to get it back, revise or rewrite it (since "Evangeline" has been published), and deliver it as a lecture when I go South and West on my Magazine expedition.

3. I have been "so still" on account of preparation for the Magazine campaign; also, have been working at my book—nevertheless I have written some trifles not yet published—some which have been.

4. My health is better—best. I have never been so well.

. . . .

6. The "common friend" alluded to is Mrs. Frances S. Osgood, the poetess.

7. I agree with you only in part, as regards Miss Fuller. She has some general, but no particular, critical powers. She belongs to a *school* of criticism—the Göthean, æsthetic, eulogistic. The creed of this school is that, in criticising an author, you must imitate him, ape him, out Herod Herod . . . For example, she abuses Lowell (the best of our poets, perhaps) on account of a personal quarrel with him. She has omitted all mention of me, for the same reason—although, a short time before the issue of her book, she praised me highly in the *Tribune.* I enclose you her criticism, that you may judge for yourself. She praised "Witchcraft," because Mathews . . . wrote it. In a word, she is an ill-tempered and very inconsistent *Old Maid*— avoid her . . .

And now, having replied to all your queries, let me refer to the *Stylus.* I am resolved to be my own publisher. To be controlled is to be ruined. My ambition is great. If I succeed, I put myself (within two years) in possession of a fortune and infinitely more. My plan is to go through the South and West, and endeavor to interest my friends so as to *commence with a list of at least five hundred subscribers.* With this list, I can take the matter into my own hands. There are some of my friends who have sufficient confidence in me to advance their subscription—but, at all events, succeed I will. Can you or will you help me? I have room to say no more.

Truly yours,
E. A. Poe

Poe to Frederick W. Thomas

May 4, 1845.

My Dear Thomas,—In the hope that you have not yet *quite* given me up, as gone to Texas, or elsewhere, I sit down to write you a few words. I have been intending to do the same thing ever since I received your letter before the last—but for my life and soul I could not find, nor make, an opportunity. The fact is, that being seized, of late, with a fit of industry, I put so many irons in the fire all at once, that I have been quite unable to get them out. For the last three or four months I have been working 14 or 15 hours a day—hard at it all the time—and so, whenever I took pen in hand to write, I found that I was neglecting something that *would* be attended to. I never knew what it was to be a slave before.

And yet, Thomas, I have made no money. I am as poor now as ever I was in my life—except in hope, which is by no means bankable. I have taken a 3d pecuniary interest in the "Broadway Journal," and for everything I have written for it have been, of course, so much out of pocket. In the end, however, it will pay me well—at least the prospects are good. Say to Dow for me that there never has been a chance for my repaying him, without putting myself to greater inconvenience than he himself would have wished to subject me to, had he known the state of the case. Nor am I able to pay him now. The Devil himself was never so poor. Say to Dow, also, that I am sorry he has taken to dunning in his old age—it is a diabolical practice, altogether unworthy "a gentleman & a scholar"—to say nothing of the Editor of the "Madisonian." I wonder how he would like me to write him a series of letters—say one a week—giving him the literary gossip of New-York—or something of more general character. I would furnish him such a series for whatever he could afford to give me. If he agrees to this arrangement, ask him to state the length & character of the letters—how often—and how much he can give me. Remember me kindly to him & tell him I believe that dunning is his one sin—although at the same time, I do think it is the unpardonable sin against the Holy Ghost spoken of in the Scriptures. I am going to mail him the "Broadway Journal" regularly, & hope he will honor me with an exchange.

My dear Thomas, I hope you will never imagine, from any seeming neglect of mine, that I have forgotten our old friendship. There is no one in the world I would rather see at this moment than yourself; and many are the long talks we have about you and yours. Virginia & Mrs. Clemm beg to be remembered to you in the kindest terms. Do write me fully when you get this, and let me know particularly what you are about.

I send you an early number of the "B. Journal" containing my "Raven." It was copied by Briggs, my associate, before I joined the paper. "The Raven" has had a great "run," Thomas—but I wrote it for the express purpose of running—just as I did the "Gold-Bug," you know. The bird beat the bug, though, all hollow.

Do not forget to write immediately, & believe me

Most sincerely your friend,

Poe.

Poe to Evert A. Duyckinck

Thursday Morning—November 13th, 1845.
85 Amity St.

My Dear Mr Duyckinck,—For the first time during two months I find myself entirely myself—dreadfully sick and depressed, but still myself. I seem to have just awakened from some horrible dream, in which all was confusion, and suffering—relieved only by the constant sense of your kindness, and that of one or two other considerate friends. I really believe that I have been mad—but indeed I have had abundant reason to be so. I have made up my mind to a step which will preserve me, for the future, from at least the greater portion of the troubles which have beset me. In the meantime, I have need of the most active exertion to extricate myself from the embarrassments into which I have already fallen—and my object in writing you this note is, (once again) to beg your aid. Of course I need not say to you that my most urgent trouble is the want of ready money. I find that what I said to you about the prospects of the B. J. is strictly correct. The most trifling immediate relief would put it on an excellent footing. All that I want is time in which to look about me; and I think that it is in your power to afford me this.

I have already drawn from Mr Wiley, first $30—then io (from yourself)—then 10 (on account of the "Parnassus")—then 50 (when I went to Boston)—and finally 25—in all 135. Mr Wiley owes me, for the Poems, 75, and admitting that 1500 of the Tales have been sold, and that I am to receive 8 cts a copy—the amount which you named, if I remember—admitting this, he will owe me $120. on them:—in all 195. Deducting what I have received there is a balance of 60 in my favor. If I understood you, a few days ago, Mr W. was to settle with me in February. Now, you will already have anticipated my request. It is that you would ask Mr W. to give me, today, in lieu of all farther claim, a certain sum whatever he may think advisable. So dreadfully am I pressed, that I would willingly take even the $60 actually due, (in lieu of all farther demand) than wait until February:—but I am sure that you will do the best for me that you can.

Please send your answer to 85 Amity St. and believe me—with the most sincere friendship and ardent gratitude

Yours
EDGAR A. POE.

Poe to Mrs. Virginia Poe

June 12, 1846.

My Dear Heart—My Dear Virginia,—Our mother will explain to you why I stay away from you this night. I trust the interview I am promised will result in some *substantial good* for me—for your dear sake and hers—keep up your heart in all hopefulness, and trust yet a little longer. On my last great disappointment I should have lost my courage *but for you*—my little darling wife. You are my *greatest* and *only* stimulus now, to battle with this uncongenial, unsatisfactory, and ungrateful life.

I shall be with you tomorrow . . . P.M., and be assured until I see you I will keep in *loving remembrance* your *last words*, and your fervent prayer!

Sleep well, and may God grant you a peaceful summer with your devoted Edgar.

Poe to Philip P. Cooke

New York, August 9, 1846.

My Dear Sir,—Never think of excusing yourself (to me) for dilatoriness in answering letters. I know too well the unconquerable procrastination which besets the poet. I will place it all to the account of the turkeys. Were I to be seized by a rambling fit—one of my customary *passions* (nothing less) for vagabonding through the woods for a week or a month together—I would not—in fact I *could* not be put out of my mood, were it even to answer a letter from the Grand Mogul informing me that I had fallen heir to his possessions.

Thank you for the compliment. Were I in a serious humor just now, I would tell you frankly how your words of appreciation make my nerves thrill—not because you praise me (for others have praised me more lavishly) but because I feel that you comprehend and discriminate. You are right about the hair-splitting of my French friend:—that is all done for effect. These tales of ratiocination owe most of their popularity to being something in a new key. I do not mean to say that they are not ingenious—but people think them more ingenious than they are—on account of their method and *air* of method. In the "Murders in the Rue Morgue," for instance, where is the ingenuity of unravelling a web which you yourself (the author) have woven for the express purpose of unravelling? The reader is made to confound the ingenuity of the supposititious Dupin with that of the writer of the story.

Not for the world would I have had any one else to continue Lowell's Memoir until I have heard from you. I wish *you* to do it (if you will be so kind) and nobody else. By the time the book appears you will be famous, (or all my prophecy goes for nothing) and I shall have the *éclat* of your name to aid my sales. But, seriously, I do not think that any one so well enters into the poetical portion of my mind as yourself—and I deduce this idea from my intense appreciation of those points of your own poetry which seem lost upon others.

Should you undertake the work for me, there is one topic—there is one particular in which I have had wrong done me—and it may not be indecorous in me to call your attention to it. The last selection of my Tales was made from about 70, by Wiley and Putnam's reader, Duyckinck. He has what he thinks a taste for ratiocination, and has accordingly made up the book mostly of analytic stories. But this is not *representing* my mind in its various phases—it is not giving me fair play. In writing these Tales one by one, at long intervals, I have kept the book-unity always in mind—that is, each has been composed with reference to its effect as part of *a whole.* In this view, one of my chief aims has been the widest diversity of subject, thought, & especially *tone* and manner of handling. Were all my tales now before me in a large volume and as the composition of another—the merit which would principally arrest my attention would be the wide *diversity and variety.* You would be surprised to hear me say that (omitting one or two of my first efforts) I do not consider any one of my stories *better* than another. There is a vast variety of kinds and, in degree of value, these kinds vary—but each tale is equally good *of its kind.* The loftiest kind is that of the highest imagination—and, for this reason only, "Ligeia" may be called my *best* tale. I have much improved this last since you saw it and I mail you a copy, as well as a copy of my best specimen of analysis—"The Philosophy of Composition."

Do you ever see the British papers? Martin F. Tupper, author of "Proverbial Philosophy," has been paying me some high compliments—and indeed I have been treated more than well. There is one "British opinion," however, which I value highly—Miss Barrett's. She says.—"This vivid writing!—this power *which is felt!* The Raven has produced a sensation—'a fit horror' here in England. Some of my friends are taken by the fear of it and some by the music. I hear of persons *haunted* by the 'Nevermore,' and one acquaintance of mine who has the misfortune of possessing a 'bust of Pallas' never can bear to look at it in the twilight. . . . Our great poet Mr. Browning, author of Paracelsus, etc., is enthusiastic in his admiration of the rhythm . . . Then there is a tale of his which I do not find in this volume, but which is going the rounds of the newspapers, about Mesmerism, throwing us all into most admired disorder or dreadful doubts as to whether it can be true, as the children say of ghost stories. The certain thing in the tale in question is the power of the writer & the faculty he has of making horrible improbabilities seem near and familiar." Would it be in bad taste to quote these words of Miss B. in your notice?

Forgive these egotisms (which are rendered in some measure necessary by the topic) and believe me that I will let slip *no* opportunity of reciprocating your kindness.

Griswold's new edition I have not yet seen (is it out?) but I will manage to find "Rosalie Lee." Do not forget to send me a few personal details of yourself—such as I give in "The N. Y. Literati." When your book appears I propose to review it fully in Colton's "American Review." If you ever write to him, please suggest to him that I wish to do so. I hope to get your volume before mine goes to press—so that I may speak more fully.

I will forward the papers to which I refer *in a day or two*—not by today's mail. Touching "The Stylus:"—this is the one great purpose of my literary life. Undoubtedly (unless I die) I will accomplish it—but I can afford to lose nothing by precipitancy. I cannot yet say when or how I shall get to work—but when the time comes I will write you. I wish to establish a journal in which the men of genius may fight their battles, upon some terms of equality, with those dunces the men of talent. But, apart from this, I have *magnificent* objects in view—may I but live to accomplish them!

Most cordially your friend,

EDGAR A. POE.

Poe to George W. Eveleth

29th of February, 1848.

I mean to start for Richmond on the 10th March. Everything has gone as I wished it, and my final success is certain, or I abandon all claims to the title of Vates. The only contretemps of any moment, lately, has been Willis's somewhat premature announcement of my project:—but this will only force me into action a little sooner than I had proposed. Let me now answer the points of your last letter.

C—— acted pretty much as all mere men of the world act. I think very little the worse of him for his endeavor to succeed with you at my expense. I always liked him, and I believe he liked me. His "I understand the matter perfectly" amuses me. Certainly, then, it was the only matter he did understand. His intellect was 0.

"The Rationale of Verse" will appear in *Graham*, after all. I will stop in Philadelphia to see the proofs.

As for Godey, he is a good little man, and means as well as he knows how . . .

The "most distinguished of American scholars" is Professor Charles Anthon, author of the "Classical Dictionary."

I presume you have seen some newspaper notices of my late lecture on the Universe. You could have gleaned, however, no idea of what the lecture was, from what the papers said it was. All praised it—as far as I have yet seen—and all absurdly misrepresented it. The only report of it which approaches the truth is the one I enclose—from the *Express*—written by E. A. Hopkins, a gentleman of much scientific acquirement, son of Bishop Hopkins, of Vermont; but he conveys only my general idea, and his digest is full of inaccuracies. I enclose also a slip from the *Courier and Enquirer.* Please return them. To eke out a chance of your understanding what I really *did* say, I add a loose summary of my propositions and results:—

The General Proposition is this—Because Nothing was, *therefore* All Things are.

1. An inspection of the *universality* of Gravitation—*i.e.*, of the fact that each particle tends, *not* to any one common point, but to *every other* particle—suggests perfect totality, or *absolute* unity, as the source of the phenomenon.
2. Gravity is but the mode in which is manifested the tendency of all things to return into their original unity—is but the reaction of the first Divine Act.
3. The *law* regulating the return—*i. e.*, the *law* of Gravitation—is but a necessary result of the necessary and sole possible mode of equable *irradiation* of matter through space: this *equable* irradiation is necessary as a basis for the Nebular Theory of Laplace.
4. The Universe of Stars (contradistinguished from the Universe of space) is limited.
5. Mind is cognizant of Matter *only* through its two properties, attraction and repulsion: therefore Matter *is* only attraction and repulsion: a finally consolidated globe-of-globes, being but one particle, would be without attraction—*i.e.*, gravitation: the existence of such a globe presupposes the expulsion of the separative ether which we know to exist between the particles as at present diffused: thus the final globe would be matter without attraction and repulsion but these *are* matter: then the final globe would be matter without matter—*i.e.*, no matter at all: it must disappear. Thus Unity is *Nothingness.*
6. Matter, springing from Unity, sprang from Nothingness—*i.e.*, was *created.*
7. All will return to Nothingness, in returning to Unity.

Read these items *after* the Report. As to the Lecture, I am very quiet about it—but, if you have ever dealt with such topics, you will recognize the novelty and *moment* of my views. What I have propounded will (in good time) revolutionise the world of Physical and Metaphysical Science. I say this calmly—but I say it.

I shall not go till I hear from you.—Cordially—

E. A. Poe.

By the by, lest you infer that my views, in detail, are the same with those advanced in the *Nebular Hypothesis*, I venture to offer a few addenda, the substance of which was penned, though never printed, several years ago, under the head of—A Prediction."

Poe to Mrs. Sarah Helen Whitman

[The letter was undated and unsigned. It is supposed to have been written on October 1, 1848]

I have already told you that some few casual words spoken of you by —— ——, were the first in which I had ever heard your name mentioned. She alluded to what she called your "eccentricities," and hinted at your sorrows. Her description of the former strangely arrested—her allusion to the latter enchained and rivetted my attention.

She had referred to thoughts, sentiments, traits, *moods*, which I knew to be my own, but which, until that moment. I had believed to be my own solely—unshared by any human being. A profound sympathy took immediate possession of my soul. I cannot better explain to you what I felt than by saying that your unknown heart seemed to pass into my bosom—there to dwell for ever—while mine, I thought, was translated into your own.

From that hour I loved you. Since that period I have never seen nor heard your name without a shiver, half of delight, half of anxiety.—The impression left upon my mind was that you were still a wife, and it is only within the last few months that I have been undeceived in this respect.

For this reason I shunned your presence and even the city in which you lived. You may remember that once when I passed through Providence with Mrs. Osgood I positively refused to accompany her to your house, and even provoked her into a quarrel by the obstinacy and seeming unreasonableness of my refusal. I dared neither go nor say why I could not. I dared not speak of you—much less see you. For years your name never passed my lips, while my soul drank in, with a delirious thirst, all that was uttered in my presence respecting you.

The merest whisper that concerned you awoke in me a shuddering sixth sense, vaguely compounded of fear, ecstatic happiness and a wild inexplicable sentiment that resembled nothing so nearly as a consciousness of guilt.

Judge, then, with what wondering, unbelieving joy, I received, in your well-known MS., the Valentine which first gave me to see that you knew me to exist.

The idea of what men call Fate lost then in my eyes its character of futility. I felt that nothing hereafter was to be doubted, and lost myself for many weeks in one continuous, delicious dream, where all was a vivid, yet indistinct bliss.—

Immediately after reading the Valentine, I wished to contrive some mode of acknowledging—without wounding you by seeming directly to acknowledge—my sense—oh, my keen—my exulting—my ecstatic sense of the honour you had conferred on me. To accomplish as I wished it, precisely *what* I wished, seemed impossible, however; and I was on the point of abandoning the idea, when my eyes fell upon a volume of my own poems; and then the lines I had written, in my passionate boyhood, to the first purely ideal love of my soul—to the Helen Stannard of whom I told you—flashed upon my recollection. I turned to them. They expressed all—*all* that I would have said to you—so fully—so accurately and so exclusively, that a thrill of intense superstition ran at once through my frame. Read the verses and then take into consideration the peculiar need I had, at the moment, for just so seemingly an unattainable mode of communication with you as they afforded. Think of the absolute appositeness with which they fulfilled that need—expressing not only all that I would have said of your person, but all that of which I most wished to assure you, in the lines commencing—

"On desperate seas long wont to roam."

Think of the rare agreement of name, and you will no longer wonder that to one accustomed as I am to the Calculus of Probabilities, they wore an air of positive miracle . . . I yielded at once to an overwhelming sense of Fatality. From that hour I have never been able to shake from my soul the belief that my Destiny, for good or for evil, either here or hereafter, is in some measure interwoven with your own.

Of course I did not expect, on your part, any acknowledgment of the printed lines "To Helen;" and yet, without confessing it even to myself, I experienced an indefinable sense of sorrow in your silence. At length, when I thought you had time fully to forget me (if, indeed, you had ever really remembered) I sent you the anonymous lines in MS. I wrote, first, through a pining, burning desire to communicate with you in *some* way—even if you remained in ignorance of your correspondent. The mere thought that *your* dear fingers would press—*your* sweet eyes dwell upon characters which *I* had penned—characters which had welled out upon the paper from the depths of so devout a love—filled my soul with a rapture, which seemed, then, all sufficient for my human nature. It *then* appeared to me that merely this one thought involved so much of bliss that here on earth I could have no right ever to repine—no room for discontent. If ever, *then*, I dared to picture for myself a richer happiness, it was always connected with your image in Heaven. But there was yet another idea which impelled me to send you those lines:—I said to myself the sentiment—the holy passion which glows in my bosom *for her*, is of Heaven, heavenly, and has no taint of the earth. Thus then must lie in the recesses of her own pure bosom, at least the germ of a reciprocal love, and if this be indeed so, she will need no earthly clue—she will instinctively feel who is her correspondent—In this case, then, I may hope for some faint token at least, giving me to understand that the source of the poem is known and its sentiment comprehended even if disapproved.

O God!—how long—*how long* I waited in *vain*—hoping against hope—until, at length, I became possessed with a spirit far sterner—far more reckless than despair—I explained to you—but without detailing the vital influences they wrought upon my fortune—the singular additional, yet seemingly trivial fatality by which you happened to address your anonymous stanzas to Fordham instead of New York—by which my aunt happened to get notice of their being in the West Farm post-office. But I have not yet told you that your lines reached me in Richmond on the very day in which I was about to enter on a course which would have borne me far, far away from *you*, sweet, sweet Helen, and from this divine dream of your love.

Poe to Mrs. Sarah Helen Whitman

18th October, 1848.

You do not love me, or you would have felt too thorough a sympathy with the sensitiveness of my nature, to have so wounded me as you have done with this terrible passage of your letter:—

"How often I have heard it said of you, 'He has great intellectual power, but no principle—no moral sense.'"

Is it possible that such expressions as these could have been repeated to me—to me—by one whom I loved—ah, whom I *love!* . . .

By the God who reigns in Heaven, I swear to you that my soul is incapable of dishonor—that, with the exception of occasional follies and excesses which I bitterly lament but to which I have been driven by intolerable sorrow, and which are hourly committed by others without attracting any notice whatever—I can call to mind no act of my life which would bring a blush to my cheek—or to yours. If I have erred at all in this regard, it has been on the side of what the world would call a Quixotic sense of the honorable—of the chivalrous. The indulgence of this sense has been the true voluptuousness of my life. It was for this species of luxury that in early youth I deliberately threw away from me a large fortune rather than endure a trivial wrong. Ah, how profound is my love for you, since it forces me into these egotisms, for which you will inevitably despise me! . . .

For nearly three years I have been ill, poor, living out of the world; and thus, as I now painfully see, have afforded opportunity to my enemies to slander me in private society without my knowledge, and thus with impunity. Although much, however, may (and, I now see, must) have been said to my discredit, during my retirement, those few who, knowing me well, have been steadfastly my friends, permitted nothing to reach my ears—unless in one instance of such a character that I could appeal to a court of justice for redress.

I replied to the charge fully in a public newspaper—afterwards suing the *Mirror* (in which the scandal appeared), obtaining a verdict and recovering such an amount of damages as, for the time, completely to break up that journal. And you ask me *why* men so *misjudge* me—*why* I have enemies. If your knowledge of my character and of my career does not afford you an answer to the query, at least it does not become *me* to suggest the answer. Let it suffice that I have had the audacity to remain poor that I might preserve my independence—that, nevertheless, in letters, to a certain extent and in certain regards, I have been "successful"—that I have been a critic—an unscrupulously honest and no doubt in many cases a bitter one—that I have uniformly attacked—where I attacked at all—those who stood highest in power and influence—and that—whether in literature or society, I have seldom refrained from expressing, either directly or indirectly, the pure contempt with which the pretensions of ignorance, arrogance, or imbecility inspire me. And you who know all this—*you* ask me *why* I have enemies. Ah, I have a hundred friends for every individual enemy, but has it ever occurred to you that you do not live among my friends?

Had you read my criticisms generally, you would see why all those whom you know best know me least and are my enemies. Do you not remember with how deep a sigh I said to you . . . "My heart is heavy, for I see that your friends are not my own"? . . .

But the cruel sentence in your letter would not—*could* not so deeply have wounded me, had my soul been first strengthened by those assurances of your love which I so wildly—so vainly—and, I now feel, so presumptuously entreated. That our souls are one, every line which you have ever written asserts—but our hearts do *not* beat in unison.

That many persons, in your presence, have declared me wanting in honor appeals irresistibly to an instinct of my nature—an instinct which *I feel* to be honor, let the dishonorable say what they may, and forbids me, under such circumstances, to insult you with my love . . .

Forgive me, best and only-beloved Helen, if there be bitterness in my tone. Towards *you* there is no room in my soul for any other sentiment than devotion. It is Fate only which I accuse. It is my own unhappy nature . . .

Poe to Annie L. Richmond

FORDHAM, November 16, 1848.

Oh, Annie, Annie! what cruel thoughts . . . must have been torturing your heart during the last terrible fortnight in which you have heard *nothing* from me—not even one little word to say that I still lived . . . But, Annie, I know that you *felt* too deeply the nature of my love for you to doubt *that*, even for one moment, and this thought has comforted me in my bitter sorrow. I could bear that you should imagine *every other evil except that one*—that my soul had been untrue to yours. Why am I not *with* you now, that I might press your dear hand in mine, and look deep into the clear heaven of your eyes; so that the words which I now can only *write* might sink into your heart, and make you comprehend what it is that I would say . . . But, oh, my own sweet *sister* Annie, my pure beautiful angel . . . how shall I explain to you the *bitter, bitter* anguish which has tortured me since I left you? You saw, you *felt* the agony of grief with which I bade you farewell—you remember my expression of gloom—of a dreadful, horrible foreboding of Ill. Indeed—*indeed* it seemed to me that Death approached me even then, and that I was involved in the shadow which went before him . . . I said to myself—"it is for the last time, until we meet in Heaven." I remember nothing distinctly from that moment until I found myself in Providence. I went to bed and wept through a long, long, hideous night of Despair—when the day broke, I arose and endeavored to quiet my mind by a rapid walk in the cold, keen air—but all *would* not do—the Demon tormented me still. Finally, I procured two ounces of laudanum, and, without returning to my hotel, took the cars back to Boston. When I arrived I wrote you a letter, in which I opened my whole heart to you—to *you* . . . I told you how my struggles were more than I could bear . . . I then reminded you of that holy promise which was the last I exacted from you in parting—the promise that, under all circumstances, you would come to me on my bed of death. I implored you to come *then*, mentioning the place where I should be found in Boston. Having written this letter, I swallowed about half the laudanum, and hurried to the Post Office—intending not to take the rest until I saw you—for, I did not doubt for one moment, that Annie would keep her sacred promise. But I had not calculated on the strength of the laudanum, for, before. I reached the Post Office my reason was entirety gone, and the letter was never put in. Let me pass over—my darling *sister*—the awful horrors which succeeded. A friend was at hand, who aided and (if it can be called saving) saved me, but it is only within the last three days that I have been able to remember what occurred in that dreary interval. It appears that, after the laudanum was rejected from the stomach, I became calm, and—to a casual observer, sane—so that I was suffered to go back to Providence . . . It is not *much* that I ask, *sweet sister Annie*—my mother and myself would take a small cottage at——oh, *so* small—so *very* humble—I should be far away from the tumult of the world—from the ambition which I loathe—I would labor day and night, and with industry, I could accomplish *so* much. Annie! it would be a Paradise beyond my wildest hopes—I could see some of your beloved family *every* day, and you often . . . Do not these pictures touch your inmost heart? . . . I am at home now with my dear mother who is endeavoring to comfort me—but the sole words which soothe me are those in which she speaks of Annie—she tells me that she has written you, begging you to come on to Fordham. Ah, Annie, *is it not possible?* I am so *ill*—so terribly, hopelessly *ill* in body and mind, that I CANNOT live, unless I can feel your sweet, gentle, loving hand pressed upon my forehead—oh, my *pure, virtuous, generous, beautiful sister* Annie! Is it not POSSIBLE for you to come—if only for one little week? Until I subdue this fearful agitation, which, if continued, will either destroy my life or drive me hopelessly mad.

Farewell—*here and hereafter—forever your own*

EDDY.

Poe to Mrs. Maria Clemm

[A fragment of the letter]

September, 1849.

. . . possible. Everybody says that if I lecture again & put the tickets at 50 cts. I will clear $100. I *never* was received with so much enthusiasm. The papers have done nothing but praise me before the lecture & since. I enclose one of the notices—the only one in which the slightest word of disparagement appears. It is written by Daniel—the man whom I challenged when I was here last year. I have been invited out a great deal—but could seldom go, on account of not having a dress coat. Tonight Rose & I are to spend the evening at Elmira's. Last night I was at Poitiaux's—the night before at Strobia's, where I saw my dear friend Eliza Lambert (Gen. Lambert's sister). She was ill in her bed-room, but insisted upon our coming up, & we stayed until nearly 1 o'clock. In a word, I have received nothing but kindness since I have been here, & could have been quite happy but for my dreadful anxiety about you. Since the report of my intended marriage, the McKenzies have overwhelmed me with attentions. Their house is so crowded that they *could* not ask me to stay.—And now, my own precious Muddy, the very moment I get a definite answer about everything, I will write again & tell you what to do. Elmira talks about visiting Fordham—but I do not know whether that would do. I think, perhaps, it would be best for you to give up everything there & come on here in the Packet. Write immediately & give me your advice about it—for you know best. Could we be happier in Richmond or Lowell?—for I suppose we could never be happy at Fordham—and, Muddy, I *must* be somewhere where

I can see Annie.—Did Mrs. L. get the Western Quarterly Review? Thompson is constantly urging me to write for the Messenger, but I am so anxious that I cannot—Mr. Loud, the husband of Mrs. St Leon Loud, the hostess of Philadelphia, called on me the other day and offered me $100 to edit his wife's poems. Of course, I accepted the offer. The whole labor will not occupy me 3 days. I am to have them ready by Christmas.—I have seen Bernard often. Eliza is expected but has not come.—When I repeat my lecture here, I will then go to Petersburg & Norfolk.—A Mr. Taverner lectured here on Shakespeare, a few nights after me, and had 8 persons, including myself & the doorkeeper.—I think, upon the whole, dear Muddy, it will be better for you to say that I am ill, or something of that kind, and break up at Fordham, so that you may come on here. Let me know immediately what you think best. You know we could easily pay off what we owe at Fordham & the place is a beautiful one—but I want to live *near Annie.*—And now, dear Muddy, there is one thing I wish you to pay particular attention to. I told Elmira, when I first came here, that I had one of the pencil-sketches of her, that I took a long while ago in Richmond; and I told her that I would write to you about it. So when you write, just copy the following words in your letter:

I have looked again for the pencil-sketch of Mrs. S. but cannot find it anywhere. I took down all the books and shook them one by one, and unless Eliza White has it, I do not know what has become of it. She was looking at it the last time I saw it. The one you spoilt with Indian Ink ought to be some where about the house. I will do my best to (find—torn) it.

I got a sneaking letter today from Chivers.—Do not tell me anything about Annie—I cannot bear to hear it now—unless you can tell me that Mr. R. is dead.—I have got the wedding ring.—and shall have no difficulty, I think, in getting a dress-coat.

Wednesday Night.

. . . also the letter. *Return the letter when you write.*